W9-ALV-247

Praise for *Transformation,*
Revelation, and *Restoration*—
Carol Berg's acclaimed Rai-kirah saga

"Vivid characters and intricate magic combined with a fascinating world and the sure touch of a Real Writer—luscious work!"   —Melanie Rawn

"A spectacular new voice.... Superbly textured, splendidly characterized, this spellbinding tale provides myriad delights."   —*Romantic Times*

"This well-written fantasy grabs the reader by the throat on page one and doesn't let go.... Wonderful."   —*Starburst*

"Both a traditional fantasy and an intriguing character piece.... Superbly entertaining."   —*Interzone Magazine*

continued . . .

"The prince's redemption, his transformation, and the flowering of mutual esteem between master and slave are at the story's heart. This is handled superbly."
                                        —*Time Out* (London)

"Vivid characters, a tangible atmosphere of doom, and some gallows humor."   —*SFX Magazine*

"Powerfully entertaining."   —*Locus*

"An exotic, dangerous, and beautifully crafted world."
            —Lynn Flewelling, author of *Traitor's Moon*

"Berg's characters are completely believable, her world interesting and complex, and her story riveting."—*Kliatt*

"Berg greatly expands her world with surprising insights."   —*The Denver Post*

"Epic fantasy on a gigantic scale. . . . Carol Berg lights up the sky with a wondrous world."
                                        —*Midwest Book Review*

"Ms. Berg's finely drawn characters combine with a remarkable imagination to create a profound and fascinating novel."   —*Talebones*

"Carol Berg is a brilliant writer who has built her characters carefully and completely. The magic is subtle and vivid, and the writing is compelling."   —BookBrowser

"A much-needed boost of new blood into the fantasy pool."   —*Dreamwatch Magazine*

SONG
OF THE
BEAST

Carol Berg

A ROC BOOK

ROC
Published by New American Library, a division of
Penguin Group (USA) Inc., 375 Hudson Street,
New York, New York 10014, U.S.A.
Penguin Books Ltd, 80 Strand,
London WC2R 0RL, England
Penguin Books Australia Ltd, 250 Camberwell Road,
Camberwell, Victoria 3124, Australia
Penguin Books Canada Ltd, 10 Alcorn Avenue,
Toronto, Ontario, Canada M4V 3B2
Penguin Books (N.Z.) Ltd, Cnr Rosedale and Airborne Roads,
Albany, Auckland 1310, New Zealand

Penguin Books Ltd, Registered Offices:
80 Strand, London WC2R 0RL, England

First published by Roc, an imprint of New American Library,
a division of Penguin Group (USA) Inc.

First Printing, May 2003
10 9 8 7 6 5 4 3 2 1

Copyright © Carol Berg, 2003
All rights reserved

Cover art by Matt Stawicki

REGISTERED TRADEMARK—MARCA REGISTERDA

PRINTED IN THE UNITED STATES OF AMERICA

Without limiting the rights under copyright reserved above, no part of this
publication may be reproduced, stored in or introduced into a retrieval system, or
transmitted, in any form, or by any means (electronic, mechanical, photocopying,
recording, or otherwise), without the prior written permission of both the copyright
owner and the above publisher of this book.

PUBLISHER'S NOTE
This is a work of fiction. Names, characters, places, and incidents either are the
product of the author's imagination or are used fictitiously, and any resemblance to
actual persons, living or dead, business establishments, events, or locales is entirely
coincidental.

BOOKS ARE AVAILABLE AT QUANTITY DISCOUNTS WHEN USED TO PROMOTE PRODUCTS OR
SERVICES. FOR INFORMATION PLEASE WRITE TO PREMIUM MARKETING DIVISION, PENGUIN
GROUP (USA) INC., 375 HUDSON STREET, NEW YORK, NEW YORK 10014.

If you purchased this book without a cover you should be aware that this book is
stolen property. It was reported as "unsold and destroyed" to the publisher and neither
the author nor the publisher has received any payment for this "stripped book."

The scanning, uploading and distribution of this book via the Internet or via any
other means without the permission of the publisher is illegal and punishable by law.
Please purchase only authorized electronic editions, and do not participate in or
encourage electronic piracy of copyrighted materials. Your support of the author's
rights is appreciated.

This one is, as always, for the Word Weavers past and present and all they bring to their reading. And it's well past time to raise a glass to my editor, Laura Anne Gilman, and her nose for nuance—no spackle!—and my agent, Lucienne Diver, for her encouragement, enthusiasm, and expertise. But mostly and entirely for the one who completes my being.

Chapter 1

The light had almost undone me. I had not been prepared for any of it, dead man that I was, but never could I have been ready for the shattering explosion of sunlight after so many years in the dark. They had threatened so often to burn out my eyes, the thought crossed my mind that it had finally come to pass. Perhaps my memory of being dragged from my cell through the bowels of Mazadine and kicked through the iron door that would take me back to the world was only another cruel nightmare.

Wrapping my arms about my head, I sank to the ground, huddling to the faceless prison wall like a pup to its dam, and there I remained until the sun slipped below the rim of the world. Only when blessed darkness eased the agony—never had I thought to bless the dark again—could I consider other pressing matters, such as getting as far away as possible before someone decided to put me back behind that wall.

Rocks and gravel cut into my bare feet as I stumbled down the rutted road and found a crossroads shrine, a mossy spring dedicated to Keldar. Just off the road sat a well-stuffed wool cart, while from the nearby shrubbery came the unmistakable sounds of a drover who had drunk too many tankards of ale at supper. I fell to my knees be-

side the spring, but no sooner had I taken a first desperate sip than five Royal Horse Guards, torches blazing in
the night, raced past at full gallop, turning up the road to
Mazadine as if the cruelest of the world's monsters were
at their backs. Breathing a prayer of heartfelt thanksgiv-
ing, I scrambled into the wagon and buried myself in the
wool.

Eyeless Keldar had never been my god. The cold lord
of wisdom had never appealed to one born into the service of his brother Roelan, the joyous, hunchbacked god
of music. But Roelan had abandoned me in the darkness.
The loving voice that had guided me through my growing had fallen silent. The hand that embraced me at my
dedication when I was fourteen, accepted my service for
seven years of glory, and sustained me through the first
years of my captivity had been withdrawn. So, as the beggar who refuses no penny dropped in his cup, I accepted
Keldar's gift and pledged him service as I rode through
the night, cradled in a wagonload of wool.

Hunger quickly became my encompassing reality.
Though half out of my head, I dared not risk a charge of
thieving or any other crime that might fix a guardsman's
eye on me, so I roamed the pigsties and refuse heaps of
Lepan, the market town where the drover left off his wool
and his passenger. Too weak and sick to fight the other
beggars for the best scraps, I would take whatever was
left and find a dark hole in which to hide, trying to block
out the noise and the light that drove me to madness.

I took my first step back toward life on the night of a
monstrous storm. Thunder echoed from the distant peaks
like giant's laughter, and if lightning was, as old wives

said, the fire of dying heroes' hearts, then there were a great many heroes dying that night. A merciless rain drove me to shelter in a stable. I huddled in a corner, drenched to the soul, shivering with the chill of death and the late spring wind. Somewhere amid murky cravings and failing senses passed a fleeting sorrow that my brief freedom had had no more value than my captivity. A final victory for those who had sent me to Mazadine, never bothering to tell me why.

While I was thus occupied with dying and regrets, the stable door crashed open to a heavy boot, followed quickly by the grunts and whimpers of a backstreet mating. The smell of wine and vomit and lust soon overpowered the aura of unclean stable and even my own filth. Only when the woman began to struggle did I realize that the coupling was not voluntary.

I did not—could not—move. I had no strength left to right the ills of the world. But then I heard crackling sparks and frantic pleading. "Have mercy! You wear the Ridemark. I'll die from your pleasuring! Oh, sir, I'm just sixteen!"

A Dragon Rider! From the ashes of my life flared one last ember, fanned by brutish laughter and wine-sotted grunting . . . and the memory of a red dragon scribed on the wrist of the faceless judge who stole my life. If I was going to die, then I would take at least one Dragon Rider with me. Hopeless fool. I could not even think how I would be able to do it.

I eased myself up the wall and edged to my right, lifting a length of rusty chain from a nail. The stable floor yielded a long spike, thin enough to pass all but its head through two links of the chain. Faster than I'd have believed possible, I stepped toward the groveling shapes. When the Rider lifted his head to bellow in his lust, I dropped the loop over it, twisting the spike so the chain bit deep into the man's flesh. His cry was cut short, and I hoped I could keep the iron noose tight for long enough that he would fall insensible before throwing me off. But those who mount the dragons of Yr and ride them to war are no striplings. He raised his shoulders and leaped to his feet, carrying me with him until he slammed me against the stable wall. Sparks shot high, spitting and hissing in a scalding rain of fire as the wind went out of me, my vision grew blurry, and I lost my grip on the spike.

Better this way, I thought, as my ribs cracked and the roaring warrior yanked off the noose, turning to finish me. But even as he raised his fist, his red-rimmed eyes bulged and died, and blood trickled out of his silent mouth. It would be a race to the last crossing, but at least no girl of sixteen, charred to ash by a Dragon Rider's mating, would accompany us. It was a satisfactory ending as I slumped to the filthy floor and the warrior's heavy body fell on top of me.

It was not in the afterlife that I next opened my eyes, nor in the rain-lashed stable, but in a shabby room that was achingly familiar. No one who has traveled the roads of the world would fail to recognize the attic room of an ill-prospered inn, the cheapest lodging to be found under a roof. A dirty sheet and a mouse-chewed blanket on a pallet that was half moldy straw, half mouse droppings and beetle husks. A flyspecked window that could not be opened in summer or could not be shut in winter, and that would always overlook the midden. A broken table for eating or writing or playing cards. I'd spent a sizable portion of the happiest years of my life in such lodgings.

". . . never saw such marks upon a living man. What think you, Narim? Is he a runaway slave? I'd not have brought him here if I'd thought it."

Fingers drifted lightly over my bare back. Where was darkness when you needed it? Would that I could pull its mantle over me to hide what I could not bear to remember.

"Not a slave. Look at the shape of his eyes, his dark hair, his height. He is clearly Senai."

The first voice was a young woman. The second unmistakably an Elhim. I could imagine the pale gray eyes examining my wreckage and the slender fingers rubbing his colorless face.

"Senai!" said the girl. "You jest! He may have the height and the coloring, but what Senai was ever brought so low as this? Smells like pigsties, he does. To have scars like these, and . . . blessed Tjasse . . . look at his hands."

Why could I not move? I was not ready to face these things myself, much less have them exposed to public view. I lay on my stomach on the straw pallet, a spider busying herself with her spinning not a hand's breadth from my nose. I felt like the carcass of a holiday pig, stripped bare and possessed of no will, no dignity, and too many memories of mortal horrors to get up on my bones and walk. And, too, rags had been wrapped so tightly about my middle that I could scarcely breathe.

"Someone has broken his fingers repeatedly. Hundreds of times, I would say."

"Hundreds . . . Fires of heaven!"

"I've heard rumors of a prisoner escaped from Maza-dine."

"Bollocks! No one leaves Mazadine alive."

Foolish girl. She couldn't see that I was really dead. The Elhim was wiser. "Who can say what is life, Callia? I think perhaps this one has known that which makes death a sweet companion. He may not thank you for bringing him here. Yet . . . he came to your rescue."

"Aye. I put the knife in the pig, but it was this one took him off me."

Time to move. I drew my knees under my aching ribs and paused to take a shallow breath. Then I pushed my-self up to kneeling, wrapped my arms tightly about my middle, and anxiously waited for the room to stop spin-ning. The girl knelt on the floor beside me and the Elhim stood next to her, slimmer than a young boy and scarcely taller, his skin fair and smooth, his hair white blond. It was almost impossible to tell one Elhim from another, all of them so fair and pale and sexless. Though we called them "he," crude bullies of every race regularly found unseemly pleasure in confirming that Elhim were neither male nor female.

The girl looked old, even at sixteen. She might once have been called pretty, but her hair was dull, her skin blotched with disease, and her light blue eyes knew too much of unnatural pleasure. Her shabby, low-cut gown of stained and singed green silk was overfull with her blowsy charms. As I sat up, she clamped one hand over her mouth, as if I were indeed a dead man waked. Her other hand gripped a flask of wine.

The Elhim cocked his head to the side and widened his pale eyes. "So your valiant rescuer wakes, Callia! Hand him your flask. A dram of wine might do the fellow good." His curly head would have come no higher than my shoulder if I'd not found it expedient to remain seated, leaning against the wall. "You are a great mystery, Senai, that begs for explanation. But for now we'll settle for a name to thank you by."

I should have said something, but I had forgotten how to form words. For the final seven years of my captivity I had uttered no sound, and it would take more than a moment to convince my tongue that the metal jaws and the lash were not waiting for me, and that the tally of seven years would not have to start all over again with my first utterance. I struggled for a moment, then shook my head, pointed to the bed and my bandaged ribs, and cupped my grotesque hands to my chest as one does when acknowledging a service.

"They've not taken out his tongue, have they?" asked the girl in horror. She soothed the thought with a swig from her flask, leaving red droplets of wine running down her chin when she pulled it away too quickly.

Shaking my head, I tried to indicate that my incapacity was a passing problem of no importance.

Callia yielded me the wine flask, wiping her mouth with the back of her hand. "That's good, then. Couldn't stomach that." She grabbed a cracked pitcher and the remainder of the ragged petticoat they had torn to bind my ribs and carried them to a peeling dresser next to the window, setting them beside a dented plate polished to a high sheen. With no conscious immodesty she removed her bodice and dabbed at her blood-streaked breasts with the rag she'd dipped in the water pitcher. "Still three hours till dawn," she said. "Don't do to scare off the customers with the blood of the last one."

I dropped my eyes, and my cheeks grew hot.

"You may be half a madman to throw yourself on a Rider in your condition, but at some time you've had some wit about you. . . ." The Elhim cast his eyes to my left wrist, where the silver mark of the Musicians' Guild lay unrecognizable beneath the scars of manacles worn for too many years. Elhim were known to be clever at numbers and puzzles and games, always poking about in mysteries and scraps from the table of life, drifting on the edges of society. They were welcomed by neither the Senai nobility nor the Udema, who filled the trades and armies and freeholds, nor even the foreigners like Florins and Eskonians, who still languished for the most part in slavery or indenture decades after their kingdoms' defeats. "Did anyone see you with the Rider, Callia?" he called over his shoulder while his gray eyes picked at my secrets.

"Nah. I was in Smith's Alley, catching my breath from a fine, strapping fisherman, when the villain takes a wrong turn from the Alewife. Drank up half their stock from the smell of him. It was dark so's I didn't see the Ridemark on him until he had me to the stable." She threw down her rag and buttoned up her dress, then came to retrieve her wine. After a long pull at it, she dropped it back in my lap and bent over me, permitting an unavoidable glimpse of what her bodice couldn't hold, while planting a kiss on the top of my head. "When you've mended yourself a bit, I'll thank you proper. Till then you can claim anything else I've got for as long as you need. I do dearly love being alive." Her eyes sparkled with more than the wine, and she skipped through the door, her footsteps dancing down the stairs out of hearing.

The Elhim watched her go, smiling a crooked smile. "Callia has charged me to coddle you until she's back. She's a kindhearted girl."

I nodded and tried to remember how to smile, even as my eyelids sagged.

"Here, here, good fellow. I dare not let you sleep just yet. See what Callia's brought you."

With effort I dragged my eyes open again and identified the smell wafting through my bordering dreams. Soup. A steaming pail of it. Narim filled a dented tin mug and held it out. "Can you manage it?" His eyes studied my hands as I carefully cradled the hot, dripping cup between my palms. I could not yet make myself look at my hands, so I concentrated on the soup, inhaling the glorious aroma—a touch of onion, a sprig of parsley, and mayhap somewhere in its past a knucklebone had touched the broth. I could hardly bear to take the first taste, for the reality could be nowhere near the glorious delight of anticipation.

I was wrong. The broth was watery, but rich with barley, and imminently, delectably satisfying. I took only a small sip at a time. Held it. Savored it. Felt it go down and outline the hollow places. Strengthening. Saving my life.

Narim was kind and let me enjoy an entire cup without interruption. But as he refilled it, he served up the question that had been quivering on the edge of his tongue. "How long were you there?"

I saw no reason to alter the dismal truth, so I held up

five crooked fingers once, then twice, then again, and two fingers more after all.

"Seventeen . . . seventeen years? Hearts of fire. Is it possible?" His voice was soft, filled with wonder and a thousand unspoken questions. But he said nothing more, only stared at me as if to map my bones.

When I finished the second cup of soup, he offered me another, and it was all I could do to refuse it. Starvation knows nothing of reason. But I had once traveled the poorest places of the world, and I'd often witnessed what happened to those who gorged themselves after too long without. Narim must have read the panic in my eyes as he hung the cup on the rim of the bucket, for he smiled and said, "It will keep. When you wake again, the ovens down below will be primed and roaring, and I'll whisper compliments to my friend the cook, who'll heat it up for you. Will that do?"

This time I managed the smile, and I cupped my hands to my breast and bowed my head to him as if he were the king's own chamberlain.

"You will return the service someday, I think," he said, putting a strong arm behind my shoulders so that I could lie down on my stomach again without too much pain. "You have returned from the netherworld with the flame of life still lit within you. The gods do not ignore such a heart."

It was kindly meant, but I did not believe him. I had no heart left.

Chapter 2

His name was Goryx. My jailer. The one sworn to bring me to heel. The only face I saw for seventeen years. He was a burly, round-faced fellow with iron biceps, a cheerful disposition, and shining little eyes that crinkled into slits when he was pleased. He lived outside my cell and brought me enough pasty gruel and stale water that I would not die. His own rations were little better, and his room, though larger than my fetid, airless hole, was windowless and dim. He was a prisoner as much as I in many ways, only he had nowhere else he would rather be.

When my god would call me, there in the darkness of Mazadine, Goryx would listen while I made my answer, and when I was done, the exaltation of the holy mystery still nourishing my soul, the iron grating of my cell would open, and his smiling face would appear. With a long-suffering sigh he would hook a chain to my neck collar and haul me out, then drop the black canvas bag over my head. Once I was secured to a chair, he would spread my hands on his worktable, clucking over them like a mother hen, stroking my fingers and commenting on the efficacy of his last work. If the bones had begun to knit back together, I would hear the rasp of the metal jaws as they were laid out on the table, and I would feel the cold steel clamped onto the finger he'd decided would be first; then one by one he would break them all again. Only when he'd poked and prodded me enough that I was awake would he chain me to the wall and begin with the lash. He was an artist who took great pride in his work, able to make it last all day, able to take me to the edge of death, yet not quite beyond. That was forbidden. I was not to die. I would not be on my cousin's conscience as long as I lived. And when he was satisfied, Goryx would put me back in the tiny cell where I could not stand up or stretch out, and he would leave me in the dark until Roelan called me to sing for him again and, like a fool, I would answer.

For ten years I endured. Roelan comforted me, whispering in my heart that my service was valued, though I could not understand why, since no one could hear me but my god and my jailer. But I clung to his voice, reveled in his glory, let his music soar in my soul while I willed the pain to pass by. Somewhere in that time, though, after so many years of faithfulness, the whispered call grew fainter, and the darkness grew deeper, and I sang the music of my heart but heard no answering refrain. Soon all that was left to me was the pain and the darkness and the shreds of my defiance, and it was not enough.

Goryx saw it. He nodded and smiled his gap-toothed smile when he peered through the grate, and said, even as he pulled me out to do it all again, "Not long now."

He felt me tremble as he laid out his tools and stroked my knotted fingers, and he heard me whisper, "No more. Please, no more. Not again."

"Yield. Obey. And there will come a day seven years

from this one when you will see me no more," he said, as he laid my bones bare yet again. "Nothing more is required of you. Seven years of obedience and you will be free to go on your way."

As he expected, the day came when I broke. I've heard that there have lived those extraordinary men and women who cannot be defeated by such means, but I was not such a one. Goryx had broken all the fingers on my left hand and had clamped the jaws on my right thumb, ready to begin. "No more," I begged. "By the Seven Gods, no more."

"Do you yield?"

"Please . . ."

"You will obey and be silent?"

Head fogged with pain, I did not answer quickly enough. So he finished my right hand, and when I begged for mercy and swore I would be silent until the end of time, he said he could not believe me. So he laid my back open again, and I thought I would go mad from it, for I had not even my pride to sustain me any longer. But his work was done. When next I heard the god's faint call, I could not answer. I huddled in the darkness and clutched my ruined hands to my breast and begged Roelan's mercy, but I could not sing for him again. The music in my heart had bled away, and I was left with only darkness and silence. And in the formless years that followed, there came a time when I no longer heard the call, and I knew that I was truly dead.

Chapter 3

In the matter of a week, Callia and Narim had me in some semblance of order. I could take a deep breath without passing out, though my constant coughing was a matter of extreme gravity, and a sneeze out of the question. Their modest fare of soup and bread, with cheese added when I could stomach it, was finer than the delicacies of a hundred noble houses where I'd eaten in my youth. I gained a little weight, and Callia said my color was improved a thousandfold—surely her casual habits in matters of undress kept the blood flowing in my face. She brought me a shirt of coarse brown wool and a pair of tan breeches that were immensely cleaner than the rags I'd worn, even a shabby pair of farmer's boots only slightly too tight, "gifts," she said, from one of her admirers. I had not yet convinced myself to speak, a failure which made me feel stupid and weak, just as when I would stand up too long and get shaky at the knees.

Callia left me with far too much time to think about what I was to do with myself. For seven years I had worked to erase every remnant of my identity, every memory of my past life, every thought, desire, and instinct. Absolute emptiness had been the only way I could fulfill the terms of my sentence, the only way I could be silent, the only way I could survive. I'd had to be unborn. In the last years of my captivity, I could sit for days and have no image impose itself on the darkness of my mind, no trace of thought or memory. Now I could not fathom what I was to do next.

By the middle of the second week, the bump on the back of my head no longer throbbed a warning every time I moved, and I could stand up for moments at a time without falling over, so I picked a night when Callia and the Elhim were both out and started down the stairs. I had depended on the girl's meager livelihood for far too long, yet I didn't have the courage to face her as I took my leave. Halfway to the first landing, the steps dropped out of my vision as if they'd tumbled down a well. My foot could not find purchase, and I tumbled headfirst down the stairs. When my cracked ribs hit the splintered wood, I lost track of at least an hour.

Fumbling hands . . . a knife in my side . . . "Come on, then, arm over my shoulder."

I tried to stay still. Every movement, every breath, sent a lance through my middle. But the hands were insistent and my feet found the steps. Fortunately Callia was the first to discover me, and she hauled me back to her room with many protests of dire offense at my attempt to leave without telling her. "A life for a life," she said. As I could not yet muster words, she made me raise my hand in an oath to stay until she and Narim had judged my condition sound. As she was in the middle of binding up my ribs again, I had no choice but to acquiesce. The swearing was not so difficult as I made it out to be. In truth I was terrified at the thought of leaving the haven of Callia's room, and I blessed the injuries that kept me from having to face the world now that I was so irrevocably changed.

Outside of Callia's window was a goodly section of roof, and I'd made it a habit to crawl out onto it whenever anyone came up the stairs. Once Callia went back to work in earnest, she began bringing men back to her room, which sent me out for most of every night. I would lie wedged in a crevice behind a chimney, trying not to listen to what pleasure five coppers could buy. At first the open sky left me sweating with unnameable, unreasoning panic, but after a few nights I didn't want to go inside anymore. As I watched the stars pass over me in their eternal pavane, I began, ever so slightly, to believe that I was free.

One hot, still night as I was sitting on the roof, watching the wedged moon wander in and out among the wispy clouds, Callia climbed out of the window to sit beside me. She carried a linen kerchief, with which she was blotting off the sweat of her most recent encounter, and a flask of wine, which she offered to me. I gave her my customary gesture of thanks and drank deep of the sour vintage.

"What do you do out here all night?" she said. "You never seem to be asleep no matter what time it is. You're always just sitting and staring."

I pointed to the dancing moon and the stars, shining dimly in its light, and to my eyes while I held them wide open. Then I pointed to the dark heights where Mazadine lurked, and I passed my hand over my eyes, closing them tight. She had learned to understand my awkward signing very well.

"You weren't allowed to see the sky while you were in prison?"

I waved my hand at the dark, squat houses crowded together in the lane, at the few stragglers abroad, at the shadowed trees of the local baron's parkland across the sleeping city, and the ghostly mountain peaks of the Carag Huim looming on the distant horizon. Then I passed my hand across my eyes again, leaving them closed.

"Nothing. You weren't allowed to see nothing?"

I nodded.

"Damn! I can't imagine it. So I guess you're making up for it out here."

I smiled and returned her flask.

She drank, then peeked over at me sideways with the usual lively sparkle in her eyes. "I've no right to ask it, but I'm devilish curious and not used to minding my own business. Whatever was a Senai doing in Mazadine? I told Narim you must be a murderer at least, for the only thing worse is a traitor, and traitors are hanged right off, but you saved my life, and your ways . . . well, maybe it's only they're such gentle ways because you've been in such a wicked state, but I won't believe you a murderer. Are you?"

I shook my head and wished she would stop.

"Then what?" She picked up my knotted and scarred hand and held it in her warm, plump one. "What made them do this?"

I shook my head again, retrieved my hand, and was glad she accepted my inability to speak. Even if I could have convinced myself to say the words aloud, I could only have told her it was to silence my music and thus destroy me. But in a thousand years of trying, I could not have told her why.

Perhaps she thought I was too ashamed to tell her. She didn't press. "You don't mind my asking? I've not offended you?"

I smiled and opened my palms to her, and she passed the wine to me again.

She changed the subject to herself and chattered for half an hour about the peculiarities of men, beginning with her father, who began using her when she was eight and selling her when she was nine. Then she branched into detailed comparisons of Senai and Udema and all the others who had the money to pay for their pleasuring. "I think it's why I'm such great friends with Narim," she said. "My other friends ask how I can go about with a gelding child, but I tell them he's the only one I know who's got nothing to gain from using me."

I was listening with only half my attention, happy I was not expected to comment, when there came a low rumbling from the west. As it swelled into an unrelenting thunder, from the western horizon rose a cloud of midnight that quickly spread to blot out the stars in half the sky. Streaks of red fire ripped across the arch of the heavens. The moonlight that flickered behind the looming darkness was carved into angled shapes by ribbed wings that spanned half the city, then was transformed into intricate patterns of green and gold swirls and spirals by translucent membranes. Red fire glinted on coppery-scaled chests so massive they could smother twenty men and horses, and on long tails rippling with muscles so powerful they could knock holes in a granite wall.

"Vanir guard us! Dragons!" Callia dived through the

window as the flight passed over Lepan—five or six dragons, soaring on the winds of night. A hot gust lifted my hair, and it was heavy with musk and brimstone, the unmistakable scent of dragon. Soon, from above the blast of flame and the thunderous wind of those mighty wings, would come their cries—long, wailing, haunted cries that chilled the soul, cries that spoke an anger too powerful to bear, deep, bone-shaking roars of fury that caused the enemies of Elyria to cower in their fortresses and bow before the power of our king. Unheard from below would be the harsh commands of the Riders, each man a tiny knot of leather and steel behind the long, graceful neck of his mount.

I did not move from my place on the roof, only craned my neck to watch their passing, telling myself every moment to look away—that only danger and grief could be the result of my gaze. Not allowing myself to think—I was well practiced at that—I clamped my arms over my ears. I dared not listen to their cries, but by every god of the Seven, I would not fail to look.

"You're a madman!" said Callia, poking her head out of the window once the sky had regained its midnight peace. "You've been put away too long." She climbed out and plopped herself on the roof beside me. "You never know when one of the cursed beasts is going to glance down and decide you're ugly or insolent or breathing . . . whatever it is sets them burning. You could have ended up as crisp as Gemma's solstice goose!"

I scarcely heard her. My arms still blocked my ears lest I be undone by the sounds of their passing, and my eyes strained to see the last flickers of their fires as they disappeared in the eastern darkness.

"Are you all right?" The girl pulled my chin around to face her, and her eyes grew wide as she gently touched my cheek. "What in the name of sense . . . ? Why ever didn't you go inside? If you're so fearful of them as to make you weep, then you oughtn't even look."

But of course I had no words as yet, so I could not tell her that my tears had nothing to do with fear.

A few days later, Callia presented me with perhaps the finest gift of thanks I have ever received for any mortal service rendered. In response to her insistence that I let her know something that would please me—my being not yet ready for the favors she was most willing to dispense—I induced her to indulge me with a bath.

"Hot water poured on you in one of those tin tubs?" She looked from the drawing I had made in the dust on the floor to my absurd mime of washing. "Can't possibly be healthy. You've still got that beastly cough. And what if it makes your ribs loosen up again just when they're getting stuck back together?"

Impossible not to smile at her. I shook my head and tried more inept playacting to demonstrate that such activity would do no harm, but rather a world of good for my spirits.

"Well, Dilsey owes me a favor. I gave her a bit of lace to wear in her hair when she steps out with Jaston the pot boy. She'll haul the water up. Are you sure there's nothing else but that?"

I smiled and shrugged.

"You'll have to hide on the roof while she brings it. I'll tell her it's for one of my gentlemen." This consideration seemed to intrigue her. That evening, when the battered tin tub was in place and filled, it took some convincing to get her to leave the room. "Are you sure you don't need help? Perhaps I ought to stay. See how it's done in case you fall ill again."

I made a silly, eye-swirling face to show her it was just one of my peculiarities.

"Are all Senai so modest? The only ones I ever get are so drunk they've wandered into the wrong district. They don't realize I'm not quite their usual thing . . . and of course in that state they have no sensibilities at all!"

I apologized as best I could without words and pushed her gently through the ragged curtain that served her as a door. Once alone, I breathed easier. It was perhaps a strange thing after so long believing I would go mad if I did not hear another human voice, but I prized the hours when Callia was gone and the Elhim did not see fit to visit.

Rarely have I felt anything so sensually magnificent as that bath. I lowered myself gingerly into the steaming water, ignoring the protest of my aching ribs and the damaged muscles in my back as I curled up in the small tub and let the water cover my head. If I could have stayed under for an hour I would have done it. But I soon breached the surface, and over me came a joyous madness to get the remnants of Mazadine off me. With the scrap of cloth I'd found in Callia's bits and pieces and the sliver of soap Dilsey had supplied, I scrubbed away layer after layer of filth until my skin was gloriously raw and the water was black. With a knife borrowed from the Elhim, I set out to trim my mat of hair to a civilized length and scrape off the seventeen years' growth of unhealthy beard. The task took far longer than it should, for

I'd not counted on the difficulties of trying to manage a knife with fingers that could scarcely bend. The tenth time the knife dropped into the water, my delight had given way to howling frustration. But I forced myself to pick it up again, using one hand to wrap the fingers of the other around the hilt and willing them to hold on. If I was to live, I had to begin somewhere.

Dilsey had left one last pitcher of clean water standing by the tub, and when I finished with the knife without cutting my throat, I stood up and poured the now cold water over myself, glorying in the feeling of being clean. I stepped out, using my shirt to dry off, and was standing in the middle of the room completely unclothed when I heard light running footsteps on the stair. I bent over to tug on my breeches, but in far too much of a hurry, so that I was left dizzy and had to lean my head against the wall to keep from falling over.

"Callia, I've come to get the bath. We've a guest who— Oh!"

I looked around to see a short, dumpy Udema girl, staring with crossed eyes and open mouth at my bare back. I didn't like to think what it might look like. As I straightened, the girl's eyes traveled upward, registering my height and, no doubt, the dark hair, straight nose, and lean features that confirmed my heritage. She backed toward the doorway, a trace of fear in her eyes, the wariness of the Udema servant who interrupts a Senai at his business. "Pardon, my lord."

I tried to calm her, holding out a hand to stay her nervous flight, but she had already run down the stairs, no doubt spreading the gossip that Callia's latest customer was a Senai whose back was ridged with layer upon layer of red and purple scars. On my first night at the lodging house the Elhim had reported rumors of a prisoner escaped from Mazadine. I'd given it no thought—mostly because I was incapable of thought, but also because I had not escaped. I had been released. The terms of judgment had been fulfilled. But now, faced with exposure, I wondered. What if Goryx had miscounted the days? What if he had released me one hour early . . . or one day . . . or one year . . . and they said the time had not been completed and I would have to start again? What if they came to take me back?

I heaved up all the contents of my stomach into Dilsey's earthenware pitcher, then leaned heavily on the windowsill and tried to get my damp shirt on, cursing my infernal weakness and my clumsy hands, praying for the wave of terror to pass. I had to leave.

When I heard running feet on the stairs, I grabbed the Elhim's knife in both my hands and backed into a corner. But it was only Narim himself who charged into the room like an owl diving for its prey. "At least three souls are on their way to the Royal Horse Guards, each in hopes of collecting a silver penny for information regarding a Senai prisoner escaped from Mazadine. If you've no wish to be mistaken for such a one, I'd say the time has come for you to quit this house for a span. Callia remains below and will attempt to distract any who come looking, but she bids you hurry."

I nodded and stuck one leg through the window, but the tin tub sitting in the middle of the room glared at me accusingly. I stopped, calling myself every name ever invented for a fool. Anyone coming to Callia's room would know immediately what she'd done. Only Senai saw any virtue in bathing, so a Senai had clearly been here. No way to hide the evidence. If Callia could not produce a likely candidate, she would be arrested. And if my cousin had decided he was not done with me . . . if it was indeed me that these guards were hunting . . . Stupid, stupid. What had I done . . . letting these good people step into the dragon's mouth for me?

"Come on, man! It won't take them long to get here. Off with you."

I closed my eyes and shook my head. Gathering every scrap of will I possessed, I bade my tongue obey me. "Danger"—I could scarcely hear so low and hoarse a whisper as I could produce—"you . . . the girl . . . must get away."

"Nonsense. Climb across the roofs. They'll search here and find nothing. We'll light a lamp in the window when it's safe to come back."

In my bones I knew it was not so. They had been hunting someone for two weeks or more, yet not announced who it was. For anyone else, for any ordinary prisoner who had escaped, they could have made up a story, but I . . . I was to be forgotten. No one was ever to know who I was or what I had been. Something had gone wrong. Either the time was mistaken or . . . who knew what else it could be? But if they took me, then they would kill anyone who had seen me or talked to me. And if they connected me to the dead Rider, it would be a long and wicked death.

"Please," I croaked desperately, shaking my head. "Believe. You'll die for helping." I was trembling with the effort of the words, feeling the darkness close in on me again . . . and the unending guilt.

"Even if they just suspect it?" His eyes were narrow and his voice angry.

I nodded, wishing I could tell him how deeply I regretted the blind cowardice that had made me stay with Callia.

"And you never told us the risk? What kind of person are you?"

It would have taken far too many words to explain it. "Go quickly" was all I could manage.

"I'll get Callia and meet you on the roof."

"No."

He looked at me sharply. "You mean to stay—to wait for them?"

"Please go."

"And so you will let some illiterate Horse Guard take your life, which Callia and I so carefully preserved, while we are forced to abandon our home for that very act of preservation? You might have saved us all the trouble and died in that stable."

"They will not kill me."

He released a monumental sigh. Then, wrapping his soft, pale eyes around my face and his hands about my own that still clutched his knife, he quieted my shaking with his slender fingers. Very softly he said, "Tell me why not."

Though everything within me demanded silence, I could not refuse him. "They are forbidden it."

A smile touched his lips. "So it is you, then, Aidan MacAllister, beloved of gods and men, the most famous musician in fifty generations, he who could transform the souls of men with his voice and his harp. The cousin of

King Devlin himself, vanished like the wind when you were but one and twenty."

I shook my head feebly.

He drew me toward the window, and I forced more words to stay him. "Save the girl. Leave."

"Foolish boy. I'll not leave you. I'm here to take you where you need to go. You are the Dragon Speaker."

I didn't know what he meant by such a title. No one knew about the dragons.

Chapter 4

My mother always told me I was born singing. She said I never cried like other infants, but wailed in a beautiful, rambling melody that varied as to my particular need. But it was in my days of glory that she said it, and always within the hearing of those who would repeat it and amplify the tale into legend. Her dark eyes would sparkle with the loving laughter that kept my head human-sized.

What I remember from my earliest days is only the music—the harmonies that played themselves unceasingly in my head, demanding to be let out whether through my voice or a harp or a whistle made of reed. I could not pass a bell without ringing it or hold a flask without blowing across its mouth, and when I had nothing else I would beat my hands upon a table or a pot or my knee, bringing to birth the rhythms and songs that crowded and bumped each other about within me.

My mother was the younger sister of King Ruarc, a craggy, vicious warrior who doted on her and took her under his protection when my father was slain in the brutal Eskonian wars. She insisted on remaining in my father's house in the country, rather than moving into the palace, which her brother had preferred. She wanted me away from our everlasting wars, she told me, for despite the claims of King Ruarc's court musicians, there were a great number of things to sing about that were not battle and blood and death. I didn't understand what she meant, and got confused when her eyes grew sad and full of tears as she talked of my father, who had been burned beyond recognition by the dragon legion of the Eskonians. Everyone else rejoiced that he was a great hero and said he lived in honor with Jodar, the god of war. Not until I was older did I associate my father with the stinking, screaming remnant of charred, decaying flesh that existed in our house for a month when I was very small.

And so I grew up outside of courtly circles, though King Ruarc provided swordmasters for me who were as fine as those he chose for his own son, Devlin, and tutors suitable for those with such close connection to the throne. But my mother spent her fortune hiring master musicians to train me in the only skills I cared about. By the time I was ten I had mastered the harp and the flute and the lyre, and I knew every song my masters could find to teach me. I could play the most intricate harmonies, my fingers flying across the strings, and I could wind my voice about the most complex melodies, so that every note was perfect and would hang shimmering in the air to join with its fellows. Every day I practiced and sang from earliest rising to dark midnight, the desire was so strong within me.

When I was eleven, my masters said that I was ready to be heard, and they arranged that I should sing at the royal victory feast marking the Eskonian surrender. The prospect was terrifying—proclaiming myself a musician before the king and five hundred of his finest warriors. Indeed the guests sniggered behind their hands when I

stood up in my gold-encrusted suit and began to play—
the king's nephew, who preferred the harp to the sword.
But once I touched my strings, my terror vanished and
my doubt, for whenever I released the flood of music that
was in me, it swept everything else away. At the end,
King Ruarc himself stood and raised his glass to me, saying he was honored that his family was touched by the
gods in so many ways. I believed I had reached the pinnacle of my life, and that my course would be straight
from that night forward.

But it was on that same night of the feast, when my
performance was long over, and the king and his warriors
well into drowning twenty years of blood with unending
flagons of wine, that I wandered the vast parklands of the
palace, cooling my fever of success, and learned that
everything I'd done, every note I'd struck and every word
I'd sung, were naught but childish play. For it was on the
night of my first triumph that I first heard the cries of
dragons.

Every Elyrian child is fascinated with dragons. Their
image is carved on every stone column and lintel and
woven into every tapestry. If you were very lucky, you
might see them flying high above the land on their way
into battle, and, until you learned the truth of their murderous power, you might call them beautiful in their towering majesty. But every Elyrian child, along with the
children of every kingdom with or without dragons, soon
learned the horrors of dragon fire—the scorched crop-
lands and forests, the flame-ravaged towns and villages,
and everywhere the scars of burned flesh and agonizing
death.

No one knew how old the dragons were. Legend said

that in ancient times dragons had terrorized the wild lands of the west, ravaging the countryside with only a race of wizards able to exist alongside them. Scholars had no real evidence of that. Indeed our history from more than five hundred years in the past was either lost or dreadfully muddled—erased, not by dragons, but by a seventy-year span of famine, disease, and anarchy that had cost us more than three-quarters of our population. In those same years, invaders from the east and north, tattooed tribes with a taste for flaying prisoners, and fur-clad horsemen who reveled in blood and destruction, had sensed our weakness and come looking for metal, gemstones, and women, ravaging our towns and cities, destroying books and culture and learning along with buildings and temples.

At some time in those Chaos Years, so the tales said, the Twelve Families of the Ridemark Clan defeated the wizards in a great battle, gaining control of the bloodstones that bent dragons to the will of men. Whatever the truth of history, the Twelve Families had made the dragons into the most fearsome weapon of war the world had ever known. For five hundred years the beasts had been pressed into the service of kings and nobles, controlled by the bloodstones of their bound Riders. Thus had the barbarians been thrust back beyond the mountains that ringed our lands and civilization arisen once again in Elyria and her neighboring kingdoms. New cities were built. Roads and herds and villages spread rapidly across the land. Trade and learning were reawakened. But still, and always, we waged war. Now that we had the power of dragon fire, our unending lust for victory and vengeance threatened ruin to everything we built.

In the very instant of hearing the dragons' screams, I stood in my uncle's moonlit gardens and felt my talent burned to ash as truly as their breath had reduced the cities of Eskonia. Standing beside a shrine dedicated to the hunchbacked god of music, I wept because I could not make their dreadful music into my own. When I returned home I could not sing or play, but only clutch my harp and rock back and forth, crying out my hunger to hear more of dragon songs. My mother feared for my reason, berating herself for encouraging my intensity so young. But my masters said that I was confused. Yes, the god of music had given me a sign on that night, they said. Was I not beside Roelan's shrine when I was stricken? But of course no beauty could ever be found in the murderous braying of dragons. The god had only used the bellowing of beasts to tear down my childish pride so that he could shape my talent to his service.

I accepted their saying, for it seemed right and reasonable that the beauty that I craved was the music of a god, not the mindless roaring of the beasts of fire who had charred my father's flesh. But in my deepest of hearts I feared that one of the Seven—perhaps Jodar, the god of war, or Vanir, the fire-tamer—had condemned me to search for harmony where it could never be found. I thought that Roelan must despise me to leave me afflicted with such a yearning.

From that day I never again lived in the house of my father. I told my mother and my teachers that I had to forsake all I had done thus far and learn my art again from the beginning until I was worthy of Roelan's favor. My mother yielded to my passion and my masters' insistence that I must obey the demands of my art or go mad. And so I found out where the dragon legions were encamped and took lodgings as close as was allowed. For hours and days and weeks at a time I would watch the beasts fly off to war, trumpeting their dreadful fury, and I would open myself to the sound of it and try to make it a part of me. Ashamed and afraid of the burden the gods had put on me, I told no one why I did what I did. My masters drifted away. They said they could not presume to teach me any more.

Only Gwaithir, my harp master, remained, being fond of me and believing a boy of eleven should not make his way alone. He saw that I was fed and clean, moved my household whenever I said—which happened to be when the dragon legions left the vicinity—and corresponded with my mother, for I had no time and no mind for anything but music. She would visit me once or twice a year, but I would kiss her absentmindedly, living wholly in the world of songs and harmonies that played out in my mind.

As time passed, I stopped thinking about the beasts themselves and the horrors they wrought and listened only to the tone and timbre and wrenching power of their cries. Some called my actions madness, but I was fortunate that my mother and Gwaithir seemed to understand, for it was in that time of mystery that I began to hear a whispered voice in my head and heart.

Sing to me.

Ease the grieving of my heart.

Transform me into that which I have been.

At first the call was not even words, but only a quiet, swelling hunger, a lonely emptiness so huge and deep that I was left shaking. I ran to Gwaithir and clung to him, terrified that I was going mad, unable to explain my tears that were so much more than fear. After a second year of listening and practicing and exploring the most basic fundamentals of my art, losing myself in a realm where only my soul and the music and the hunger existed . . . only then, tentatively, quietly, in a way that had nothing at all to do with the complexities I had mastered as a child, did I begin to sing again. And only then did the one who called me speak his name.

I am Roelan.

Thou art my own, my beloved, and I will cherish thee until the dayfires burn no more.

Sing for me, beloved.

The god of music himself had claimed me for his own.

Gwaithir told me that on the night I first sang for Roelan, sitting on the ruined walls of Ellesmere at moonrise, he'd felt the breath of the god raise the hair on his arms and his neck. As for me, on that same night when I was thirteen, I first heard the god's answering song—quiet, distant music that raised me out of my body so that I believed that I was standing on a mountaintop, gazing down upon a lake of fire.

I did not perform in public for three full years—until I turned fourteen and Gwaithir presented me for membership in the Musicians' Guild. The guild had been formed after the Chaos Years, a promise to Roelan that never again would the world's songs and music be lost. Although every musician supported and honored the guild, few were accepted as members, for the applicant's talent, memory, and mastery of the art had to be exceptional. Those of the guild were exempt from service in the king's armies, and every household, whether noble or peasant, was open to them. Unlike lesser performers, they received no pay, but they never wanted for food or drink or a roof or company. Membership in the guild would be freedom to travel as I wished, giving myself wholly to the god. But first I had to prove myself worthy. Talented though he was, Gwaithir was not a member, and no one of my age had ever been admitted.

As we entered the Guild Hall in Vallior, a splendid performance space of wood floors and walls, polished to a golden glow, and a domed ceiling painted with scenes of the hunchbacked god playing his harp, Gwaithir fidgeted nervously. He was terrified that I would fail, terrified that I would die in battle before the world could hear the music I could make. But before he left me, I laid my hand on his shoulder and said, "If he does not want me, he will be silent, and I'll know he has some other path in mind. If he wishes me to serve him in this way, I will not fail."

And so it was. I sat on a stool in the center of the cavernous room, a room alive with echoes, and I faced ten of the finest musicians in the realm—names of legend. They had heard nothing of me since my childhood triumph at the victory feast, and likely assumed that the onset of manhood had ruined my voice. The steward at the door had told Gwaithir that the guild committee had agreed to hear me only out of respect for him and a nagging remembrance that I was related to the king.

For my part, I could not have told anyone how many were there or who, for I was making my heart quiet so as to listen for Roelan. "Master," I whispered in my deepest silence. "It is thy servant, Aidan, who awaits thy call."

In moments, it came—a torrent of sensation, sweeping

through me like a summer hurricane, pounding fire
coursing through my veins, stripping my lungs of breath
until I could draw myself together and sort out his words.
No longer did I hear an echoing emptiness, but the loving
voice in my heart.

Beloved, soothe my uttermost sorrows.

Transform me.

Make me remember.

My teacher. My master. My god.

I sang that day of homecoming, of searching a frozen
earth for a place remembered, though lost for uncounted
ages of the world. I sang of adventures along the way, of
constant leaving and forgetting, of the weight of years
and the passing of time so that the searcher feared his
cause was lost. Gwaithir said I had the judges in tears by
the end, but all I knew was that Roelan answered me. In
his song that only I could hear, the searcher found his
heart's desire—a lake of fire in the heart of winter snows.
There he met his brothers and sisters long estranged, and
the joy that flowed within me held me riveted, mesmerized until the last echoes of the god's refrain were gone.

"Where have you learned it, boy?" said one of the
judges, as I shook off my daze. "Whose hand has guided
yours on the strings? It is the sound of the wind your fingers pluck. Your voice sings the glory of moonlight on
the snow, the music of birds, the whisper of winter mist."

"The god of music guides my hand and voice," I said,
as will every musician who respects the gods. I did not
tell them that Roelan schooled me by speaking in my
heart or that he sang in answer to my music or that he had
disciplined me to find beauty even in the harsh bellowing
of dragons. It seemed pretentious to say I knew how my

god did what he did. It was mystery and took no honor from him to remain so. They did not need to know.

And so it was that my wrist was marked with silver on that day, and I was proclaimed a guild singer dedicated to Roelan.

For seven years I traveled the length and breadth of all known lands, my life an unending celebration of beauty and mystery and joy. I refused no invitation, shunned no venue as too remote or too dangerous or unworthy, and I took no payment save food and shelter, for there was nothing that could match the gift of my life. I was the voice of a god, and I carried his joy into noble houses and into lepers' dens, into palaces and the poorest quarters of great cities. I sang before the king, and I sang for his soldiers in the field of battle, and I sang for the stunned and starving victims of war in their squalid tenements. When King Ruarc died, I sang his funeral dirge, and when my mother lay consumed by her last illness, I sang her through the crossing with words of those people and things she had cherished. And when my eighteen-year-old cousin, Devlin, was crowned king of Elyria, I made my obeisance with my harp in my hand. But always I returned to the dragons, watching from afar as their Riders screamed the commands that would force them to obey, listening to their pain and wild fury and grief, and making it my own.

I had always gotten along with my cousin Devlin. Until the days of my rebirth at eleven, we met on every family and state occasion, always shuffled off to eat and drink together and amuse ourselves while our elders carried on adult business. The rivalries that one might have expected for two highborn youths so close in age and family—I was six months his junior—were made moot by the difference in our passions. He claimed to have no ear for music, and I made no secret of my disdain for the arts of warfare and statecraft, which were all that interested him. I complained bitterly to my mother that I had to waste time with fencing and riding, while Devlin did not have to spend equal time with my strict flute master. But we found things to do and had some good times, and we did not dread our rare meetings.

I saw my cousin very little in my three years of madness or my years in the guild. If he felt any jealousy that I was already at the pinnacle of my profession while he was still "the boy" riding in his father's massive shadow, it was surely blunted by the certainty of his ascension to the most powerful throne in the world. Devlin was his father's only son, his four sisters long married off to distant nobles who were strong allies but no threat to his inheritance, and in five hundred years no king of Elyria had lived beyond the age of fifty. The high price of using dragons to wage war was that there was no end to it. The devastation they wrought on land and cities and people was so terrible that there was no shifting of loyalties or blending of peoples or softening of borders, no forgiveness and no respite from vengeance.

A year after his coronation, when I was eighteen, I sang at Devlin's wedding to a beautiful girl of impeccable Senai breeding, and a year after that I sang at his infant son's anointing as Prince of Thessin, heir to the throne of Elyria. I did not speak to my cousin on either occasion, but I did spend an hour with his son as we waited in the gardens for the anointing ceremonies to begin. The child, draped in heavy finery and held at arm's length by an exasperated waiting woman, was wailing endlessly, threatening to sour the harmony I'd brought to honor him.

I had no experience with infants, but when the waiting woman began to curse at the child, I offered to make an attempt to quiet him. I picked for a moment at the sound of his lament, and then began to sing in counterpoint to his cry. Where he would raise it up a tone, I would go down, and when he would pulse in demanding rhythm, I would smooth it with a gliding arpeggio. When he pierced the sky, I sang quietly of the earth, and before long he hushed and opened his eyes wide. I smiled as I sang, and he made some earnest cooing. I sang another round, and he followed every inflection with his own chirping until he was laughing and waving his tiny hands.

The child's wide-eyed delight at the lullaby I created for him on that sun-drenched summer afternoon opened a new world to me. He laughed and gurgled and held tight to my finger as it plucked the strings, giving me a thread of purity and innocence and unfettered delight to weave into the tapestry of music. Over the next two years I sent him a little flute from Florin and a silver llama bell from the high mountains of Godai, a music box with tiny soldiers that marched about in circles, and a drum from the wild men of the eastern wastes. I wrote him letters every month, telling of where I'd been and what I'd seen, delighting in thinking of him as my family. I hoped to get a chance to meet the child again someday to thank him properly for his gift to me.

It was in the fourth year of Devlin's reign that I received an urgent summons to his palace in Vallior. I had just returned from two months' journeying in Eskonia, and I was staying with a prosperous merchant family, the Adairs, who had befriended me when first I began traveling and sought a place in one of their caravans. They had a son named Gerald who was close to my age and, once he got over his awe at my fame and position, became my closest friend. He was sturdy and sensible, but took very well to adventuring and made it a habit to show up whenever I booked passage in one of his family's caravans. We saw a great deal of the world together, he pursuing his family's business looking for interesting merchandise and healthy markets, and I pursuing the work of my heart. The Adairs also had a daughter a few years younger than I, sixteen at the time I was summoned to see Devlin. Alys was fair and intelligent, good at poking fun at Gerald and me, who tended to take ourselves far too seriously where women were concerned. Yet I had begun to think that if Roelan ever left me room for other passions, I might well find myself hopelessly attached to her perfect green eyes. I'd had no thought of roots in the seven years of my journeying, but it was the fourth return to Vallior in a row that I'd found myself at the Adairs.

When the royal summons came, I excused myself regretfully from a fine and lively dinner, spruced up my attire, and debated whether to take my harp. I finally did so. It would be awkward to have to send for it if music was wanted. Why else would Devlin call for me?

The small private garden was elegantly manicured with mounds of perfect flowers, squared-off shrubbery, and a copper fountain in the shape of a rearing dragon that spewed water instead of fire. The evening was cool, the lingering light soft on the green, and, as always, I kept an eye upward to see if there was any trace of red fire in the sky. I didn't have to wait very long. My cousin swept into the garden from a brilliantly lit wing of the palace, and he was as elegantly attired as his garden, green satin shirt and tight black breeches, and a black silk cape, its clasp a golden dragon with ruby eyes. He'd grown a beard since his coronation, so he looked more than six months older than me. Perhaps the weight of the golden circlet on the dark hair so like to mine had also done its part. I dipped my knee, and he gestured me up. We were still exactly the same height.

"You're a hard man to catch," he said, motioning me to walk beside him down the flagstone pathways. He had always been restless.

"I've not spent three nights running in the same bed for seven years," I said.

"The price of your calling, I suppose."

"True enough."

"I'll confess I never thought your name would be better known than mine." I listened carefully, but heard no more than wry observation. "I've had people tell me you are touched by the gods, and I tell them that when you were eight years old you set your hair on fire as we were scaring bats out of Wenlock Cavern, and I had to throw you in the lake to put it out."

I laughed. "Perhaps it was the god who sent the storm as we rode home that day to make sure the fire was out."

"Indeed. I never thought of that."

We walked awhile in silence. It seemed best to wait for him. At last he stopped alongside the dragon fountain, and he was not thinking at all about the childish adventures we had shared. His eyes were like obsidian as they bored into mine. "You've just returned from Eskonia." It was a statement, not a question.

"Yes."

"What were you doing there?"

Easy to say something frivolous. Everyone in the world knew what I did. But he was not asking the question lightly, so I responded with the same seriousness.

"I sang in fifteen cities and uncounted villages, at more than a hundred weddings and coming-of-age feasts, and possibly that many funerals. I explored the ruined temples at Horem, and I spent the night alone in an ice cave at the top of Mount Pelgra, though I can't tell you why, except that I heard the howls of the Denazi wolves and the song of the snow lark that I had never before heard. I refused no call and no invitation and no opportunity to learn, as is my duty and my habit . . . and my pleasure."

I would have guessed he could repeat my words exactly, so intently did he listen, and he was listening to far more than words. Perhaps we had more in common than I'd thought.

"You went to Cor Marag."

The slightest twinge of . . . it was not guilt, but something else—pride, shame, rebellion?—touched me. Cor Marag was where the northern dragon legion camped when they were quartered in Eskonia . . . as they had been when I was there.

"I still love to watch them. Never outgrew it." I smiled as I said it, but my words fell like lead between us. Lies are heavier than other words. Of course, I did not enjoy watching dragons and thinking of what they did. Listening was something else, but I still could not explain why. It was just easier to lie and let it pass.

"So I hear. You follow them. Wherever you travel you find where they are, and wherever they are, that's where you travel."

I said nothing. I certainly couldn't deny it, but to discuss something so intimate, so holy, with a man I scarcely knew . . . I'd not told anyone why I did what I did, not since the night when I was eleven and my music masters insisted that Roelan had used the dragons to punish my pride. It was mystery. It was between Roelan and me and could not be explained in words. But Devlin seemed to want words.

"Aidan, tell me why." In that moment he was speaking to me as a cousin, not a king, and if I'd understood it, perhaps I would have made some attempt to explain, and my life would have been very different. But I was too much used to living in my own world, and I could not see into his.

"I go where my god commands me." How stupidly prideful it must have sounded.

He shook his head in exasperation. "Stay away from them."

"I don't—"

"Just stay away. Don't be seen anywhere near them. Anywhere. Do you understand me? I won't have it. I have no ill will toward you, but this . . . whatever it is you're doing . . . it will stop now. You are forbidden to be within a league of any dragon legion. Forbidden."

I stood stunned at this pronouncement, and by the time I sputtered out the words "Devlin, listen," he was gone. At the doorway into the lighted palace he was met by a huge broad-faced man in the uniform of a Dragon Rider. The fellow's imposing stature, as well as his bald head, hawk's bill of a nose, and full curling lip, announced him as Garn MacEachern, the high commander of the Ridemark and the Elyrian dragon legions. They conferred for a moment, but by the time I recovered my wits and ran to the steps, they had disappeared inside. Two guards barred my way. The chamberlain who had shown me to the garden appeared silently at my elbow and pointed me discreetly to the side gate that led out of the palace.

Devlin left Vallior the next day to lead his warriors against the rebellious state of Kythar far to the east, so I was unable to get an audience. His chamberlains said it was to be at least three months until he returned.

A few weeks later I journeyed into Aberthain, a small country in the southwestern hill country whose king was Devlin's vassal. King Germond had three dragons in his service. Unlike most rulers, he kept them close to his palace, and with them the noble hostages he had captured from his enemies. His capital city was quite vulnerable, and to have the symbols of their strength so near gave his people heart. Though Devlin's warning echoed in my mind, I could not refuse when Germond asked me to sing at his son's coming-of-age feast.

King Germond's dragons were bellowing ferociously as I lay in the fine bed in his palace. I could not sleep for their cries. So I made my way to the barren wasteland where they were kept and sat upon a high, rocky promontory overlooking their encampment. They roamed restlessly across the desolation, vomiting fire that blazed red and went out quickly because there was nothing left to burn, and their voices thundered with anger and sorrow.

Some time in the deeps of that night I began to sing, and it was as if the whole chorus of the Seven Gods sang in me. My heart came near bursting with the glory of the music.

Three days after my return to Vallior I was arrested in the middle of the night and charged with treason. Aiding the enemies of Elyria, the two officers said, though no specific accusation was ever made. Naively, foolishly, I demanded audience with the king. I insisted on knowing what were the charges, and I claimed that I was so well known that people would hunt for me and find out what injustice was being committed. But the only information I received was when an officer who remained in the shadows raised his hand to have the burly, hard-faced men drag me away. On his wrist was the red outline of a dragon—the Ridemark. I kicked at a lamp, rolling it toward the tall man, and as the oil pooled and flared into brilliance, it showed me the hawk-nosed high commander of the Ridemark clan.

In a spiraling nightmare of horror and despair, I was forced to watch as the Adairs and old Gwaithir and my manservant Liam and every person who had any personal dealing with me was slaughtered in a secret execution, and a faceless, hooded judge with a red dragon on his wrist pronounced the sentence that would send me to Mazadine. My voice was to be silent for seven years, and only then could I be free to go . . . as long as I did not go anywhere near a dragon.

Chapter 5

The refuse heap where Narim had told me to wait lay next to a butcher shop. The hot days had brought the foul mess to such ripeness that even the most abject wretches of Lepan avoided the place. As I crouched beside it in the lingering evening, I did my best to stifle my coughing and get a decent breath without inhaling, a more difficult feat of breath control than anything I'd done when I was singing. If I'd had anything left in my stomach it would not have stayed there, and with enormous regret I considered my glorious bath that seemed far more than half an hour past.

Count to a hundred, I told myself. *If they're not here by then, I'll go. There's bound to be a boat to steal somewhere along the river, or a wagon going south.* But even as I glared at the rats sitting boldly on their treasure trove of rotting rubbish, I knew I could not leave Callia and Narim to the searchers. No one else was going to die for me. Count to a hundred and I would retrace my steps up the steep embankment to the butcher shop roof and across a half dozen rooftops to the inn where the Elhim was trying to persuade Callia that she had to abandon her life or die. Just as I was about to start back, I heard voices in the lane.

"Vellya's pigs! What charnel house is this? Only for you, Narim, would I dump a good customer and come to such a place. The soldiers wouldn't have bothered me at all if they'd found me with an assistant magistrate."

"Quiet, girl! There are things you don't understand."

"I daresay— Oh, there you are!" The flushed, buxom Callia in her shabby green satin bustled past the waiflike, chalk-skinned Elhim. She brushed her hand over my clean-shaven face and examined the rest of me thoroughly. "You look right fine. Maybe there's something to this bathing. Now what's all this about us getting killed because of you? My place has been searched a deal of times. Found it more profit than trouble. Searchers always have money—for bribes and all—and they like spending it on fun instead."

"I'm sorry," I rasped, looking helplessly at the Elhim. He folded his arms and looked amused.

"So you've got a tongue, do you? Just like a Senai to use his first words in a month to tear up a woman's life." Callia set her hands on her hips and screwed her face into a frown. "I'm not going anywhere until you tell me why you're so important."

"If you want her to do as you say, you're going to have to trust her," said Narim. "She's a businesswoman and isn't going to abandon it lightly. And you'd best make it quick."

I think he just wanted me to confirm what he'd guessed, but I wasn't ready to do so, so I gave Callia only the most important detail. "When they took me . . . before," I said, struggling to get out so many words at once, "they killed everyone in the house where I lived . . . everyone close to me: servants, friends . . . everyone."

"Why would they do—" Shouts and screams and an explosion of orange flames from the way we had come interrupted her. Callia gaped at me. "They've fired the Drover! Who, in the name of Tjasse, *are* you?"

"He'll tell you all about it later," said the Elhim. We took off jogging down the dark twisting alleys of Lepan, past deserted shops and dimly lit taverns, past muddy sties, stables, and smithies reeking of coal and ash, always taking the downward-sloping ways that would lead us to the slow-moving Lepander River. Few souls were about in the night. Drunks sprawled in corners, lost in blissful stupor. A growling beggar whose face was ravaged with seeping burns lunged at Narim from a dark doorway, and the Elhim had to struggle fiercely to get away. A few late revelers staggered out of a tavern, but no one else prowled the dark lanes—not at first. The Elhim was taking us to a friend's dinghy tied up down by the docks. If we could just get through the town fast enough . . .

But every hundred paces I had to stop and cough, allowing the stitch in my side to subside, persuading some meager reserve of strength to seep back into my legs. I had tried to keep my body from atrophying completely in prison, but with poor food, little space, and the pain of constant injury, it had been impossible. "Sorry," I gasped for the hundredth time as I bent double, leaning on an empty bin behind a fishmonger's stall. The heavy, ripe air and the steepening pitch of the cluttered lanes told me we were nearing the river, but I had tripped on a rusty wagon tongue and couldn't get moving again. Torches had flared into life all over the sleeping city. Shouts and the pounding of feet and the clangor of armed men on horseback came from every side, the noise grating in my head. "Go on. I can't. . . ."

Callia grabbed a dark apron from someone's washing and wrapped it about her like a shawl. Glancing over her shoulder nervously, she tugged at my arm. "Come on. Can't leave you after all this trouble. I'm shiv'd if I'll let you get away without explaining."

"Look, Callia," said the Elhim, "head down past the slave docks. Go north until you come to the old customs house. There's an alehouse just past, and an alley between. Down the alley you'll come to some stone steps leading down to the river. The boat will be at the bottom of the steps. Wait for us there. We'll be less noticeable if we go separately."

Callia must have been wickedly afraid, for she didn't argue at all. She only laid her hand on my cheek and said, "A life for a life. Be there." Her breath was sweet and only faintly tinged with cheap wine. Silently she slipped into the shadows.

"Now you," said the Elhim. "We'll take it slower. It's not far. But listen to me . . . if we get separated or the boat's gone or something happens to me, find your way to the Bone and Thistle on the Vallior road. Ask for Davyn and tell him I've sent you. He'll help."

The distance to the rendezvous may not have been far, but our journey was very slow. We cut through the ramshackle riverfront district, constantly forced to backtrack. Parties of armed men roamed the city, asking questions of clusters of sleepy residents.

"Murderer on the loose," they were saying.

"A Senai gone mad from dragon's breath, I heard."

"Madman. Fired the Drover 'cause he didn't like the ale! Copped a whore and said he'd gut her if he didn't get his money back."

Narim, his back flattened to a stable wall, whispered in my ear, "At least they aren't saying you were dissatisfied with the woman. Callia would be most disturbed at that." I was too tired to appreciate his humor.

Roving bands of ruffians were taking the opportunity to harass people in the streets. In one alleyway we stumbled over a dead Elhim whose face was pulp, bloody clothes half ripped from the slender, mutilated body. His purse had been cut from his belt. Narim was no longer smiling when he locked my arm in the vise of his fingers and dragged me onward.

Staying low, we scuttered across a wide lane, ducking into a stinking alley that sloped sharply downward. Its far end opened onto a broad embankment choked with weeds and rubbish, overlooking the dark, foggy ribbon of the Lepander.

"Down there," whispered the Elhim from just behind me, nudging me toward a broken stone path that led down the embankment. "Go on down to Callia. I'm to leave a token so my friend will know who took his boat."

I nodded, praying my watery knees could get me down the stone steps. Somewhere in the yellow fog, water rippled into a backwater with a soft plopping noise. The steps seemed to go on forever. But eventually my searching foot sank into mud instead of jarring on stone. Across a muddy strip was the vague outline of a dinghy bobbing gently beside a plank walkway, dark against the dark water. No sign of Callia—not until torches flared behind and before me to reveal a broad-shouldered man with a hard, cruel mouth holding the terrified girl by the throat, a knife pointed at her eye. Before I could move, a thick, hairy arm was clamped about my own throat, and my right arm was twisted behind my back.

"Well, well. Senai nobles are keeping low company these days. Don't you know you can get crabs from bitches like this?" said the one holding Callia. I didn't have to see the red mark on his wrist to know he was a Dragon Rider, and a very angry or very drunk one, unable to control his inner fire. Orange sparks spit and hissed wherever he held the girl close to him. She whimpered softly. "We'll protect you, Senai. Our sovereign will appreciate that his family's seed is not being dispensed in such unworthy vessels." Then, with no more thought than plucking a fowl for his supper, the Rider whipped his knife across Callia's throat and shoved her to the ground. Mud spattered her cheek, the eyes that had sparkled with so much life fixed in terrified surprise.

"Bastards!" I cried in my useless, croaking whisper. But outrage produced no magical surge of strength to prevent my ending ignominiously with my own face in the mud. While they wrenched my arms behind me and locked manacles on my wrists, black despair descended into my soul. If it had been in my power to will my heart to stop beating, I would have done it . . . especially if I could have taken every villainous Ridemark warrior with me.

"Didn't teach you well enough, did we?" said the murderer, wiping his bloody knife on my cheek. "We'll tell Goryx not to be so dainty with you this time." With heavy boots and the dragon whips they carried at their belts, he and his companion proceeded to give me a taste of what they had in mind. But they had no more than gotten started when they abruptly stopped again.

Shouts and heavy blows continued, but they had little to do with me, for which I was immensely grateful. My bonds made movement impossible, even if I'd had the strength to try or the fortitude to ignore the fresh indignities that had been laid over my already battered self. I was barely lucid enough to keep myself from drowning in the mud. But the proceedings were very odd. The Elhim could not be putting up such a fight as I heard. Somehow in my groggy confusion I envisioned an irritated Callia standing up in her green satin, the blood trickling down the front of it from her gaping throat, and throwing the heavy bodies into the river with a resounding splash. Or perhaps the splash was my face falling into the mud as I slipped into insensibility.

I didn't want to open my eyes. The terror that I would see nothing but darkness was so absolute as to allow no other thought to pass through my mind. In the same way I dared not move lest I feel the damp straw, or the manacles about my wrists and ankles, or the iron walls so close about me that I could touch all four plus ceiling and floor at once. I dared not breathe lest I smell the stink of my fear and the foulness of my den of living death. Desperately I fought to stay on the far side of the boundary between sleep and waking. Better not ever to wake up. Better not to know.

". . . not yet ready for visitors. But I thought you ought to see . . ." The whisper came from the waking side, but learning who it was meant opening my eyes.

"By the Seven!" Vaguely familiar, that shocked, angry voice. "They'll pay for this. Do what you can. As soon as he's fit to talk, send for me."

Clothing rustled and footsteps receded—furious footsteps on wood floors—then water dribbled close by my ear. Warm wetness on my naked back, stinging at first . . . then soothing . . . and on my face and my arms. Mumbled cursing as the gentle ministrations touched my hands. Sometime in between I was rolled onto my back, a position I could not bear after seventeen years of constant lashings. When I heard a dismal moan and concluded it was my own, the invisible spirit crooned comfort—a spirit that, from the sound of it, was surely embodied in an elderly gentleman.

"Only a moment, laddie; then we'll have you over again. I can see it would pain you. Let me get you cleaned up and make sure we've left nothing untended; then we'll send you off to sleep away your hurts."

My eyelids were still too heavy to open and became more so once a spoonful of something sticky-sweet slid down my throat. So I let myself continue the dream that rather than fouled straw, I lay on cool, clean linen sheets, and not on a stone floor, but on pillows as soft and embracing as a new bride. And I dreamed that it was not Goryx, but a gentleman minister of Tjasse, the goddess of love, who tended my wretched body.

Moonlight teased at my eyelids, peeking through a tall window beside the bed. By the way my limbs were tangled in the pillows and the way my stomach rumbled in hollow annoyance, I surmised that this night was not the same as the one on which I'd been brought to this delightful place. A candle gleamed softly from a silver holder sitting on a carved wood mantelpiece. The light revealed a large bedchamber furnished with comfort and elegance to match the delicious bed. Across an expanse of shining wood floor, a white-haired gentleman sat in a cushioned chair, snoring softly, his head resting on his hand.

I shifted my position carefully in preparation for sitting up, pleased to feel a noticeable improvement in my overall well-being. I was attired in a fine linen nightshirt, loose at the neck, no sign anywhere of the torn and muddy clothing I'd been wearing by the riverside.

About the time my legs dangled off the edge of the bed, the gentleman woke with a jerk and promptly knocked off his spectacles. "Bother," he mumbled as he picked them out of his lap, gave them a wipe with a handkerchief clutched in his left hand as if left there for exactly such a purpose, jammed them back on his nose, and looked up to find me watching him. "Oh! I say . . . good. Good, good, good. How are you then?"

"Better," I said, managing to get the word out without my stupid stammering, though my voice was still hoarse and harsh, scarcely more than a whisper. The sound clearly bothered him, for he jumped up, grabbed a flat wooden stick from a tray of physician's implements, and stuck it down my throat to take a look, setting off my lingering cough. Then he felt around my neck with his fingers and peered at me closely.

"They didn't . . . cut you . . . damage your throat on purpose when they did these other things?" His lip curled as he said it.

I shook my head, a cold sweat rippling over my skin.

Such mutilation had been a looming horror in the dark-ness, and, practically speaking, if someone wanted me silent, it would have been far simpler than what they'd done. But Goryx always said that if he damaged my throat, I could not demonstrate my obedience sufficiently. Of course, by the end it didn't matter.

"There's some redness, a little swelling. This cough most likely. I've given you something for that. But this other . . . the sound of it . . ." Without knowing more, I wasn't going to help him. He peered over the top of his spectacles. "Lack of use. That's it, isn't it? They've had you locked up and forced you silent. He said something about that."

I acknowledged his guess, though it seemed based on real information and not just insight, like the Elhim. The Elhim . . . The physician was certainly not one of the strange pale race, but I wondered. "Narim?" I said.

"What's that?" The old man poured red wine from a crystal decanter and handed me the glass.

"Do you know Narim?"

"I know no one by that name. Was it the girl? A girl was found dead beside you."

I ignored his question and gazed at the wineglass, en-visioning Callia's face as she relished her wine, just like she relished everything her impoverished life had brought her.

"You knew the poor dead girl?" He spoke respectfully. Didn't call her a whore, though it had been written all over her for anyone to see.

"She was my kind rescuer. As are you. Thank you." I raised the glass to him . . . and to Callia . . . and drank deep, promising myself that her short life would not be forgotten.

"It's my pleasure. You— Well, clothes are laid out for you when you're feeling up to it. Washing things on the dresser. I'll arrange for dinner to be sent. My master is most anxious to speak with you, but I'm insisting you take things slowly, so we'll hold him off awhile yet."

I cupped my hands to my chest and bowed my head in appreciation, noting how when his eyes flicked to my hands, his mouth hardened into a grim line. "Gentle Roelan, preserve us," he mumbled as he left the room. He knew who I was.

I was tempted to follow him out the door and discover who was his master, my benefactor. But the bed was far too comfortable. I drained the wineglass, set it on the physician's tray, and sprawled out on my stomach once again.

Fine smells . . . roasting fowl . . . hot bread . . . My eyes blinked open. A covered silver tray sat beside the bed exuding fragrances that made my stomach do back flips. The candle on the mantelpiece had burned down a third of its length. An hour had passed. Though my physician friend was gone, I didn't think I needed to wait for him. With a glutton's delight, I plunged into the tender roast fowl, stewed apples, delicate cheeses and pastries.

The decanter of wine had been refilled, and I required a good measure of it as I awkwardly coaxed a silver razor to scrape two days' growth from my face. When I'd last looked in a glass, I had been twenty-one, impossibly healthy, and filled with the unutterable joy of spending my life doing what I loved most. I had been immeasurably graced by the gods, and everyone had always said they could see it in my face. Now I was thirty-eight or thereabouts and had touches of gray in my hair and the reflection of Mazadine in my eyes. It was a dead man who looked back at me.

Lacking a dead man's luxury of immobility, I donned the simple full-sleeved shirt of dark blue, the black breeches and hose, and the good boots that had been left on a chair. All were exactly my size except for the breeches, which had to be belted in considerably to accommodate the lack of meat on my frame. I'd probably lost a third of my weight in prison.

Only after I'd poured another glass of wine and sat in the physician's chair by the cold hearth did I notice the harp that lay on a round table next to the door—a small harp, just the size I had carried when I traveled, its polished rosewood frame glowing richly in the candlelight. I moved over to stand beside the moonlit window—as far from the harp as I could get—and tried to ignore the resounding silence that was in the place where my heart used to be. It was perhaps not a good time for my cousin, the king of Elyria, to walk into the room.

The years had not passed lightly over Devlin. His face was lined with too much sun and wind, and coarsened with too much wine. We had been of a size in our youth, but now he carried almost as much bulk as his father, who had been a bull of a man. A long scar gleamed white on one tanned cheek, and his eyes told me that he had seen a great deal of death.

How do you greet someone who has stolen half your life, murdered your friends, and destroyed your heart? I could not speak—would not give him the satisfaction of hearing the donkey's bray he had left me to replace the songs of a god. Instead I poured the remainder of my wine onto his polished wood floor and dropped the goblet beside the pool, splattering shards of glass and red droplets all over the room. Then I stood in silence, waiting for him to explain why he had chosen to offer me a day of comfort and healing after sending me to the netherworld for seventeen years.

He gazed at me unblinking, unspeaking, and I thought it must be to see if I was afraid. But after a moment it came to me that he wasn't sure how to begin. When he did, his voice was soft and intense. "I didn't know." His hands fidgeted with his sword belt, but he did not drop his gaze or stammer. "I want you to believe me, Aidan. I had no idea. Until three weeks ago this night, I did not know you were in . . . that place . . . or anything of what was done to you."

He must think I've gone mad, I thought, *to try this tactic with me.* His servants were still killing my friends, shackling my wrists, and laying on their whips.

"Of course I am responsible. I won't deny it. The gods have given me duties every bit as mystical as those you professed, no matter how distasteful you may find the work of kings. I wanted you silenced. It was necessary. Those around me who are accustomed to carrying out my orders . . . they heard my wish and they saw to it and I was well content. But never . . . never did I mean for it to happen the way it did. I should have asked. Should have made certain. But . . . well, I won't make excuses. It changes nothing. I should have asked, but I didn't."

He moved to the table and poured himself a glass of wine. "Three weeks ago I told one of my aides to find you. You'll appreciate this one," he said, closing his eyes and shaking his head. "I needed to ask you a favor. By the Seven . . ."

When he faced me again, his ruddy color had deepened and his eyes glittered. "My aide was astonished at my request. 'Your Majesty,' he said, 'he is disappeared. You know. We all assumed that you . . . that he . . . We understood that he was taken care of as you commanded.' His smirking was insufferable. 'He's not been seen in all these years, so we presumed him dead or as good as.' I couldn't believe no one had told me. I looked into it, began asking questions I should have asked seventeen . . . oh, gods, Aidan, seventeen years . . ."

His dark eyes searched deep. I suppose he saw what he had done, for he dropped his gaze abruptly. At least he didn't say he was sorry or that he wished he hadn't made his desire so clear. He had already told me that it had come out as he wanted. That was enough to condemn him.

"I'll not insult you by offering what you would rightly disdain coming from me, nor can I relax the restriction that you saw fit to disobey, but if there is anything else . . . ask and it shall be done."

I would have preferred to remain silent, but the rage that had been building as he spoke could not find its outlet until I knew the most important thing. And so he heard what voice I could muster, his face burning scarlet as I croaked, "Why? No one ever bothered to tell me why I had to be silenced. You never told me."

Disbelief shot from his eyes directly into mine, shifting instantly to astonishment. He averted his face. A moment's hesitation and he strode toward the door. By Keldar's eyes, he wasn't going to tell me!

"Devlin!" I wanted to strangle him.

Perhaps it was the sight of the harp lying useless on the table that made him give as much as he did, for he paused beside it for a moment, then spoke over his shoulder, a break in his voice making it sound as if he were truly sorry. "You were bad for my dragons, Aidan. You made them uneasy. I wish it could have been different."

The door swung shut behind him.

Chapter 6

I walked out of my cousin's house that same night. He chose not to prevent me. By the time I found my way to the front doors through dark, deserted rooms full of shrouded furnishings, the old physician was waiting with a cloak, a heavy leather purse, and an expression of great distress. He opened his mouth several times, but he must have been commanded not to speak to me, for nothing ever came out.

I wanted nothing from Devlin. If I'd had other clothes to wear, I would have stripped off the ones he'd given me, but necessity ruled, and I took the cloak as well. The leather bag of coins revolted me even more, but necessity ruled in that wise also. No one else would forfeit his or her life by helping me, so I would take Devlin's blood money to use until I could fend for myself. I could not say I would rather starve. Only those who have never starved can say that.

It was a long, slow walk into the nearest village, but the old physician's remedies and two days of uninterrupted rest had done marvels. Or perhaps my anger sustained me until I could take a room at an inn, eat a bowl of the landlord's porridge for a predawn breakfast, and collapse on a sagging bed.

Even then I could not sleep. The consideration that my ruin had been a mistake, that the Adairs and Gwaithir and Callia had died for nothing, was infuriating to the point of madness. I made his dragons "uneasy." Uneasy! By the Seven Gods, what did that mean?

Hours of reviewing our conversation and reliving the occasion of our last meeting before my arrest took me nowhere. It was well onto noon by the time I gave it up and slept the clock around once again. My dreams were filled with questions, but even more with rage. I killed Devlin more than once that night, cruelly, viciously, without remorse, and so vividly that I woke up sick and shaken, expecting to find blood on my hands. I had planned to be on my way that day, to hunt for some back-water town where I could start over again, where I could become someone else and forget everything that had been. But the insistent, bloody resolution of my dreams showed me how futile it was to attempt such a thing before I had made some peace with myself and whatever gods might exist to hear me.

So I used my cousin's gold to buy a horse and a flask of wine, and I inquired where I might find a shrine dedicated to Keldar. I rode through the hot morning and turned off the road at the place I'd been told, winding slowly up a worn path to a grassy, rounded hilltop. In that place of unchecked winds and uninterrupted vistas stood an ancient stele graven with the closed-eye symbol of the blind god. At its base were laid faded bundles of wild thyme and rosemary, lovage and pennyroyal, herbs whose sweet fragrances would be carried on the back of the wind, finding their way to the god, bearing with them the prayers of those who left them.

I had no herbs, but I uncorked the wine—red and sour, as Callia had relished it—and poured half of it on the ground beside the herb bundles. I begged Keldar for the wisdom to unravel the puzzle of my life and find a path that was not solely the way of vengeance. I was mortally afraid. As a man who has lost one leg sees an enemy's sword poised above the other, so deep was the terror of my dreams. I had never killed a man. To follow the way of vengeance—the only way that seemed clear—would surely destroy whatever was left of me. Yet on any other path I would be as blind as Keldar and risk stumbling back into the horror I had just escaped. If the blind god could help me find my way, then I had to ask.

The hot wind blew. The dry ground soaked up the wine. But my soul remained cold and silent, the familiar ritual providing no comfort. I sat leaning on the stele, drank the rest of the wine, and considered kings and dragons and prideful musicians who did not listen well enough when given warning. My imprisonment had been no mistake. Devlin had wanted me silenced, but not harmed, and he thought he'd gotten it—but how? To assert that mine had been the best-known name in Elyria and every neighboring kingdom was not false pride. How could I have disappeared so abruptly and my cousin not have known of it? What had been said on the day after I was dragged from my bed?

If Devlin believed I was somehow a threat to his dragons . . . that would explain a great deal. Only the dragons kept Elyria in control of her vassal kingdoms and prevented her from being upended by petty tyrants or overrun by the barbarian hordes from beyond the borderlands—the wild men with braided hair and a loathing for civilization. But why would he think it? "Uneasy"? What did that mean? He assumed I knew, and when I told him I didn't . . . whatever it was he thought I'd done, he was still afraid of it. His need to leave me in the dark had outweighed his purpose, the "favor" he was going to ask of me.

I was at a loss. Neither answers nor vengeance would bring back the dead. Narim had urged me to go to an inn on the Vallior road and ask his friend Davyn to help me, but I could not imagine what help some Elhim clerk might offer. Besides, Narim might have been questioned and his friends compromised. I had no desire to cross paths with my cousin's Dragon Riders again. And so, since I could think of nothing better, I threw the wine flask into the distance, returned the way I'd come, and reclaimed my room at the Whistling Pig. I would wait for Keldar's guidance.

The common room of the Whistling Pig was no different from those of a thousand poor hostelries along the roads of Elyria. A huge, soot-stained hearth with a friendly fire that filled the room with smoke and was never allowed to go out. A hodgepodge of tables, chairs, barrels, and crates, with a few splintered ones piled in a corner. Greasy, dark-wood walls hung with boars' heads. Plain food, endless ale, and always a tall stool to welcome a wandering musician. I sat in the darkest corner, hiding behind a brimming tankard while I listened to the talk, trying to let myself be drawn back into a world I had almost forgotten.

It didn't take long to catch up with the news. Little had changed since I'd been hauled off to Mazadine. Elyria was still at war with everyone who did not swear fealty to

her king, and no kingdom with dragons enough to face
those of Devlin or his vassals would swear fealty to a
king who had charred their fields and cities with dragon
fire. Gondar was the current battleground, a wealthy
kingdom far to the south that was jealous of Elyria's control of the rich mining country on their common border.
The locals said that Prince Donal, Devlin's son, commanded the Elyrian troops on the Gondari border. The innocent child . . . now nineteen or thereabouts . . . facing
the brutal horrors of dragon warfare . . . I ordered another
ale.

A moment of general sensation was caused by a tooth-
less tinker newly arrived from Lepan who told of the
great uproar in the city four nights previous when two
Dragon Riders had washed up on the riverbank with a
number of quite fatal holes in them. According to the tinker, a manhunt, the likes of which he had never seen, had
scoured the city. But the culprit was still on the loose, and
the dragon legion commander had vowed to hang the villain on the walls of Lepan by his entrails.

"They say one man did it?" asked one of the listeners.

"I wouldn't want to go against the man who could take
out two Dragon Riders," said a thick-necked farmer who
could have tied a knot in an iron bar.

"I'd shake his hand," said another, who wore one withered arm and the savage evidence of dragon burns on half
his face. "Ridemark clansmen think they own the world.
Bring nothing but ruin. Good riddance to 'em."

"I've heard they mate with the beasts," said one of the
barmaids, leading the conversation into progressively
wilder speculation on the nature and habits of the mysterious clan who wore the Ridemark on their wrists.

I lost track of their talk, for it was only the tinker's story that held my interest. Two Riders killed and thrown in the river . . . the hunt through the streets of Lepan . . . It was all backward and inside out. The Riders had been the hunters and had captured their prey and taken him to their king, only . . . It came back to me then how they had begun to beat me, then stopped abruptly. And I had imagined someone throwing bodies into the river, only I'd thought I was dreaming because I'd been kicked in the head. If the dead Riders were the ones who had attacked me, then who had delivered me to Devlin? Why would Devlin's men kill his own Dragon Riders?

The evening grew late, and a serving maid stuck a pair of ducks on the spit, the grease hissing and spattering. The room was thick with smoke. More people arrived. Two Elhim quietly eating soup were shoved out of their chairs by a local herdsman who wanted their table. The landlord used a broom handle to force the Elhim to wipe up their spilled soup with their own clothes. Once the momentary sensation was over, the travelers, farmers, and shopkeepers grew mellow in their ale and dropped their conversation out of hearing. A few Udema began arguing loudly about whose turn it was to pay for the next round. All so familiar, yet I had no more part in it than if I were watching a puppet show at a midsummer fair.

"A song," said the landlord. "Anyone here to give us a song?"

I gripped my tankard between my palms and took a long swallow while a stocky Udema youth stepped up to the stool and proceeded to sing "Morgave's Lament" in a breathy, off-key tenor. I shut my ears and tried not to remember singing that particular song, a soldiers' favorite, in the starlit field where King Ruarc's troops lay waiting nervously for the steel-helmeted warriors of Florin to attack. The soldiers had besieged me when the song ended, loading me down with so many medallions and rings and clips of hair to be delivered to wives and lovers when I returned to Elyria that my manservant had torn pages out of a book to write each name and wrap each token so we could keep them straight. It had taken me two months, but I had delivered every one. The battle had been a bloody one. Few of the tokens would ever have been reclaimed.

While the patrons stamped their feet in approval, and the stocky youth gaped at the acclaim and began another song, I rose, dropped one coin on the table and another in the musician's cup, and started up the stairs. About the time I reached the first landing, three brawny ruffians burst through the door, bringing the room to silence. Two of them were wielding swords. Their leader had a broad, flat face with a deeply cleft chin and cold blue eyes that seemed to bulge outward from his brow ridge. He swept the room with his gaze, then motioned for his companions to search the room.

"What's all this?" demanded the landlord, a paunchy man with red hair. "You've no right—"

"We're hunting the bastard who murdered our brothers. The one who shelters him will be dragon fodder . . . and his family . . . and his village . . . and his woman's village."

My stomach shrank to a knot as they began circling the room, forcing everyone to show them their hands. The landlord would remember. And the pretty barmaid who had wrinkled her nose in disgust as I'd fumbled my cup and my coins with my grotesque fingers. I retreated into the shadows and ran lightly up to my room, grabbed my cloak, and peered out the window.

Three lathered horses pranced nervously in the yard. No guard remained with them to see me shinny out the window and drop to the ground. A few awkward, fumbling, cursing moments in the stable as I tried to grip buckles and straps; then I abandoned the saddle that had come with my horse, settling for a bridle. Grateful again for my mother's insistence that even a musician should ride as befitted a warrior's son and a king's nephew, I threw myself on the back of the horse. I took him slowly out of the stable to the road, then urged him into a gallop, hearing shouts behind me. I had chosen the horse carefully, and he was well rested, but I didn't breathe easier until I was three leagues down the road with no more sign of pursuit.

I was more than passably familiar with the roads of northern Elyria, having traveled there a good deal in my first years singing. For a week I stayed on the back roads, buying supplies at a village market, and spending the first few nights under the stars, trying to put distance between Lepan and any sighting of a Senai with crippled hands. Why would Devlin send his thugs after me not two days after allowing me to walk out of his house? Just like the bodies in the river, it made no sense . . . unless Devlin hadn't sent them. On that first night I spent a long time beside my tiny fire wondering if Devlin had as firm control of his dragon legions as he thought. The thought was unsettling, like the tremors before an earthquake. The

Chaos Years were only a few hundred years behind us; not much time at all.

When my supplies ran low, I stopped at a pilgrim's hostelry, a meager shelter for those visiting a local shrine to the twins Vellya and Vanir, goddess of earth and god of fire. In the holy cavern visitors could wander by torch-light among pits of boiling mud that reeked of brimstone, deep crevasses where spouts of fire shot up from glowing rocks, and rocky maws of simmering water that would periodically shoot towers of steam to the cavern roof ten stories above. I skipped the pilgrimage to the cavern and resumed my journey after sharing the common soup pot and sleeping on a hard mat in the shelter. I spoke to no one, asked no questions, and sought no news. My hands stayed inside my cloak.

Fortunately the roads were mostly deserted, for I had begun talking to myself aloud. Anyone who heard me might have reported a madman on the loose. I needed to work the rust and hesitation from my speech. It was too noticeable. So I worked at the repetitive diction exercises my singing masters had drilled into me, and I searched out saxifrage and coltsfoot and candlewick and boiled them in water, inhaling the steam or drinking the tea to ease the irritation of my throat.

Only once, as I stood on a rocky overlook and watched the sun set over the Carag Huim with the color of drag-ons' fire, did I attempt to turn my speech into a song, that same "Morgave's Lament" I had known since I was five. But the first three notes fell dead in the quiet air. I could not hear the next one in my head, could not feel the words blossom from the unfolding melody, could not summon the passion that would weave together the notes and the words and grow them into so much more together than they were apart. And so I faltered and broke off . . . and cursed myself for a fool to think it even possible that I could make music where none lived any longer.

On the next day I passed a roadside shrine dedicated to Roelan. The graven visage of the hunchbacked god was nestled in a grove of willows next to a well-tended pool. I stopped there awhile, gazing at the god with the falcon on his crooked shoulder. In the hot stillness of the afternoon I forced myself to look inward, to lay myself open, to listen and feel as I had not permitted myself for half an eternity. But though my ears came near bleeding with the effort, the world was silent. I left the shrine without an offering for the god. I had nothing to give him.

At the end of my second week on the road, I arrived at the city of Camarthan, a fair-sized market town of graceful domes and arches built of warm yellow granite and white marble. It was nestled in the green foothills of the Carag Huim, the Mountains of the Moon, that bounded Elyria on the west. No major trade routes passed through the city, but myriad minor ones, ensuring that its marketplace provided the most interesting and exotic fare of any in the kingdom. The people were friendly and open, and perhaps because of their constant exposure to new things, their city had always been the best place to try out new music. The region lay under the protection of the Duke of Catania. In the past when I had visited Camarthan, the duke had been a cultured, well-educated man. When I had come there to sing in his marble-columned festival pavilion, the duke's wife had tried her best to entice me to settle in Camarthan as a member of the court and a mentor for their son, who at fifteen was a more than passable harpist. I had refused her, explaining that I was pledged in service to Roelan and must go where the god called me. The duke had graciously offered me a home for whenever the god permitted me to settle. It was perhaps foolish to go back to a place where I had been well known, but it was a convenient destination when I had no other in mind. The old duke's son now ruled Catania. Assuredly our paths were unlikely to cross.

I left my horse in a clean public stable, asking the owner to find me a decent saddle with large buckles that an "aged servant with poor eyesight" could manage. Then I spent a nervous hour in the local shops, finding new clothes that were less fine and less memorable than those my cousin had supplied, and a better knife than the one I'd gotten from a barmaid at the Whistling Pig. I sought out a glover's shop deep in a deserted street and bought some loose-fitting doeskin gloves that I could manage to pull on over my wretched hands so that perhaps their appearance would not be so noticeable. The gloves served dual purpose: except on the very hottest days every joint I had ached miserably, and my hands and feet were cold all the time.

By the time I'd taken care of these matters, I was shaking with exhaustion from three weeks' traveling in constant fear and the terrifying exposure of the city streets. Along with my pride and my defiance, I had used up the last of my courage in Goryx's chamber. Once mortal necessity was satisfied, I could think of nothing but to find somewhere to hide. So I sought out lodgings in a modest quarter of the city, the streets frequented by clerks and laborers, drovers and journeymen. To remain anonymous in the poorest streets of any town is always difficult, for many residents are looking for information to sell, and no one has enough occupation to keep them from watching each other. But in the streets where people are hurrying about on their own business, no one has time to look too closely.

I, of course, had no business, a matter I was going to have to rectify before too many weeks passed. My cousin's purse would not refill itself. But I constantly put off taking action. I couldn't force myself out of my room except to find something to eat, and even then I would make my purchases and scurry back to my lodging like a rat to a hole. A glance from a passing stranger would make me break out in a sweat; a casual word would force my stomach into spasms of terror. I imagined Dragon Riders awaiting me around every corner with manacles and whips. Life became a shriveled mockery, more dismal, I think, than the refuse heaps of Lepan . . . until I spent the next-to-last silver coin from my repugnant hoard. Left with no choices, I had to take up life again.

Chapter 7

My first ventures out in search of a new start were into Camarthan's marketplace. The tree-shaded market was crowded and busy, with a good number of escape routes should I draw unwanted notice. The first day I forced myself out for an hour, the next for two. I drifted from one display to the next, never speaking to anyone until I chided myself that all the work I'd done while on the road was gone for naught if I let my voice rust away again. So I asked a few questions about the origins of the exotic artworks, fabrics, and furnishings one could see in the market, satisfied when the words came out without the harshness of my first days of speech. For a week I would fly trembling back to my hiding place as soon as my allotted time was done. But as the days passed uneventfully, I gained confidence. After two weeks I would spend the whole day in the market, listening to the babble of commerce, watching the ebb and flow of sellers and buyers, and actually beginning to see some of the things at which I looked.

Inevitably, I was drawn to a harpmaker's stall. I had passed by it ten times before without stopping, but on one beautiful summer afternoon, an elegantly dressed young woman sat tuning a small rosewood harp with ivory keys under the hovering eye of the old craftsman. Her shining dark ringlets shook with her frustration.

"It won't tune," she said. "Why would I buy it? It doesn't matter that it's lovely to look at."

The white-haired man crinkled his brow and answered her, but in the language of Florin, not Elyria.

"I don't understand your gibberish," she said when he was done. "I won't buy the harp if it won't tune properly."

The man tried to explain again, but the frowning young woman shook her head in annoyance.

"He's telling you to tighten the nut three times, then let it back to the right tuning, rather than coming up from under," I said. "It's often better that way with a fine instrument." Precision and loving care had gone into making the three beautiful harps displayed in the old man's stall.

"You understand this nonsense he speaks?" asked the woman.

"Well enough."

She did what I told her and was soon playing the richly toned instrument and singing in a sweet but thin voice. "Ask him if his price is firm," she said after a few moments.

"What did he tell you?"

She told me, and I had no need to query the man. The price was eminently fair. But I did as she bade me, though at the same time I complimented the harpmaker on creating such a fine piece.

"Do you play?" he asked, smiling with relief.

"Not anymore. But anyone would be proud to play an

instrument so well crafted." Then I told the woman, "He says his price is firm. And I'll advise you it's a bargain."

"Well, then. It does sound nice."

With slender, agile fingers she counted out her gold and silver coins. As she walked away, I also turned to go, but the old Florin called to me. "Sir!" And when I looked back, he bowed politely as Florins do. *"Vando zi. Estendu zi na."*

I returned the politeness. "Thank you, and may your gods walk with you also."

The stall next to the harpmaker was occupied by a leather merchant who displayed a wide variety of wares, from bags and wallets to lightweight leather armor and saddlery. The florid, balding merchant had watched the interchange with the harpmaker intently. As I hurried past, he called out, "Senai! A word with you, if I might."

Very tempting to pretend I hadn't heard; I wanted desperately to run away. But I paused and clasped my gloved hands behind my back as if I had all day to answer.

He was a prosperous man by the look of his beige silk shirt and well-cut leather breeches and vest. A Udema— short, stocky, sturdy, and fair-haired like all his people. Jaw like an anvil. "You speak the language of the Florins?"

"Yes."

"And know their customs? When to bow and all?"

"Yes." I had absorbed languages and customs just as I had devoured the sounds of cities and countryside and wild lands. All of it was music.

"And for others besides Florins. Is it possible you know them too—like the tongue of the Breen?"

"Why do you ask?"

"There's a beltmaker, a Breen, who sits on the far side

of the market. She does fine work, but her designs are too odd for Elyrians. Looks as if she's not had a fair meal in a twelvemonth. I'd hire her to do some of my tooling, but she doesn't understand when I ask her. I was going to propose—if it wouldn't be taken as an insult to so worthy a gentleman as yourself—to offer you a consideration if you would speak to her on my behalf. It would be to her benefit as well as mine."

The perfect answer to my dilemma. For days I had scoured my head for ideas of how I might earn a living. I had examined every stall in the market, tried to judge every passerby as to what he did and whether I could do it too. Though involvement in music would be risky and painful, I had resigned myself to hiring out as a singing master or as a harp or flute teacher—cheaply, of course, as I could not demonstrate the lessons. But everything else I knew, every skill I might possess or learn in a reasonable time, seemed to require hands that worked. I could write only with difficulty and none too legibly. My stiff fingers could not build instruments or transcribe music or keep accounts. My ruined back muscles were so weak that I could not do anything that required strength, even if I could get past the inevitable questions asked of a Senai hiring out to do ordinary labor. But I had not even considered my experience with languages.

"I could speak to the beltmaker," I said, trying not to sound too eager. "No consideration necessary. But perhaps you have further needs in the area of translation and interpretation . . . ?"

He narrowed his eyes, drawing his broad brow into a knot. "You wouldn't know how to approach a Raggai

chieftain about selling some of his goldwork, now, would
you?"

"I once lived for a month in a Raggai village. Raggai
are very protective of their goldwork, unless the buyer
becomes a member of their family—a matter of a few
pigs and a cask of brandy. And, of course, a family member can do as he likes with his brothers' or sisters' work,
as long as it brings honor or profit to the family."

A beneficent smile blossomed on the Udema merchant's face. "My name is Alfrigg. . . ."

After a bit more dancing about, Alfrigg agreed that he
could well use a permanent translator, especially since he
was on the verge of expanding his business. "And your
name, sir?"

"Aidan . . . MacTarsuin."

"Ah, I see."

I had named myself "no man's son." Alfrigg would assume that I was a younger son, dispossessed by some
family dispute. Such was often the case among Senai
families. The situation produced a class of well-educated
but impoverished clerks and priests, artists and actors
who never quite fit into any society. I did not contradict
his belief. Dispossessed was quite accurate.

Further discussion revealed that Alfrigg hailed from
the town of Dungarven in eastern Elyria. He had appren-
ticed to a butcher, but discovered he had more luck with
hides than meat. He had bought out his apprenticeship
early, and now ruled a flourishing business and a family
of seven children with a despotic hand. He liked Camarthan for its location and friendly atmosphere, but as
he saw the caravans pass through, visions of a leathery
empire floated behind his blue eyes.

When I suggested that I could perhaps give him a preview of what customers in other regions might look for—that Eskonians wore small leather pouches with the dust of their ancestors in them, for example, or that the Breen felt it important to have the name of their household gods on everything they used—he slapped me on the back and crowed in delight. "Vanir bless me, but I always thought Senai the most useless of all Earth's creatures. All their reading and writing and dabbling, politics and playacting . . . pshaw! Even Elhim and donkeys have better purpose. But you, good sir, will make me a rich man, a very useful endeavor indeed." After a quarter of an hour of negotiation, Alfrigg brought out a red enameled flask of uziat—the fiery brandy Udema used to seal every contract—and two tiny cups. "May our association be long and profitable, Aidan MacTarsuin!"

I worked mostly as an interpreter at first, helping Alfrigg negotiate with traders whose caravans passed through Camarthan. Occasionally I advised him on the cultural aspects of his stock. In addition, I translated letters and documents, though I hinted that I had always hired scribes to write for me and was thus uncomfortable penning documents for myself. Fortunately, Alfrigg's Elhim clerk was quite capable.

Though merchant trading was nothing I had ever felt an interest in pursuing, the days were busy and interesting, leaving me little time for fear or regret. Nights were more than sufficient for that. Someday I would have to take up the search for the truth of my life. But first I needed to get a few things in order with myself. If I flinched at every sound, I could not hear the subtleties

I needed to hear. If I shied away from people, I could not ask questions unremarked. My employment seemed a good first remedy.

My body presented a challenge equal to that of my cowardly spirit. I could not walk five steps without panting in exhaustion. How could I ever get close enough to the dragons to discover why my cousin said I made them uneasy? More to the point, how could I have any hope of getting away again to do something with the knowledge? And so, on every morning I was in Camarthan, I rose early to go walking in the rugged hills. At first I could scarcely cover half a league in two hours, spending most of my time collapsed against a tree or a boulder wondering if I would ever again be able to move or to breathe. But after a month or so it became a little easier, and after three months I was able to run all the way to the top of Mount Camar itself, where I could see all of Camarthan and all of western Elyria spread out before me in the dawn light. It was a distance of more than two leagues each way. The beauty and peace of the Carag Huim and the dry, clear air were healing for my lungs if not my spirit, and they enabled me to face Alfrigg and his cohorts with equanimity.

"Aidan, lad, I've a proposition to put you." Alfrigg settled back in his "business chair," an ample creation of padded leather, studded with brass. He was in an expansive mood, having just concluded an excellent deal with a saddlery in Vallior. "I've not done right by you. We've set our agreement for your pay, and I can't have it said that I renegotiate contracts before their term, but you've done good work these few months. My clerk tells me you've been moving from lodging house to lodging house as if you'd trouble paying. I don't like that. Looks bad to the customers . . ."

"No need to concern—"

". . . and so I've talked to the wife, and we've decided you will move in with us. We've plenty of room, better food than you'll get anywhere in the district, and, as you take on more responsibility, it makes good business for you to be here. It will give us time to get to know each other better." He waved me toward the straight wooden chair on the other side of his desk, as if expecting to negotiate the details right then and there.

Alfrigg's house was large and lively, his wife a wise, witty, and skilled housematron. Udema custom encouraged a prosperous businessman to shelter his most valued and trusted employees. As these were almost exclusively other Udema, it was a great compliment he paid me. Indeed, the prospect of a homely house, offering comfort and company, out of the public way was very attractive. Though I no longer cowered in my room for days at a time, I ate my meals alone and kept my gloves on and did indeed move from one poor lodging to another every few weeks. No man with half a mind would refuse his offer. But the last generous family who had given me a home had all of them been murdered.

I remained standing, pretending I didn't see Alfrigg's gesture toward the chair. "Though I thank you immensely, sir, and your wife, too, for such a kind offer, I cannot."

"Why ever not?"

"I just . . ." I fumbled frantically, but no logical reason

came to mind. "Please understand, my family . . ." I couldn't even finish it.

"Ah, yes, your family." His fair complexion scarlet, he burst from his chair, shoving aside the flask of uziat that sat waiting to celebrate our closer relationship. "What would they think? How could I be so stupid as to believe a Senai might prefer a Udema house to a rathole?" Before I could stammer out a denial, the door had slammed behind him.

Alfrigg did not forgive me the slight. We worked well together, but never again with the ease of our first days. He made unending references to "those with refined sensibilities who cannot even remove their gloves lest they be contaminated with a Udema's touch." It grieved me to have wounded him so sorely, as he was a kind and generous man, but I could not recant without opening up more questions than I was willing to answer.

Soon after this debacle, Alfrigg's Elhim clerk found a new position with the duke's court, and another Elhim was hired to replace him. His name was Tarwyl, and he looked very much like Narim—as all Elhim looked very much like Narim. He was quite competent and seemed gentlemanly and good-humored. After the first week of his employment, he asked if I knew of a good place to take lodgings, as he was new in the city. And perhaps I could show him about?

I gave him the name of a few decent houses I had used in the past months that would accept Elhim as residents, but at the same time I made it clear that I did not keep company with others who worked for Alfrigg. Tarwyl did not seem offended and made no further attempts at fa-

miliarity. Elhim likely got accustomed to such slights. I
despised myself.

And so the days passed. I did not speak to the old harpmaker again, though occasionally I would sit under a tree
in the marketplace and listen as customers came to try out
his instruments. Sometimes the old Florin himself would
play, and I would listen, longing for the sounds to come
alive inside me. But there was only emptiness. Only silence.

For the rest of that year I worked for Alfrigg. I began
accompanying him on journeys into Eskonia, and
Aberthain, Kyre, and Maldova, helping him hire agents
to receive his merchandise from the caravans, sell it, and
send him back the money. He tried to get me to cross the
Sea of Arron to set up a new agency in Ys'Tarre, a remote
kingdom reputed to be exceptionally wealthy and acces-
sible only by sea, but, with profound apologies, I declined. I'd always had a weak stomach on the water. I told
him I would go anywhere in his service, as long as I
didn't have to travel in a boat. He gave me a generous
bonus when the first caravan returned from Eskonia with
a healthy profit. When he presented it, he did not offer me
uziat, though the red enamel flask sat ready as always on
his desk.

On one of our trading journeys, I at last learned what
the world believed had happened to Aidan MacAllister,
beloved of the gods, the most famous musician in Elyria
and beyond. The caravan stretched out as far as the eye
could see in a gray and dismal downpour, wagon after
wagon flanked by armed riders. I was hunched over in

the saddle in aching misery, my cloak pulled snug against the rain, and the reins wrapped tightly about my hands because the pain in my fingers prevented my grasping them properly, when one of the guards pulled up to ride next to me.

"Say, MacTarsuin, I've been meaning to ask . . . have I met you before?" He was a wiry, middle-aged man with a tangle of gray-streaked brown hair.

"I don't think so," I said, pulling the hood of my cloak lower.

"Name's Sinclair. Been riding caravans since I was a lad. Thought maybe I'd seen you riding with us back when Master Gerald ran things. There was a leather merchant often sent his man with us in those days."

My pulse raced ahead of me ever so slightly. "Master Gerald?"

"Master Gerald Adair. It's the Adairs what used to own this lot, back fifteen, twenty year ago. Fine gentleman he was, and his father before him."

"But he doesn't own it now?"

"Gor, no! It was a wicked happening. The whole family of 'em gone: Master Gerald, the old man, his good lady, the daughter what was just come womanly, a fair and sprightly girl. Burned to death. All of 'em. Their house caught fire in the night. A servant what escaped said a lamp got spilled and caught the wall hangings. You probably heard about it. It was the same time as Aidan MacAllister disappeared—you know, the singer. Some say he died in the fire with them."

"I'd heard he disappeared. Just not how or when."

"Well, he was great friends with Master Gerald, and there was talk in the caravans as how he had an eye for

Mistress Alys. After the fire he was never seen nor heard no more. A pity. Never heard the like of him and his harp. Would take you away from what ailed or what troubled, show you things you never thought to see, and when he was done, he'd set you back down wherever you'd come from, only better. Eased, you know, so things weren't so hard. A loss to the world it was when he went away. I've wondered . . ."

It was as well he needed no prompting for his rambling conversation. I remained mute, cold rain dripping from my hood.

"As I said, a number say he died in the fire or was grieved so by it as he couldn't sing no more. But I've heard another story. Dragons flew over Vallior that night. A few months later a Dragon Rider was going around the taverns and alehouses, saying he saw Aidan MacAllister come to the dragon camps at dawn the next morning, talking wild about how the dragons had torched his friends. Said MacAllister took up a sword against the dragons and got himself burned dead. That's the story I believe. Somebody like that—friendly with the gods and all—don't just die in his sleep or give it up when his woman gets roasted."

In the autumn of that year I hired an Elhim scribe and had him write a letter addressed to the curator of the royal archives at Vallior. The letter stated that I was compiling a list of unsolved cases of treason as a service to the Temple of Jodar. The god of war bore a virulent hatred for traitors, I said, and the temple could use a list of missions to prescribe for penitents wishing to expiate their own failings by taking Jodar's vengeance. I was looking for incidents between fifteen and twenty years in the past. The scribe looked at me strangely, but I said only that we all did service to the gods in our own private ways. And I paid him very well and promised him more work if he was discreet.

If the crime of which I had been convicted—the incident in which I had "aided the enemies of Elyria"—had been recorded at all, then I had to assume the case had never been publicly closed. From Sinclair's testimony and other references I'd heard, no hint of scandal was attached to my name. I wouldn't have expected it. As my name was linked to his own, my cousin would have seen to that.

But my case must never have been filed. When I received an answer to my query, nothing in the two pages of missing battle plans, stolen horses turned up in enemy cavalry, and other such occurrences could possibly have been related to me. Only three cases had anything to do with dragons.

In one incident in the dragon camp at Cor Damar, three Dragon Riders had been slain as suspected spies. The three had been causing havoc in the camp with their dragons. Another Rider had turned his own dragon on the three, slaying both Riders and dragons to prevent further trouble. The investigation had uncovered no cause for the three Riders' defection. I had visited many towns and villages near Cor Damar that year, a satisfying time when I felt that I had moved up a whole level in my skills, but as far as I could remember I had spoken to no Dragon Rider and done nothing that could be remotely connected to the incident.

The second case occurred at Cor Neuill, the winter lair

just north of Camarthan. A Dragon Rider had been found knifed to death after a midwinter's feast, and a Ridemark child had disappeared. The dragon lair had been in chaos that night and the murderer/abductor had never been found. In truth I had sung in the camp only two days previous and had been scheduled to perform at that very feast, but my mother had been taken ill, and I had canceled the remainder of my performances in Cor Neuill.

The third incident involved the escape of two Kasmari hostages being held in the dragon camp at Aberthain. I well remembered my visit to Aberthain and the night of glory when I sat on the ridge above King Germond's dragons and sang with the gods. The coincidence was sobering. But the hostages had escaped days after I had left the kingdom, and ample witnesses could have testified as to my whereabouts. In truth I had traveled so widely, there was likely no crime in the kingdom that had not occurred before, during, or after my presence. So it seemed I had dredged up nothing of any use.

Winter came and my bones ached so that I could not sleep. I could not hold a cup without clamping both my palms around it like an infant. When I refused Alfrigg's offer of hot, spiced wine to celebrate his oldest daughter's betrothal, he threw down his cup and stormed from the room. His wife, Marika, frowned at me in puzzled exasperation, then followed after him silently as I stuffed my useless fingers in my pockets.

The Gondari war had worsened. Elyria had warred with Gondar for as long as I could remember. Gondari assassins had killed my uncle King Ruarc's father-in-law and were suspected in a hundred other deaths. These occurrences had always been resolved in Elyria's favor, in a rain of dragon fire. But now the Gondari had come by dragons of their own and were raiding unhindered into Elyrian lands. They had evidently slaughtered every inhabitant of three Elyrian border villages and delivered their heads to Devlin in a gold casket. No one in Camarthan could understand why Devlin and his son didn't blast the Gondari and their dragons into oblivion. The disputed gold wouldn't melt, they said.

On a bitter evening in the last month of the year, when the snows lay deep on the roads into Camarthan, I sat huddled before the roaring hearth in the common room of my latest lodging house, wishing I dared stir up the coals or move even closer without setting myself afire, when a young serving girl set down a tray of ale mugs and announced, "Dragons in Cor Neuill."

Some patrons grumbled a curse, saying how they'd hoped this year might be different and the fiery devils not come. Others argued that the dragons were the only reason a man could sit and drink a mug of ale in peace without some ax-wielding barbarian splitting his skull and ravishing his wife. One laborer moaned that now the legion was returned, he'd have to go to the Ridemark camp for work. He said he'd rather stick with lower pay working for local folk, but his wife wouldn't let him.

I sat staring into the flames, wishing my creaking joints would be eased and my terrifying thoughts vanish up the chimney with the smoke. The dragons always came to Cor Neuill at year's end. To take the beasts into the snows they hated, to practice battle maneuvers in the ice-laden wind, to reaffirm who was master and who was servant . . . these were profound symbols of the Riders' control. Deep in my innermost self I had known that when the dragons came, I could no longer put off my search for the truth.

And so my time of waiting came to an end. On the next morning I went to Alfrigg and proposed a new enterprise—that he should supply the Dragon Riders their leather armor. It was true, I said, that the commanders of the Riders refused to speak the common tongue of Senai and Udema, using only the ancient tongue of the Ridemark clan. But he, Alfrigg, was fortunate, for I knew the clan speech, so that when he ventured into the dragon legion's camp, he could take his interpreter with him.

Chapter 8

An exceptionally tall and broad-shouldered Elhim met us at the southern watchpost of Cor Neuill and led us down the ribbon of trampled mud and snow to the headquarters of the dragon legion. The weather had deteriorated all day, and pregnant clouds hung low over the snowy peaks. Alfrigg grumbled continuously as he hunched in his fur-lined wool cloak against the fine stinging sleet. "What use is the world's richest contract if I'm but another scrap in the An'Huim glacier?"

The Elhim, shivering in his thin, shabby cloak, cocked a pale, frosted eyebrow at the massive leather merchant on his tall horse, as if trying to imagine the anvil-jawed Udema frozen in a river of ice. But his only comment was, "Not far to go, your honor." Then he bent his head forward again, a damp lock of fair hair falling over his left eye. He slogged down the gently sloping road, leading us toward a squat, stone building that might be perched on the edge of the clouds, for all we could see beyond it.

I was shivering, too, though my cloak was quite adequate. Terror and cowardice are far more potent than any winter storm. Now that the day had come, I could scarcely keep from turning tail and riding as fast as I could go, as far from any dragon as I could get. On my lips was an unending prayer to Keldar to show me what I needed to see on this visit, as I could never attempt such brazen stupidity again.

Smoke drifted lazily from the chimney of the headquarters building and from the campfires scattered among the hundreds of tents, only to be swirled away by the gusting wind. Having sung at Cor Neuill several times, I was familiar with the layout of the encampment. The commander and his adjutants slept in the permanent quarters, while the foot and horse soldiers and aides, the cooks, grooms, herdsmen, and other functionaries that hovered about a clan encampment were relegated to the tents. Not the Riders, though.

The Riders lived with the dragons down in the vast bowl of Cor Neuill that lay hidden in the storm beyond the headquarters building. Each man ate and slept, lived and fought with the dragon to which he had been bound in a rite so secret that no one outside the Twelve Families of the Ridemark had ever witnessed it. In that rite the Rider was attuned to his dragon's bloodstone, a thumb-sized jewel of dark red that the man would wear for every moment of his life from that day forward, slaying his own mother if she but laid a finger on it. The jewel allowed the Rider to impose his will upon his bound dragon, controlling its rage and directing it wherever he chose. With the stone he could also control other dragons in a limited fashion and protect himself from their assault. And the jewel infused him with fire that made his skin spark when touched, a matter of mortal consequence to anyone the Rider touched when drunk or angry.

As far as anyone knew, no one outside the clan had

ever possessed a bloodstone or ridden a dragon. Even within the Twelve Families the privilege to ride was reserved only to a select few. Legend said you could tell at birth which child of the clan would ride the dragons, for his mother's birth passage would be scorched as he came into the world, and his eyes would burn with golden fire. Perhaps it was true. In all my observations, however, it was only cruelty and arrogance that flamed in a Rider's eyes, and the knowledge that no man was truly his master. They cared only for the honor and traditions of the clan, nothing for territory or power beyond their own. They lived only to destroy, leaving to kings and princes the business of whom to burn.

A hundred hard eyes glanced our way as we rode through the encampment. Interest waned just as quickly, and they turned back to their business of mending harness, darning socks, sharpening weapons, and cooking supper over the fires that struggled bravely against the gusty wind—the usual activities of a military camp. Accompanying them were the usual smells of woodsmoke and bacon, horse dung and leather, and, as in all Ridemark camps, the faint odor of brimstone. There were women about, not the whores and gap-toothed washing women found everywhere that soldiers lived, but sturdy, capable, cold-eyed women dressed in the same black and red capes as the men. The women of the Twelve Families rode to war with the men, performing most duties equally with their clan brothers, except for riding the dragons.

A sullen young woman took our horses and led them toward a lean-to on the side of a substantial stable, while the Elhim directed us through a leather-curtained door into the blast of heat from an open hearth. Some thirty black-caped men and a few women occupied the wide, shallow single room of the headquarters. Many of them were clustered around a large map table. At the far right end of the room three warriors conferred with an officer seated at a folding field desk. Chests and trunks were stacked about the room, and two Elhim clerks stood over them, ticking off items on lists. Even in a Ridemark camp, Elhim's skills with numbers were useful. Several young aides darted about filling drinking cups from steaming pots.

The curtained-off areas in the corners of the room would be sleeping quarters, and just across the stone floor, opposite the door we'd entered, was a wooden door that led outside again. Few who were not of the Twelve Families were ever allowed to pass that door, so I had been told on the visits in my youth. Few would have any desire to do so, of course, for the doorway led out to the rim of Cor Neuill and the horror that lived there.

The Elhim took us to the man at the field desk, a giant of a man, well past middle age from the evidence of the scant, grizzled hair on his boulder of a head, but with the muscled chest and tight girth of a man half his years. His nose had been broken at some time, for it resembled a hawk's bill, and as he turned his cold, light eyes away from his subordinates to look at us, I shriveled inside. Of all the ill luck . . . of all the commanders who could have been assigned to Cor Neuill, it had to be the high commander himself. Garn MacEachern, the very man who had stood in my cousin's garden the day I was warned away from his dragons, the very man who had watched from the shadows as I was arrested and condemned.

Panic throttled my tongue. Fear must have been written all over my face, for Alfrigg raised a frost-rimed eyebrow at me as he waited for me to speak. What half-crazed rat had ever walked so boldly into the fere-cat's lair?

"The leather merchant and his man," said the Elhim haltingly in the tongue of the Ridemark clan. "Come to present the proposed contract for supply of Riders' armor to the commander and quartermaster."

Alfrigg bowed respectfully, yet kept his jaw lifted and his broad back straight. "Your excellency," he said. "Greetings of Jodar and his six brethren to you."

I bowed, too, quickly turning sideways between Alfrigg and the commander as Alfrigg had instructed me. Not looking at either party, I translated the merchant's words. Alfrigg was a masterful businessman, dealing as much in his uncompromising honesty and self-confidence as in leather goods. He knew his bargaining would go better if he kept the attention focused on his own open face and imposing presence rather than on any intermediary, no matter how necessary. It suited me well to have MacEachern's gaze drawn to Alfrigg and not to the rivulets of sweat dripping down the sides of my face or to the gloved hands that I clasped behind my back to keep them from shaking. Astonishingly enough, my words came out clear and calm, absolutely at odds with the chaos inside me. Perhaps Keldar was guiding my performance, as Roelan had done so often when I was young.

With me to translate and his Elhim scribe to write, Alfrigg had corresponded at length with the quartermaster, a thin, squinting man with a tic in one eye, so that much of what was to be discussed that afternoon was mere formality for the benefit of the commander. The Riders were impressed that the merchant had brought his own interpreter. I made sure to stumble and grasp for words just enough that they had no need to ask how I had grown so facile in their tongue. A great many songs were composed in the language of ancient Elyria. And, too, Goryx my jailer had spoken nothing else.

After the brief formalities of agreement, the two scurrying aides brought a tray of tall pewter goblets steaming with pungent spiced wine. My throat was parched. But even the blazing hearthfire had not yet warmed the blocks of ice in my boots or the throbbing lumps in my gloves, and I dared not fumble a cup right under MacEachern's nose, so I shook my head at the pockmarked young man who held the tray. Alfrigg glared at me furiously. Because I was Senai, my refusal could be viewed as an affront to my Udema employer, or, even worse, as an affront to the Ridemark clan. Most Senai, even impoverished younger sons who were forced to seek employment, scorned those of the Twelve Families as "mongrel"—neither Senai nor Udema nor of any other identifiable heritage. Those who had climbed to so high a rank as MacEachern and had reached the inevitable conclusion that they could never be accepted into Senai society were very sensitive to Senai insults. I needed to smooth things over quickly.

"Master Alfrigg," I said, just loud enough that the Riders could hear the honorific, "as the weather is so unsettled, I will forgo the honor and pleasure of taking refreshment with you and the commander and proceed with the duties you have assigned me. Please command me, sir."

The curl of MacEachern's full lip told me that I had succeeded in earning his scorn by thus abasing myself to a Udema. Alfrigg, of course, assumed I was snubbing him again and could not hide his irritation. "I would not presume to hold you here while you could be useful elsewhere. As always you show excessive attention to your duties." He then proceeded to ask if I could be shown examples of the Riders' gear and perhaps clarify with a Rider a few of the requirements noted in the contract. The financial and delivery details, which Alfrigg and the quartermaster were to sit down and solidify, needed no interpretation.

MacEachern nodded curtly and summoned our Elhim guide, who had been standing quietly beside the door since our arrival. The slight was easy to interpret; clearly I was not worthy of a guide from the Ridemark itself. Well and good. I did not want his esteem. "Take the merchant's servant to speak with Bogdar. Request my brother in my name to answer whatever is needed." With that we were dismissed.

Alfrigg and the quartermaster retired to a vacant table with their ledgers and scrolls. MacEachern wagged his finger at one of the officers who had moved away upon our arrival. But as the Elhim and I pulled our cloaks tight about us and headed out the wooden door on the northern wall of the room, the commander leaned back in his chair, sipping his hot wine and watching us go. I hoped it was just his relishing the idea of a Senai serving a Udema merchant that made him stare, but I couldn't help wondering if there was some way he could see through my cloak to the purple scars on my back or read my soul to discover my hatred for him and my loathing for what he had made of me.

Once the Elhim pulled the wooden door closed behind

us, I breathed easier . . . at least until the icy wind sucked my breath away. We stood on an exposed outcropping of rock, roughly semicircular in shape, approximately forty paces in any direction. The flat side was the long northern face of the headquarters building, and the semicircular perimeter was a waist-high wall of granite slabs. Directly opposite the wooden door, at the apex of the circular wall, was a gap wide enough to walk through. The wind had scoured the rock platform clean of snow save in the corner to my left, where a crusted, roof-high drift obscured the joining of the wall and the building. Beyond the wall, above and below and in any direction, was the storm, layer upon layer of thick gray clouds, their undersides shredded by wind-driven sleet and snow.

When the red and gold lightning split the boiling clouds, an observer might reasonably conclude that somehow the seasons had become confused and sent the harbingers of summer rain into the winter sky. But the mistake would endure only until their eardrums shattered with the noise—not thunder, but the screams of dragons—soul-wrenching despair, mindless hatred, raw, murderous bloodlust that tore at the very center of your being. No being in the universe could fail to be turned to quivering jelly by the trumpeting bellow of dragons. No tongue but would invoke the Seven Gods and beg for their protection at the sound. No ear could hear in it anything of beauty, joy, or harmony. For years I had tried to understand how the most terrifying of cries could be the tool of the most gentle of gods, how Roelan could transform the cruel and brutal screams of beasts into music of such power that I was left trembling in ecstasy. I had never found an answer.

Perhaps the shock of MacEachern's presence had lowered my defenses. Perhaps it was the terror that had en-
gulfed me since I had entered the camp, or merely the
fury of the tempest and the proximity of the beasts, but
when the inevitable moment came, I could no longer protect myself as I had on Callia's roof. I could not close my
ears or force my thoughts away when the cry shattered
the gray afternoon. For the first time since my release I
heard a dragon's roar.

"Roelan!" I cried, unthinking, unheeding, doubling
over in agony. No pain I had endured in Mazadine could
match what I experienced on the ramparts of Cor Neuill.
The unbridled wildness tore at my chest as if a knife had
opened me and a great claw ripped out everything inside.
The noise hammered relentlessly in my head, causing red
smears in my vision, as if immortal Vanir had set up his
fiery forge behind my eyes. I clenched my frozen hands
to my breast. "Roelan, have mercy."

The god did not see fit to answer, but as a wing of
green and copper gossamer split the cloud a seeming
hand's breadth from my face, then was swallowed up
again, the Elhim caught my elbow and put his mouth
close to my ear. "Steady, my friend. The path is steep and
narrow and will be iced over." His calm, quiet voice
eased the pain as a salve soothes a burn.

"An old wound," I whispered, though he made no remark on my odd behavior. "The cold affects it wickedly.
I always forget." No one with a dram of intelligence
could have accepted my feeble explanation.

"May you be healed of all your hurts," said the Elhim,
guiding me firmly toward the gap in the wall. "Bogdar is

encamped very near the bottom of the path, so it will not be far. We'll not be required to go around the valley."

Somehow his steady reassurance enabled me to regain control, to close my ears and focus on the ice-glazed path that zigged and zagged down the cliff face through the clouds, seemingly without end. The blustering wind whipped our cloaks. A great gout of flame spurted just beyond the next turning of the unsheltered path. The sleet turned instantly into a spray of hot rain; the ice on the path melted away; and melted snow dribbled down my neck from my hair. The Elhim flung his arm out, pressing me against the cliff face, a deed well done, as the blast of hot, brimstone-tainted air that followed might have toppled us—especially the slight Elhim—off the steep path.

"Thank you," I said as we headed downward again, dropping below the thickest part of the clouds into sheets of driving sleet. From the last traverse, we looked down upon a desolation of soot-blackened puddles and frost-rimed skeletons of trees, of scorched, barren rock and frozen ruts. In the distance, arcs of fire spanned the valley like hellish rainbows. Immediately below us and around the perimeter of the valley wall were vast, stinking stockades of pigs and cattle and other herd beasts brought in never-ending streams to feed the dragons.

The Elhim led me through a milling herd of nervous, bleating sheep, deftly avoiding the wet, dirty beasts and the worst of the foul mud. Once past the stockade gate, we followed the track up a slight rise toward a shelter scarcely larger than a soldier's tent, consisting of little more than three stone walls and a roof of sod tilted toward the back wall. The fourth side had no wall but a leather curtain, and it faced the center of the valley. Another identical shelter stood some fifteen hundred paces beyond the first, and, though I could not see it for the sleet, another beyond that one, and another, creating a ring around the wasteland—a ring of power. In each of the dens lived a Rider wearing a bloodstone.

A dragon could not pass between two bloodstones unless commanded by its Rider, and then only in fearsome torment, thrashing its tail and blaring its cries, requiring every mote of strength and control its Rider could bring to bear. When I was a boy living in sight of dragon camps, I had watched the beasts try to escape the Riders' Ring. Only for the first few days in a new encampment would they attempt it. After that they stayed as far from the ring of bloodstones as possible. Individual Riders would leave on occasion to take their mounts out on patrol or maneuvers, or to go drinking or whatever else they did, but rarely did they leave a gap of more than two in the Riders' Ring, as the wide spacing made it extremely difficult for the remaining Riders to control the dragons. Riders lived with their beasts and desired nothing more, so it was said. Their clan brothers of the Ridemark made sure they wanted for nothing.

When we reached the first shelter, the Elhim called out, "*Denai* Bogdar! A visitor!" We heard no response save a howl of wind flapping the leather curtain. "I say, sir. Bogdar! A request from the *Tan Zihar*." As did many Ridemark servants, the Elhim spoke mostly Elyrian, laced with common words of the ancient speech.

"He's not there."

We whirled about to see a bear of a man standing behind us, carrying a wine cask on one shoulder as if it were a pillow. He could have palmed a boulder, his hands were so large, and like every exposed part of his body they were covered with thick, wiry brown hair. His mustache and beard were trimmed close around his protruding jaw, but the rest of his hair he wore long and knotted into a thick braid that fell halfway down his back. So much hair must have done somewhat to keep him warm. His bulging shoulders and oaklike arms were bare where they emerged from a leather vest that hung open to display the wiry forest of his massive chest. Tight leather breeches and thigh-length boots completed his attire, along with the purplish-red, square-cut jewel gleaming at his throat, held on with a leather strap. The eyes under his thick, overhanging brow were everything I knew to expect from one who wore the bloodstone at his throat and the dragon mark on his wrist—contemptuous, uninterested, and as friendly as an adder's eye.

"Bogdar's gone to stand watch on our royal pain in the ass." He jerked his head toward the center of the waste-land. "Won't be back until the night watch."

Royal pain . . . "Hostages," I said in surprise. "You've hostages in camp."

"Florin brat." A frost-glazed mudhole hissed when he spit into it. "Make a dainty sweetmeat for my kai." His kai . . . his bound servant . . . his dragon. The dragons were never given names.

While I considered the wretched plight of a hostage—a royal child, more often than not—forced to live in a stone hut in the center of that bitter wasteland, shivering in the frigid weather, surrounded by the unending terror of bellowing dragons and their hellish fire, saved from gruesome death only by men such as this one, the Elhim launched into the purpose of our visit. ". . . and so, *Denai*

Zengal, it is the *Tan Zihar*'s wish that this man's questions be accommodated, the better to provide for you and your noble brotherhood."

It seemed ludicrous that such a man as Zengal would consent to answer the mundane inquiries of a leather merchant's assistant, but in fact he agreed easily and led us to his own place, the next link in the chain of the Riders' Ring. Just outside the leather curtain was a firepit with a haunch of mutton dripping over the fire, filling the air with its savory aroma. A neatly stacked pile of logs and kindling lay beside it. The Elhim and I warmed our hands as Zengal summoned an Eskonian slave to replenish the stack. The slave was chained to a wood cart that he would drag from one Rider's hovel to another every miserable waking hour of his life. The Rider gave the spit a turn, dropped his wine cask just inside the leather curtain, and led us inside.

As one who had visited every possible type of dwelling from caves to grass-roofed shacks, from refuse heaps to palaces, and who had spent a considerable time around military camps, I believed I knew what I would see when Zengal pulled back the leather curtain of his stone hovel—spare, utilitarian, unclean except for the weaponry that would be honed and oiled and ready in its proper place. But the shelter was nothing at all like I expected.

Following the Rider's lead, I dodged a hanging lamp of silver and crystal and removed my muddy boots before stepping onto the layer of rush matting and thence onto the wool carpet of finest Eskonian design. The hut was small, no doubt, and sparely furnished, but the bed was a knee-high mound of fine, thick furs from the rarest of

beasts like snow leopard and tundra fox, and I didn't need
the evidence of women's undergarments strewn about to
note that it was large enough for more than one. The
clothes chest was polished sirkwood, bound with gold-
studded straps, and a row of golden goblets set with
amethysts stood on a small shelf on one wall. His
weapons were of the same quality: a dagger with a curv-
ing hilt of silver, chased with gold, an Eskonian scimitar,
its guard inlaid with jade. Hung in a place of honor was a
plain coil of oiled leather, each of its three strands knotted along its considerable length and tipped with steel. I
came near heaving up my long-forgotten breakfast at the
sight of it. A dragon whip. Designed for a hide a knife
could scarcely penetrate, for scaly flanks and leathery
skin encrusted with stonelike jibari, not for human flesh,
not over and over again until the underlying muscles
were useless and the skin screamed at the slightest touch.

"Well, do you want to see or do you not?" In one hand
Zengal held a goblet of wine and in the other a pair of
dark-stained leather greaves he had just removed from a
hook on the wall. The Elhim sat cross-legged on the carpet with pens and paper, looking up at me expectantly,
ready to take notes as I had asked him to do. "They must
fit exactly or you can't grip with the knees, and they have
to be thick—dragon scales are like knife edges—but flex-
ible enough to bend and hold. You see?"

For the next hour he showed me every piece of the
specialized garments the Riders needed to survive astride
the deadly monsters: the elbow-length gauntlets, the
chin-to-groin vest, the stiffened-wool mask and helm to
prevent sparks from igniting hair or damaging eyes. By
the time we were finished, the Elhim had ten pages of

fine-scripted notes, and Zengal stood naked but for the bloodstone at his neck. He downed his fifth cup of wine, unconcerned as the icy wind from the uncovered side of his lair frosted the hair on his massive body. No foolish Senai modesty here. I shivered inside my wool layers, thinking of Callia. I wanted to smile at the remembrance of her teasing, but the red mark on Zengal's wrist goaded and mocked me. I ached to strangle him and every Ride-mark villain.

I managed to examine every piece of the Rider's equipage without fumbling or dropping it. I asked how it might be improved, what measurements should be taken, everything that I might be expected to ask and nothing beyond it. Zengal answered willingly and at length, as will any soldier when discussing the necessities of his profession. Only once were we interrupted—when a dragon bellowed so near that the blades on the wall quivered in the firelight and the earth rumbled beneath our feet. While I battled to display nothing of the weakness I had shown the Elhim, Zengal fell silent and stepped to the edge of the rush matting, staring out into the gloom. Several answering blasts seemed to disturb the Rider, but not enough to prevent his downing the rest of his wine and refilling his cup yet again from the cask. He turned a blank face to me as I knelt on the carpet pretending to in-spect the pile of scorched armor. I swallowed the lump in my dry throat and said, "That's a fearful sound. I never thought to be this close to the dragons. And I'll confess it's damned uncomfortable when they sound so ... angry."

Zengal snorted. "They've no minds to be angry with.

It's the way they are—vicious, bloodthirsty. The way they will always be."

While continuing to check the Elhim's notes against the leather goods, I asked him common questions about dragons. Seemingly uninterested, he answered nonetheless. Sparks swirled in the wind beyond the doorway. Another cry came, closer than the last. I felt the blood rush from my face. The Rider burst into bellowing laughter. He bent over me, somehow more fearsome in his nakedness than if he were armed. "Are you afraid a dragon is going to stick his tongue in my lair to taste your sniveling flesh? Rest easy, tailor. They've been fed this sevenday, and you're far too bony for their taste. As long as you're with me, you need fear Davyn here as much as you fear a kai."

When the Rider named the Elhim who sat an arm's length from me, I almost lost the thread of my questioning. Davyn—the name Narim had given me to find help on the Vallior road. Coincidence. Of course it was coincidence, I thought . . . until I handed him the Rider's gauntlet and found his pale eyes fixed on my own. By the Seven Gods . . . He knew who I was. But I had no time to dwell on it. I was rapidly running out of things to ask about the Rider's garb, and I'd scarcely begun working up to what I needed to know.

"It doesn't upset them, then, when strangers are about . . . doing things they're not used to? Even if I were to start ringing bells, say, or yelling or screaming?"

The Rider spit into his firepit and dipped another goblet of wine from the cask, sucking it down in a single breath. "Upset? Do you think these are Senai ladies? There's nothing in the world can upset a dragon. Can you upset a volcano? Can you disturb a lightning bolt? Can you offend a whirlwind? They do what they do, and lucky for you and everyone like you, I and my brothers don't let them do it unless we tell them." He turned his spit once again, then settled himself, still naked, on his bed of furs, sucking down yet another cup of wine.

I wanted to scream at the man. I wanted to ask him why Callia lay dead, and Gerald and Gwaithir and Alys, and all the rest. Nothing made sense. I'd never been closer to a dragon than the rim of this very valley. I'd never touched a Rider until my feeble attempt on Callia's attacker. I'd never done anything they could consider a threat. Anything.

"Aye," I said. "The Riders protect us all . . . even the vile Florin spawn who sits out there in the center of all this." I pulled on my boots as if to go, then stood up waving my hand at the wintry desolation. "How is it done . . . to keep a hostage alive out there with the dragons?"

Zengal belched and shrugged. "We make another ring," he said, his words slurred with drink. "Three of us with the brat every hour of every day. Damned waste of time playing nursemaid. They always end up dead, after all." He stroked the golden cup in his hand and turned it so the firelight made the jewels gleam. "But the rewards are fine enough."

"I heard a story once that a hostage escaped from a dragon camp, right past the beasts. How could—"

In a move so light and quick as to belie his size and state of drunkenness, the naked Rider pinned me to the stone wall with a callused hand about my neck. Sparks flew in the deepening gloom, stinging my face and neck, and the thick, sweet odor of wine fouled what breath I could get. "It's a lie!" he screamed. "All lies, those stories. There were no kai in the lair, no Riders. They'd all been sent away. Ordinary soldiers were guarding the hostages . . . paid by spies for their treachery. No black-tongued singer could make the kai let hostages go free. It is impossible!"

"Of course not," I squeezed out, gasping and choking, my neck starting to blister with the touch of his hand. "I would never believe it. Just wanted . . . Just curious. That's all."

The Elhim backed away, fumbling at the knife sheath at his belt.

Zengal shook me as if to make sure I was paying attention. "The devil set out to shame us because his father was burned by the kai. He bribed, tricked, lied, let everyone think the Twelve Families had grown weak. But we saw it stopped, didn't we? Taught him, didn't we?"

"Yes," I croaked. "You taught him. Silenced him forever."

The Elhim had a dagger raised to strike, but whipped the weapon behind his back when the Rider let go of me and stumbled toward his wine cask again.

"I should go," I said, trying to will strength into my knees and flatten myself against the wall to keep my distance from the Rider. "You've been extremely helpful, Excellency, but I've taken far too much of your time."

Zengal grunted, staggered past me, and fell onto his fur-lined bed. The wine cup dropped from his hand, the spilled wine soaking eagerly into his fine carpet.

I would not have been human if I did not look on the bare, exposed back of the drunken Rider, thinking of the dragon whip on the wall and the moment's satisfaction it promised. It wouldn't even matter that I would be dead in the next moment. But my hands could not grip, and I had no strength, and nothing would be changed . . . except perhaps myself.

I carried with me the image of Goryx and his beatific smile as he left me broken and bleeding in my cell after a day's beating. He would touch my wounds, then lick his fingers and his lips and groan softly, his small eyes bright with unholy pleasure. When I had looked in the glass at my cousin's house, my face bore no resemblance to the one I had worn for my first twenty-one years—only death and emptiness where Aidan MacAllister, beloved of the gods, had once looked back at me. But I knew the face of evil, and the face of death was preferable. I pulled on my boots, tightened my cloak about me, and stepped out into the storm.

Chapter 9

I wanted to ask the Elhim how he had come to be employed at Cor Neuill, but I had no wish to linger in the valley, and the long trek up the steep path took all of our concentration. The footpath into the lair had been purposely left difficult to discourage casual entry, but the storm had made it even more treacherous. Snow and sleet had accumulated in dangerous, outsloping patches packed hard by the wind and the falling temperatures. The clouds closed in, forcing extra caution, as we didn't want to walk off the cliff at the end of a traverse. My foot slipped twice, but I managed to keep my balance, left with only a sick lurch in the belly as I looked into the bottomless, swirling clouds beyond the edge.

We were on a particularly steep portion of the path when both of the Elhim's feet slipped off the track. He scrabbled for a purchase on the icy rocks, all the time sliding sideways, downward, and outward. Knowing that my hands could not hold him and my shoulders had no strength to haul him up, I threw myself across his body, hoping my weight could hold him to the ground until he could find a foot- or handhold to pull himself to safety. I wedged my feet in a shallow depression in the rock and locked my arms around a protruding boulder, so that we wouldn't both slide off the edge. Against the howl of the wind, he grunted and strained in quiet desperation. It seemed an hour until he squirmed back onto the path and out from under me, but it likely took me longer to get my arm unstuck from the crack between the boulder and the cliff wall.

Sitting with our backs against the rock, we let our heartbeats return to a normal rhythm. The Elhim grinned at me. "The dragons may think you're too bony, but I think you have exactly the proper balance. Any heavier and I'd be flat. Any lighter and I'd be dead."

I smiled back at him, then nodded my head up the path. It was too cold to stay still. We got gingerly to our feet and trudged upward.

Not long after that near disaster, I became horribly disoriented. Faint stars peered at an unlikely angle through whipping clouds and encroaching night. Sure I had missed the path and was ready to walk off the edge, I halted, flailing my arms to find the anchor of the cliff face. Once my hand touched the rock and I crept forward a few more steps, I realized that the displaced stars were actually glimmers of lantern light leaking out from around the shuttered windows of the headquarters building. We hurried up the last pitch to the rock platform.

Despite my anxiety to be away from Cor Neuill, I laid a hand on the Elhim's shoulder as he reached for the door handle. "What are you doing here, Davyn?"

He smiled broadly. "Waiting for you, Dragon Speaker." Then he yanked open the door and motioned me inside before I could ask him what, in the name of sense, he meant.

The business of the dragon legion continued inside the

headquarters, unchecked by the early onset of night. A hard-faced woman, flanked by two warriors with drawn swords, sat at a table dispensing coins to a line of bedraggled drovers and carters. Other men wearing the black and red of the Twelve Families were carrying piles of blankets and crates of supplies out to distribute in the encampment. The local populace might be eating their horses or selling their children to buy half-rotted turnips, but those of the Ridemark would eat their fill and sleep warm if there were stores to be had anywhere.

Alfrigg and the quartermaster were still huddled over their accounts, but to my relief MacEachern was nowhere to be seen. Two empty wine flasks and a third only three-quarters full stood in the midst of the ledgers and papers, which was usually a sign that Alfrigg was in control of the negotiations. The red flask of uziat stood ready at his elbow.

"Master Alfrigg," I said, bowing when my employer looked up. "I have the information you desire. The Rider Zengal was most helpful. I would venture to say the Riders have no needs we cannot accommodate reasonably. We should be able to send Tarwyl and Jeddile down here tomorrow to begin taking measurements."

Davyn laid his notes on the table in front of Alfrigg and withdrew while the merchant perused the close-written pages. "Unusual materials? Special designs?"

"It's all there, sir. Very little different from your estimates."

"Excellent!" He seemed to have forgotten his earlier aggravations in the flush of success. "Tell this gentleman the same, and that if he'll agree to our last set of figures, we'll make our first delivery one month from this day."

I told the quartermaster what Alfrigg had said, as if he were truly unable to understand the words himself. *Agree,* I thought, *so we can be out of here.* Now that I'd had a chance to ask my questions, I wanted nothing but to get safely back to my room in Camarthan, where I could consider what I'd been told. But to my dismay the quartermaster read too much into my words and decided that he should hold out for a lower price, so we entered into two more hours of haggling. Now that the interpreter had returned, the signs and nods and pointing they'd used while I was in the valley would no longer suffice. Every word had to go through me.

Back and forth the two men went with the details of their contract, each point to be argued, considered, re-stated, and argued again: how many, how much, what day, what hour, what conditions . . . until I wanted to scream at them to agree or be damned. The noise in the room grew louder as more day laborers came in to collect their pay. A group of officers argued loudly about plans for a mock battle and contingencies for worsening weather.

Two servants stoked the fire in the massive hearth, so that the room grew stifling. A red-faced Alfrigg, already sweating from the wine and the intensity of his financial sparring, loosened his thick outer tunic. "You'd think we were in the belly of one of these dragons."

I did not respond. A mistake. Irritated at having lost the last point in his engagement with the squint-eyed quartermaster, he took out his frustration on me. "What kind of high and mighty fool stands there in a heavy cloak? We've got several more points to discuss before we're done, so you might as well resign yourself to deal-

ing with us lowly peasants. Take off the cloak and put
your mind on our business."

It was true that sweat was running down my face, and
my garments were drenched underneath the wool cloak,
but I dared not remove my cloak lest my failure to remove my gloves be noted. "I would prefer not, sir," I
said. "How shall I answer the gentleman's last query?"

From the bundle strapped to the back of a hollow-eyed
woman in the paymaster's line, the strident, unceasing
squall of an infant raked the senses like glass on steel.
Everyone was shouting to be heard over the din, and in
the midst of all of it, the shutters began to rattle. Smoke
billowed back down the chimney until it became hard to
see. A number of people, including myself, began coughing. This was not the wind.

The rumbling grew louder and the ground shook,
sending a crate of metal cups crashing onto the stone
floor, and toppling the wine flasks that stood in the midst
of the contract papers. Fearing we would have to start all
over again, I reached out with my clumsy hands to sweep
the papers aside before they were drenched with the dark
red wine. But at the same moment, the dragons skimming
the rooftop screamed out their hate. Distracted and nervous, I staggered against the table, forced to close my
eyes and try to block out the fire that seared my mind,
tore at my lungs, and set my skin blazing, lest I cry out as
I had on the path into Cor Neuill.

Two strong hands clamped my wrists to the table. My
heart stopped. My eyes flew open in horror-struck certainty of exposure.

But it was only a puzzled Alfrigg, staring into my face
with genuine concern as he held down my hands. "Aidan,

lad, are you ill?" I would have sworn that the cacophony fell into absolute silence just as he said my name. No one in the room could have missed it. "You look like death."

"No," I stammered, cursing the moment's lapse when I'd told him my true given name. "I'm fine. Why are you—"

"You've laid your gloves in the wine. Take your hands out of them or you're going to drip all over everything."

"I'll be careful."

"Don't be a fool, boy. Take your hands out of the gloves."

Of all the ridiculous images that fate could contrive to illustrate mortal danger . . . There was I, surrounded by my enemies, leaning over the table with my gloves soaking in a puddle of wine, determined not to show my hands lest I be returned to horror and lose my reason. Across from me was the uncomprehending Udema, equally determined that my hands would indeed come out, lest I mar his contracts and cause him to lose face. And there was no possible way to tell him of all he might lose if I did as he asked and was recognized.

"Alfrigg, please," I said softly, but his iron grip did not relax.

"We wouldn't want to risk losing all our work. This miser is on the verge of signing." He spoke through clenched teeth, his face flushed with more than the heat of the room.

With every passing moment another eye turned our way. I had to end it quickly. Only the quartermaster was close enough to see, and for a brief moment I thought the gods had decreed that everything would turn out all right, for Davyn poked his head in front of the squint-eyed clansman, saying, "Excuse me, Excellency. I will clean up this mess."

The Elhim distracted the quartermaster just long enough for me to yank my wretched hands from the gloves. I drew them immediately into my cloak, but not quickly enough, for the leather merchant's jaw dropped, his irritation replaced in an instant by curiosity and pity. Alfrigg was a good and kind man.

"Vanir's fires, Aidan, lad. What have you done to your hands?" Alfrigg's voice was not designed for intimate conversation. "Here, let me see." He drew my arm into the light.

"Alfrigg, please don't," I whispered, but it was already too late.

The quartermaster shoved the Elhim aside. "Aidan? Was that the name? 'Aidan' who has something wrong with his hands?" He peered into my face. "Osmund, summon the high commander instantly. Tell him we've discovered something most intriguing about one of our guests." He slid around the table toward Alfrigg, who held my left wrist in his powerful grip and stood gaping at my misshapen fingers. A smile blossomed on the pinched face of the quartermaster as he gazed on the work of his clan brother. "Derk, Vrond," he shouted. "Bind these two!"

Alfrigg looked up to see the two guards running toward us with drawn swords. Immediately he dropped my wrist and went for his own weapon. His confusion in no way hindered his deadly intent. He would kill the man who touched him or me, even if the attacker was a member of the Ridemark clan in the heart of their camp. I couldn't let him do it.

Using every scrap of strength I possessed, I laid my left arm across the Udema's head, knocking him against the stone wall. I had no doubt that the blow pained me far more than it did him. But it dazed him long enough for me to grab my dagger from under my cloak, clamp one hand over the other on its hilt, praying I could hold it long enough for my purpose, and press it to his throat.

"You'll not take me, Udema," I shouted. "You've been MacEachern's pawn the whole time, haven't you . . . toying with me . . . leading me into this trap?"

Alfrigg was mumbling curses. I had only a moment before he gathered his wits and realized he could flick me off him like a fly. Only a few moments beyond that and the others would recover from their confusion and realize that Alfrigg was certainly not MacEachern's pawn. Before they dared attack him, I had to convince them he was not my pawn either. I hated what I was going to do.

"I'll not allow it, Udema scum!" I screamed, jamming the dagger into the fleshy part of his shoulder, twisting it enough to ensure there was plenty of blood and plenty of pain, but not enough damage to truly hurt him. "You'll never get me back to Mazadine!" He couldn't have heard my whispered apology, as he was roaring a blistering litany of curses and maledictions of such creative grotesquerie that the gods themselves could never have heard the like.

Unable to get enough purchase on the dagger to pull it out again, I left it in him, leaped backward, and ran for the rear door. My chance of escape was so small as to be invisible, but I would not stand still and let them take me. Quickly I retraced my own rapidly disappearing footprints across the snow-covered platform to the gap in the wall. They would assume I'd take the downward path. Beyond the gap the path was dark enough and the wind fierce enough that they wouldn't expect traces. But I leaped onto the wall itself, and without even thinking how impossible it was, ran lightly along its snow-packed top to the corner where the ice-crusted snowdrift lay piled all the way to the roof of the headquarters.

I didn't quite reach the roof before the door burst open, spilling torchlight onto the windswept stone. Flattening myself against the mountain of snow, I dared not breathe until the shouting crowd of warriors disappeared through the gap in the wall and down the path. Quickly I scrambled the rest of the way to the peak of the rooftop, just in time to see a second wave of men follow the first toward Cor Neuill, and a third, smaller group fan out in front of the headquarters.

MacEachern soon arrived at the headquarters running, met by the quartermaster at the door. "Where is he?" the commander screamed.

"Bolted. Into the valley. Before we could—"

"You let him go for the dragons? Gods' teeth, you fool!" With the back of his hand MacEachern bashed the quartermaster in the head, knocking him to the ground. "Incompetent idiots. I should have all of you flogged. What if he— Everlasting damnation!" He stormed through the leather curtain, while the quartermaster picked himself up from the snowy threshold and followed slowly on his commander's heels.

For half an hour I lay on the roof, the sweat on my face turning to ice, my clothes freezing hard under my cloak. It might have been prudent to wait until MacEachern was finished dispatching his searchers and emptying the headquarters building of the unpaid carters and laborers, but I could stay no longer. I had to go while I could still move. My joints were already so stiff I dared not lower myself behind the roof peak when another party of warriors returned. My gloveless fingers could scarcely bend. So I crept carefully down the pitch of the roof to the corner of the building nearest the stable and the lean-to where visitors' horses were tethered. Gritting my teeth, I dropped to the snow.

From the corner of the building to the open-sided shelter was twenty-five paces across open ground within plain sight of anyone stepping out of the headquarters doorway. I pulled up the hood of my cloak, crammed my frozen fingers close to my body, praying them to warm up enough that I could convince my horse to do my will, and stepped out of the shadows. Slowly. I fought the temptation to make a dash for it, instead forcing myself to shamble across the snow, as if sent to do cold, unpleasant, boring duty at the stables. The distance seemed as vast as the frozen wastes of Sunderland, where men travel over ice for days on end to reach the next village. Every shout made me cringe, as I expected to see one of the shadowy forms outlined against the campfires pointing a finger my way. Every movement in the swirling snow induced my feet to move faster. But I kept it slow, and with relief passed into the shadow of the shelter, only to come near leaping out of my skin when a hand fell on my arm.

"Hold! Hold!" said the ferocious whisper as I raised my arm to use as a bludgeon again. "My skull is not half so thick as the Udema's, and it would be a shame to crush it after saving it only two hours ago."

"Davyn!" I sagged limply against the thick timbers of the shed.

"Well done," he said. "Using the roof. They're sure you've gone to steal a dragon, so they'll search the whole valley before they figure out you're still up here. And you'll be far away by then."

Yes, get away . . . My limbs felt like dough. "My horse," I said thickly. "I've got to get going."

"Not *your* horse. If anyone found it missing, your ruse would be spoiled. Besides, your horse doesn't know the way and would get you lost and frozen."

"The way?" I felt dull and sluggish. I hadn't even considered where I could go. Of course Camarthan was no longer safe.

The Elhim led me into the stables and past the line of nervous horses, most of them still skittish from the passage of the dragon flight. But in a corner box stood a smallish roan, peaceably champing at a bucket of oats until he caught sight of the Elhim and whinnied agreeably. "Hey, ho, Acorn," said Davyn, patting the horse's nose and producing an apple that the beast happily snuffled off his palm. "Acorn will carry you," he said, noting my skeptical assessment of the undersized horse. "I promise your feet won't drag the ground. And he's carried heavier men than you. Give him his head, and he'll bear you safely."

"In the dark . . . ?"

". . . and the storm He's an intelligent horse. He knows where to take you."

"Yours?"

"He allows me to ride him, and he will allow you. Now be quick."

Davyn held Acorn's head as I mounted, and he spent a goodly time whispering in the horse's ear before stepping back. "Give him his head, and don't be concerned. You'll be met by friends. Tell them I'll be along as soon as it can be done inconspicuously."

"But I—"

Footsteps crunched beyond the stable doors. Davyn pressed his fingers to his lips and laid a hand on Acorn's nose.

"Don't touch me, you creeping ferret." It was Alfrigg. "You'll not hold me here another moment. I'm going back to Camarthan and search out the egg-sucking, flea-bitten Senai pig. I'll nail his hide to the walls of my shop. I don't care what he's done. I'll gut him with his own bloody knife, I will."

A quiet murmur was identifiable as the quartermaster's high-pitched voice, but I couldn't catch his words before Alfrigg broke in again. "No, I don't need a guide. I was riding these roads before you were whelped. And in worse weather. Why did I ever think I needed a Senai tongue-flapper? Tell your commander the deliveries will commence as soon as one or the other of us has slit this highborn bastard's throat."

Never had I been so glad to be despised. From the vehemence of Alfrigg's curses, I was reassured that I hadn't hurt him too much, and, as they were letting him go, I must have done enough for the moment. "I need to warn him," I said softly. "They're letting him go now, but—"

"The Udema will be warned that a rival merchant in one of his new territories has sworn an oath to eliminate him and his family. He'll be on his guard. And he'll be watched."

As the hoofbeats died away, the Elhim led Acorn to the end of the stables farthest from the headquarters. My relief had warmed my blood, and I motioned for him to give me the reins. "Wrap them around," I said, as he looked dubiously at my gloveless hands. "Yes, I know . . . give him his head. But I'll feel better with something to hold on to."

"If he falters, tell him *thanai.* It will remind him."

Thanai—home. "Davyn . . ." I tried to etch the Elhim's likeness on my memory so I could recognize him if we ever met again. Broad shoulders for an Elhim. Fair skin stretched over fragile bones. A deep cleft in his chin. Laugh lines about his eyes that hinted he was far older than the twenty or so years he appeared. The curl of pale hair that was forever drooping over his left eye.

"Perhaps next time you'll believe it when someone offers you help. Now, be off. I'll be missed soon." He whacked Acorn's rump, and the horse ambled slowly out of the stable, immediately turning away from the camp and into the whirling wilderness of snow.

In the matter of moments the camp was swallowed by the night. I could not tell whether we were heading east or west or over a cliff or upward to the stars that I trusted were still sparkling somewhere above the storm. Strange. For the first time in six months I was not afraid. There was something reassuring about going blind into the storm, as if I were indeed resting in the palm of the eyeless god.

Chapter 10

I called on Keldar a number of times during that frigid night. Not in fear. Just a soft reminder that I was still there in the blustering wind and unending snow. I didn't want him to forget about me. The night was bitterly cold, my lips and nose and fingers so ominously dead to the touch that I longed for the familiar ache in my hands just to prove I still had them. I was horribly thirsty, but I had no water, no food, no means of making fire, and no shelter but the feeble defense of my cloak. For seven years I had been a traveling musician, priding myself on how little I needed in the way of material comforts, but I had never been trained to survive like a soldier in the field, with nothing. Every time I thought I had been brought as low as a man could fall, I slipped a little further. Why was I yet living? The god of wisdom must have a plan for me, for all knew that horses were beloved of Keldar, and only a horse stood between me and the long, cold descent into death.

To keep my mind off my misery and prevent any panic-induced attempt to head Acorn for Camarthan, I kept trying to make some sense of my interview with Zengal. The Riders were afraid of me. It was the only possible conclusion—their hatred, their determination to force me silent, their defiance of Devlin. No wonder the king was worried. It didn't matter whether I was his cousin or his brother or his wife or his child. If he had to choose between me and his dragon legions, he had only one possible course. Devlin's dragons kept Elyria and his vassal kingdoms in existence.

Those of the Ridemark clan considered themselves above politics. Each of the Twelve Families chose to serve the ruler it considered the best tactician, the fiercest and craftiest opponent, the most ruthless war leader, or the best paymaster. Once sworn in fealty to a lord, the only thing that would make the Riders bend their honor and defy him was a threat to the superiority of their position—that is, a threat to their dragons. But why in the name of the Seven would they think of me as a threat? My brain came to a standstill whenever I hit this question. I would back off and try another path, but always I came back to it.

It could not be that I made the dragons "uneasy," as Devlin said. Zengal claimed that nothing made them uneasy. But the Rider had exploded in anger and defensiveness when I mentioned the escaped hostages. He had spewed out contrived stories and rote excuses. And then what had he said? *No black-tongued singer could make the kai let hostages go free.* If the Riders really believed I had made the dragons disobey, caused them to reject the control of the bloodstones . . . Vanir's fire, no wonder they were ready to kill me! But why would they think it? A series of remote coincidences? I knew nothing of dragons save the sounds of their voices that a god had used to inflame my music.

"Idiocy!" I shouted on the hundredth occasion I

reached this impasse, inadvertently jerking the reins wrapped about my frozen hands. Acorn pulled up abruptly.

"No . . . no . . . I'm sorry." What had the Elhim told me to say? For a panicked moment I could not remember. It was too dark; I was too cold. I'd been awake and afraid and freezing far too long. "Go on, Acorn. Have your head. You know the way. Go home to your . . . home . . . yes. *Thanai!*"

With a snuffle, the sturdy little beast took off plodding again and I leaned forward, burying my face in his wiry mane. "Thank you, Acorn . . . Keldar, all praises be sung to your name." I did no more thinking on that long night's journey, but drifted in and out of sleep, holding on by sheer instinct, for I had nothing of will left. I dreamed fitfully of dragon wings and unclimbable mountains of snow, of Callia laughing as she bled out her life on her green silk dress, of Goryx smiling and fastening the cold metal jaws on my fingers. . . .

"No! No more. Please no more." I screamed as he began to break them one by one. I fought to make him stop. I felt like I was falling, though my bonds held me tight while lights flashed about me, and he kept on—one after the other. "Have mercy," I sobbed. "I will be silent until the end of the world."

"I'm sorry, my friend," came a familiar voice. "We had to get your hands untangled from the reins. It was a long, hard journey, but you're safe now. You'll be warm again in time."

Hot wine was poured down my throat until I gagged, and something heavy and blessedly warm was wrapped about my shoulders.

Another voice. "Lift him onto the litter. Careful!"

"On his stomach, not his back. Hurry and get him to the fire. Of all the ill luck to have such a storm. One would think the Seven would arrange it otherwise." There was a great deal of laughter at that.

They should not blame the gods. The storm was surely Keldar's doing. If I was blind, then so were my pursuers blind. I was settled gently on my stomach. My hands— which were not broken, only frozen—were wrapped in warm cloths. I felt the unmistakable jostling of being carried. "I'll be all right," I said, my words muffled in the soft fur under my face. "I'll be all right if I can just sleep for a year or two."

Friendly, hearty laughter broke out around me. I wished I could see who it was, but I was carried close to a blazing bonfire, where I caught only a glimpse of a dozen pale gray eyes and a great deal of fair hair before I fell so deeply asleep I could not dream.

The smell of new-baked bread and hot bacon drew me out of the luxurious darkness into the gray light of a cold dawn. "I'm sorry we can't let you sleep for a year, but I think I've brought you fair recompense. Am I right?" An Elhim—and I was certain it was Narim—sat cross-legged beside me, holding out a plate piled high with meaty slices of bacon still sizzling from the fire and thick chunks of bread dripping with butter. Behind him a bonfire showered sparks on at least five Elhim who were stuffing blankets and pots and tins into enormous saddle packs. I lay on the snow-covered ground swaddled in thick blankets, close enough to the fire that my face was hot.

"You've brought me the only thing in the world that could induce me to move," I said, maneuvering myself so I could sit up without exposing any part of me to the cold air. "Though it looks as if you were going to force me to it fairly soon anyway." One of the Elhim began throwing snow on the fire, which hissed in protest and sent out huge spouts of steam.

"We need to be on our way. The storm has passed, and we assume you will be pursued. You came on Acorn." His face wore a cast of worry that I eased by passing on Davyn's message around a mouthful of butter-soaked delight.

"Ah, good," said Narim. "Davyn is the best and bravest of us all. You were recognized, then?"

"I was a fool. Came near getting another good man killed . . . and this Davyn, too, if anyone gets wind of what he's done. You and your friends would do well to keep your distance. You've saved my life yet again—and I do thank you most truly for all this—but my best repayment will be to stay away from you."

Narim smiled and shook his head. "Since we found you in Lepan, your life has never been truly in danger, Aidan MacAllister—not because you are the cousin of the king, but because you are the nearest thing the Elhim have ever had to a hope of redemption. Whatever debt you acknowledge to me or my kin, you will have ample opportunity to repay . . . if you come with us. Many will risk whatever danger is necessary to keep you safe."

"I don't understand. How is it that you and Davyn . . . ?"

"And Tarwyl is over there loading the horses. You have a number of friends. I've no time to tell you all of it

right now. We must be off before the Riders start looking
this way. Only know that as long as one of the three of us
lives, you will never go back to Mazadine."

"But—"

"Hurry yourself or you'll get stuffed in a saddle pack."
He threw my boots and cloak at me, and after that a heavy
shirt and a pair of thick woolen gloves—my own spare
shirt and gloves that I'd last seen in my rooms at Camarthan. I thought of the quiet Elhim who had taken
lodgings across the passage from me and wondered if he,
too, would appear among my rescuers.

Riding in a saddle pack didn't sound all that bad, for
the air outside my cocoon was bitterly cold and thin.
Acorn had brought me a good way up in the world. As I
pulled on my outer garments and relinquished my blankets to the busy packers, the sun shot over the eastern
horizon, banishing the lingering grayness and drenching
the world in the blinding blue-white brilliance of winter
morning.

We were camped on a high, wide plateau, looking
eastward over a panorama of rolling hills and valleys unrecognizable beneath their mantle of snow. The world
might have been newborn in that dawning, for there was
no sign of human handiwork anywhere to be seen in all
the lands laid out before me. Behind me rose a sheer face
of pink-tinged granite rising sharply into the deep blue of
the western sky—Amrhyn, the towering grandsire of the
Carag Huim, the impenetrable Mountains of the Moon.

My spirits, lifted by the kindness of the Elhim, sank
abjectly when I saw Amrhyn. Where within the bound-
aries of heaven and earth could we go from this place except back the way we'd come? For centuries men had

attempted to conquer the heart of the Carag Huim, but found no passage save those to the south of Catania or far to the north in the realm of frozen wastes. Every attempt ended at an unscalable cliff, a gaping chasm, or an impassable slope of dangerously crumbled rock left by an avalanche. Every man who claimed to have found a way into those mountains had been proved a charlatan, and it was widely accepted that the gods intended for us to contemplate such awesome works as the Carag Huim from a respectful distance. Even the Dragon Riders stayed away from this mountain range, calling it a place cursed by the gods. But I was in no position to question my rescuers. I had nowhere else to go.

In a quarter of an hour I was astride the faithful Acorn, plodding up a winding way toward the cliff face. I could not call it a trail. Narim and Tarwyl rode single file in front of me, and two others behind. Two stayed back to wait for Davyn.

All day we traveled through impossible ways: paths that appeared to lead over cliffs, yet would turn abruptly to follow a narrow ledge bearing downward. Valleys with no outlet until you squeezed between two giant boulders and passed through a dark cleft in the rock to emerge in an open vale. Impossible slopes of dangerously loose talus that turned out to be more stable than they appeared. Sometimes it was difficult to see exactly how we got to where we were going, for the blinding sun on the snowy peaks forced me to keep my eyes squeezed to narrow slits. Surefooted Acorn followed his brethren, and I came to think that perhaps only the horses really knew the way.

About midday Narim called a halt. We cracked the icy shell of a noisy brook to refill our waterskins and let the horses drink. While Tarwyl handed around hard, sweet biscuits and dried meat, the other three Elhim talked of the trail and the weather.

"Isn't Alfrigg going to miss you?" I said to Tarwyl, when the conversation lagged.

The deep-voiced Elhim nodded solemnly. "My cousin has taken my place at the merchant's shop. Curiously enough his name is also Tarwyl, but he's much less efficient than I. I would guess he's already made some terrible errors in the accounts and is very likely to be sacked any day now." The four Elhim broke into merry snorts and chuckles.

The Elhim were so difficult to tell one from another, I could well believe his story. "And you"—I spoke only half in jest to the fourth Elhim, who indeed bore an uncanny resemblance to the fellow who had lived across the passage in Camarthan—"I would guess you have a cousin who has moved into your rooms? One who is perhaps as much a thief as you, who seems to have acquired every stitch I own and brought it here?"

His pale skin had a leathery texture to it, and he had a terrible, red-rimmed squint to his eyes, as if he'd been in blinding sunlight far too long, but he managed to tilt his eyes cheerfully at my question. "Indeed, my cousin plans only to stay a few more days. The room is really not at all suitable."

"Why? Why are you doing this?"

Every attempt at more serious questioning was gently but firmly put off, and we were back in the saddle before I had a single clue as to where we were bound and how in the name of heaven they had managed to find this passage into the Carag Huim. Our path took us ever higher and ever westward into the heart of the mountains. The stark ranks of ice-clad peaks rose sharply into the heavens on every side of us, and the snow lay deep upon the trails we followed, so that our going was often little more than a crawl. I began to believe that we were indeed going someplace where the clan would never find me.

Evening came early on the eastern flanks of Amrhyn, leaving us in chilly shadows at the hour when the rolling lands we had escaped were still basking in the gold of afternoon. We were climbing a saddle between the main bulk of Amrhyn and one of its towering shoulders to the north. It was the steepest ascent we had made. Impassable, every other traveler would have declared it, unless they saw the narrow thread of rock wall supporting the path that crisscrossed the slope.

"Only a little farther," called Narim, who was in the lead. "Have a care as we descend, Aidan; the horses always try to run down this ridge." He wore an odd smile as he disappeared over the top. I understood it when I reached the crest and saw what lay beyond. Not another frozen wasteland to be traversed. Not another stretch of tundra broken only by stunted junipers and ice-shattered rubble, not a snow-filled bowl, but a vast green valley dotted with lakes and springs, patches of evergreen forest dusted only lightly with snow, and everywhere herds of deer and elk and small, sturdy horses that could only have been Acorn's relations. A flock of birds rose from the trees at the passage of a wild boar. I could scarcely comprehend such a marvel. In the distance a geyser shot twenty stories into the heavens, and an eagle soared joyously on the warm air that rose from the valley floor, lapping at my toes.

Even if I'd been able to form a question, my companions had already abandoned me, riding at full gallop down a broad, winding road that traversed the steep hillside. Acorn pulled anxiously at the reins, and I knew what he wanted. I clamped my arms around his neck and shouted, *"Thanai!"*

Like an arrow released from a bow, the horse raced after his fellows, all the day's weariness shed in the warm air and the exhilaration of home ground. Down, down, recklessly, wildly. Even as I hung on for my life, I found myself laughing in manic delight. Into the evening woodland, startling deer and at least one black bear nosing an overturned rock, back into meadowlands, leaping one streamlet after another, circling deep, blue pools that steamed in the cooling evening. All the way across the breadth of the valley and into a rocky enclave where sheer walls made a protected corner and a stream trickled from the mouth of a cave through a bed of mossy rocks.

The others were already off their horses, embracing a group of perhaps twenty Elhim who stood just in front of the cave. I pulled up Acorn so as to approach more slowly, rather than careening into the crowd and tumbling off into the arms of his laughing kin as Tarwyl had done. My intent was not to make my arrival dramatic, only civilized, but as I rode toward them silence fell. Every one of the gray eyes turned to me, and every fair head bowed graciously. There had been a time when I was accustomed to such attention, accepting it as an honor to my god and a challenge to prove myself worthy of his favor. But all that had changed. My face grew hot. As I slid off Acorn's back and stroked the good beast's neck with whispered thanks, a tall Elhim in a long gray robe, leaning heavily on the arm of a younger Elhim, stepped forward to greet me. His white hair was braided and fell to his hips. His pale, parchmentlike skin was creased with a fine tracery of white wrinkles. And his gray eyes were filled with such a vast knowledge of joy and sorrow, good and evil, that I thought he must be the oldest person I had met of any race.

I held out my hands in greeting, but the old Elhim did not take them. Rather he cupped his papery hands before his breast and bowed deeply, saying, "Greetings, Dragon Speaker. In the name of the One Who Guides and in the name of the Seven, I bid you welcome, and in the name of every Elhim that breathes the air of the world, I offer you our fullest gratitude for your coming. Everything we have is yours to command. Our lives are in your service before every other, and whatever we can do to ease your path is only your single word from being accomplished. You are the hope of our people, and our joy in your presence is beyond description."

How could I answer such a kindly greeting full of such flowery nonsense? There was clearly some mistake, and honor bade me acknowledge it. I had so many guilts earned fairly through my own pride and folly and carelessness, but this one . . . Whatever had I done to convince an entire people that I was worth putting themselves at such risk? I cupped my hands before my breast and returned his bow. "Good sir, I am honored by this generosity your people have shown me at such risk of their lives and fortunes. Your words humble me. But in truth I cannot accept such gifts when I believe them to be misdirected. You call me by a title I do not know, and speak of hopes of which I am ignorant, and you seem to

have expectations that—much as I would desire to offer
you service—it is very unlikely I could fulfill. There
seems to have been a terrible mistake."

I expected consternation, dismay, shock, perhaps
anger, but instead I got sad smiles and sighs of resignation.

"You see, Iskendar? As I told you. Incredible as it may
seem, he has no concept of what he is"—Narim spoke
from behind the shoulder of the elderly Elhim—"or of
what he was."

"But if he is as we have judged him, all we have to do
is tell him our story," said the old Elhim. "Of course, we
thought the deed was closer to accomplishment, but what
is a matter of a few years after five hundred?" His eyes
glittered, their sharp edges cutting away my skin as if to
see what lay beneath.

"I'm afraid . . ." Narim flushed and eyed me nervously. "Well, of course we will tell him and see what can
be done. I swore to bring him here safely, and, thanks to
my brave kin, I have accomplished it. A deed well worth
doing, as Aidan's is a heart worth keeping in the world.
But whatever else comes of it is up to the One. I would
hold no great expectations. Many things have changed
since we last breathed hope. Many things."

"You've done well, Narim. As you say, the One will
decide the outcome."

I followed their exchange with no splinter of enlight-
enment. It came to a point where I could no longer tolerate ignorance. "Tell me, Narim, and you, good sir. What
is it you think I can do for you?"

The ancient Elhim answered, while Narim chewed one

of his fingers and watched me closely. "We have hopes you can make them remember."

The hair on my arms and my neck rose up as if brushed by a finger from the grave. A knife turned in the hollow of my chest so that I could not get out the question except in a whisper. "Who?" I said, and even then I did not know if I could bear the answer.

"The dragons, of course. The Seven who are the eldest and their sons and daughters who lie enslaved with them these five hundred years. If it is to be anyone at all, then it is you who must free the dragons that are named by men the Seven Gods."

Chapter 11

"Of course we're not saying the dragons are gods." Nyura, the servant or aide who seemed attached to old Iskendar's arm, had jumped in quickly at my shocked denial. "Far from it. No god could kill so viciously or allow himself to fall victim as the dragons did. It is only that many things humans have perceived as the powers of a god are perhaps not supernatural in their origin. Listen to our tale and judge."

They had led me deep into a torchlit cave while I was still lost in dismay and outrage. I was so caught up in what I had heard and what I was yet to hear that I absorbed no impression of the cave, save that it was large, clean, and pleasantly warm, and a number of people lived there. And scarcely had we sat down on thin quilted pallets than the tale had begun. . . .

"From the beginnings of time the Elhim and the dragons roamed the lands of Yr: the Mountains of the Moon and wild forests and plains that lay beyond them to the west. In summer, we Elhim would climb the peaks and hunt and fish in the mountain vales, and in winter ply our trades and crafts in the lower lands. The dragons would fly all spring, summer, and fall, hunting game in mountains and valleys—there was plenty for all—and in winter they would go to ground, sleeping away the coldest months, emerging only when the rivers were free of ice."

It was Tarwyl telling the tale, his sober clerk's manner replaced by the misty-eyed, harmonious language of an experienced loremaster.

"It was always a day of celebration when the dragons returned in the spring, of rejoicing at the birth of the year. They would soar overhead, their cries of joy and delight filling us with joy in our turn. In the first spring flight we saw the new-hatched younglings, soft and scaleless, their awkward, half-spread wings still glistening sticky white. The elders flew beneath them, bathing them with gentle fire, making a rising of the air with the beating of their wings until the younglings could fly on their own.

"We listened to them bellowing and trumpeting and shaping sounds of great variety, but for centuries we did not understand them. Only gradually did we come to think that there were meanings in their songs as truly as in our own. When they sang, we felt the power of their emotions reflected in our minds: their joy in their young, their pride in the wisdom of their clans, the beauties of earth and sea and fire, the hardships of hunger and death, and only a passing interest in those who shared the earth with them. But they knew we were not beasts and never did they harm us.

"We grew curious, of course, as the years passed and we found no other creatures who sang so clearly of life. We began to suspect that their sounds were words, and that the emotions and images we saw in our minds were theirs. Exploring deeper into the Carag Huim, we found the caves where they slept and the valleys where they played. We studied their sounds and tried to imitate them, but that was not possible. Their bones and muscles are so different. We did better when we used their images to form our own words. And when we shaped our words into formal patterns of speech similar to their own, the dragons understood us without study or practice. Early in the year after their spring waking, we would speak with them, interpreting their answers through both words and images they placed in our minds. But as the days faded toward winter, they were no longer able to communicate, as if they had grown wild again.

"But we learned how they hatched their younglings, and how they hunted. And we learned what they disliked—cold and snow—and we learned what they feared—the red gems we called bloodstones and the sour herb called jenica or dragonsbane. The gems were found deep under the mountains in a hole called Nien'hak—the pit of blood—and the dragons said the stones took away their will. Jenica grows high on the tundra, and we learned that if they ate it, it would make them groggy and sick and unable to fly. And after many years of observation we learned the secret of their speaking—the lake they called Cir Nakai.

"Every spring when emerging from their caves, the dragons flocked to a lake that was fed by a deep, cold spring, drinking their fill of the clear water as the sun set. They did not return to the lake until winter, so its effects wore away and they gradually grew wilder until their fall mating and long sleep. It would be so to this day if it were not for the abomination the Elhim wrought upon them."

Fifty or more of the Elhim had gathered around the small fire with us, listening in solemn and sad attention. Their posture spoke of hope that this time the story might end a different way, while their faces displayed the knowing sadness that it would not. Wine was passed, a cup placed in my hand, but I could not drink it.

"There came to the world twenty years of terrible drought," Tarwyl continued. "Mighty rivers became roadways of caked mud. The Carag Huim were bare of ice and snow. The herds of elk and deer grew scant. The Elhim had grown increasingly fond of some new lands across the Carag Huim—what you now call northern Elyria, especially this region of Catania—as they were so much easier to tame than the lands of Yr. In those days, no one else had settled so far north. In the drought years, life here in the northlands was abundant compared to the southern and eastern climes. It was said that in the fifteenth year of the drought nothing at all grew in the lands south of what is now Vallior, and that to the east by the Sea of Arron, people were driven mad by drinking seawater when no fresh could be had. Plagues arose, and the barbarians began their raiding. And so came Senai from the south and Udema from the east, looking for fertile lands and good hunting, water and safety.

"We went out to welcome them and succor them in their need, but were dismissed as no more than children. Our houses were taken by Senai, our fields were tilled by Udema, and we were barred from our own hunting grounds. Any who resisted were slain. These other races were so large and so obsessed with their male/female duality that we didn't understand them at all. But two things we saw quite quickly. If we didn't do something to prove ourselves worth noting, we would be exterminated. And when the newcomers caught their first sight of the dragons, they were terrified."

I wanted to cover my ears. The Elhim's words were like a bleached skeleton sprawled on the desert with a rusty knife blade lying between two ribs. Truth. Uncompromising. Unavoidable.

"We spoke to the dragons and asked for their help, not to harm but only to frighten the humans away. But they could not understand our need. Even common words cannot always transmit common thought, and dragons had no concept of territory or greed, deception or conspiracy. They could not understand the kind of danger we faced. They would not help us, and every sevenday another of our villages fell to the newcomers. And so the Elhim gathered together and devised a plan—a terrible, unholy plan that even in our direst need we knew was wrong. We sent our kinsmen into the mountains to gather jenica— every sprig or leaf that could be found. We sent diggers into Nien'hak to dig up the bloodstones—every pocket, every vein, that we could see. And when winter came and the dragons went to sleep, we threw the jenica into the lake—poisoned it—and cut the bloodstones so that there was one for every dragon."

Several of the listeners had closed their eyes and crossed their arms upon their breasts.

"When came the spring awakening, we watched from the crags. As the dragons drank their fill of the lake at sunset, they fell still and sick, and they cried out in pain and fear, 'Oh, children of fire and wind, what ill has befallen us?' And when they grew quiet, we crept near. In horror we saw that while the older dragons were only groggy and unmoving, every youngling lay dead. A few of us faltered at this grievous outcome and wanted to halt the plan. But others prevailed, saying it was too late. Who knew what the dragons would do to us in their wrath?

"When the dragons revived from their sickness, an Elhim holding a bloodstone stood beside each one. We thought the bloodstones would keep them docile, but instead the beasts went mad. We tried to calm their fury by singing the songs we had learned from them—the songs they sang to their own younglings when the little ones were frightened. Five hundred Elhim died in the dragons' waking, scorched to ash and bone, but the others, those who held the bloodstones, though bathed in the white fire of the dragons' uttermost rage, did not burn. Whoever had carried the stone into that dragon's fire became its master, able to control the beast with his will and his voice, the Elhim, the stone, and the dragon inextricably bound together from that day.

We wept for our dead kinsmen, and we wept for the glorious dragons who were sent forth at our command and terrorized our enemies with fiery death. Not until we left our refuge in the mountains to see for ourselves did we know how terrible was the plague we had unleashed. We had made of the countryside a wasteland. No spring came to Catania that year, only the fires of the dragon summer.

"But the tally of our sins was not yet complete. Once our struggle was won, we fully intended to let the dragons go free, but we did not know how. When we tried destroying one of the stones, the dragon went on a rampage, uncontrollable by any means at all. We had to bring other dragons around to kill it. We used our dragon lore, tried every method we could think of, every holy rite we knew, to no avail. The burden of the dragons was so terrible and so wrong that we eventually went to the humans for help, hoping that they had some skill or insight or god-magic that would show us how to set the beasts free.

"Only twelve Senai and Udema families yet lived in Catania—yes, you begin to see how it goes. We begged their forgiveness and told them all we knew of dragons, pleading for their help. But to our horror they did not free the dragons either. Instead they took the stones for themselves and said that only they would control the beasts. They would not believe that the dragons were sentient beings who could speak if allowed to drink the water of Cir Nakai. They had never known the glory, only the terror of their destruction. They believed that the wordless power in their minds—the images of joy and love, fire and earth, water and wisdom that sang in their hearts when first they came to our lands—were visions from gods, not the speech of dragons. We told them the names of the seven eldest dragons: Tjasse and Vellya and Vanir, Keldar and Audun, Roelan and Jodar, but they believed in magic as children do and took those names for their gods. How was it they still felt the presence of the gods, they asked, when the dragons were bound by the bloodstones? But that, too, would fade as time and madness and killing took their toll. As the dragons grew wild, the gods fell silent, and only the Elhim knew why."

Narim took my untouched cup of wine and set it aside, then signaled me to stand. All the company rose and moved silently, deeper into the cave. As we walked toward a dark opening in the back wall of the cavern, Tarwyl walked beside me and continued his tale.

"The dragons have produced no younglings since that wicked day, so every dragon that dies in our wars is one soul lost to the world forever. And the longer the dragons are forbidden the water of the lake, the less likely they can ever regain their rightful place in the world. The longer they live under the influence of the bloodstones, the further they slip into wildness.

"All these years we have tried to discover how to redeem our sin and free the dragons from the bloodstones. As more humans came north after the Chaos Years, founding their new kingdoms on the cruelty we began, we sent our kin into every part of the world seeking an answer. In five hundred years we never saw a spark of hope.

"But some twenty-three years ago we heard whispers of disturbance among the Riders. It was clear there had been . . . incidents . . . where they had lost control of their dragons. Any man or woman who spoke of this rumor was instantly slain, but Elhim are everywhere and hear everything, unnoticed by most people. It was Davyn who first heard one who called himself a servant of Roelan touch a harp and bring forth the music of dragons, and in a voice that would sear the soul, sing about a lake of fire. . . ."

Tarwyl's voice drifted away. Narim took my arm and gently propelled me through a dark, rounded passage, lit only by a circle of red-gold light at its far end. I was as cold and numb as if I were still in the heart of the storm, terrified as I had never been. As we approached the circle of light, I pulled back, whispering, pleading. "No. Please, no more. Have mercy. . . ."

Narim tugged gently. "I know how hard this is," he said softly in the dark. "Iskendar and the others don't understand about Mazadine. But you have come so far and heard so much, the truth is already a part of you. It is so painful, so terrible, because in your deepest of hearts you have always known—from the first night in your uncle's garden. There is no blame to you, for what good was the knowledge without the understanding to go with it? Come and open yourself to all of it; then perhaps your healing can begin."

I walked toward the red light and emerged in a high mountain basin open to the west. Nestled in the bowl of harsh cliffs and ringed with a broad gravel shore was a glassy lake blanketed with steam and fog in the cooling air. The bloodstained sun lay round and bloated on the horizon. Its red light on the still water and the rising vapors created an image of fire, as if the whole basin were ablaze . . . as had its image in my mind from the earliest days of my glory, when first I began to hear the voice of my god.

On the gravel shore of the lake of fire, I sank to my knees and rocked back and forth silently, aimlessly, my arms wrapped tightly about my middle. Unlike in my boyhood fervor on the night I had first seen the lake of fire in my visions, I did not weep. I had no tears left. I had nothing left. I had often wondered why I clung to life so fiercely in Mazadine and after, and until that moment I had never had an answer. But now I knew . . . now that it, too, was gone. Music and courage, pride and love, dignity and friendship, joy and hope—all the elements that had formed my life, giving it shape and substance and worth—all had been left behind in the Riders' bleak fortress. But I had come out still bearing the knowledge that I was once beloved of a god and had given him everything I possessed. Even though Roelan had abandoned me, I had believed that something in me was worthy of a god's favor. Surely Keldar or Vanir or Vellya . . . one of them . . . would see it and show me his face and give me a reason to keep breathing. But the voice in my heart had never been a god. It had been a beast.

NARIM

Chapter 12

I sat on the high, narrow rim of rock that separated Cor Talaith, the warm, green valley the remnants of my people called home, from the bowl of rock that held Cir Nakai, the lake of fire where we believed the dragons could find their minds again. On that morning, as every time I perched on that dangerous, wind-scoured sliver of crumbling granite, I wondered to which side I would topple if I were to lose my balance. How much was required to remove the stain of terrible error? Was the sacrifice of all purpose save expiation enough? Was the abandonment of all growth and development of our people enough? Would it come to our extinction, as some among us believed, and if so, would that be enough—and would it be worth such a price? And where in such a weighty reckoning was calculated the price of one innocent man's life?

I should never sit still and think. I knew which way my heart would lead me if I just kept moving, but when I sat still I always ended up on that knife edge and realized I could fall either way.

Far below me in Cor Talaith where the winds were warm and the grass was green, three of my kin and a tall, lean figure—a human male—worked at building a bridge across a steaming fissure that was one source of the warm air that blessed our valley. The bridge would greatly shorten the way from the fertile meadow where we grew our wheat to the caves where we lived and the waterfall where sat our mill and granary. I watched the man struggle to lift a small stone from the cart he had driven from the rockfall on the north side of the valley. He scooped it onto his forearms and bent his knees to get the leverage and strength he could not get from his back, then gathered it to himself and carried it to the growing pile beside the scaffolding at the edge of the fissure.

It had been difficult to persuade the man to stay in Cor Talaith once he had convinced Iskendar and the others that he could offer us no possible hope of redemption. The only way he would accept the refuge we offered was if he had work to do. He had begged me for some hard physical labor that would drown his desolation and fill his emptiness with exhaustion. I owed him that. I had been the instrument that stripped away his last defense against despair. That I had also given him labor that would make him stronger—already after six weeks he could lift stones of ten times the size he could at first— he might or might not thank me as he traveled farther on the terrible road I had laid down for him. Though I cared a great deal for Aidan MacAllister and grieved for the horrors he had endured—and those he had yet to endure—neither love nor sympathy would sway my purpose. Thinking might, if I sat too long on the rim between Cor Talaith and Cir Nakai.

A red-tipped hawk shrieked a cry of triumph and dived toward the wide, barren shingle that bordered the lake as I started down the slope of jumbled rock and hardy, gray-green tuck grass that would take me into Cor Talaith. Preoccupied with my moral dilemmas, I wasn't looking where I was going, so I almost ran into the tousled figure trudging upward.

"I guessed you'd be up here."

"Davyn!"

My friend clapped his sturdy arms around me, making dents in my ribs with the greeting. "I finally got loose. There was an ugly uproar in Cor Neuill these past weeks. Thought my legs were going to get run off carrying their messages—but fortunately the fellow I replaced got healed of his wasting fever, so I was able to turn over my duties to a more experienced clerk."

"Well done. I've not rested easy since I saw Acorn come home without you."

"How is he? I didn't want to speak to anyone until I'd talked to you. Did all come about as you expected?"

Davyn was not referring to his unflappable horse. I nodded toward the distant group of laborers. "He exists. Nothing more. If anything, I underestimated the impact our story would have on him. By the time we were done with the telling there was so little of him left he might as well have been standing naked before us. He had no difficulty convincing the others that our hopes were irrevocably ruined—and so our leaders are well satisfied."

"By the One!" My best friend stood perhaps a head taller than me and had shoulders like a young ox—well, at least for an Elhim—so that even in his rumpled weariness he was a formidable presence, especially when his eyes flashed in such righteous indignation. "How can we have fallen so low?"

I clapped him on the shoulder and pointed him back down the hill. "Because few of us have your withering intelligence, your unswerving sense of honor, or your implacable understanding of right. If we were all like you, we'd never have gotten ourselves into this mess."

Davyn shrugged off my hand and grinned wryly as he headed down the slope. "An odd compliment to one who's spent the last half year living a lie."

"Who better to live a lie than one with such steadfast devotion to truth? You never get confused."

Davyn broke into the infectious laughter of the terminally good-hearted and stopped just ahead of me, gracing me with an exaggerated bow. "And who is this stranger, this self-proclaimed cynic and prince of devilish conspirators? It cannot be the same Narim who is trying single-handedly to save a race from its own weaknesses." He put his hands on his waist. "I happen to believe, good Narim, that you've never done a single dishonorable thing in your considerable span of years."

I laughed and shoved him out of my way, hurrying downhill faster—ahead of my friend so he could not read in my face how wrong he was. "You must make yourself known to MacAllister. He's asked after you often, afraid you've reaped severe consequences for his escape. I think you'll be good for him. He's stayed very much apart from the rest of us. Doesn't speak except for what's necessary. Asks no questions. Shows no interests except to work until he drops. You could poke a knife in him, and he would not bleed."

"I would have thought he'd be easier with you or Tarwyl. He doesn't know me."

"Tarwyl is back to Camarthan to make sure everything is cleaned up, and I . . . I've been trying to ease the last of Iskendar's and Nyura's concerns, so I haven't had the time to spend with him. Everyone else is a stranger, and he feels the burden of their ruined expectations—even if they're imaginary." And, of course, it was part of my plan to leave the fullness of Aidan MacAllister's desolation on display. My kin had to be absolutely convinced he could do nothing . . . and only then . . .

"You've not introduced him to Lara, then?"

"No. She's not come around. Just as well. Less suspicious if it occurs by chance. But it needs to be soon. If we're to make an attempt this year, we've got only six weeks to get him ready, and until we know more, her knowledge is everything we have. She'll have to judge whether he is capable, whether any of this is worth pursuing."

"But Narim, after what happened in Cor Neuill . . ." Davyn stopped again, blocking my way, looking intently at my face. "Surely he told you of it. I wouldn't expect him to understand, but you . . . I knew you'd read the signs. You *did* get his story about his visit to the dragon camp?"

I couldn't tell Davyn about my fence-sitting—that I couldn't face MacAllister without a tidal wave of guilts getting in the way, that I was too cowardly to face his despair. I couldn't tell Davyn those things, for then he would ask me why I took it so much to heart, and I would have to tell my dearest friend what I had done. "Not exactly. There wasn't time. The storm on the night of his escape was so bad, and he hasn't been much for conversation since then. He is so low."

Davyn laid his hands on my shoulders, and his eyes were swimming as he spoke, ever so softly. "Narim, he heard them. It almost killed him when they would trumpet—a bellow not anything out of the ordinary way—but he felt it so deeply. I watched him three times over. It's what caused him to be discovered, because he couldn't hide what it did to him. The first time was so vivid, he called for Roelan. I had the strangest thought that it might be Roelan himself flying over us."

I couldn't believe it. I'd been so convinced of what the singer believed about himself that I'd not even probed for the single bit of information that might have alleviated my own despair. Even yet I wouldn't let myself believe what I'd heard. "You're sure?"

Davyn didn't answer, only raised his eyebrows at me.

"All right, all right." A prickling began in my chest and flushed my skin, until even the roots of my hair quivered with unaccustomed life. I tried to remain calm . . . to check for problems . . . to be sure before I let myself feel it. "Could anyone else have seen it?"

"No one was with us the first time. The second came while we were in a Rider's hut, but the devil was too drunk to notice. The quartermaster and the Udema were close enough to see when the third one came, but they were preoccupied and didn't know what they were seeing. They would chalk up everything to fear."

"The link is still there."

Davyn smiled at me with a radiance no Elhim had seen in five hundred years. "Just as you predicted. It means we can proceed." He laughed out his joy and as before I was caught up in it. By the One, I felt young again, as if the dragons were beating their wings underneath my heart. I shouted and whooped and tumbled the laughing Davyn to the ground, then ran down the hillside leaping over boulders as if I were sixteen again, not five hundred and sixteen.

AIDAN

Chapter 13

Steady . . . pull . . . don't jerk . . . roll up the strip of scented pine . . . longer than the last. Ignore the burning of muscles too long unused . . . too damaged . . . too tired from long days' labor. Ten more planks to smooth, each with two edges and two faces, leaving flat, white surfaces ready to drill and peg and join to make tables or benches or doors or walls . . . no matter what . . . The end is the work itself. Bend your aching fingers around the wooden handles, darkened with the touch of countless useful hands . . . not yours. These knotted, ugly appendages that once danced over sweet-singing strings . . . will them to grip and draw the knife along the grain . . . steady . . . half the length . . . three-quarters . . . make the curling strip longer than the last. Endless planks from endless trees. Endless curls of resinous pine to throw in the fire which snaps its smoky pleasure at the tidbit. Over and over. Don't think. Just do. Again and again until your arms are molten lead and your eyelids sag. Only then stagger into the corner where the straw mat and wool blanket will enfold you in oblivion for one more night. Steady . . . pull . . .

"So what does old Vanka plan to do with this mountain of lumber?"

I straightened up and squinted at the Elhim who stood in the woodshop doorway, trying to discern the subtle features that would distinguish this one from five others who could be his twin. But for once, even in the wavering light from the woodshop hearth, I had no difficulty. The broader-than-usual shoulders, the shadowed cleft in the chin, the lock of hair fallen over his left eye. "Davyn?"

"Right. Safely home."

I nodded as I set the knife for another pass. "I'm glad. Truly." There was nothing else to say. Too bad that he had risked his neck to save me when I couldn't do what they wanted me to do. To sing again. Heaven and earth . . . they wanted me to sing to the beasts of fire and death and set them free.

"Have you eaten?" he said. "I'm heading over to see what I can glean from supper. I've not had anything since I got in this afternoon."

I always had to review the day to decide whether I had eaten. I seemed forever hungry, though eating was never very appealing. On most days I would rise at dawn when no one but Yura, the morose cook, was awake. He would give me a packet of bread and cheese or cold turnips, and I would carry it with me, eating as I drove the cart to the southern end of the valley to begin loading more stones for the bridge. The Elhim gathered morning and evening to eat in the refectory in the large cavern, chattering, visiting, and enjoying each other's society. They extended me a kindly welcome, but I knew better than to imagine I was good company. My presence could be nothing but a dismal reminder of their disappointment. Even Narim avoided me. So I stayed away. When the early darkness

fell I would retreat to the woodshop that the stubby Vanka
had turned over to me while he was building a storehouse
at the southern end of the valley. There I would eat the
rest of my rations and work until I dropped. A straw pallet and two blankets in the corner of the woodshop saved
me the long trudge to the cavern.

"I don't—"

"I smelled Yura's sausage pie earlier. If you've never
tasted it, it's well worth the walk over there. Everyone
else is already done with eating and off to other business.
I'd like the company. We ought to know each other better, since we own each other's life."

I must have looked puzzled, for he laughed, and his
gray eyes crinkled into the fine lines that proclaimed it
was his habit to laugh a great deal. "It's an Elhim custom.
When you save a person's life, that life belongs in part to
you. You can delight in its pleasures and grieve at its sorrows—and you are obligated to participate in its future
course. Since you have saved my life, and I, by virtue of
my sturdy friend Acorn, have saved yours, we had best
get on with our delighting and grieving and participating,
had we not?"

"I don't think you've made a good bargain. My future
prospects are somewhat limited."

"Most Senai would not think an Elhim life worth saving, so we won't make any judgments yet as to who gets
the better of our trade." Davyn had a winning way about
him.

I began to stack the finished planks against the wall,
and without saying anything more, the Elhim took up a
broom and began sweeping up the curls and slivers of
pine and tossing them on the fire.

"Your mount is well taught," I said. "I felt a right fool venturing into that storm with nothing but a cloak and a horse."

"I wondered if it was your curses I heard on the wind that night. Fortunately Acorn and his kind have no need for teaching. Have you been out among the herd? They're a marvel—even in such a marvelous place as Cor Talaith."

While we finished tidying up the woodshop and banking the fire, Davyn told me of the small, sturdy horses that roamed the valley, and how they allowed themselves to be haltered and ridden, but maintained a streak of independence. "If they get the yen to graze the south meadows, don't bother trying to lure them north to hunt or haul wood. Might as well try to get a Florin to eat fish." He propped his broom back in its corner. "So do we eat now?"

"I'll confess—when I was ten, sausage pie was my favorite," I said.

"You won't look back after eating Yura's."

We walked slowly across the end of the valley through the moon shadows cast by rocks and trees and outbuildings scattered across the meadow. A number of sheds and workshops were clustered in a broad, grassy pocket created by the sheltering cliff walls. A bend in the valley hid the place from view until you were right on it. An orange glow flared from the forge as we walked past and the clang of ironwork rang out—Bertrand the smith often worked late—but the noise soon faded away as we passed through a dense grove of tall, thin firs. A stream burbled through the trees into the meadow, sparkling in the silvery light. Davyn inhaled deeply of the bracing air—air just cold enough to make my long-sleeved wool shirt welcome, along with the gloves I'd put on by habit. "I do dearly love coming home," he said. "I stay away too much."

"It's a beautiful place." I said. "Quiet." Indeed I could not bear the thought of returning to a city—the noise and crowds and unending fear. Earth's bones, how I hated being such a coward. "It's kind of your people to let me stay awhile."

"You can stay as long as you like. No one knows of this place. Even the rare Dragon Rider who takes his mount so far into the god-forbidden mountains overlooks such a small green blot in the middle of the snow as Cor Talaith."

"But surely—"

"You are only the second gallim—non-Elhim—ever to come here. We are very different from other races, as you know. We have to earn our way in the world, for we're too few to be self-sufficient, but since we're neither physically powerful nor warlike, it's good to have a sanctuary. Our roots are here, no matter where we vines go wandering. And it's important that we have a place . . . secure . . . private . . . especially at certain times in our lives. . . ."

His words left the subject hanging. There were questions I should ask, things no human had ever known about the Elhim—why they were so different, how was it possible for them to have children, or did they—and I had the sense that Davyn was ready to answer if I asked. But I was so tired I couldn't think—the very state I did my best to achieve every day, and I was doing well to force my feet to move one in front of the other. I should have stayed in the woodshop.

Davyn seemed comfortable with silence, and we entered the lighted mouth of the great cavern without further conversation. He rummaged about the deserted kitchen and came up with two mugs of cold cider and two plates of savory sausage and vegetables in a rich brown crust still warm from the embers of the supper fire. We ate our meal, and then he offered to clean up the plates and mugs if I would unroll two pallets from the stack kept for those who had no specific quarters in the warren. I never saw Davyn join me, for as soon as I had rolled out the thin mat, I was asleep, dreaming of murderous dragons who caught me up in their sharp talons and deposited me torn and bleeding into the dark heart of Mazadine.

When I awoke, sweating as usual with my night terrors, Davyn's mat was rolled up again, though the two other Elhim who had been sleeping when I arrived were still snoring quietly. I put away my mat, then sat beside the hot spring that welled up in a basin at one end of the room and went through my daily ritual of shaving. It always took me a number of tries, dropping the knife or fumbling it enough to nick the skin, but I refused to let my beard grow. I hated wearing a beard. It was a measure of my life's condition that getting my face scraped every morning without slitting my throat had been for so long the highlight of my days. Though it was too small a change to be called progress, the activity had become a little easier—on that morning only three fumbles and no blood.

I padded quietly between the sleeping Elhim toward the refectory, stopping short at the doorway. Davyn was sitting at the far end of a long refectory table, drinking tea with Narim, the two of them talking with a woman. She sat cross-legged on the floor next to the hearth, her chin propped on one hand. Her long brown hair was caught in a braid that fell over one shoulder, leaving a few unruly wisps to obscure the features of her narrow face. She wore a dark green tunic belted with flat metal links, brown breeches and vest, and tall boots that covered her slender legs up to her knees. She was arguing in low, intense tones with the two Elhim while with her right hand she absentmindedly poked a chunk of sausage skewered on a fork into the flames.

". . . don't know why you insist you need him. I can do everything you want. I know the ritual, and—"

"Hush, girl. Others will be about soon," said Narim. "You can't do it alone."

"I don't need any bloody weakling Senai to share what is mine by right."

"Live through what he's endured before you call him weakling," said Davyn. "Your skills and knowledge are indisputable, but his heart must guide our enterprise."

I cursed myself for a fool. They had not believed me. They still thought that by wheedling and plotting they could get me to do what they wanted. Davyn was no different from the rest. It was time to leave Cor Talaith. My own griefs were hard enough to deal with; I didn't need those of an entire race. As facing hypocrisy so early was unpalatable, I turned to walk away, but was too clumsy to escape unnoticed. Returning to the narrow passage, I bumped into the hanging bell used to call the Elhim to supper. I wasn't able to muffle it fast enough, and Davyn called out to me cheerfully. "MacAllister! Good morrow.

Sorry our passages aren't designed for Senai height. Come join us."

"Not today," I said. "I really need to be on my way."

"It's scarcely light enough to see your own feet," said Davyn, smiling in his friendly way. "Surely your labors can wait a half hour more. We'd like to have a word with you while the place is quiet. We have someone—"

"I mean I need to leave Cor Talaith. I've taken up space here for too long."

Narim said nothing, and the woman concentrated on her sizzling sausage, though she was either pretending or she liked it well charred on the outside. It was a frowning Davyn who tried to dissuade me. "The hunt was still furious when I left, even after more than a month. They're patrolling every road in Catania, examining every traveler. You'll never get through."

"Are there no other ways out of here?"

"Only north into the wastelands or a very long trek down to Raggai—and neither one until the snows melt."

"Then I'll have to risk Catania. I need to get on with my life and let your people get on with theirs."

"You must do as you think best. But Tarwyl is due in next week. He can tell us how things go in Catania. If there's a chance—and you still want to go—I'll take you out myself."

A startled Narim cast him a sharp look, and Davyn answered it without ever taking his eyes from my face. "It is your choice to go or stay. That will not change. But no matter what hopes we've had or given up, we'd not want you taken again by the Ridemark. Will you wait for Tarwyl's word?"

I had no grounds to argue. My discomfort at their plot-

ting was no reason to be a fool. "It seems reasonable.
Thank you—again. If I'm to stay awhile longer, then I'll
feel better if I get back to work and pull a bit of my
weight at least." I nodded to the three of them. Davyn did
not smile, but only relaxed his concern. Narim sat expressionless, tapping his thumb on the scrubbed table.
The woman glanced up as I took my leave, brushing the
wisps of hair from hostile blue eyes with the back of her
hand. I carried the image of her—a disturbing image—as
I left the refectory and made my way to the stables, where
I hitched the mule to the wagon in the dawn light.

The left side of the woman's face had been severely
burned at some time in the past. Her light brown skin, so
smooth over her fine bones on the right side of her face,
was crumpled into a scaly pink disaster on the left. The
intrusive ugliness halfway across her cheek and brow dis-
torted the outer edge of her eyelid to give a permanent
droop to the left of her blue eyes. But more disturbing
than the remnants of painful injury to features otherwise
pleasing was the flash of red from her left wrist—not a
burn, but a red dragon scribed on her skin. A woman of
the Ridemark. Her presence made no sense at all. The
Elhim had rescued me from the Riders. Their goal was
the ruin of the Ridemark, to free the dragons that made
the clan powerful enough to manipulate kings.

A creeping unease prickled my skin as I drove the
sluggish mule across the dewy fields. If I could not trust
the Elhim and their account of events, then I was once
again left with no idea of what had happened to me. I reviewed every event of the weeks since I had gone to Cor
Neuill, but by the time I began to lift the stones from the
towering rockfall into the wagon, I had come no nearer a

conclusion. Only one thing kept intruding on my think-ing: If they had lied about their relationship with the Rid-ers, then perhaps they had lied about other things, more fundamental things.

"Good Keldar, show me the way." For the first time in six weeks the familiar plea came to my lips without a surge of disgust following it. But as I crammed my fin-gers under a skull-sized knob of granite and bent my el-bows, scooping the stone onto my wrists and forearms and hefting it high enough to dump it in the wagon, I called myself every name for a fool. There were no gods.

Furiously I crouched and lifted another, and another. Then a larger one than I had before. It was getting easier. My shoulders protested but I managed it, distracted as I was by thoughts and memories, making no more sense of them than at any other time.

Work. Forget. I hammered at myself in the rhythm of the stones. I knew truth when I heard it. The story Tarwyl had told on the night of my arrival was truth. It just wasn't everything.

When I had loaded all the mule could haul, I drove across the valley floor to the bridge site by the gaping fis-sure. Steams and smokes hung over the fissure as always, but the breeze cleared them enough to see that the Elhim builders were not yet working. Only one figure sat atop a stack of lumber in the angled sun, watching me pull up.

"Good morrow, Senai." Nyura, old Iskendar's constant companion, was a nervous, fidgety sort of person who looked as though someone had shoved all his features into the center of his face, neglecting the broad expanse of pale blandness around the edges. Iskendar and Nyura had spoken to me fairly often in my first days in Cor Talaith. Iskendar, the leader of the Elhim community, would ask if I needed anything and would I not consider sharing their table. I could feel his unspoken hope: Perhaps if I took part in friendly society, learned more of the Elhim and their sin, felt enough compassion for their five hundred years of penitence, perhaps then I could find it in myself to sing again. Would it were so easy. I thought I'd made it clear that there was no substance to his hopes, considering it a measure of their acceptance that they sought me out so rarely anymore. But of course the morning's events had proven me wrong. And here was the fluttery Elhim hovering about again.

"How fare you, Aidan MacAllister? Iskendar sends his greetings and asks how we may serve you."

"Nothing has changed. Thanks to the kindness of the Elhim, I'm well. But I've trespassed on your hospitality too long. I need to be on my way."

He didn't seem too surprised. "We'll regret losing your company."

"I'm sorry I can't be all you wish me to be."

"Rest easy. We'll find another way."

As I began to unload the cart, the Elhim watched, rubbing his chin thoughtfully, as if deciding how to proceed with a conversation doomed to go nowhere.

"Tell me," I said, "if it is not too private a question . . . I understood there were no women among the Elhim."

I don't know what he expected from me, but it clearly wasn't that. He gaped for a moment, but he soon gathered his wits and answered smoothly, dismissing the topic as if to get it out of the way as quickly as possible. "No. We do not possess the duality of your species. We are of only one kind, neither male nor female. If you have other questions about such matters . . . well, we do consider these things private, but not secret, if you understand me. If you were to develop a close friendship with one of us—of longer study than a passing acquaintance such as I am privileged to have with you—I'm sure that friend would be happy to discuss it further. You understand. . . ."

"Of course. I was just curious because I heard a woman's voice in the great cavern this morning. Talking with Narim."

"Ah. Now I understand. It was surely Lara you heard. A sad story that. You saw her scars? She was brought to Cor Talaith as a young girl—some eighteen or twenty years ago now. Frightfully burned. The fool of a child sneaked into the lair at Cor Neuill and tried to ride a dragon. An astonishing feat to get the beast away at all, but it turned on her. We allowed her to stay here. Did our best to heal her injuries."

"So she *is* of the Ridemark?"

"Well, yes. But her own people wouldn't have her back after she trespassed their laws."

"And she still lives here?"

"No. No. She lives on her own. Wanders the mountains and the northlands. Narim says she hires out to guide caravans through the northern passes. It was Narim who found her and cared for her. She comes back here from time to time to see him. You could say we're the only family she has."

"Ah. I see." I let the matter drop while I finished unloading the cart. It didn't explain what she had to do with me, but I didn't think Nyura was going to tell me that anyway. No wonder she sounded so bitter. Family and clan, tradition and honor were the very sum of existence to those of the Ridemark.

The Elhim kept watching from his perch, only a persistent tapping of his foot on the ground indicating he was not yet finished with our conversation. Though the air was pleasantly cool, the breeze had died away, so nothing mitigated the rays of the sun as I worked. I was almost done with the load. When I stopped to wipe the sweat from my face, Nyura took the opportunity to speak again, glancing at me with his close-together eyes. "I've a bit of news I thought might interest you, though I've wondered . . . after hearing of your terrible imprisonment . . . Well, perhaps you have no concern, as you have every right to despise the lot of them."

His speech was hesitating, yet in every pause he would watch me, casting his pale eyes on me and then away again. I kept working and let him spin it out. "Your cousin, King Devlin, has a son . . ."

In that pause he did indeed see my interest sparked. I could never forget Donal, the infant who had shown me the truths of innocence, purity, and undemanding love to weave into my music.

". . . nineteen now. A fine youth by all accounts. Leading troops in the Gondari war."

No surprise. I'd heard as much in Camarthan.

". . . but no one understood why the king and the prince did not smite the Gondari, as their forces are superior. We've learned that the Gondari have taken the young prince hostage."

Hostage! Donal . . . my cousin's child and so my cousin, too . . . the infant grown to fair youth, held in squalor and bitter cold, murderous heat and unending ter-

ror, surrounded by savage bellowing and the vomit of
fire, day and night. Absolutely without hope. If his father
attacked the Gondari, the youth would be chained to a
post and seared with dragon's fire—not charred to ash in
an instant, but left to die slowly in agony as long as they
could make it last. And if Devlin held back, his son would
languish in his prison forever until he died coughing up
blood, or shivering with untended fever, or banging his
head in madness against the stone walls while the dragons screamed their triumph. Stalemate. Forever.

In that instant I understood what was the "favor" that
Devlin was going to ask of me on the night of Callia's
murder. He believed I could free his son. He thought I
could sing and make the dragons let Donal go, as had
been done in Aberthain. No wonder he claimed he didn't
know what had been done to me. No wonder. He had
been so agitated, so tentative. He was going to go ahead
and ask . . . until I said I didn't know what I'd done. At
that point he couldn't ask without revealing what he'd
been determined to destroy. To keep his dangerous secret,
he'd had to sacrifice his son. *Fires of heaven, Devlin . . .*

Until that moment I had not actually believed what the
Elhim told me I had done, that my music had somehow
made the dragons grow restless and disobey the commands of the bloodstones. I had been sure it was all a
mistake, a devastating, life-destroying misunderstanding.
But now . . .

I looked upon Nyura's pale face, not thinking of him
at all, but of my cousin's child in a prison more hopeless
than Mázadine. I could not hate Devlin enough to rejoice
in such devastation. I closed my eyes and envisioned the
trusting, helpless infant I had known in an hour of purest

joy. "Would that I could sing for you," I whispered. "If there were a god to hear me, I would beg his grace to sing you free."

The sound of horses brought me back to the present. Nyura was riding away toward the caverns, no doubt insulted by my long distraction. The bridge builders were arriving with a team of horses dragging a load of huge timbers down the road. I greeted them, and then drove slowly back to the rockfall to get another load. After working until sunset, I moved to the woodshop and smoothed rough timbers into usable planks until I could not lift the drawknife one more stroke.

Though the work drove me to exhaustion as I wished, never could I rid myself of the image of Donal trapped in horror. Uninterested in Elhim society, I did not return to the cavern, but bedded down in the woodshop, as had been my custom for the past weeks. Deep in my dreams that night I heard the bellowing dragons, no music in their cries, only wild and savage murder to the ears of a youth standing at the threshold of manhood without hope. The dragons screamed, haunting and dreadful, until I woke shaking in the dark corner of the woodshop and glimpsed a slender figure outlined against the dim glow of the banked fire. The figure had an arm upraised, and glittering in the light of a flaring ember was the deadly blade of a knife on a course for my back.

Chapter 14

I launched myself at the lower half of the slender silhou- ette, shooting up one hand to hold the dagger-wielding arm at bay. We toppled onto the sawdust-covered floor, but my assailant writhed and struggled and squirmed out from under me. I hadn't enough hands to hold him still, yet keep the knife a safe distance from my vital parts. Fortunately my legs were longer than my attacker's arms, and I was able to plant a foot firmly in his gut. A pained grunt followed and a massive expulsion of air, debilitat- ing enough to relax the hand holding the knife and allow me to back away crabwise from the cloaked and hooded figure. My arms felt like water.

Not sanguine about any further combat, I pulled my- self up to get away. But I was desperately curious and reached out to flip the hood from my opponent's face. At the same moment he raised the knife again with a furious growl. The better part of wisdom commanded me to de- part, even in ignorance, so I ran.

My morning excursions in Camarthan served me well as I streaked through the moonlit meadows and wood- land. By the time I reached the great cavern, I had left pursuit behind and given a bit of thought as to what I was going to do next. On consideration, waking my hosts to say one of their number was trying to murder me seemed unproductive and unwise. Instead I sank to the ground in the shadows, flattening myself to the cliff wall just beside the mouth of the cavern, thinking I might see who would come slinking through the doorway while honest people slept. With surprise on my side, I could drag the villain before his own people and have evidence of my accusation.

But as the hard, brittle stone dug uncomfortably into my back, the damp grass soaked my breeches, and my blood lost the heat generated by midnight attacks, I began to laugh. I rolled onto all fours, a position that stretched and eased my wretched back, and I laughed until tears dripped from my face onto the soggy ground. Anyone who came on me in that time would have thought me mad.

You can't let go, can you? I said to myself. *Was there ever such a cowardly fool as you, Aidan MacAllister? To run away from a shadow who offered you nothing but what you have already? What dead man fears a knife? And what idiot thinks a villain will come walking through this door when there are undoubtedly fifty other entrances hidden in these cliffs? Why do you hold on? Let it go, fool.*

If my midnight visitor had renewed his assault at that moment, I would have bared my breast and guided his blade with my grotesque fingers. But no one came, and at some time I collapsed into a sodden heap and slept until first light, when fingers began poking at me.

"MacAllister! Aidan! Dear god, are you all right?" A hand clamped my wrist and probed about my head—seeking a pulse or an injury, no doubt—then rolled me onto my back before I was awake enough to prevent it. My inadvertent groan at that painful posture only intensified his efforts to locate a wound, so he pulled open my shirt and would have ripped it right off of me if I'd not gathered my foggy wits.

"I'm all right. Please don't." I pushed the hands away and sat up to greet Davyn, whose wide-eyed fright was yielding to a flush rosier than the dawn light.

"I thought . . . seeing you out here like this . . ."

"It's a long story," I said, "and not one I care to publish. Not very flattering to my Senai warrior heritage."

"But—"

"I'm all right. I'd rather talk about breakfast. I don't think I ate anything at all yesterday, and as it seems I'm inescapably attached to living for today, at least, I might as well get on with it."

"Of course. Yura was just lighting the fires when I came out."

We ate Yura's breakfast porridge, thick, hot, and satisfying. Then, leaving Davyn still mystified, I took myself to the stables and the rock pile and the bridge and the woodshop. I worked hard enough that I could not entertain a single thought except how to persuade my body to do what I demanded of it. And when I buried my face in the straw-filled mat in the corner of the woodshop late that night, I held the faint hope that I might never wake again.

I did, of course, to another dark figure lurking in the shadows, but this time instead of using a knife, my visitor beckoned me with his voice. "Wake up, slugabed, and come with me. We need to talk."

"Don't want to talk," I mumbled into my pallet. "Use the knife. I shouldn't have stopped you last night."

"It doesn't matter what you want, Aidan MacAllister."

At last someone was being honest with me. But as I recognized the voice as Narim's, I decided that such a judgment was premature.

"So talk," I said. "Tell me something that is absolute truth."

"You are not dead."

I bleated in disbelief. "You're a fool," I said, and pulled my blanket over my head.

"That is certainly truth. But not because of what I just said. One could as easily say that *you* are the fool, mourning the loss of your gods. The gods are still there. You just don't know their names, and for a Senai to admit such a thing is beyond the capability of the species."

"I've seen no evidence to contradict my belief," I said. "Not in a very long while."

"Ah, my friend, you are still lost in the darkness. How much more wondrous are gods who can create such beings as humans and dragons and Elhim, than your paltry deities who speak with borrowed voices."

"I do not deny that I am and have been a fool."

"But a live fool. Come with me and let me prove my contention."

"Why should I?"

"For Callia. She deserves a reason for her death."

I stared at the pale-eyed Elhim who crouched in the darkness like a wolf waiting for the last embers of the watchfire to die away. "Bastard."

"If that's the worst you have to say of me before we're done, I'll count myself fortunate . . ."

Silent and furious and wide-awake, I pulled on my boots.

". . . but then, of course, it is impossible for an Elhim to be a bastard. Our young have only one parent, so we know nothing of marriage or nonmarriage, thus nothing of bastardy. We've never really understood the insult intended."

The moon hung low in the west as we hiked for two hours across the valley, following an obscure track that wound its way between slabs of layered rock until breaking out onto a desolate hillside. Somewhere in the dark expanse of scrub and grass, sparse, stunted trees, and broken bits of reddish rock shone a faint, steady light. We headed for it as directly as one could without being a goat, and it soon resolved itself into a lantern, held aloft by none other than Davyn.

"So you've agreed to try this?" he said anxiously. "We'll be with you the whole—"

"Well, he didn't exactly," said Narim. "I bullied him into it a bit."

"Bullied? Ah, by the One, Narim. What have you done?"

"He wanted only truth. Complete truth. I told him he wasn't dead. That was about as complete as I could get. Telling, bullying, truth . . . He's not going to believe anything until we show him."

"But Narim—"

Davyn was interrupted again, this time by a muted rumbling as of a distant storm or a blustering wind heard from inside a thick-walled fortress. But the stars shone cold and still, growing in brilliance as the moon sank

below the western peaks. Our cloaks and hair lay unmoving in the quiet chill of midnight.

"Is the woman already in place?" asked Narim uneasily.

"Yes. But we've time. You must prepare him."

I stood still, arms folded, determined to go no step farther until I heard an explanation. Narim screwed up his
face at Davyn, then motioned for me to sit down. I found
a convenient rock that put my face at a level with his.

"Someone tried to kill you last night," he began.

"Was it you?"

He looked startled at my question, and if the light had
been better I would have said he turned red. But Davyn
had taken the lamp up the hillside and was scrabbling
about a pile of crumbling rock. "No. No, it was not . . ."
An edge to the way he said it told me that he was quite
capable of killing, and would have no qualms if he believed such an action necessary. I listened more atten-
tively after that. ". . . but I know who it was, and the
attempt has made us change our plans. Move before
we're ready. We weren't going to do this for a few weeks
yet."

"Who was it?" I didn't want to lose the critical answer.

"I'll not tell you that. It's of no importance. There are
those of us—some, not all—so blinded by fear that they
can no longer see possibility. To them, safety dictates that
the world remain as it is. They believe you represent the
extinction of the Elhim."

"But why? I've told you—"

"That is, of course, the most important part. The why.
Something has given them pause, a reason to disbelieve
your saying. They know you're the only one capable.

They've only to think back to the first time you heard a
dragon's cry in your uncle's garden."

   Now it was my turn to be surprised. "How in heaven
and earth do you know of that?"

   Impatiently Narim cut me off. "We know everything
about you from the day of your birth until the day of your
arrest. Elhim have sources of information everywhere,
and we used every one of them to learn of you. We know
what you told your singing masters that first night, and
what you told your mother, and how you lived the next
three years and every year thereafter. Don't you see?
We'd been waiting for centuries for someone with your
gift. In the days when we were friends, the dragons told
us there were a few—a very few—people who could
touch their minds. 'Nandithari' they called them—
Dragon Speakers—who could understand their speech
even when they were in their wildest state at year's end.
They told us that those rare beings had an open and quiet
heart, ones who could listen so well they could distinguish the sound of one bird's flight from another. When
we heard you sing, we knew you were such a one."

   Why wouldn't they listen? Narim of all of them should
know. He said he understood what it meant to me to discover that my life had been a lie. One more time I tried to
convince him. "I cannot help you," I said. "Even if there
was a time when I could, even if I wanted to more than
life itself, I cannot. No amount of wishing, no amount of
words or storytelling, threats or pleading or plotting can
put back what is gone." I held out my scarred, knotted
fingers. "Inside me the damage is worse than this. Far
worse. What heart I possessed is dead. My music is dead.
Why won't you believe me? If I could make it not

so . . . heaven and earth, Narim, don't you think I would?"

The Elhim said nothing, only shook his head and took my arm, silently demanding that I should follow him. I let him pull me off the rock and lead me up the hill to where Davyn stood before a dark, round hole about a hand's breadth taller than I. A pile of brush lay to the side of the yawning emptiness. Another rumbling. This time I felt it in my feet, as if a storm lay beneath the earth.

"What is this place?" I found myself whispering as if standing at the entrance of a tomb, my neck prickling with the unreasoning dread that the tomb was my own.

Narim still said nothing, but followed Davyn and his lantern into the dark hole, dragging me along behind him. The passage was nothing like the airy warrens of the Elhim caverns, but only a cramped dirt chute through the side of the hill, a giant rabbit hole or worm's den, bored smooth by an inhabitant the diameter of a man's height. Downward. Ever sloping, gently, inexorably down. It was warm, very different from the cool caverns of stone, and quite dry. Only a few side passages, and the place smelled of dirt and roots. We might have been burrowing straight to the center of the earth.

We had been descending for at least half an hour when I caught the first trace of brimstone in the still air. Unwittingly I slowed my steps, but Narim pulled me onward, still saying nothing. My friend Gerald Adair had been deathly afraid of dark, enclosed spaces, abandoning me when I would sing in the coal mines of Boskar or the hovels of the poorest of the poor. He would have gone mad in that long tunnel. I had teased him unmercifully about it, but I was beginning to understand his fear.

Another quarter of an hour and a faint gleam ahead of us turned out to be another lantern like ours, abandoned alongside a large, empty leather sack at the opening of a wide side passage. Davyn set our lantern beside the other, trimmed it to a soft glow, then motioned us forward. Narim whispered in my ear, "Fifty paces from the crossing." I couldn't help but count the steps in my head. The silence was as palpable as the warm air, more heavily tainted with the rotten, sweet smell of brimstone. Mixed with the stink was a thick, ripe, animal smell . . . musky . . . dragon.

"Where in the name of all sense are we?" I said with scarcely more than an outward breath.

Neither Elhim spoke, but I got my answer soon enough. A faint smudge of light in the heavy darkness marked the end of our journey, and when I saw what was beyond, I was transfixed with wonder and terror and astonishment.

We stood in our tiny dark hole high on the wall of a vast cavern, not one polished and furnished and home-like, as was the Elhim refuge, but crude and rough in its gigantic dimensions, blasted from the roots of the earth and lit by burning heaps of rubble. The cavern floor was pitted with boiling pools of luminous green and milky white, cracks and fissures that vented steam and smoke enough to make the walls drip and the hot air heavy and oppressive. In between the pits and pools were half-rotted carcasses and bones of every imaginable size. When I was forced loose from my paralysis enough to take a breath, I gagged at the stench of brimstone and carrion and the musky, decaying foulness of a beast too long confined.

For the cavern was occupied by a copper-scaled mon-

ster five times the height of a man and twice that in length
even with the spiked tail curled beneath it—a sleeping
dragon. The patterned wings of green and copper were
folded into bony ridges on the massive flanks, and the
monstrous head was lowered to the ground, the gaping
nostrils spewing only weak and intermittent spurts of
flame in rhythm with the harsh blast of its breathing. The
horny brow ridges were as thick as logs, as were the coverings that encased razor-sharp talons that could rip the
hide of an elephant as if it were paper. The armored flesh
was crusted with stony parasites like the hull of a ship
long docked, and the folds where the head joined the
long, muscular neck were deep. This dragon was un-
thinkably old.

From behind me Narim made some movement, and it
took me a moment to judge what it was he did, but when
I saw the tiny figure far below us standing on a jutting
outcrop of red rock, I shook my head in disbelief. The
woman Lara stood almost in the beast's face, just at the
level of its eyes. She wore leather breeches and tunic,
elbow-length gauntlets, and a stiffened-wool helmet—
Rider's armor. At Narim's second signal, she raised her
hand and shouted so that her words echoed through the
thick foulness of the air and bounced from the moss-slick
walls of the cavern. She spoke in the ancient tongue of
the Ridemark, her voice stern and commanding, unyielding in the force of her will. *"Arrit, teng zha nav
wyvyr . . ."* Wake, child of fire and wind. Wake from the
sleep of dying and heed my command.

There was a pause as the echoes died away, as if the
very orb of the world stopped its spinning dance about
the sun, holding time in abeyance. My soul cried out in

dread, commanding me to hide before time took up its path again. Thrumming, insistent panic begged my feet to run. But instead I sank to my knees, Narim and Davyn at my shoulders, their thin, strong fingers digging into my flesh as if to hold me together. When the beast began to move it was too late.

"Speak your name, beast," commanded the woman.

The huge body shifted uneasily, the battering ram of a tail slamming into the cavern wall, the very movement causing the rumble that shook the ground. Rough breath and a snort of fire as its head lifted up slowly, and then the eyes came open. Glaring red eyes, swirling pools of scarlet flame glazed with films of ghastly white, filled with wild, unreasoning hatred—the gaze that could transfix a victim in horror while the furnace within was readied to release volcanic breath that would flay a man and cause his blood to boil right through the veins. The woman was sure to be incinerated.

"Speak your name; then return to your winter's death. The snow still lies deep upon the hunting grounds, and your brothers and sisters will not heed your call." She held her hand in the air, and in the short, fiery bursts from the waking beast's nostrils, I saw the flash of dark red in her fingers. A bloodstone—a kai'cet, the Riders called it. Heaven and earth! But every speculation as to how she had gotten away from her clan with one of its treasures, or how she had learned to use it, a woman—one who would never have been considered for training in the secrets of the Riders—all of that was lost when the dragon gaped its jaws and belched out a garish rainbow of fire that arced over Lara's head. The thin trailer of water cascading down the wall behind her erupted in steam, and then the beast released a roar that shook the foundations of the world.

The tide of sound broke over my head as if the ocean itself had reared up in a single mighty wave and commenced to drown the history of humankind, only it was not an ocean of water, but an ocean of fire. I believed in that moment that my life had come to its ending, that my flesh had been scorched away, that my entrails had turned to bloody vapor just as the waterfall had vanished in steam, and that my bones lay burning on the hard-packed earth of our hiding place. Despair and grief and memory were erased, wonder and curiosity dismissed in a torrent of pain. I could not scream, could not pray, could not weep, for every part and fiber of my flesh quivered in the agony of burning. And yet it was only an instant—less time than the swinging of a pendulum—and I could look upon myself huddled on the now quiet ground, my spasms held in the steady grip of the two frightened Elhim, and I could read the word that had been seared into my soul with pain and fire.

For that single instant I hung suspended out of my life, and I formed that same word, whether only in my mind or on my tongue I did not know, and I reflected it upon the sender with my spirit's whisper. *Keldar.*

And in that same instant outside of time, I heard his answer, so faint as to be unnoticed by any who had not lived in silence for seven endless years: *Beloved.*

Chapter 15

What words can describe that instant of contact? *Lightning* is too cold, *majesty* too weak, *glory* too dim, *salvation* too imprecise, *devotion* too impersonal. Whatever soul it was that spoke to me in that breathless moment, whether god or dragon, pulled me from the brink of disintegration, and I clung to its word as a drowning child to a father's outstretched hand. So much grief and regret and tender concern was wrapped in it that I did not believe I could encompass all of it in a year of remembering. He knew me, called me by the name Roelan had given me when I was young, the name my god had sung when filling the world with music. All the horror and disgust I'd felt upon learning that the voice of my music was a murderous monster was swept away in the flood of this creature's care for me. A being with such capacity for love was no beast. My soul was touched with the remembrance of joy, and my companions had no idea of it, for I could not tell them, could not move or speak without letting go of the fragile moment.

"In the name of the One, what have we done?" said Davyn, lifting my drooping head and raking his worried gray eyes over my face.

"Only what was required. If he cannot bear it, then best to learn it now."

"Narim"—even as their faces flickered orange and gold in the reflection of dragon flames, Davyn stared at his friend with scandalized disbelief—"you've not told him any of it, have you?"

"We need to get him out of here."

"Narim, my oldest friend, his life is not ours to use as we will. By the One, his very eyes bleed."

"By the time he was in our hands, there was no way to tell him. A man in despair cannot choose rationally. And somehow in the past two days, for some damnable reason I cannot see, the others have guessed what we already know. They've tried to kill him once and will not give up now they've judged him a danger."

"That doesn't make this right."

"Ordinary estimates of fairness or justice have no relevance when the survival of an entire race is at stake. As of this moment, Aidan MacAllister is either on his way back to life or he is truly dead. I cannot think he would prefer to be where he was. Now let's get him out of here so we can judge which way he's gone."

All this was gibberish to me. They raised me to my feet, led me up the long tunnel, and sat me on the rocky hillside facing the rose-streaked silver of the dawn, letting the quickening breeze of morning sweep away the lingering stench of brimstone and decay. Though I struggled to hold on, the last echoes of Keldar's voice began to slip from my grasp. Helplessly I felt it go, reaching after it with such aching misery and grief that I must have groaned quite audibly. Only then did the words of the two Elhim begin to filter into my head, and I began to wonder again who it was who wanted me dead and what in the universe I was going to do about what had happened.

"Dragon's teeth, did he fall off the ledge?" Someone else had come up behind me, someone my mind told me ought to be dead.

"No," said Davyn. "He's not spoken since the dragon's cry, and we don't know but what we've killed him with it. Some of us are a bit more concerned than others."

"Is he so afraid of a stupid bellow? Every child in Elyria has heard worse, though perhaps not in such close quarters and lived to think about it." It was the woman Lara. Though I did not look up, I could smell the charred, stinking leather of her armor. Her blackened gauntlets dropped to the ground five paces away, next to the pack from the tunnel. "I told you it was a waste of time. If the beast is ever going to 'speak,' it won't be when we wake it up from winter sleep. How do you know it even has a name or can remember it after so long?"

"Keldar," I said softly, pricked to unwilling response by her casual dismissal. "His name is Keldar."

"By the One! Keldar. We suspected as much." Davyn rolled over on his back and chortled at the sunrise in unmuted glee. "Who could imagine it?"

"You heard him? He spoke the name?" Narim crouched in front of me, peering into my face, less ready to be excited than Davyn. "Was there anything else? Was it in the sound or in your mind?"

"He guessed it couldn't see," said the woman scornfully. "He saw the growths on its eyes and called it by the blind god's name. He heard nothing but the bellowing of a beast, as we all did."

"I'd never seen a dragon's eyes before," I said. "Is he truly blind?"

She snorted and did not deign to answer.

Narim ignored her. "Was it the same as when you would hear Roelan?"

I shook my head. "Very different. Just as clear, but it's never been so . . . painful . . . so hard . . . so intense. Narim, I . . ." My voice was much calmer than I felt. My whole being was in chaos. My mind was a jumble of exquisitely sharp images, the sensations coming and going in flickering bursts: the eye-searing brilliance of the fiery rainbow, the feel of the warm dirt beneath my hands, the shattering cacophony of the bellowing, the choking fetor of dragon. Half a moment of breathtaking clarity—no more—and then the image would evaporate. But no sooner had I adjusted to the silence of the morning than it burst upon me yet again. It was as if someone repeatedly stabbed a stiletto into my head and yanked it out again. I had to force my attention to every word being said—even my own—or I would have heard or spoken only half of them.

I had things I needed to say, but Davyn interrupted my hesitating speech, rolling onto his side and propping his face on his hand. "It was inevitable that it be more difficult," he said eagerly, his eyes flashing in the winter sunrise. "Part of it is you, of course. The vileness done to you. The injuries you've suffered. But most of it is the dragons themselves. They've been captive for so long, held in this wild state, that we weren't sure it would be possible to reach them . . . even for you. Even at the height of your power, right before your arrest, Narim worried that you'd not be able to reach them in the way that's necessary. Roelan, perhaps, but, of course, we can't know which one is Roelan."

Roelan. My "god." A dragon. Unbelievable. "But you said that I . . . affected . . . more than one."

"That's true. Never all of them. Perhaps only Roelan and the other six eldest were changed by your music. We don't know. For a few years after you disappeared, certain dragons still showed the changes you had wrought, and so we had hopes that you were with them in some way, but over time . . ."

"Ten years," I said. "Roelan's voice grew fainter from the first day, and after a while there came a time when I couldn't— After ten years he didn't answer anymore." I was only an instant's separation from that desolation; only the single word shimmering in my memory kept it away. Davyn gazed on me with sympathy, while Narim walked away, sat himself on the weedy hillside, and stared expressionlessly into the morning.

"We came to believe you were dead," said Davyn softly. "We had no idea where they'd taken you. The One who guides us surely led Narim to Lepan."

I needed answers. Clarity. "What of this dragon . . . Keldar?" Even as I spoke the name, my intellect tried to convince me it was impossible. Denial would put me back in the prison of my despair, yet acceptance was surely the madness I'd fought so hard to hold at bay.

Davyn glanced at the woman who had shed her reeking leather armor and was packing it carefully in her bag, studiously ignoring us. "Ah, yes. Well, some eighteen years ago, not long before you were arrested, this dragon flew out of Cor Neuill, ridden by a brave and enterprising young girl of thirteen. She'd been determined to ride for many years, even following the legion into battle, where she managed to get herself a bloodstone from a fallen Rider. It was not this dragon's—Keldar's—stone, its dekai'cet, as they call it. The dragon linked to her stone had been wounded when its Rider fell. The clan had destroyed the beast, of course; they've never learned to link a new stone to a dragon. But Lara was convinced that with a bloodstone of her own, she could ride any dragon—as indeed she proved. Her courage and skill were indisputable. But the mistake she made was assuming that only the *bloodstone* enabled her to get the dragon out of the lair. In truth we believe that *you* made it possible. You'd been to Cor Neuill only two nights before. The lair was in chaos: dragons disobeying their Riders, threatening them, breaking through the Riders' Ring, when she decided to make her attempt."

Lara stuffed the gauntlets into her pack quite savagely, and it struck me that she didn't particularly like this part of Davyn's story.

"She planned to take the dragon back to the camp to prove to her clan that she could control the beast, but the dragon refused her command to turn. To command a dragon with a bloodstone that is not the one bound to it from the beginning—the dekai'cet that its own Rider carries—is extremely difficult, which is why dragons without linked stones must be destroyed. And this dragon had another destination."

"The lake?"

"We don't know. But he brought her into the Carag Huim, and she tried very hard to get control. The beast flew straight into a cliff. . ."

I could envision the drama played out before me: the

child goading the dragon to madness with the hated jewel . . . the struggle . . . the disaster . . . and the agonizing fire.

"Well," said Davyn, seeing in my expression that I understood enough. "They both survived. Narim found Lara and brought her to Cor Talaith. Until about five years ago we didn't know what had become of the dragon. Lara searched through the mountains and eventually found him in this cavern, where he had gone to heal or to die. Since then she's—"

"Enough," said Lara, hefting the heavy pack onto her slender shoulder. "I won't be talked of as if I were an ignorant beast like the one down below us. Hear this, Senai." Her blue eyes flamed, and the terrible scars on her left cheek quivered red as she tossed her long braid over her shoulder. "I am a daughter of the Ridemark, and no matter what my people say of me, I've not betrayed them, only taken a kai'cet, as is my right. I do not believe dragons have minds. I do not believe they can speak. I do not believe that some cowardly Senai harp player ever has or ever will make them something they are not. All I want to do is ride one of them without burning, and since my own people won't allow it, this is the only hope I've got. Now, Davyn, I'll thank you to stop talking about me."

Lara marched furiously past Davyn and me without so much as another glance, but to my surprise, when she strode past the bemused Narim sitting on the hillside, the Elhim reached out a hand to her, and she clasped it firmly before continuing on her way. Narim put his chin back on his knees and went back to his meditation.

"He nursed her for over a year," said Davyn softly.

"Made her move her limbs so they would not be left un-usable, every hour of every day, when she could not do it without screaming. He scoured the hills and the cities for remedies to ease her and heal her, and prevent as much scarring and deformity as he could. She cursed him for it, but now there is no bond deeper than theirs. She is torn apart by her longing to be accepted again by her clan, and her love for Narim, and her fear that he is right about the dragons and she is wrong. And she does dearly want to fly."

The sun baked away the dew on the gray-green scrub, and we watched Lara's straight, slim figure dwindle as she descended into the valley. Then I saw no alternative but to get back to the truth of what had happened in the night. I had to accept it, and the Elhim had to know.

"I thank you for this," I said. "What happened here was something marvelous, something unexpected. I'll never forget it. But now"—my conclusion had been reaf-firmed as I had listened to Davyn and Lara, feeling Narim's expectant gaze on my back—"if you believe that I can speak to him again or regain . . . anything else . . . Davyn, I was dying. When I heard him and spoke his name and heard . . . what I heard . . . I was already leaving my body behind. If it had been more than a sin-gle word, even a heartbeat longer, I'd never have gotten back. I'm sorry. I still can't help you." A crippling irony. They had given me something to live for, and I couldn't claim it without dying. Not a satisfactory conclusion, but perhaps enough to keep me going awhile longer.

Davyn sighed and gazed ruefully at Narim. "We should have warned you."

"Narim was right," I said, trying to ease his distress. "I

wouldn't go back. I'm sorry—you'll never know how sorry—that I can do no more."

"But that's the whole point," said Narim, popping up from his reverie at last and standing over me. His gray eyes drilled into my soul. "You've shown us you can survive this kind of raw contact, however difficult it might be. The connection—your gift—is still there. And so we can try the next step. You see, I have a plan. All we have to do is keep you alive."

My head was beginning to hurt. "Keep me alive?"

"I had hoped you could stay in Cor Talaith while you were made ready, but that's impossible. And we can't send you out where the Riders or your cousin might find you. Everyone seems to want you dead or captive."

"I'm sure he's noticed," said Davyn.

"So there's only one place I can send you. It won't be easy, but I'll convince her."

Davyn rolled back onto the ground and groaned dramatically. "You can't be thinking it. She hates him more than Garn MacEachern does, and her temper is worse!"

"Wait," I said, their words running together in a muddle. "Tell me what you're talking about. What plan?"

Narim crouched down in front of me. "This dragon you've named Keldar is injured. Fortunately an injured dragon keeps himself in winter sleep until his injuries can heal or he dies. But Lara has learned to rouse him, as you saw, and command him with her stone. She has driven beasts into the cave to feed and strengthen him, so we hope that when spring comes he might awaken on his own. Now that we've found you, we can give him the next gift we've prepared. We've built a sluiceway to his cave to send in water from Cir Nakai."

"The lake water," I said dumbly. "You think you'll be able to speak to him."

"No. We think that *you* will be able to speak to him."

Speak to a dragon. Not in the way I had thought of as speaking to my god, but as one natural creature to another. As in the tale from Elhim legend. I could not imagine it.

"The one who attempts it cannot be an Elhim," Narim said, a forced patience in his voice. "We are anathema to the dragons and likely would not live past his first glimpse of us. Nor can it be Lara. She carries a bloodstone, and besides, she—"

"She doesn't believe," I said.

"Exactly. How could she possibly reach him? You are the only person in the world who can get us the answer."

"The answer for what?" I was numb. Uncomprehending.

"You must make Keldar tell you how we can release his brothers and sisters from their binding to the bloodstones. Then we can bring the dragons back to the lake so they can take their rightful place in the world once again."

Davyn had been watching and listening, letting Narim's intensity carry the burden of revelation, but as I struggled to comprehend what they wanted of me, he broke in, the stray lock of hair falling inevitably over his soft gray eyes. "You must understand the risks, Aidan. We don't understand how you were able to reach them before or if it's possible for you to do it again after all that's happened. We don't know if it's even possible to speak to a dragon. It's been so long—five hundred years since the dragons have tasted the water of the lake of fire.

There may be nothing left in them to be awakened by it. They are so wild, lost in their blood frenzy and hatred."

Slowly I shook my head. My experience of the night told me that there was a mind and a soul in the being that was Keldar—buried impossibly deep—but I had touched it and I knew.

But Davyn would not let go. "You will have to walk into that cavern, stand helpless before a creature who has slain ten thousand humans without regret. If he does not wake with the change of season, then he will have been roused with the very device that drives him into madness. The chance of success is so small as to make me begin writing your epitaph the moment you agree."

What choice was there to be made? *Beloved*. The echo of the word made me tremble with awe and wonder and the last hope of life.

"So where is it you want to put me?" I said.

A corona of satisfaction illuminated the pale Narim, while a tired Davyn rubbed his forehead, smiled wryly, and answered. "He wants to send you into a dragon's mouth even before your confrontation with Keldar. He thinks to have you live with Lara."

Chapter 16

.

"Have the Senai harp plucker stay here? You're out of your mind!" A red-faced Lara stood in front of a low, thick-walled stone hut half-buried in the sparkling snow-drifts of a mountain meadow. From the position of her hands on her slender hips, Narim had made a singularly grave error in his carefully wrought calculations. The sharp-edged breeze that so belied the brilliant sunshine of the morning pulled curling wisps of brown hair from her taut braid and flicked them at the scarred left side of her face. But the chill of the wind was as nothing to the frost of Lara's tongue. "I'll not have it. I've few enough supplies laid in, not a single feather bed, no silk draperies or cushions, and no food fit for refined tastes. When I said I'd help you in this madness, I never, ever agreed to nursemaid any Senai popinjay."

"Ah, Lara, was ever a woman so passionate in her loyalties as you?" said the slender Elhim, pale as snow next to Lara's angry flush. "Davyn laid me a wager that Aidan and I would be creeping into the back caverns of Cor Talaith this night with your boot print on our backsides . . ."

Lara nodded as if Davyn were the only intelligent creature she'd known in a lifetime.

". . . but I told him that, being the sensible person you are, you would agree that there is no rational alternative."

"Not on—" Lara tried to interject, but Narim had a way of pouring out his words in a tide that swept all other conversation out of the way.

"If we send Aidan back to civilized lands, either your people or his own will take his head or his freedom, and if he stays in Cor Talaith, the Elhim will do the deed. For a man beloved of the gods, he is sorely in need of protection from those of us of lesser state, and nowhere is he less likely to be set upon than behind the security of your sword."

Lara rolled her eyes. "Why do you believe anything he says? Thousands can witness to his lies. Ask those who've fled before the Gondari dragon fires. He once sang to them of peace and beauty, but have they ever witnessed anything like that? He gets only what he deserves."

But Narim did not relent. "And, of course, my friend is not exactly accustomed of late to the privileges and comforts of his noble relations. Lest you've forgotten, your own clan has hosted him for seventeen years. And for the past two months he's had to put up with the poor hospitality of Cor Talaith. I think he'll be less of a burden than you believe."

Narim's gray eyes were the portrait of ingenuous innocence, but his words had me squirming. I wanted nothing more than to stuff my cloak in his mouth. I hoped Lara would send us away so that I could deal with him as I so sincerely desired, but instead she turned her rigid back to us and slammed her palm into the heavy pine door of the hut. It swung inward, and she disappeared inside. The door remained open.

"I do believe I heard a welcome," said Narim, tugging on my arm. "Best get inside before she changes her mind."

"Perhaps we'd better rethink this," I said, standing my ground. "I can hide in Camarthan. It's a big place and I know it well. Or Cor Talaith. You've said it's only a few who want things to remain as they are. I'll just stay out of their way."

"You and Lara must come to an accommodation. Your lives will depend on one another. It's only five weeks until the time of the dragon's waking, and we must be as prepared as we can be. The dragons should be flying over the lake of fire, not enslaved to the Twelve Families of the Ridemark. If you and Lara cannot do what is required, we might have to wait another whole year, a year in which thousands may die, in which your life and our enterprise will be at risk every moment. . . ."

A year in which Donal, my cousin's child, would remain captive in the dragon camps of Gondar. Donal was the only human being yet walking the earth to whom I could claim any tie of affection—a fragile wisp of a connection that would most likely be dissolved in an instant if we were ever to meet in person. But if anything in the realm of possibility could prevent it, I would not let him suffer the fate to which his father and the wretched state of the world had condemned him. I took a deep breath and followed Narim into Lara's hut.

If I'd not been wary of the woman already, I would have burst out laughing when I stepped inside. Everything I had expected of a Rider's lair and had not found in Zengal's den in Cor Neuill was laid out before me in Lara's domain: greasy food bags and empty wineskins, worn-out sharpening stones, woolen leggings, battered pots, and old boots strewn from one end of the straw-covered stone floor to the other. The hearth was streaked with fifty years' soot, and a month's worth of ashes was packed into its corners, scarcely leaving any space for the yellow, gasping fire. A trail of dropped kindling and dried mud clots led from the door to the half-filled wood box, and the battered trestle table that served with three rickety stools as the only furnishing was littered with dirty cups, inkpots, wood shavings, half a loaf of bread so dry it had developed cracks, and ten shriveled apple cores. A jumble of leather scraps and the bag of Rider's armor were tossed in a corner beside an untidy pile of blankets.

Her weapons would not be in the mess. I glanced about casually. Sure enough, hanging in a place of honor beside the door were a bow of polished yew and a well-oiled scabbard with an immaculately gleaming sword hilt sticking out of it. Beside them was the inevitable—a carefully coiled dragon whip. I was sorely tempted to run away as far as I could go.

Cursing under her breath, Lara kicked a bag of onions out of the corner farthest from the hearth. The bag split and dusty brown orbs began rolling about the floor. "You can sleep there," she said, pointing at the space she had emptied. "I hope you brought your own blanket. I've none to spare."

"I'll manage," I said. "Even without feathers."

I shouldn't have said it, but the words burst unbidden from my tongue. After so long alone . . . to willingly share lodgings with a daughter of the Ridemark . . . If there was indeed a god watching, I wanted him or her to know that I appreciated the joke.

Narim kept his face grave and discreetly angled away from my own, while stepping quite viciously on my foot. Nothing of jest was manifest in his words, however. "We've five weeks to get him ready, Lara. I'm trusting you to teach him well. We've brought the materials you specified, and I'm leaving you the journal."

Lara seemed on the verge of throwing her errant vegetables at me until Narim's words brought her up short. "Your journal!"

Narim shrugged as he pulled from his pack a small, thick leather volume in a condition so fragile I thought it might disintegrate in his hand. "If it's ever to have any use beyond historical oddity, it will be now with the two of you." He placed the book in Lara's hand and tapped his fingers on it fondly, removing them with clear reluctance. "You'll have a care with it?"

Lara clutched it to her chest. "Every care. I promise."

"Good enough." Narim clapped me on the arm. "Behave yourself, Aidan, lad. The girl has a wicked way with a dagger. I'll stop by in a few days to see how you're getting on. For now I'd best get back to the warrens. Our doubters may believe you've gone back to Camarthan with Tarwyl, but they expect me to be at our meeting tonight with a new plan to redeem our souls—one they can be sure will change nothing."

Lara and I both followed Narim outside. Hard to guess which one of us most regretted his leaving. As he passed beyond the edge of the trees that bordered the open meadow, he turned and waved, and I would have sworn a huge grin crossed his face. Two voices mumbled curses as we turned back to the hut without looking at each other.

Lara did her best to ignore me, jabbing at her fire and throwing a few sticks on it, shoving aside the litter on her table to make a place to—very purposefully and vigorously—sharpen her dagger. I unloaded the bags I'd carried the three leagues uphill from Cor Talaith: two bulky rolls of leather, a cloth bundle of leatherworking tools, a flat tin of thick, foul-smelling grease, a heavy round of cheese, a bag of dried beans, and a few other supplies to augment Lara's stores. I pulled out my blanket, and after a few moments' consideration that included a sideways glance at Lara honing her blade that was likely sharp enough to dissect a flea, I left the hut. It was perhaps five hundred paces to the edge of the trees, and I made the trip three times, hauling back soft pine branches to use for a bed. By the time I was finished, the sun was already low, and my stomach was reminding me of how long it had been since Yura's oatcakes and my farewell to Cor Talaith.

Even if Lara had given me reason to think she was interested, I was not yet ready to break bread with a member of the Twelve Families, so I merely set the supplies on her table, cut myself a piece of cheese, and retreated to my corner. I would have dearly loved to heat a cup of water over her fire and drop in a few of the chamomile leaves I'd brought, but before I got up the courage, Lara hung one of her battered pots over the sputtering flame and threw in a few bits of onion and smoked meat. It smelled unspeakably delicious. My cold cheese sat heavy and unsatisfying in my stomach . . . at least until the onion started to burn. Lara yanked the pan from the grate, stabbing her spoon at the mess as if it were an annoying insect and scattering ashes and sparks all over the hearth. Darkness fell quickly and the cold crept through the thick stone, so that I wrapped up in my blanket and my cloak before Lara had eaten her concoction. I fell asleep wondering how on earth we were ever going to get beyond this silliness and do whatever it was Narim had in mind; assuming, of course, that I didn't end the night with a knife between my ribs.

Familiar nightmare shoved me beyond the threshold of sleep while the light seeping around the edges of the shutters was still gray. The morning was bitterly cold, and as I struggled to lace up frozen boots with nonworking fingers, I wondered sluggishly how it could be only five weeks until spring. Perhaps the dragons could tolerate more cold than I. If I had the choice of it, I'd sleep until the heart of summer.

Lara was still a shapeless roll of gray in the corner of the room farthest from mine. I knew she was there from the soft puffs of breath frost that drifted upward from the direction of her head. It was the only softness about her that I had seen. I pulled on my heavy wool shirt and my cloak and my thickest gloves, then quietly opened the door and slipped outside. The crags of the Carag Huim were just beginning to take shape in the predawn stillness, and the rolling snowfield of the meadow was taking on a life separate from the dark line of trees to the south and west and the rocky heights to the north and east.

I needed to be moving, so I tramped around the hut, finding what I was looking for on the west side of the house: a neat, knee-high pile of split wood, an ax with its head buried in a thick stump, and a wooden sledge with snow runners under it and a rope tied to one end. The ax would be of no use unless two good hands came with it. I could scarcely manage the knife I shaved with; anything heavier was impossible to grip securely.

So I hitched the rope over one shoulder and hauled the sledge across the meadow into the trees. Making sure to keep my bearings, I searched until I found a downed tree large enough to be worth the bother of stripping its branches and dry enough to make it possible for me to do so. Using my boots and my forearms to break off the branches, I managed to fill the sledge, and then began the long trek back.

The meadow was flushed with fiery pink when I emerged from the trees, and a thin trail of blue smoke rose straight up from the hut's chimney. She was awake. Only the prospect of a fire and something hot in my belly convinced me to go inside rather than find something else—anything else—to do. But she hadn't murdered me in the night, so I unloaded my broken branches next to the cleanly hewn and split logs, then carried an armload of my gatherings into the hut.

She was hacking at the loaf of dried bread with her well-honed dagger, making more crumbs than edible portions. From her glare as I dumped the branches in the wood box, I guessed that the night hadn't warmed her feelings about a Senai houseguest. The dragon whip was still on the wall, so I couldn't say my feelings had changed either. How had I let myself get talked into this?

"I've brought some herbs—chamomile, meadowsweet, wintergreen—for tea," I said, all plans of clever conversation sunk into mundanity in an instant of her hostile attention. "Would you care for some?"

"I've got what I like," she said.

I nodded and dug my tin cup from my pack, stepped outside to fill it with snow, then set it beside the tiny fire. Opening the packet of herbs came next. Her scorn scorched my back as I fumbled at it in my heavy gloves. Finally I got a pinch of the finely crumbled leaves and dropped them in my cup that was only a quarter full of water once the snow had melted—scarcely two mouthfuls. Sighing at the delay, I retrieved another handful of snow and slipped it into the cup.

"I won't cook for you," said Lara, her pointed chin stuck out defiantly. "You'll have to do for yourself, even if you have to get your hands dirty."

"I would never expect you to," I said. "I'll do my share of whatever's needed and try not to get too much in your way."

She snorted as she threw one of my sticks on the fire. "These will burn for exactly no time. Do you understand what an ax is for?"

"I have a vague notion."

Things didn't seem to be going well. At least she didn't complain about my using the fire. For a little while, every time she turned her back I'd throw on another branch until the fire was big enough to put out a little heat and get my precious cup steaming. The tea was pungent, and I felt it settle pleasantly into my cold extremities. It made me slightly less inclined to abandon the whole enterprise and take my chances in Camarthan.

Lara soaked her dry bread in warmed honey. I munched on a cold oatcake and used my cup to melt more snow. While she spread the rolls of dark leather out on the floor, I cleaned my knife and took my cup of warm water outside. Time for my daily ritual, and I wasn't about to do it where the woman could gawk. A careful half hour and no nicks later, I had my gloves back on and no beard, and I was huddled by the hearth trying to decide if Lara would be any more hostile if I burned up all the wood in one day. Better think about something else.

"So what is it Narim wants you to teach me?" I said.

"The whole business is idiocy." She was kneeling on the floor beside her materials and she raked me with a scornful eye. "I'm to instruct you in the lore of dragons. He wants you to learn the words, ritual words that should never be used by anyone outside the Twelve, and other words he's got written in his book. And we're supposed to fit you out with Riders' armor." Her hatred for this idea had her hands clenched so tight, I thought she might cut her flesh with her fingernails.

"Riders' armor?"

"He thinks it's going to protect you when you walk into that cavern and the kai tries to burn you. I told him it's a waste of time. Why would you need it, if you're so friendly with the beast?"

"You're right. It doesn't make sense."

I think she was astonished that I would agree with her about anything. I certainly was.

"Well, it doesn't matter," she said. "I've given my word, so there's no getting out of it until you realize this is slightly more dangerous than playacting and decide your noble skin is too precious to risk." She dragged her bag into the middle of the floor and pulled out stiff, charred leather greaves that stank of the same grease I'd hauled up the mountain—something like rotted hay and lamp oil. "Hold these up to your legs so we'll know how much bigger we'll have to make them."

All that morning, while I found a dented pail by the woodpile and proceeded to clean out her firepit, Lara cursed and measured and cut. I tried on every piece of her armor so she could see where she needed to make changes to fit me. But when she thrust her gauntlets at me and said to take my own gloves off and put hers on, I gave her my spare pair of gloves instead, saying they would do as a pattern.

"You must be a tender flower indeed who can't take off his gloves inside. Or is it you're afraid of dirtying yourself with a Rider's touch?"

"Modesty," I said, then scraped another shovelful of ashes from her hearth into the pail and swore to myself that the next time I saw Narim I would shake him until all his secrets fell out of his head. It was going to be a long five weeks.

By the time darkness fell I had a healthy fire and a fine bed of coals, and Lara had a good-sized stack of shaped leather pieces. Her floor was littered with scraps. I had thrown some of my beans into a pot of hot water, and they had simmered enough to make decent soup. Only as a concession to habit drilled into me by my lovely and gracious mother did I offer Lara some of my soup. The woman grimaced, pulled out a strip of dried meat, and began chewing on it. I took that as a refusal.

"I suppose you've never worn real armor, being protected from fighting as you were," she said.

"No."

"Probably don't even know how to hold a sword."

"I was taught."

"Ah, yes. Senai think of themselves as warriors and play at it when they're children. I suppose even you did that."

"Yes."

"Will you spar with me? I need practice. Elhim are too small."

"No."

She nodded knowingly, as if she had expected nothing else, then leaned her back against the legs of the table and stuck her boots near the fire.

"I heard you sing, you know. People fought to get closer to you. To touch you. To give you rings and letters and locks of hair to take to their families and lovers. They begged you to sing again and again until dawn came. I never understood it."

I finished eating and kept my eyes on the fire. "What words are you supposed to teach me?"

"Narim says you know the true language." She had switched to the tongue of the Ridemark, the odd inflections and slurred endings blunting the harsh edge of her speech.

"There was a time when I was fluent. I've forgotten a great number of words, but not the sounds of it." I, too, used the old speech and did not pretend to fumble with it as I'd done in Cor Neuill. Sometimes you have to enjoy what petty triumphs you can scrape together.

"Hmmph." I had the feeling she was disappointed that I'd said it right. "Well, first lesson then. You are to address the dragon as *'teng zha nav wyvyr.'* "

"Child of fire and wind."

"You know it already?"

"I know the words. You said them when you woke Keldar."

"Right. So I did." Absentmindedly she brushed the wisps of hair back from her face, exposing the ugly remnants of disaster. "So you understood all of what I said that night?"

I repeated the commands she'd used in the old speech and also in common speech. Remembering words was as much a part of me as breathing.

"I'm surprised you remember it so exactly. You were a puling mess that night."

I decided then that it was not the scars or the drooping eye that marred Lara's face, but her ever-present sneer— the curling lip and the acid tongue so ready to wound with the greatest possible pain. Or perhaps she bore scars that were worse than the ones I could see. Of all men I should know how the damage inside could distort the face one showed to the world. I wanted to be angry with her and wipe her sneer away. But like the fool I was, I sat there feeling inordinately guilty that my existence could cause such hatred as to twist a well-proportioned face into meanness. No point in getting angry at her digging. She had no reason to understand. "That was after," I said.

She opened a small tin box that sat on the floor next to her pallet and pulled out Narim's worn leather book. The light was long gone, but she refused to move closer to the fire. Likely trying to stay as far from me as possible. The flames cast an angry red glow on her terrible scars and gleamed on the shining, dark brown braid that fell over her shoulder.

"What is the book?" I said as she leafed through the pages, looking for what she wanted, running her finger over the words as I had seen many do who came late to reading. The Twelve Families were not known for scholarly leanings, especially for their women.

"Narim's dragon journal. Everything he's learned that has anything to do with the beasts. Drawings, notes, lists. Pages and pages of words he says were used by dragons. Impossible stupidity." She looked up sharply. "You're not to touch it. Not ever."

"I wouldn't think of it."

She returned her attention to the book. "Here." She pointed to a page. "This is where he said we had to start. Test your memory now, Senai. Here are the fifty words for wind. . . ."

Not since I was a child had so much information been forcibly thrust into my head. Lara took her bargain with Narim very seriously, but she seemed determined to see me stumble. I, of course, was not about to allow it. She would speed through the lists of words and the guessed-at meanings, like the fifty for wind: *wyvyrri,* the fine, light airs of autumn, perfect for soaring high; *wyvyar,* the heavy, damp gusts of spring; the variants for storm gales and hurricanes and whirlwinds, for dangerous downdrafts that would threaten youngling fliers, and for the heated rising airs of summer. . . . Then came fifty for the texture of the air, and for the taste and smell of it a hundred more. Lara would give me each of them once as rapidly as possible, then quiz me on them randomly, mixing them with the groups that had come before.

Some of the words I already knew, not the syllables themselves but the thing they described, for they were exactly what Roelan had spoken to me when I was young and living, when I wove them into my music and believed I had discovered the heart of the universe. That made my night's work easier, though after three hours and three hundred words, I began to think my head would burst. But I refused to be the one to call a halt, and we continued on through midnight. We finished the eighty-seven words that described lights in the heavens: stars, moon, and twenty variants of sun, lightning, and the colored veils of northern climes. Then, as if by mutual agreement, Lara shut the book, and I began to bank the fire. Though Lara could not have known it, it had been the most delightful evening I had spent since the night before I was arrested. Though it seemed such a foolish and impossible purpose, it was good to know my mind could still work, and it allowed me to touch the past in a way other than grief, regret, and longing.

All that week during the daylight hours Lara cut and prepared the leather for my armor, variously soaking and shaping the pieces over wooden forms, heating them, and rubbing them with the stinking grease Narim had obtained for her and other substances she had already. She would not let me help or even watch what it was she did, saying it was the lore of the Ridemark and not to be shared. And I was forbidden to touch the journal, which she kept locked in a tin box with the key around her neck. So I was left to occupy myself. I resumed my morning runs, continued my awkward wood gathering, and gradually took over preparing our meals. Lara had set a trap in the woods to catch an occasional rabbit or squirrel. I checked hers and built a few more well out of her sight. She would have scorned my clumsy creations as crude

and ill made—indeed, any child could have done better—
but she didn't criticize the meat I brought in with them.

With childish eagerness I anticipated the evenings
when we would work on the words from Narim's journal.
When I had mastered them, Lara began to guide me
through the meticulous drawings from the fragile pages.
Narim had insisted that part of communicating with a
dragon was interpreting its movements. So Lara taught
me the physical characteristics of dragons: how the wings
were shaped, how the eyes had multiple lids and, in the
daytime, changed color according to the color of the sky,
how the head moved when the beast was angry or pleased
or listening. When we had reviewed all the drawings, she
said we needed to work using something more substantial. That was when I balked.

A huge boulder pile lay on the north side of the
meadow. Lara had hacked out crude steps in a massive
chunk of granite to match the stepped scales on the
dragon's haunch that allowed a Rider to climb on. In the
top of an adjacent rock she hammered steel spikes to
match the barbed protrusions on the beast's shoulder. She
then demonstrated the Rider's mount, running lightly up
the narrow steps, arcing the steel hook on her whip handle up to the shoulder barbs in a perfect throw and catch,
and shinnying up to the top. Jumping down lightly, she
offered me the whip. "Your turn. Narim says you have to
learn, in case something happens to me and you have to
ride. To bring the beasts to the lake if things should ever
get so far." The very words were gall in her mouth.

I could not touch the thing. Even if I'd not had the
deep-rooted horror of dragon whips, they were of no use

to me. To haul yourself up, you had to be able to grip. "If I were ever to ride, I'd have to use another way," I said.

"There is no other way. You can't mount from the front, because you'd be dead from the poisoned barbs on the edge of the wings. From the haunch to the shoulder can be half again the highest distance you can reach— even with your height. You can't climb in between. The scales protrude enough to hold on to, but the first attempt would slice off your fingers even with the gauntlets. The scales of the neck are sharp, but nothing like those on the flanks."

"A good thing I won't need to ride, then." I tried to pass it off lightly, for I didn't want her goading me about it. "You don't want me to do it anyway. Teach me something else."

She made a great deal of fuss, calling me a weakling and a coward, settling on the explanation that I was too ashamed to fail in front of one who was not Senai. That was near enough the truth that I kept my mouth shut until she tired of hearing herself.

The part that still had me confused was what Narim actually expected of me. That night as I melted snow for tea and she worked the damp pieces of my gauntlets to soften and shape the leather, I asked her the question that still had me doubting. "Even if I can learn how to free the dragons from the control of the bloodstones, what's to prevent the clan from taking them right back? As long as they possess the stones, won't the Riders just go through their rituals again?"

Lara squirmed, as she always did when I referred to Ridemark secrets. "Why would beings with minds sit still for the Riders to imprison them again? Supposedly the only way it happened the first time was that the Elhim poisoned the lake of fire with jenica. Narim thinks the freed kai will be 'wary.' "

"But you don't believe it."

She snatched the journal from the table and locked it back in its tin box. "It's all fairy tales. I believe the moon will be eaten by the Great Wolf in the northern sky before I ever hear the speech of a dragon."

I couldn't say that I disagreed with that.

By the end of three weeks I supposed Narim would say we had come to an accommodation, but no one observing her insults and my silence would think we had made any progress at all.

Chapter 17

A few days after the incident at the boulder pile, I woke in the night suffocating, convinced that Goryx had dropped the canvas bag over my head and was stroking my back with his coiled dragon whip, his usual gesture of macabre affection as he prepared for the first lash. I jerked upright bathed in sweat, throwing off the blanket I had inadvertently pulled over my head against the cold. Still shaking, I crept to the hearth and threw on the rest of the scraps from the wood box, trying to stir up the banked coals of the fire. It refused to flame again, so I hurriedly pulled on boots and cloak and went out in search of more kindling. I was desperate for light.

The moon was three-quarters full and bathed the snowfields in cold silver so bright I could see my shadow. As I stood leaning on the weathered rail used for tethering horses, taking deep gulps of the frosty air, trying to banish my terrors with space and freedom and the beauty of the night, I heard a muffled cry from inside the hut. The door flew open, and Lara stood outlined in the doorway, her blanket clutched around her shoulders, her moonlit face dazed and bewildered, pale with panic. No sneer. No curling lip. "The fire," she mumbled. "Something woke me and it flared up."

A spare, eloquent moment. No wonder she always stayed so far from the hearth. "I'm sorry," I said. "The scraps I'd thrown on must have caught. I didn't think of it waking you." Didn't think of the horror flame must raise in her, a necessity for life, yet always a reminder of her agony. "Forgive me. I'll watch until it's safely banked again." Of course she would seek cold darkness to soothe her nightmare, as I sought light to ease my own.

"Why were you messing about with the fire? What are you doing out here?" Suspicion and mistrust followed close on regained composure.

"Summons of nature," I said, shifting my eyes to the moonlit crags. Her boots crunched across the snow until she was standing so close I could sense her breath on my cloak. I had never been a good liar.

"You've been out here too long for that. Too long for one who gets frostbite if he's more than three steps from the coals." She stood beside me, her head scarcely reaching my shoulder. "You're shaking now. Why—"

Her abrupt silence forced me to look at her. She was staring at my hands that rested on the rail. I'd been in such a hurry that I hadn't put on gloves, and so grateful for the moonlight that I hadn't noticed the cold. Quickly I snatched my twisted, ugly appendages back into my cloak, then fixed my eyes on the moonlit peaks. Her boots crunched again, and it was a cold hour until I could force myself to go back inside. I couldn't explain why I hated it so fiercely that she had seen.

Nothing changed after that night. Lara did not mention my hands, which was fine with me. Even if she were capable of it, I did not want her pity, any more than she would want mine. She had more words for *sniveling weakling* than dragons had for *wind*. No service I offered was welcome, and no word I spoke was met with anything but derision. The only reference she made to the night's exposure was three days later, when she threw an awl, two rolls of leather thongs and strong sinew, and a stack of leather pieces down in front of me, telling me to thread the lacings through the edges so my Rider's breeches wouldn't fall off. "I don't have time to do all of it," she said with an unreadable expression. "Are you capable of doing your part, as you claimed?"

"I can do whatever I need to do," I said. And so I did. Slowly. Painfully. Mumbling curses as the awl slipped out of my grasp a hundred times for every successful hole. Trying to will the thongs and sinew through the tool and the stiff, oiled leather, when a hundred clumsy attempts had me wanting to beat my head on the table. Such a small endeavor, yet for three days it loomed far larger than anything having to do with sentient dragons or the redemption of a people. I utterly forgot where I was and what I was doing and what were the true measures of accomplishment and failure.

I would have preferred to fight my battles outside of Lara's view, but she never said anything. Never watched me. Never seemed to take notice of my driving frustration or my seething anger or my sporadic outbursts of satisfaction at my all-too-rare successes. At first I was sure it was purest Ridemark contempt. But when she wordlessly laid a second stack in front of me while I still stared in exhausted triumph at the first, I glanced up quickly in dismay. On her lips was the glimmer of a smile. It was so faint, such a remote and inconceivable grace, that I called

myself seven names for a fool. Most likely she was enjoying the sight of a Senai struggling with such mundane
labors . . . but it hadn't looked like that sort of smile.

Our work went on, preparing for the equinox, the day
the ancients said the eye of the world began to widen with
delight at its bride, the earth—the day Elhim lore said the
dragons would stir from their winter's sleep. Lara was
quite serious about keeping track of the days. On the wall
above her sleeping pallet she had used coal to mark off a
crude calendar, and each morning she carefully checked
off another square. She had certain days noted with circles and half circles and crescents which I took to be
phases of the moon, the equinox with a large X, and other
days with marks of no easily discernible shape. One of
the latter fell at the beginning of my fifth week with her.

All that day she seemed distracted and nervous, absolutely unlike herself. We worked on my armor, and for
once I accomplished more than she. The greaves were
done, ready to lace about my legs. The breeches were
done, thick and stiff and uncomfortable. I was sitting on
the floor wrestling with the first two pieces of the vest
and the sinew that would bind them together, the material so much stronger than leather laces, and so much thinner, and far more difficult to grasp.

"I'm going out for a while to . . . to check the traps,"
Lara announced in late afternoon, tossing aside the stiffened wool she had been shaping into a helm.

"I checked them this morning," I said. "Only two fox
kits not fit to keep."

"You let go more than you keep," she said in irritation,
throwing on her cloak and shouldering her bow. "And
you'd eat the same thing every meal of the year. I'm tired

of cheese and oatcakes, so I'm going to find something better. I'll be out past nightfall." I knew better than to question the sense of such a venture.

"I would never doubt you can take care of yourself," I muttered, my frustration at the task she had set me forcing my words louder than I might otherwise have said them. She heard me and turned blazing red, which was another mark of an unusual day. At any other time she wouldn't have listened, or if she'd listened, she wouldn't have cared. The door slammed so hard behind her that a pot of oatcakes fell off a shelf, and the flat, dry cakes shattered into crumbs on the floor.

I dropped my work and gazed idly about the hut, puzzling over the strange course of the past weeks. It was then I noted the mark on Lara's calendar. I examined it more closely than I'd dared before, and the splotch on this day resolved itself into a D.

Dragon? Departure? Discovery? All our work at lists of words prompted a torrent of possibilities.

The sun slid lower in the thin, watery blue of the sky. I salvaged a broken oatcake and melted a slab of cheese on it.

Deviltry? Deception?

An icicle, the last holdout against the afternoon warming, splintered on the stone doorstep, shattering the stillness.

Duplicity? Danger? Death?

I donned my cloak and set out after Lara in the failing light. Though an hour had passed since her departure, it was easy enough to follow her, for though the remaining patches of snow were crusty and brittle, they were better walking than the muddy strips of meadow in between. In-

teresting that the small, firm boot prints went nowhere
near the trees where our traps lay. I trotted at a good pace,
first skirting the meadow, then climbing a steep track up
the ridge at its eastern end. By the time I reached the top,
the first stars had poked through the deepening blue. The
bloated bulge of the moon pushed over the eastern horizon beyond a landscape wrinkled like an old man's face
with rocky ridges like the one on which I stood. Lara's
trail led me deep into the narrow valley between one
ridge and the next. I bore south around rocky slide areas
and stunted pine trees growing out of the rock, their roots
scarcely grasping the dry slopes. The going was tricky in
the dim light until the moon rose high enough to take up
its hotter brother's duties in the sky.

Some three hours from the hut, I believed I had lost the
trail, and I considered going back. I wasn't at all familiar
with the crumpled wasteland, and to stay out all night had
its own risks. The first touch of the morning sun would
alter the snowy landmarks. As I sat on a rock to rest and
take my bearings, I realized that fifty paces beyond my
position, behind a cluster of boulder stacks standing sen-
tinel like a giant's wardens, gleamed a pool of light that
was far too yellow and far too unsteady to be moonlight.

I scrambled up the steep side of the ravine and crept
forward until I had passed the boulder stacks and could
look down on a small, protected grotto where a smoky
fire flickered next to a half-frozen pool. Lara stood beside
the fire, locked in a fierce embrace with a man.

I was stunned . . . and unreasoningly embarrassed.
Never in all my considerations had I come within fifty
leagues of the idea that Lara might have a lover. Why had
I thought that because such a blessing was inconceivable

for me, it was equally inconceivable for a young woman so filled with passionate life? Her hatreds were for me and my kind, not for everyone in the world. And her scars, so dreadful on an otherwise pleasing face . . . I rarely noticed them anymore. Why shouldn't some other man develop the same blindness?

But as quickly as my view of the world was set so profoundly askew, it was reversed again. Lara stepped away from her visitor, but left her hands in his, and I looked back and forth between the two figures and gaped at the revelation. He was of exactly her height, with the same pointed chin, fine-boned cheeks, and huge eyes. He wore the same dusting of freckles across his straight nose, the same generous mouth. Only the breadth of shoulders and back, and the chin-length trim of the gold-brown hair distinguished him . . . and, of course, the finished perfection of his face. He could be no one but her brother.

". . . all arranged," he was saying in earnest excitement. "We can go this very night. Everyone is waiting to welcome you back, to give you every privilege that is yours by right."

"I can't believe it." Lara bit her lip and wrinkled her brow while examining his face as if to capture every morsel of information left unspoken.

"You were only a child. They've finally come to understand it. A strong-willed child with a warrior's heart and your family's stubbornness. These are virtues, not crimes. The only crime is that it's taken them so long to see it."

"You heard this with your own ears? From the high commander himself?" Tentative. Touching on the very edge of hope.

"He showed me the order of pardon. The moment you're back, he'll proclaim it to the Council of Twelve."

Controlled and wary, Lara pulled back a little, while still clinging to his hands. "But he'll never let me ride." She was not accustomed to hope.

Never had I seen anyone show such triumph as Lara's brother when he produced his gift. "He has promised to consider it. He will hear you. He said to tell you, 'Riders are born, not chosen. It is a precept to which we've not always been faithful.' Lara, it's as good as done."

Lara hung limp as he swung her about joyfully, then pulled her back into his fierce embrace. "By the gods, little sister. You will be the first. A woman will ride for the Mark, and you will show them the true heart of a warrior."

"To ride for the Mark. Oh, Vanir's fire, Desmond."

She could scarcely speak, and, even as I struggled with my dismay at her betrayal, I caught my first unfiltered glimpse of Lara. Everything I had yet seen of her—except perhaps for that first handclasp with Narim and the brief moment of her night terror—everything had been but layer upon layer of armor, the shell she had fashioned from scars and pain, from loneliness and bitterness. All of it fell away in the moment of her brother's pronouncement, revealing a woman of pride and dignity and lonely strength, whose face shone like a second moon. I had never thought of her as beautiful until that night, never heard the music in her voice, the simple melody laced with her glorious passion. At the same moment I began to be afraid for her. Surely she could sense the danger, the dissonance that marred the harmony of this family reunion.

Lara sank to a fallen tree that had been pulled up to the fire like a garden bench, and her brother crouched on one knee in front of her. I brushed away a clump of stickery jackweed that the wind had lodged under my nose, and edged carefully down the snowy, rock-strewn hillside on my belly, not thinking of danger in my craving to hear more.

"What's changed then?" she said. "A tradition so long bound. I never thought . . . never in the last instance believed they would relent." Yes, she had seen it. Already her shutters were being drawn again.

"I don't know. I've hammered at it so long with every one of the twelve councilors and they've always been deaf to me. Every year for eighteen years another failed petition—"

"You have been my true knight, brother."

"Then a few weeks ago, MacEachern himself summoned me. He wished me to fetch you right away, but I said our regular meeting was still three weeks hence. He was surprised I didn't know where you lived." Long grievance festered beneath Desmond's devotion, pushing him to his feet to step away from Lara.

"You know why I can't tell you."

"Well, now you're to be a Rider of the Mark, you'll no longer have to live with these divided loyalties. It will be your own people who claim you now, and your family and your high commander who shape your path."

The young man began adjusting the fittings of his saddle as if to accommodate two riders, so he couldn't see Lara's countenance freeze. I saw it and felt a knot in my gut loosen one notch.

"Desmond, did the high commander say anything

about what he wants from me when I return? Surely he expects some payment for this honor he does me."

Yes, I thought. *A good question. Listen well to his answer. Though he is your brother who cares for you, he has but one heart to give. No question where it is lodged.*

"Want from you?" Desmond turned to her, puzzled. "Nothing but what you've wished to give him all these years—your loyalty and service. Come on. We can be home before dawn."

Lara kicked at the fire, scattering the coals until a cloud of sparks flew about her like a swarm of fireflies. "I've got to think it over." She flung the words into the air casually, like the sparks from her boot.

Her brother's jaw dropped in shock and disbelief. "Think it over? Lara! What is there to think about?" Anger hardened his pointed jaw. "You will come with me. The head of your family commands you."

She chucked him playfully under the chin. "Don't fret, sweet Desmond. It's only I've got a bit of business to finish, some debts to pay. This is so unexpected. I've got to get accustomed to the idea." She laughed uproariously, but with far too little mirth to my ear. A dangerous laugh. I just wasn't sure for whom.

Desmond looked confused. I certainly was. Fatally so, for I was oblivious to the brush of the bushes behind me and the soft grit of footsteps in the crusted snow. Only when the leather strap stung my neck and tightened about it and I was flipped backward onto the hard ground did I know there was a fourth member of our little nighttime party. A heavy boot stomped on my wrist, and my hastily drawn knife leaped out of my fingers of its own volition. A vast landscape of wind-coarsened skin, pitted with deep pores and tufted with wiry red hair, exuding a virulent odor of onion, presented itself a hand's breadth from my nose. That was all I was able to see before he sat his massive bulk on my chest and stomach, making unnatural white stars bloom from the hazy darkness. While I fought to squeeze in a breath, I felt leather straps being wound tightly about my wrists.

"Well, well. What has Vanir set before us? A tasty morsel of a Senai spy? Of a Senai devil?"

The weight was lifted from my chest only to be followed by a powerful jerk on my wrists that insisted I get up on my feet or be dragged down the rocky slope on my face.

"Look here, brother Desmond! Didn't I tell you that one had to be wary of the wild creatures that inhabit this wasteland? I've trapped us a Senai fox."

Lara snapped her head around as I hobbled into the firelight, only to be pulled up short and collapsed to my knees by the skilled hand of the Rider and his dragon whip. The thong about my throat ensured I could say nothing. Desmond sneered down his straight nose as if I'd crawled out of a dung heap. Before he could speak, Lara shoved him aside. "You!" she said in disgust. "How dare you come creeping after me? Sneaking, nasty beggar."

"Who is it, Lara? Tell me. And tell me what he's doing spying on you."

Unreasonably I wanted to warn Lara of the dangerous undertone in her brother's cold baritone. But the woman quite effectively undercut both my desire and my ability to speak when she laid her gauntleted hand into my mouth so hard I rocked back on my knees and gagged on

the blood that ran down my constricted throat. Clearly the
D was not only for Desmond, but also for *duplicity* and
double-dealing, and most certainly for *danger*.

"He's beastly Senai filth," said Lara, fury boiling out
of her like molten lava. "He was found wandering in the
mountains half-frozen. The same ones who took me in
sheltered him, so I couldn't deal with him as I wished."

"And what would you suggest we do with him, girl?"
asked the red-haired man, addressing Lara with such in-
solence that a true brother would have bashed him.
Desmond only listened.

"Take him with you if you wish," said the woman. "Or
strip him and tie him to a tree for the wolves to find. What
do I care for any Senai?"

Lara was not finished unsettling her brother even yet.
Now she was done with me, she turned on him with the
fullness of her anger. "There are more important matters
here than a crippled Senai who cannot even lace his
boots. Tell me, Desmond, who is this clan brother? All
these years we've come together in secret, and I've asked
but one thing: that for my safety and the peace of those
who saved my life you not reveal our meeting place to
anyone. Yet clearly this man is here by your leave. How
do you explain it? Is this a new betrayal or has he been
here at every meeting?"

Desmond stammered like a nervous squire on the eve
of his first battle. I, struggling to clear my muddy head,
had no little sympathy for him.

"Rueddi is a clan brother of the Fifth Family, a Rider
in training. MacEachern suggested I bring him to help
protect you. He feared this escaped prisoner might be
hiding nearby and that he might try to prevent you taking

your rightful place. You know"—he regained a bit of his injured dignity—"surely you understand who this Senai is."

"He could be MacEachern's bastard for all I care," said Lara. "But you had no right to bring anyone here— even a clan brother—for any reason."

"I did only as our high commander bade me. He *will* have this Senai, Lara. No king, no god, no man or woman will prevent it. The black-tongued devil should never have been released from Mazadine. It was a terrible mistake. The one who told us that seven years of silence would destroy the singer and break his perverted connection to the kai—that one lied to us. We're going to take back our prisoner and bury him forever."

Panic devoured my reason and with it all my subtle listening. Better to be dead. I strained against the sharp-edged leather thongs until my wrists bled, and the whip grew tighter about my throat, smearing the world with red. I rolled and lashed out with my feet, first at my red-haired captor, then at Lara and Desmond, but Riders are very skilled with their whips, and I was pulled away choking and gagging. Then a boot landed in my side, leaving my legs as limp as rags, and I had to spend all my energy to take another breath. Somewhere beyond the pounding of my blood and the rasp of my starved lungs, Lara was speaking calmly and coldly.

"So the promises you've made, my pardon, the hope that I would ride . . . they were nothing but what? A ruse to draw me out and find out what I knew of the Senai? To snare him if he was nearby? All lies, then? Do the Twelve think I'm in league with this devil?"

"No! I didn't mean— Of course not. The high commander knew the man had escaped into the mountains. He thought it possible that the same ones who helped you would help him. I was going to ask you if you'd seen him. MacEachern does not trust the Elhim, not after—"

Lara pressed her finger firmly over Desmond's mouth. "Do not prattle. My trust will not be won by words. If you love me, brother, you must show me that I'm the true prize you seek. Leave this helpless Senai vermin for the wolves and take me home. When I step into Cor Neuill, I will have put my life in your hands, so I require this proof of your saying: Take back the most important prize and abandon the lesser. And if I am not the most important, then I no longer have any clan, any family, or any brother."

"Lara!"

"I'll not be used as bait. I'll not have my honor suspect. And I'll not be made a fool by lies and treachery. Prove your words by your deeds, Desmond."

I had never met man, woman, or beast so mystifyingly unpredictable as Lara. If she were to kiss me full on the lips at that moment, I could as easily believe I was poisoned as that she cared one whit for me. If I'd not been so sick and terrified, I might have laughed at Desmond's dilemma. As it was, I spit blood from my mouth, shifted my cheek that rested on a sharp-edged stone, and watched his face register every conceivable emotion as he gazed from his beloved sister to his despised enemy. She had put him in a wicked fix and me in worse. A wolf's howl echoed eerily from the rocky heights. I was going to lose either way.

Desmond recovered admirably, though if Lara believed his words honest, she was a fool beyond saving.

"There is no question here," he said, not explaining why his decision had taken so long if there was no question in his mind. "You are my first and most sacred quarry—to retrieve you from exile and restore you to your rightful place. I had thought we could bring the Senai as our triumphal gift to our clan. But if you say it is not a worthy gift, if you believe I see his capture as anything but long-delayed good fortune for our house, then so be it. We will dispose of him as you say. The gods will silence his foul tongue."

"And what of your friend, brother?"

"Rueddi is in my debt. He will carry out my wishes. Exactly."

The red-haired man bowed to Desmond and smirked at me, even as he pulled tight on the strap around my neck.

Events moved quickly after that. Scarcely two heartbeats and I was left hanging in the freezing night, my wrists secured to a sturdy pine bough above my head, my feet scarcely touching the ground. Lara had seen to the binding; then Rueddi had ripped the cloak, gloves, shirt, and boots off me. My clothes were now scattered across the clearing and down the gorge after being laced generously with blood from a deep cut on my arm. As he led his horse from the bushes Rueddi gave me a playful lash with his whip, and by the time I won the battle to keep from crying out, Lara leaped up behind Desmond, and the three of them rode into the night.

One by one the scattered coals of Lara's fire winked out. The rivulets of blood on my back and my arm and my face froze, and one by one my extremities went numb. The wolf's howl split the night, closer than before.

I could hear the change in key as she smelled my blood on the wind.

A race, I thought dully. The wolves were closer, but Rueddi would certainly be back. Desmond had no intention of leaving me to gods or wolves either one, not when his high commander wanted to bury me himself. Forever. My thoughts began to wander as I hung there slowly freezing in the moonlight. Who had told MacEachern that seven years of silence would destroy me?

I had believed for so long that I was dead, that no amount of pretending to breathe and eat and sleep would ever be able to revive my heart. But my betrayer had been wrong and I had been wrong. Life in all its oddity kept nipping at my heels like a playful pup, daring me to give it up when I had loved it so dearly. Just when I was convinced that poor humanity was alone in the universe and that it mattered not a splinter what happened to me, a being that was not a god, but was beyond all human capacities, had spoken to me with love. And just when death had declared itself inevitable, a woman who had no reason to care for me, who had unfailingly asserted her scorn and dislike, had given me a chance to live. Lara had called me a helpless cripple who could not lace his boots. But she had seen me lace up the armor, and she had chosen the mode of my binding and the branch and the tree. Intriguing possibility stirred me to movement.

I decided early on that my surmise must be wrong. The pine branch from which I was suspended was a hand's breadth in diameter, and the chances of breaking it were depressingly slim. It would be easier to uproot the blasted tree, I thought, as I hung limp and exhausted after the fruitless effort of pulling downward on it. *Uproot . . .* I

considered the trees I'd seen on my journey, scarcely
grasping the rocky soil with their gnarled roots. My
prison tree jutted out from the steep embankment almost
horizontally. I slid my feet to my right and pulled on the
branch again, this time from the slightly different angle.
Moved another handspan to the right and pulled again.
Again and again until my arms were covered with blood
from my wrists, and my shoulders refused to move again.
Then I started the other way. Move the feet; pull. Again;
pull.

It was no use. My small reserve of strength gave out. I
was too cold. My feet were dead stumps, and I couldn't
move them anymore. I stumbled and hung from my raw
wrists, unable to get my lost feet under me again. All I
could do was hang there like meat on a hook and pretend
I heard a cracking somewhere above me ... until I
slumped completely into the dirt and first the branch, and
then the tree, fell on top of me.

Quiet rustlings and feral moans drifted from behind
the boulder stacks. I sprawled facedown on the cold
ground, the tree trunk a deadweight on the backs of my
thighs. Perhaps I should have felt lucky the tree hadn't
landed on my head, but that didn't occur to me as I tried
to worm my way out from under it. The branches scraped
and stung, leaving an occasional warm rivulet of blood
trickling across my skin. The bindings about my ankles
became hopelessly tangled in the branches, and my wrists
were soon stretched awkwardly to one side of my head,
so raw I could not bear to pull on them again. It seemed
so ridiculous.

I laid my head on the cold ground to try for more
leverage, and not two handspans from my nose I saw a

soft orange glow—one of the coals from the fire, a good-sized chunk only half-burned. The coal distracted me from my futile writhings. Softly I blew, over and over, praying the coal to take fire to frighten away the encroaching predators and so that something of me would be warm. Hands and feet, legs and arms were long dead. Soon my face and lips were frozen so that I could not even tell if I was pursing my lips to blow on the reluctant coal. At the end I had to rest, to lay down my head and forget the padding steps in the deepest shadows.

"Come on," I mumbled thickly as my eyelids closed and froze shut. "Get on with it."

"No, damn you, don't go to sleep. Gods of night, what a mess. Was anyone ever so inept as a Senai?" She had come back.

Chapter 18

"Are you going to sit up and drink this or am I going to have to pour it over your head?"

Steam tickled my nose. Meadowsweet and wintergreen. Pungent and soothing. The best remedy in the world for general aches and pains, of which I had an abundance. The blazing bonfire that seared my face so pleasantly was quickly bringing my frozen parts back to uncomfortable life. I would really rather sleep. Lara had interrupted me just as I drifted off, cutting me loose from the tree, dragging me across the ground, and throwing my cloak on top of me while she built up the fire.

I was lying on my side an arm's reach from the flames, shivering under my cloak, the tin cup just in front of my nose. I didn't look up, afraid I might provoke Lara into leaving again while still in possession of that steaming container of salvation. But as usual I couldn't resist a word.

"I thought you weren't going to cook for me." My teeth were thawed enough to chatter unmercifully, blunting the careful precision of my wit.

"I decided I would rather cook than dress you. Found your precious herbs in your pocket. If you drink it, then maybe you can take care of yourself."

Slowly I eased myself to sitting and held out both shaking hands to let her slip the cup between them.

She held back for a moment. "It's very hot."

"It doesn't matter. The sense . . . the feeling . . . doesn't work right."

I clenched my palms about the cup and got it carefully to my mouth, letting the hot liquid begin to quiet my violent shivering and settle into the bruised places.

"I never thought you would uproot the whole tree. The branch was rotten. One good jerk should have broken it." She sat herself away from the fire where I couldn't see her face, wrapping her arms about her knees. My skin shrank around my aching bones when I saw the dead wolf just beyond her, an arrow protruding from its side.

"I wanted a big fire."

She laughed then, a quiet laugh that flowed softly about us like the lowest arpeggio on a fine harp. "Have you no blood in your veins? I don't understand you at all."

"I do murder in my dreams," I said.

She shook her head. "You weep in your dreams. You scream without making a sound." She stood up, threw a branch onto the bonfire, and wandered away for a bit. When she came back, she tossed my bloodstained shirt and gloves onto the ground in front of me. "We need to move."

"You think they'll come back?"

"Desmond will bring the legion. I had to kill Rueddi."

"Vanir's fires. Lara . . ." There was nothing to be said, of course. No comfort possible for one whose hopes were shattered so irrevocably. Not from me, certainly. And she'd want no thanks from me either. "Do we need to warn the Elhim?"

"When we get to the kai's lair, I'll light a watchfire on the peak. Narim will see it and understand. We should have three days' head start. The clan knows the Elhim sanctuary is in the Carag Huim, but not exactly where. I left Desmond afoot, and it will take him at least that long to get back, gather the legion, and find Cor Talaith. Meanwhile, we'll have his horses."

The kai's lair. Keldar's lair. In all the minutiae of the past weeks, our great enterprise had grown indistinct. "Are we ready?"

I donned my bloody clothing as quickly as I could, while Lara brought the horses from the far end of the grotto. She didn't answer my question until she wrapped the reins of Rueddi's horse about my gloved hands. Then she looked me full in the eye, her own clear blue ones bleak and hopeless. "I don't believe it matters in the least."

We rode back to the hut, taking a slightly longer, but less steep, route than we had walked, and collapsed on our blankets just before dawn, knowing we could not proceed without rest. I woke first, sometime near midday, and Lara jumped up soon after, diving right into our preparations as if I might be thinking of leaving her behind. We worked for an hour, saying little except to agree on what we needed to keep with us: a bit of food, our armor, a flask of brandy, the fireproofing supplies, Lara's weapons.

We left the hut by separate paths just as the light took on its midafternoon slant. Lara led the horses across the open meadow to the northern end of the valley, where she would point them down the trails leading into the wild lands of northern Elyria, hoping to lead any pursuers astray. Then she would set out directly west on a difficult route through steep, rugged terrain where her passing could not be easily tracked, before turning south to our rendezvous. I took the well-trodden path into the nearby forest, where we set our traps and gathered wood, dragging the sledge behind me to muddle the footprints so no one could tell if they were old or new. Once deep in the trees, I buried the sledge in the snow and set off on a southwesterly course, masking the signs of my passing by climbing steep rockfaces and walking in barely thawed streams, soaking my boots miserably. We could not risk being followed.

The stars claimed it was almost midnight by the time I topped a high saddle and saw the jewellike glimmer of Lara's watchfire blazing on a barren hillside. Half an hour later, I collapsed on the ground beside the fire. I had scarcely begun thawing my fingers enough to give full attention to the fat partridge spitted over it and the onions roasting in the coals, when Lara started instructing me as to our next move. "We've got to decide how we're going to—"

I covered my ears. "Please, no! You can't mean me to listen until I've had a chance to taste this magnificent bird." I knew we had a thousand things to consider, but my stomach was groaning with delight at the smoky scent. "And I've lugged this brandy about with me for at least five hundred leagues, so I want to get rid of it as well. I think this night warrants a little celebration." I pulled out the stone flask that held our only spirits and waved it in the air. She scowled and started to complain, but I was tired and feeling fey, and didn't let her. "Call it wanton indulgence stemming from my Senai decadence."

Under Lara's ferocious glare, I downed my share of the overblackened fowl and rock-hard onions, and only then did I savor the first sip of brandy. Tossing the flask to her, I settled close to the fire, closed my eyes, and let the smooth liquor trickle down my throat. I peeped out from under my eyelids, and watched her shake her head at me, then swig from the flask in the soldier's way—no savoring, no settling, only one long pull. Then she threw the flask at my belly so hard I might have lost what I'd already drunk if I'd not been ready for it. I took another mouthful. Only after it had burned its delightful way to my tired knees did I sigh and admit that indulgence had to give way or I would fall asleep. "So now to business."

"I have to tell you what we're going to do."

"An excellent plan. No matter how many words are stuffed in my head, I have no idea how to address them to a dragon. Educate me."

She pursed her fine lips in prim disapproval. I always seemed to bring out the worst in her. "Narim's journal says the Elhim would stand on a high rock near the dragon's head. They would raise one arm high as they spoke their greeting, then let it drop to their side when the dragon acknowledged them, holding their bodies very still. Excessive motion or any gesturing with arms or hands was irritating to the dragons. The Elhim didn't know why . . . whether it was rude or distracting or what. And there's more." Lara pulled the tin box from her pack and extracted the journal, moving only close enough to the fire to enable her to read.

" 'The dragon doth hold her peace after her saying,' "

she read, " 'and lowers her head if the speaker doth not likewise.' " Lara screwed her face into a frown and directed it at me. "So you need to pause as you speak. The last thing you want is for the dragon to lower its head. The nostrils flare and the head is lowered just before it burns."

"Noted," I said. "No flared nostrils. No lowered heads. And I must pause between . . . words? Sentences? More to the point, how do we get the dragon to remember the rules?"

Lara stared at me without expression, the heat of the fire laying a most charming flush upon the smooth, tanned skin of her unscarred cheek. "There is a cistern just outside the cave. The Elhim have filled it with water from the lake and built a sluiceway from the cistern into the cave. On the day Narim brought you to me, he opened the sluiceway so it would fill the pool inside the cave."

"The water, yes. And the dragon?"

"Tomorrow I'll wake the kai, and we'll see if it will drink the water. Narim's journal says that the beasts can't resist the water once they've so much as touched it. If it drinks, I'll unlink the kai'cet. As this stone is not the dekai'cet—the stone bound to the kai in the beginning— I will then have no control over the beast."

"Then I shall say hello with appropriate pauses and without distracting gestures."

She nodded.

"And then he'll most likely roast me."

Lara clutched the journal fiercely to her breast and spoke through clenched teeth. "The kai do not have minds. They cannot speak. They are wild and dangerous and vicious. Why do you believe otherwise? The Elhim are the only race with these legends. There are no Senai stories of speaking dragons. In all your songs, you never knew one, did you? They are not mentioned in any Udema legends, nor in those from Florin or Aberthain or other kingdoms. And certainly there are no such tales from the Ridemark. You're a fool! Why will you throw your life away for a myth?"

"Because it cannot be myth. . . ." And there in the starry midnight, as the brandy and the fire burned the chill from my soul, and the night wind shifted into the south, a first warm zephyr to blunt the frosty edge of winter, I told Lara of Roelan. I told her things I had never told anyone: of the mystery I had lived, of experiences I had come to believe should not die with me if we should fail, as Lara assumed we would. Someone had to know what had happened to me and find out the truth of it, for whether it was gods or dragons, there was power and magnificence in the world that should not be allowed to vanish. And, inevitably, my tale led to Mazadine, and I told her of that, too.

She listened quietly, resting her chin on her fist that was clenched tightly enough to tell me she was not quiet inside herself. I poured out my life in an unceasing stream of words, whether from the prompting of wine or dread of burning or something else I could not yet name. I spoke more words that night than in the previous eighteen years together, and when I was done, I felt empty and at peace, sure against all reason that I had left my soul's legacy in hands that would take care of it. I had implicit trust in her honor if not her goodwill, and it seemed to make it easier that she despised me so.

A long time passed before Lara said anything. Perhaps

the dragons' pause was the same—deep, respectful consideration of all that had been said, even when babbled by a lower being. When she spoke at last, she offered no maudlin sympathy, no pity, no bracing words, no advice or shocked avowals of shared retribution that I could not possibly allow. All the pointless, well-meant offerings I had dreaded from the generous souls I had encountered since my release—Callia, Alfrigg, even Davyn—Lara eschewed. She understood, and she accepted, and her questioning was to answer her own purposes, not to seek remedy for me. I wished there were a way to tell her how grateful I was for her quiet listening, but I could think of no words that she would welcome.

"So it is not your hands that prevent you from taking up your music?" she said.

"Even if I could pluck the strings, it would be nothing but noise."

"And do you hope that by speaking to this kai, you'll somehow—"

"I have no more hope than you did when you heard your brother's offer of redemption. Hope was gone long ago. If I could just come to some understanding, gain some bit of knowledge that would tell me it was not all for nothing, that would be enough."

"So you think to avenge yourself on the king and the clan. Turn the dragons on them."

"What use is that? My cousin is paying a price far greater than I could ever extract from him. Goryx is not worthy of my honor. And where's the justice in taking revenge on the entire clan of the Ridemark? They'll pay enough if we take the dragons away from them."

She shook her head. "What kind of coward are you?"

"I'll confess to that crime. Someone told MacEachern that seven years of silence would destroy me. That one is the only target who might be worth my aim. Your brother knows who it was. MacEachern knows. In one moment, I want to strangle them until they tell me, and I can throw the bastard into a dragon's fire. But in the next, I want nothing more than to find a place to hide and forget that dragons exist. Coward. No doubt of it. But *I'm* the one who didn't listen when Devlin warned me, who didn't question enough. My pride kept my mystery private; my willful blindness kept me ignorant. What if I were to find out that it was all my own fault? How could I live with that?"

Lara was silent for a while, tapping her fingers on her jaw. Then, suddenly, words burst from her like a summer tempest. "You Senai always think you know everything. Listen to me. Every day after I was burned, I prayed that the one responsible would have his throat severed or his tongue cut out. I prayed his soul would rot and that he would live with the knowledge of it every day of his life. So if you believe that heartfelt prayers are answered, then it is I and not yourself or some mysterious betrayer that you must blame for your torment. I fully intended your destruction. And don't deceive yourself that I've given it up."

I was astounded. "But why? You didn't know I had anything to do with Keldar . . . with your burning. You still don't believe it. I'm not sure I do."

Her eyes glittered in the firelight. "Oh, I knew well who to blame. Your crime was committed long before I took the kai from Cor Neuill."

"I don't understand."

"I told you once that I'd heard you sing. Well, it wasn't only when you came to Cor Neuill before your arrest, but another time long before that. When I was eight years old, you sang in the camp at El'Sagor in Florin. . . ."

I remembered it. The first time I had ever sung for the Twelve Families. I was only sixteen. It had been a hot, dismal night, the sultry air pregnant with warning, constant lightning arcing in pink and purple forks across the heavy clouds, exploding in earsplitting thunder. The clansmen were determined to hear me, though, and did not disperse even when the storm broke in wild torrents of rain and turned the plain into a sea of mud. As ever in my years of service, I had no choice but to heed the call, though I had never felt so small as the moment I climbed up to sit on a rock wall in front of a thousand warriors in the midst of a storm from the eye of the world.

But at the very moment I touched my harp strings, the rain and wind ceased, as children called to silence by their mother's hand. Whispers of awe rippled through the crowd; though to me, a youth living in constant wonder, it was but another manifestation of my master's care. The clouds, flickering with soft veils of color, hung low and thick, as if the gods had sent them to shelter and protect me. On that night I never had to strain my voice to be heard as I might have in such a wide-open venue, but was able to shade and color it, and entwine it with the soft clarity of the strings to bring to life my vision. And on that night Roelan had graced me with music of such soaring beauty that even after so many desolate years my breath faltered in my chest and my empty soul ached to remember it.

"You sang that night of flying, of soaring on the wings

of the wind until the rivers were but threads winding through the green earth, until the sky was black velvet, and the uncountable stars sharp-edged silver. You made such an image in my head. I could feel the power of muscle and sinew beneath me, and the surge as the wings spread to capture the wind. Such wild and glorious freedom you promised that from that night I could think of nothing else. I took an oath on my father's sword that I would one day fly on the back of a dragon. I swore that I would take that young and handsome Senai singer with me to show him it was as beautiful as he said and that a girl of the Ridemark could make his holy visions come true. I loved you, Aidan MacAllister. I worshiped you. For five years your face and your voice and your images never left my mind. But when I finally got to fly, it was nothing like you said, for I fell out of the sky into the fires of the netherworld. Never has there been such hate in the world as that I've borne for you. If I weren't bound by my debt to Narim, you would already be dead."

I sat mute as the storm of Lara's bitterness broke over me. What else was there to do? To tell her I was sorry would be to trivialize what had happened to her, as if a few meaningless words from hated lips could cleanse the pain from her memory or the scars from her body. I wanted to tell her how I admired her strength and her honesty, and how I grieved for all she had lost, but she would think it mockery. And unless I could be sure that what I offered had nothing to do with pity or some clumsy, selfish attempt at absolution, I could offer her nothing else. I would not serve up the very dish that I despised.

But something else held me motionless and dumb as

we sat beside the dying fire, an awakening of such desire . . . unreasoning, unexpected, laughable had it not
been so terrifying in its magnitude that it left me trembling at the edge of control. I was thirty-eight years old,
and since I'd left the nursery, I had scarcely touched a
woman other than my mother. For twenty-one years I had
been consumed by mystery, and though I sang of human
love and physical desire, in my mind and body they were
always transformed into my single passion. My music
had been the sum of everything I knew, everything I felt,
everything I wanted. I was never lonely until it was far
too late to do anything about it. But on that night on the
hillside above Cor Talaith, when Lara told me that she
had once loved me—even with the affection of a mesmerized child—only then did I begin to understand how
much I had missed.

I had no idea how to offer love or how to recognize it
when it was offered to me, though I was fairly certain it
did not come from those who told you in the same breath
that they wanted to slit your throat. Neither our "accommodation" in pursuit of Narim's plan nor our evening of
soul baring gave me any leave to offer comfort with my
arms or any reason to think she would view such an attempt with anything but scorn and revulsion. Lara had set
me into absolute confusion, and I could not sort it out. So
I sat by the fire, and she sat in the darkness, each of us
alone behind barricades of silence, waiting for the dawn.

The morning came dull and mournful, the world swaddled in thick wads of cloud holding in the damp. Lara
was up before me, scattering the ashes of our fire with her
boot as ferociously as if they were enemy soldiers. If I

was confused, Lara seemed very comfortable with her anger and hatred. I called myself the hundredth name for a fool when I remembered the longings of the past night. No matter that they seemed to resurface with equal ferocity at my mind's touch. It was easier to bury such things in the light.

Lara struck out across the barren, rolling hillsides without a word, as if she didn't care whether I came with her or not. Indeed, I considered standing my ground and refusing to go until we got a few things settled between us, but I had the distinct sense that her straight back would have disappeared just as quickly over the next ridge. I sighed and trudged after her, pulling up the hood of my cloak against the cold rain that began, inevitably, to drip from the sky.

It was only an hour's wet and dreary walk to the bulge in the earth where Keldar lay. I tried to give some thought to our coming endeavor, but the immediate misery of wet boots and the visible enigma of Lara made such absurdities as conversations with dragons retreat into fantasy. Even when we descended a rocky stair into a broad, barren valley littered with scorched rock and skeletal trees, then dropped our gear beside a jagged, gaping maw in the face of a sheer cliff—even then I had trouble believing what we were about to attempt.

I tried again with my question of two days before. "Are we ready for this?"

Lara, clearly feeling no need for further discussion on any matter, pointed at the bag of my unfinished leather armor and began to don her own.

I dragged out the breeches and pulled them on, clumsily knotting the laces. "What's this stuff that makes it smell so vile?"

"Vigar helps fireproof the leather. The secret of its making belongs to the Twelve."

"As long as it works."

I had no helm or mask. They'd not been finished when we took flight. Lara pulled hers from her bag, glanced at me, and then threw them on the ground and walked into the cave. Her back dared me to say anything. As she couldn't see me do it, I smiled after her and wished fervently for more time. The soft rain pattered on her discarded gear and into my face as I looked upward and imagined the sun and blue sky that were hiding behind the heavy clouds. Though the peaks and high valleys still wore their smooth mantles of white, spring was lurking in the Carag Huim. I could feel it in the soft edge of the air, and hear it in the trickle of water beneath the skim of ice at my feet, and smell it in the scent of the rain as it stirred the damp earth to life. The world sat poised, waiting, and with all of my being I embraced it. Then I followed Lara into the darkness.

Chapter 19

"Be ready." Her quiet command from above my head was clear and steady. She might have saved herself the trouble of saying anything so useless. How could one prepare for what was to come? The last time I'd visited that vast, stinking cavern, I'd come a gnat's breath from dying. And on that day I wasn't even *trying* to listen.

I pressed my forehead against the cool stone and fought to quiet my sudden panic, to ignore the sighing rumble of dragon breath that came from beyond our rocky niche like the gusting precursors of a thunderstorm.

Put it all away ... lingering regrets, awakened desires, hunger for justice and revelation. You must listen. Everything depends on your listening ... on hearing what it has been given you to hear, even if it is the sound of your own death.

Beyond the monstrous breathing there was ... what? The bubbling of steaming mud pits, the trickling of the cascade on the cavern wall behind my puny shelter, the faint, harsh cry of a hawk from where the world lay beyond the cave entrance far to my right, the sharp echo of hoof on stone. Across the pitted floor from the pile of red rocks, two of the small, sturdy Carag Huim horses sipped peacefully from a pool of black water not twenty paces from the monster's head. They paid no heed to the bony jaws that could gape and breathe fire upon them or snatch them up, a tasty tidbit to soothe the hunger of dragon dreams. And of course there was the sound of Lara's stiff leather, creaking as she moved, the scuff of her boots as she climbed the rocky steps to stand upon the topmost boulder of our pile, the rampart of our little fortress so ominously streaked with black.

Then her clear voice sang out to rouse the monster. "Awaken, child of fire and wind. Wake from the sleep of dying and heed my command." The hot, humid air moved uneasily. "Wake from winter's death and take your place among the mighty of the world. I command you drink your fill of the water of fire and life."

Open your ears, Aidan MacAllister, and listen. It is the gift you have been given. . . .

I felt his breathing change from nature's rhythm to the tempo colored by waking will—a mighty will, pulsing through the cave. An ominous growl vibrated the stone at my head and beneath my feet. The cry would come at any moment like the blast of a thousand hellish trumpets. I had to be ready, but what preparation can mute the scream of a thousand tormented souls, the rolling thunder of a thousand hurricanes? I raised my arms to cover my head just as he bellowed. The sound reverberated through my very bones until I was sure they must be shattered to dust; searing pain tore through my chest like a hot knife used to carve out my heart. My knees gave way as I fought to keep from crying out. Through my closed eyelids, even sheltered as I was by the rocks, I could see the brilliance of fire. A shower of hot droplets fell from the air, but I forced myself still. If Lara was a victim of

the dragon's waking, I could do nothing for her, but if she
was not, then she would tell me when to come, and I had
to be able to hear it.

The first bellow subsided into a series of horrific
growlings and snortings, accompanied by rock-shattering
blows that could be nothing but the beast's mighty tail,
slamming into the cave walls. Astonishingly, in the midst
of it all, I heard the soft whickering of horses and an unconcerned clopping of hooves.

"MacAllister!" The quiet call pushed its way through
the throbbing of my head, and I let out the breath I'd held
since her last word. I hauled myself up three boulders
until my eyes were on a level with Lara's boots. Her
leather-clad hand held the bloodstone like a pulsing heart.
She called down to me softly. "The kai drinks. Come
quickly, but stay low."

I scrambled up to the top of the flat red rock, crouching as low as the bulky leather armor would allow, and
looked out over a poet's vision of the netherworld: steaming mud pits, brimstone-laden smoke obscuring the view
of burning rubble heaps, rotting carcasses. And the beast
itself, repulsive, horrid, its head not fifty paces from me,
the white-filmed eyes of scarlet flame, open and fixed in
malevolent, unseeing madness on the bloodstone, even as
it poked its snout into the black pool. Bursts of steam shot
upward as gouts of flame streamed from its nostrils.

Ludicrous. Lara was right. Intelligence and sentience
were far more likely present in the wild horses that shared
the pool or in the very rocks of the cave than behind those
devil's eyes.

"I'll move to the mouth of the cave," said Lara, keeping her arm stretched high and her eyes fixed on the

dragon. "We must put distance between you and the kai'cet. Count fifty; then I'll say the words that release my command. I can reclaim control if you don't wait too long to tell me. Do you understand? At the first sign of trouble, call my name."

"Thank you" was all I managed to say, my wit completely abandoning me as I looked up at the worry on her face and yearned—foolishly—that it was for me. "Fifty, forty-nine . . ."

Slowly she eased down from the rock, keeping herself and—more important—the bloodstone exposed to the wakened monster, calling to him, "Hear me, kai! Drink your fill and open the doors of your mind."

The dragon raised its head from the water to follow the movement of the stone, and it rumbled ominously, rippling the muscles of its towering shoulders and the long copper barrel of its throat, flexing its wings so that I caught glimpses of swirling green and gold gossamer. It could not stretch its wings fully, of course. No cavern in my knowledge was so large it could hold a dragon's wings unfurled.

". . . forty-one, forty . . ."

Lara disappeared into the gloom, and I was alone with the restless monster.

". . . thirty-four, thirty-three . . ."

One of the wild horses nipped at another who had pushed him away from the water. The dragon shifted its head toward them and the rumbling grew louder. The smoke from the corners of its mouth shot upward.

". . . twenty-three, twenty-two . . ."

The rumbling took on an edge of brass, tearing at my

head until my vision began to blur. I would have sworn that the dragon's red, leathery nostrils moved.

". . . fourteen, thirteen . . ."

Frantically I blinked my eyes and willed the throbbing aside. I had to be able to see. The horses cantered one after the other about the pool. What were the words? The nostrils flared wide. *Gods*. I stepped backward, ready to dive off my platform, but it was almost time.

". . . five, four, three . . ."

Crusted with jibari, the barnaclelike parasites that grew unchecked until blasted with dragon's fire, the monster's head rose up. The long, scaled neck twisted, the mouth gaped wide, revealing the brown leathery tongue. Another deafening bellow sounded, threatening to rob me of my reason. Every particle of my being was on fire. If the dragon spoke in its roaring, I would never be able to hear it. All my skill at listening would be of no use if I was deafened by the pounding of my blood. I could hear only the roar, different this time, a soaring note. Triumphant. Wild. He was free of Lara's bloodstone. I hadn't needed to count to know it.

The horses seemed disturbed at last and trotted across the floor of the cave. The dragon's head moved to follow them, and the nostrils flared again, spewing thin trailers of flame, but despite the sweat that broke out beneath my stiff and stinking leathers, there was no full blast of fire. The horses left the cave, and the dragon shifted its head back to the water and drank again.

Now. The time has come. Take the words and weave into them your memories . . . of Roelan and mystery . . . of joy and faith . . . of the years of dedication to one who was as a god to you. . . .

I raised my right arm. "*Teng zha nav wyvyr,* child of fire and wind, hear me." He heard me, though I could scarcely force my voice above a whisper. The head turned toward me, and the cruel, slavering mouth. As I opened my mouth to say the next words, the nostrils flared wide, once, then twice, and the low-pitched rumble changed to hatred . . . bestial fury . . . death . . . . I heard it even before the massive head began to dip.

"Lara!"

As my shout was annihilated by the blast, I turned and leaped from the rock. My hair burst into flame as I sailed downward beneath the arc of fire. Stumbling over the rocks as I landed, I smothered the back of my head with my gauntleted hands, then dropped to my back to ensure no untended spark found a path through the leather vest. A flash of red, boots narrowly missing my head; then Lara was screaming commands from above me. Flame lit the ceiling of the cavern, and the unending screech of the damned threatened to burst my brain from my head. I rolled to the side with my hands over my face and hot drops streamed from my eyes like tears, but they were dark as they soaked into my gauntlets. When silence fell, I struggled to all fours, then straightened and climbed slowly up the rocks.

She sat with her arms wrapped about her knees, beads of sweat running down her scarred cheek, the bloodstone gleaming in her hand. The dragon's eyes were closed, though remnants of his fury burned everywhere in the cavern.

"What happened?" she said, craning to see the back of my singed hair and charred vest while grinding out a spark with her boot. She wasn't even out of breath. "I couldn't see."

I told her.

"Fool! Why didn't you call sooner? I told you if the nostrils flared—"

"He didn't burn the horses. The nostrils flared, but his head never went down. Not until he was facing me."

"Are you saying the fire was aimed only at you? That the kai knew the difference between you and the horses? Impossible."

I flopped down on the rock beside her. "That's the way it seemed."

"This kai cannot see. It burns what moves, what disturbs it. Even after drinking the water."

"Except the horses."

"The horses were quiet. It didn't know they were there. It aimed at you because you spoke. I've brought every manner of deer and mountain sheep, wild pig and goat in here. They squeak and grunt and bleat, and it burns them all. Every one. Every time. The water made no difference."

"Horses are sacred to Keldar."

"Nonsense."

"Bring in the horses again. Wake him again and you'll see. He knows what's food and what's not."

She glared at me in angry disbelief. "And so it thinks you are food?"

"No. He tried to burn me because he hated me." Even as I said it, I was more convinced.

"You can't have it both ways, Senai. Four weeks ago you said it spoke to you 'with love.' Today it hates you. What's the difference?"

That, of course, was the essential question. "I don't know. The words. The weather. Today he was free of your stone." My head ached miserably. I was nauseous with the stink of dragon and carrion and the fireproof grease on the leather. The stink . . .

"He smells us." I wanted to shout it out, but my head hurt too fiercely.

"What?"

"That's the difference. Stupid of me not to think of it. He can smell the difference: horses, deer, pigs . . . Riders."

"We've never seen evidence they can smell anything. They burn and kill whatever moves unless it holds a bloodstone."

"And any Rider who wields a bloodstone—the thing that drives it mad—wears armor like this." I drew off my gauntlets. "They all smell alike. Who's to say dragons would kill any human if they weren't commanded so by their Riders?"

"You've no proof. You know nothing of dragons."

"We've no time for proof." I stripped off my vest and the breeches, the boots, and the greaves. "Wake him again."

"You can't mean this."

"Give me time to wash off the smell." I jumped down again and dodged a pile of burning bones to find my way to the waterfall. Standing in the shallow pool at its base, I scrubbed my skin and my clothes with handfuls of sand. Lara stood beside the pool watching my antics with angry astonishment.

"You're mad. Absolutely mad. If it weren't for the

armor your bones would still be burning. They'd hear your screams down in Cor Talaith."

"If it weren't for the armor, I'd be talking with Keldar."

"I won't do it."

"Lara"—I stepped out of the pool dripping and shivering though the cavern was not at all cold—"it's the third day. Your brother will have the legion at our door anytime now. If this is going to happen, if the gods—whoever they are—wish the dragons to be free, then we've got to find the way right now. Help me."

She hadn't moved, and I was closer to her than I had ever been, close enough to know that beneath her leather vest she was quivering, strung tight as an archer's drawn bowstring. Her face was carved from rose-colored granite, but her brown hair was shining and I wanted nothing more than to bury my face in it and forget about everything else in the world.

Lara, of course, brought me quickly back to my senses. She shrugged with a muttered curse and turned her back, climbing the red rock tower once more. I watched her go; then I set off an entirely different way, circling the steam pits and jumping cracks in the stone until I reached the edge of the dark pool, twenty paces from the dragon's head. The water trickled into it from Narim's stone trough, water stolen from the fiery lake of my visions. I settled myself on the stone and looked up at the copper-scaled head so close I could feel the hot breath from the raw, red nostrils. I did not look over my shoulder. No need. I just raised one hand briefly, then rested it in my lap again and held myself ready.

As I knew it would, her voice rang out soon after. "Awaken, child of fire and wind. Drink of the water of fire and live. Be troubled no more by the stone that galls you so sorely . . . and harm not the fools who put themselves at your mercy."

I smiled to myself and awaited the onslaught.

Chapter 20

I am a warrior born. My father was a Dragon Rider, seventh wingrider of the First Family of the Ridemark, and the Riders of our line had been no less than a tenth flanker for nine generations. In Gondar, in Eskonia and Florin, in the farthest provinces of Elyria, never did the line of Govin reap anything but honor and victory for the clan. From the first days of my memory I believed that the blood of the Ridemark flowed true within my veins and that I was destined to follow in the footsteps of my ancestors.

We did not live as the soft races did. My family—mother, brother, two grandmothers, two uncles, one aunt, and three cousins—slept in a tent twelve paces square. We owned only what we could carry on our backs as we followed the legion from one encampment of mud and beast-filth to another. Warriors cannot afford comfort; it brings weakness. I could not understand how anyone who slept under wood or stone held up his head without shame.

My father lived with his dragon. We were sure to see him once a year when he came to mate with my mother to keep her his wife. And he would always return if he heard any report of disrespect or disobedience from

Desmond or me. Whenever a dragon flew above our tent, I imagined it was his, and I held my head high.

My fighting skills came early. I stood still for no insult from my older brother or any Ridemark child. I did not lower myself to fight children of other races, but frightened them with my whip and did as I pleased. In the strip of mud between our tent and the next, I played at strategy and tactics with bits of wood and stone, choosing wild dogs and prowling cats as my enemies if I could find no one willing to stand up to me.

And on the day that Desmond began his training to prepare him for our family's rightful place as a Dragon Rider, I stepped forward, too. I told the Ridemaster that I was also ready, though I was only six instead of eight. I knew the Rider's oath and the Twelve Laws. I could hook my whip and climb anything. I could recite the names of our heroes to the tenth generation and the names of our enemies from the beginning of time, and I could argue the long grievances that festered in our hearts. But on that same day I learned the hard truth no one had bothered to tell me before: that females could render any service the Twelve Families required except ride to war on the back of a dragon.

For three days I raged and wept every time I saw Desmond take his whip from its hook and leave for his training in the lair. "Quit your mewling," my father told me, "or I'll marry you into the Twelfth Family, where men take multiple wives. You'll not be allowed to speak save with your husband's leave or show your shameful face without a veil." My mother slapped me and said, "What worthy warrior requires a beast to shed our enemies' blood? The swordwomen of your clan fight along-

side the men who are not Riders born. That is enough."
By the time I was eight I was resigned to the belief that
unyielding honor was the only true glory of a clansman.
Though I was not happy with it, it would have to do.

Then Aidan MacAllister, "beloved of the gods," came
to our camp. His music—his glorious music that my
clansmen swore came from the fire god Vanir himself—
turned my head inside out. I lived in the visions he made
that night. I felt my hair streaming behind me as I soared
through a world of wind and clouds and stars, and from
that time forward I could think of nothing but flying. No
warrior can be at peace when his master denies him the
weapon he was born to wield. I resolved to ride upon a
dragon, even if my clansmen cut out my heart for it. Because of Aidan MacAllister I forsook my oaths and betrayed my honor. I lied to my commander. I hid. I plotted.
I stole. And for the span of two heartbeats I owned the
wind and clouds and stars. Then came the terror and the
screaming and the fire.

Aidan MacAllister had cursed my life, and when I saw
him in Cor Talaith, I relived every moment of the horror
he had brought down on me—the day I fell from the sky
burning and knew it was just retribution for my sins. Is it
any wonder I hated him?

Narim told me the Senai had been a prisoner of the
Ridemark all those years since my fall, but I would not
believe it. No Senai singer, so weak, so soft, so cowardly,
could survive seventeen years in a Ridemark prison.
"He's been hiding," I said, "while I'm forced to live forever with what he's done." The everlasting ugliness I
wore on my face. A lifetime of exile from my clan. There
was no going back to the Ridemark. I had done the un-

forgivable, and the price on my head was almost as high as that on MacAllister's. I would not be killed or imprisoned, but have one hand cut off so I could not steal and one foot cut off so I could not run. I would live in servitude baser than any slave. I was sure that the despicable Senai was using the Elhim, weaving tales with his lying tongue to win their sympathy, making them believe he was their savior so they would protect him from our justice. "He was a spy," I claimed in my unending arguments with Narim. "He was sent into Ridemark camps by Senai nobles to corrupt our honor."

So why did I not kill him? If will alone could shed blood, MacAllister's veins would have been emptied at my first glance. But I was bound to Narim's wishes, a sacred debt because he had saved my life. It was enough to drive me crazy, so sure was I of my hate.

But then the singer came to live with me, and all my beliefs were confounded. I scorned him for huddling by the fire, and he offered to share his tea. I reviled him for his cowardice at the kai's lair, and he made me soup. I ridiculed his noble ancestry, and he laughed at himself and cleaned my hearth. I drove him unmercifully in his schooling, and he devoured it as if I'd gifted him with jewels. No matter how I goaded him, he would not get angry and free my revenge from Narim's bond. I had never known a man of such gentle ways and teasing humor, and I could only chalk it up to weakness, because I had no other way to explain it. I counted him pitiful . . . until the night I first saw his mangled hands.

I remembered well the long, slender fingers that had touched the strings of his harp and drawn forth his cursed visions—everything about the tall Senai youth who had

corrupted my soul was imprinted on my memory—and I
knew no accident and no disease could have transformed
them so precisely into that hideous ruin. It made me think
Narim's story might be true, and where I had seen only a
hated enemy, I began to see a man.

I despised my weakness and redoubled my effort to
prove him a fraud. But I found steel beneath his soft-
spoken manner. I could not break him. Despite his struggles with the tasks I set him, he lived with everything of
gentleness and grace. So I decided that, though I could
not trust him and could not forgive him, I could not let
him be sent back to those who had done him so ill.

Then came the night by the kai's lair, the night he
poured out all of himself in his fear and in his longing,
and I was at last convinced that everything I had seen of
him was truth. I tried to persuade myself that I still hated
him. To give it up was to forswear vengeance for everything that had happened to me, and to lay open my own
actions . . . oh, curse the world forever . . . like cutting
through ripe fruit and finding only black and rotted pulp.
But I could not maintain my hatred, though I forced myself to say the words where he could hear them, as if another hearing could make them real. I wanted to make
him fear me, as was right and proper. But my truest hope
was that he would tell me one more time that he had not
meant to do me harm. I wanted him to agree that people
could cause the most dreadful horrors with the best of intentions, and that my confession had made him see things
in a new light. I wanted him to absolve himself of his
crime and thereby absolve me of mine. But he retreated
into silence, and I damned myself for a fool.

Narim, my old friend, my only friend, how could you

do this to me? You knew what he was. You knew the utter impossibility. You have the wisdom of five hundred years. How could you not guess what would happen? What warrior weeps when she sets out to do battle?

And so came the morning of our venture into the kai's lair, the moment Aidan stripped off his armor and sat unprotected in the path of the dragon fire. I stood on the rock in the lair of the blind kai, and for the second time that day I raised the kai'cet—the bloodstone—and called out its power. "Awaken, child of fire and wind. . . ." The kai bellowed with fury, crazed at being dragged from sleep again.

The fires blazed, reflecting in the still pool until it glowed orange like the lake of its origin, revealing the man who sat beside it, holding his belly as if a warrior had speared him in the gut. His eyes were fixed on the kai's head. He would have no escape if the beast belched fire. As for the beast, its mindless hatred was aimed at me. For as long as the kai'cet and I held sway, MacAllister was safe. If he was right, then once I moved far enough away and released control, he would be able to speak to the beast. It would not happen. Aidan MacAllister was going to die.

Well and good. What do I care? He is Senai. My enemy. Let this playacting be done with.

But I had given Narim my word to do as the Senai commanded, so I climbed down from my perch and held the kai'cet high. I moved quickly toward the cave mouth, screaming at the monster to keep his attention on me. The kai lashed his tail against the stone, drumming the walls until it sounded as if the doom of the world was come.

The round opening high on the western wall, where Narim had first brought MacAllister to see the dragon, disappeared in an avalanche of dirt and rocks, its earthen roof collapsed by the force of the blows.

"Hold your burning!" I screamed, as the nostrils gaped and arrows of orange flame darted from them, blackening the ceiling of the cavern. MacAllister did not move, only watched. I knew he was afraid and in pain, yet he neither cried out, nor begged me to stop it, nor ran, nor hid, nor covered his eyes.

"Drink, beast!" I yelled. "Taste the water of life!"

The head came down as if jerked by an invisible tether, yielding to my will, hiding the man in a cloud of steam as its snout dipped into the water.

Now. It has to be now.

I blew softly on the bloodstone until it glowed so brightly my gauntlet looked drenched with blood. Then I whispered the words it had taken me two years to wrest from my clan: sneaking, spying, creeping about like a lair rat until I learned the secrets denied me because I was not a man. *"Ze vra deshai, kai."* I release you from my command, slave.

Halfway between the cave mouth and the boulder pile was a deep crack in the floor with a wide ledge just below its rim. One could stand on the ledge and duck below the level of the floor to hide or peek over the edge to watch the dragon from safety. The stinking smoke venting from the depths of the crevice would mask my smell. While the kai bellowed, I dropped onto the hidden ledge, then raised my head to peer across the floor of the cave.

It was perhaps a hundred paces from my hiding place to the pool. Though I could see only MacAllister's back and a bit of his right side, I had a clear view of the kai towering over him. It stretched its neck and tossed its head, spewing short, hard bursts of red-orange fire and smoke. The man stretched his right arm upward.

Be still, fool. But I had no gemstone to command men. Beneath the constant muted roar of menacing breath and fire, of hissing scales and moving air that never ceased when the kai was awake, I heard the man's soft words as clearly as if we were sitting at my own hearth. *"Teng zha nav wyvyr . . ."*

The dragon stopped in midstretch, and began to move its head from side to side on its long neck like some huge, ugly flower swaying with the wind. Left to right and back again . . . searching . . . searching . . .

Holy gods, Aidan . . . be silent . . . don't move. But my will was not enough to stop him.

"Hear me, noble Keldar."

The red snout opened wide, and the neck curled downward. I could not bear to watch, yet I could not hide. The monstrous head shifted right, then left. Hunting.

"I crave speech with thee, wind treader, cloud splitter, lover of your earthbound brothers who fly on four hooved legs through the lower airs."

The words of the ancient speech took life from the singer's tongue, somehow grown wider and deeper than the dry syllables we of the Ridemark use. He believed the music of his heart was dead, but he was wrong. I heard it in that hour as clearly as I had heard it when I was eight.

I held my breath as the dragon tossed its head again, spit a geyser of fire upward so that sparks rained down from the cavern roof, then roared until the earth shook. But I did not close my eyes.

MacAllister, his face still turned upward, held his hands over his ears and, when the cry subsided, spoke again, his clear voice strained, but unwavering. "My hearing bursts with thy call, mighty Keldar, until I am drowned with it. Softly, wind treader. A youngling am I in my weakness. As the whispered air of the burning season enter my heart, lest I be crushed by the power of thy voice."

The kai dipped its head sharply toward the man; the red slits in the snout gaped, pouring out yellow smoke. But instead of belching fire, the beast lowered its massive chest and its barrel-shaped neck until they rested on the rocks and bones. It might have been returning to sleep, but its blind, wild eyes remained open, and its head was angled away from the man, as if turning an ear his way or ensuring that no escaping thread of fire singed the one to whom it listened. *Impossible.*

After a pause, the soft, deep voice began again. "I am the human servant of thy brother Roelan, graced in my youth with the gentle breath of his spirit. . . ."

MacAllister's voice dropped out of hearing as the dragon grew quiet and still. I dared not creep closer and risk distracting the beast, for even the tiniest spurts of flame could sear the singer's flesh from his bones if the dragon moved its head. A hiss of steaming breath spewed from the beast, and in the midst of it a low, wavering noise, a grating sound that made my teeth hurt and my gorge rise. Never had I heard such sounds from a dragon, but they were not speech—not even the "pleasant variety of sounds" Narim had described in his journal. How long would MacAllister remain in such danger before he could admit that he had failed?

It was over very quickly. The kai's three sets of eyelids—the transparent ones, the soft green ones, and the hard copper-colored ones—slid over its diseased eyes, and the hissing breath took on the low rumble of dragon sleep. The grating noise was gone, and so, I supposed, were the hopes of the Elhim. The success of the day was survival. Yet moments passed, and then more. MacAllister did not move. He needed to get away. Oftimes the beast would shift in its sleep, and if he was in its path . . .

I scrambled out of my hiding place and slipped cautiously between a rotting carcass of a herd beast and a slime-filled pit toward the singer and the dragon and the pool. "MacAllister!" I called softly. Not a twitch or a shiver.

Soon I was running, jumping across jagged cracks in the stone, yet keeping my footsteps light. "Aidan. Are you all right?" Only when I dropped to my knees beside him and felt the beat of blood in his scarred wrist did I know he was alive. Though I wanted to scream at him, I forced my voice low. "Get up, fool. Do you want to die here? It shifts its head while it sleeps." I gripped his arm and shook him until his head came up. His dark eyes that knew so much of horror and despair were pools of grief.

"Move your sorry bones away or the kai will fry you like bacon," I said. Imaginary flames crawled up my back.

The singer shook his head and whispered, "He won't."

Damned stubborn, cursed man. "Just because you were lucky while it was awake doesn't mean—"

"He's dying. He won't move anymore."

"Of course it's not dying. Not any time soon, at least. Narim told you. The kai go to ground after an injury to die or heal. We think—"

"He can't heal. He's broken inside, diseased beyond help. That's what I felt from him the first time when Narim brought me through the tunnel. I wasn't dying; *he* was. The only thing that's kept him alive is yearning for his brothers and sisters to sing him on his way. If only I could do it." MacAllister stood up slowly, rubbing his hands along his upper arms as if he were cold and gazing on the sleeping dragon like a drunkard gazes on his wine-skin. "I tried to comfort him."

"Are you saying the kai told you this?" Without thought I moved away from him, and his eyes shifted from the dragon to me.

"You think I'm mad."

"I heard no speech from the kai."

MacAllister shook his head. "Hearing? No, I suppose not. I've never . . ." He rubbed his brow with the back of one hand. "It was very . . . subtle. I got only part of it. But I'm not mad. Or at least no more so than I've been since I was eleven." He smiled then, a sweet, sad smile that wiped away the lines pain had written on his handsome face. "I'm just a bit more tired."

The kai lay still, but the bursts of fire and smoke from its nostrils told me it was no nearer death than in any hour in the past three years.

"I'm leaving," I said. "If you can bear to part from your charming friend, you can come, too. Then you can tell me what else it said." And I would weigh it well, for it would either be lies or lunacy. But I would not look into Aidan MacAllister's eyes while I judged him.

It had been early morning when we entered the lair, and I was sure that no more than two hours had passed, but the sky was dark when we stepped out of the cave.

Though the rain was only a dismal drizzle, the clouds
boiled purple and black, and from the direction of Cor Talaith orange lightning flickered unceasingly. Deafening
thunder pealed through the mountains, caught by the
jagged ridges and bounced from one to the other. The
stench of burning set us both to coughing.

"We'd best find a cave of our own, or we'll have to
take shelter with Keldar," said MacAllister. "The storm
will be on us in moments."

But as he hoisted the pack he'd dropped just inside the
cavern, I watched the sky to the east. I listened to the thunder and the roar of the wind beyond the ridge, the wind
that moved no tree limb within our sight. "It's no storm,"
I said, the truth hammering home with the power of a
dragon's tail. "It's Desmond." The clan had come.

Chapter 21

The sun hung between the lower edge of the clouds and the dark horizon, casting long, angular shadows as MacAllister and I walked down into the hellish ruin that had been the Elhim's sanctuary for more than eight hundred years. Heavy rain had left the valley floor a sea of hot, black mud, and the air was clogged with choking steam from charred rocks quickly cooled. Nothing within our sight lived—no blade of grass, no tree, no bird or insect. Not the least sign remained that any creature had ever lived in Cor Talaith. The end of the vale, where the granaries, the smithy, and the woodshop had stood, was barren. We slogged through the ankle-deep mud, thinking only to get to the warrens to see if any Elhim yet lived.

During the assault we had sheltered in a rocky cleft half a league from the kai's lair, not daring to stay too close to the lair, lest the attacking dragons discover their kin and draw the Riders to him. The Senai had spent the next four hours with his head buried in his arms. We could not escape the constant screaming of the kai wheeling overhead, and if a single dragon's cry opened him to madness, then the sounds of a dragon legion in full assault must surely drive him there. But no sooner had the skies fallen silent than Aidan jumped to his feet, ready to search for survivors.

"Not yet," I told him. "If there's to be a third wave, it will begin in less than half an hour. And even if they're done, we can't go in until it cools down. The rock would melt our boots right now."

"They don't understand it," he said, leaning his head against the split cliff wall that formed our haven. "All these years we've used them to kill our own kind, and they don't understand why we don't eat each other, too."

"Did the kai tell you that today?" Sometimes he had me fooled into thinking him sane; then he would start talking about dragons.

"No. Roelan told me long ago. I just didn't have the words to understand." He pulled his cloak tight around himself. "The battle's over; I can't hear them anymore. The rain will have the ground passable by the time we get there."

In truth I had no desire to wait.

The Riders had found the Elhim's cavern. The cliffs around its mouth were black and scarred, monstrous boulders, burned and shattered by dragons' tails, blocking three-quarters of the entrance. As MacAllister had surmised, by the time we hiked into the valley the rain had cooled the rocks enough to touch. We scrambled over the rubble, our boots slipping on rain-slick soot, until we could wriggle through the narrow opening and drop from the boulder pile into the cave.

We had no need for a torch. Fires still raged in several tunnels. Careful to avoid the smoldering ash piles, we covered our faces with our wet cloaks and picked our

way across the charred hollow that had been the refectory
and gathering hall. No use to look for anyone there. On
the far side of the great room we saw the first blackened
bones. At the same moment we both yelled out, "Hello!
Is anyone here?" No answer.

We took separate routes through the warren, turning
back only when heat or flames blocked our way. I found
five or six more corpses, all burned in varying amounts.
I had no great affection for most Elhim, but they had sheltered me and allowed Narim to care for me. They did not
deserve this. Neither Narim nor Davyn were recognizable
among the dead. I straightened the charred bodies, crossing their hands upon their breasts as was the Elhim custom and left them where they lay.

Returning from one blocked corridor, I heard voices
and hurried down the passage that led to the lake of fire.
The Senai was kneeling by two corpses . . . no, only one
was a corpse. The other gripped the singer's cloak with a
blackened hand, croaking out the last words of his hateful life.

". . . told him . . . told him . . . best to leave it be.
They'll never remember. They'll kill us all. But he won't
let it rest. He's mad, and all of us are servants of his
scheme. His plan is not what you think. He calls you
Dragon Speaker"—Iskendar spewed his bile in death
even as he had in life—"but he makes you Death Bringer.
You trust him, but he will betray you again, as he betrayed us all. The girl knows his schemes . . . his
plans . . . You will destroy us all." The old man wheezed
and struggled for breath. "Ask him why there is an Elhim
named for every dragon. Ask him what he found in
Nien'hak. Ask him how the Twelve knew . . ."

"What betrayal?" said MacAllister when Iskendar stopped. "How the Twelve knew what? Iskendar, tell me. . . ."

The old crow, ignoring the Senai's pleading, gave his death shudder and lay still. The second corpse would be Nyura. The two bitter old fools had rarely been more than two steps apart.

The Senai loosened the blackened claw from his cloak and laid it and its fellow gently across Iskendar's breast. He began to speak, so softly I could scarcely hear him. "Across the ages walks the race of One, the Single, the Children of the Whole, never alone, but joined since the dawning. . . ." The words of the Elhim death hymn. He probably knew the death hymns of every race. The words should be sung, of course, and on the second discourse he tried. "Across the valley of time walks the race of One. . . ." Ten, fifteen tones of unmatched purity, such beauty in his voice that I could almost glimpse the welcoming vale for myself. But he faltered. His voice cracked and the music fell sour in the hot, stinking air. Bowing his head, he cupped his terrible hands at his shoulders in apology. "I'm sorry . . . so sorry."

I stood silently, waiting for him, trying to think what I was to tell him. He would want to know of Narim's plotting. Perhaps at last he would be a proper man and figure out the truth of the world. How you could trust no one. How kindness and care were but the pretty face on scarred ugliness.

But when he got to his feet and noticed me standing by the wall, he had only one question. "What was he talking about . . . Death Bringer?" From the look of him you'd have thought he had torched the old Elhim himself and was asking me to mete out his punishment.

"He was a mad old man," I said. "He was dying. You can't endure a dragon's fire and speak anything of sense."

My words hung weakly in the air. MacAllister stared at me unblinking until I had to turn away.

"Come on," I said, starting down the passage toward the lake. " Let's find a place to spend the night. I'll tell you more of Iskendar and his plots and his hatred of Narim, and you can tell me what you think you learned from the kai." He followed without argument. How could anyone be so naive?

We had counted no more than fifteen bodies in the ruin. No way to tell how many more Elhim had been completely consumed in the attack, but the tracks on the lakeshore told us that many—most of them, perhaps— had escaped. Narim had escaped, I had no doubt.

We made camp in a sheltered cove a quarter of the way around the lake, where there was a broad stretch of sand. MacAllister fell onto the sand without speaking and was asleep before I could get my pack off my back. I made a fire, cooked barley soup, and sat leaning against the rocks, wondering what in the name of Vanir the fire-tamer I was doing.

Glaring sunlight scorched my eyes, forcing me awake. My back ached. I was still sitting up, and flies were gorging themselves on my untouched soup that had spilled into the sand. MacAllister was kneeling by the lake bathing his face and head. I considered pretending I was still asleep—perhaps for an entire day or until the Senai tired of waiting and took his inconvenient questions away. I had no reason to stay with a madman who believed he spoke to beasts.

As I watched him through the slits of my eyes, he removed his shirt and dipped it in the lake, then squeezed it out and spread it on a rock in the sun. In all the weeks of our sharing my hut, even on the night we left him hanging for the wolves, I had never gotten a good look at his back. When I saw my clansmen's work, it was as well I had eaten none of my soup the night before. MacAllister came away from the lake, dried his face and hair with the hem of his cloak, and stretched out on the sand on his stomach.

Only after an hour, when he had put his shirt back on and poked up the fire, did I let my eyes come open. I felt dirty. Shamed. But to a man or woman of the Ridemark, a life debt is a chain that binds beyond reason, beyond decency. I had no choices.

"I've seen more tracks up a gully on the other side of the lake," he said when he saw me stirring. "I think most of the Elhim got away. They must have heeded your warning beacon. Now, tell me. . . ." His face was expectant. His questions had not been washed away with the previous day's filth. Best to attack, lest I end up in a position with no escape.

"Iskendar and Nyura and their circle had not left Cor Talaith in a hundred fifty years and swore they never would. It's their own fault they got caught here."

"I don't understand what Iskendar was trying to tell me. He spoke of plots . . . of destroying everyone. What is Narim hiding?"

"Narim has been trying to protect you from Iskendar and the others. That's why he had to be so brutal, so secretive, why he had to stand back while you fell into despair. All those weeks he stayed away from you for guilt at not telling you of his hopes. If you didn't believe you were dead, then Iskendar wouldn't either. But for some reason, the old crows decided you were still a threat. Something Nyura told you one morning out by the bridge. Narim didn't know exactly what was said. . . ."

At last I had told MacAllister something he didn't know. "About Donal," he said. "Nyura told me that my cousin Donal was a prisoner of the Gondari."

"Well, whatever you said on that day made them believe you were not . . . incapable . . . as they wanted you to be. They were afraid of you. They had to be sure you wouldn't try to help, and when they came to believe you would . . ."

". . . they decided to kill me. I understood that already."

"Exactly. So Narim sent you to stay with me."

"So what was Iskendar talking about? What Narim found . . . his plan . . . betrayal . . ."

I picked at a hard lump of bread I'd pulled from my pack, and it crumbled in my hand. "Narim allowed you to go into Cor Neuill even though he knew there was a risk you would be recognized. He had to see what happened when you were near the dragons. And then he brought you to Cor Talaith to save your life. There's plenty of guilt to go around, and Iskendar wanted to make sure you felt it. It was my fault that Desmond suspected the Elhim. It was your fault that his suspicions were confirmed. As soon as Desmond knew you were here, Cor Talaith was doomed."

"I shouldn't have come."

"Narim knew you would never agree to stay here if you suspected what might happen. That's why he hid it from you. That was his secret. So in a way Iskendar was right. Narim betrayed you by letting you go into such danger. By lying to you. He betrayed the Elhim by allowing you to come here when he knew the likely consequences."

"Death Bringer . . . Why did he say that I would destroy us all?"

"What do you think would happen if the dragons were taken away—freed? Wars of vengeance. Invasion—barbarians pouring over the mountains. Iskendar believed a human wouldn't think of the consequences. But mainly Iskendar hated Narim. He held Narim responsible for this attack, and even as he died he wanted revenge. There's no surer way to defeat Narim's purpose than to make you mistrust him."

"How can I trust him?" He ran his fingers through his dark hair. "Lies, secrets, deception . . . you've not given me much to work with."

That was certainly true. I wasn't good at this word twisting. "You can either believe the one who tried to kill you or believe the ones who saved your life. Narim wishes you no ill. He and Davyn and Tarwyl and the others have risked everything to protect you. I'll swear it on whatever you choose. By my honor as a daughter of the Ridemark, I'll swear it."

I did not look away as the Senai stared at me, weighing my truth. Everything I'd said was truth. Just not all of the truth. But I was no Udema shopkeeper who could not meet the tax collector's eyes as I fingered my skimmed-off tally in my pocket. I didn't know whether he believed me or just decided there was no purpose in asking me any more, for he gathered up his meager provisions and jerked his head toward the track that led up the ridge beyond the lake of fire. I stuffed my food bag back into my pack and took out after him.

After half an hour of hard climbing, MacAllister broke his silence. "How old is Narim?"

I was surprised at the question, so surprised I couldn't think of a convenient lie. So I revealed what Narim would rather have kept secret. "Older than you can imagine."

"It was Narim who poisoned the lake and enslaved the dragons, wasn't it? All those years ago. He had studied the dragons, and he was clever, and he figured out how to do it, thinking he was saving his people."

"He was only sixteen. An infant by Elhim standards. They were desperate. He never meant it to be forever."

I was ready to bring out all the arguments Narim had concocted over the years to explain what he had done, but I didn't need them. MacAllister nodded his head and kept walking. "Whatever Narim's guilt, it doesn't matter. We all have our guilts. You can tell him I'll do whatever I can."

One more time I named him a weakling fool. But only in the front of my mind.

The day seared our eyes with its brightness, the drifts of dirty, ice-crusted snow scattered across the lower slopes of the Carag Huim receding even as we passed.

MacAllister was quiet as we walked. His face was hard, his shoulders tight, and I had to double-step to keep up with him. What was he thinking? He replied to my

inane comments about the path and the terrain and the
weather with the fewest possible words.

We stopped at midday to eat and rest, and I decided
we'd best get clear on our plans before we came to settled lands. "Since this kai didn't tell you what to do next,
we'll have to find Narim."

MacAllister looked up in surprise. "Oh, but he did tell
me."

"The dragon? It spoke to you?"

"Yes. Certainly."

"The journal said they formed words—a variety of
sounds that made a language—like men and Elhim do. I
heard nothing like that."

MacAllister frowned thoughtfully. "It's hard to describe. You're right; it was nothing like the journal said. I
spoke as we practiced . . . I asked what I had to do to set
the others free, but his answer . . . it was certainly not
words as we think of them." His wonder at his own telling
erased the dour expression he had worn since Cor Talaith.
"It's just been so long . . . he's so wild . . . his words have
become mere patterns of tone and inflection. Only slight
resemblance to speech. More like music. I had to shape
the sounds into words myself, so I missed a great deal, I
think."

Easy to guess that his madness would take the form of
music. He was so calm and sure of himself . . . and it was
all so stupid. I jabbed my knife into a slab of hard cheese
and almost sliced off my finger. "What did he answer,
then? Did he tell you a magic spell? Or perhaps he says
you must ask each dragon politely what's needed to set it
free?"

"No." His gloved fingers fumbled idly with a dried

apple while his mind went back to that fetid cavern. "He knew all about what happened when I was in prison, as I grew . . . weak . . . and Roelan grew wild. He seemed to know I couldn't sing again, though that part was confusing, and he kept saying something like 'let the desert loose the wind.' He said I must 'find my own'—that I must hunt down his 'brother bent with the sadness of the world.' I think he means me to find Roelan."

"It would make sense, would it not? Since you were such close friends."

MacAllister laughed, an exasperated, hopeless laugh, but filled with good humor. "It might make sense to a dragon, but he didn't tell me how to identify Roelan, or how to speak to him without the lake water, or what he meant when he said I had to become Roelan's 'third wing.' "

Shock had me on my feet. "Become his—" I choked before saying the words. No one outside the Ridemark was to hear them. No one. If any clansman spoke them carelessly, even in his own tent, his tongue would be severed instantly by his wife or his children or his parents.

"You know what it means," said the singer softly, watching me stuff the cheese and my waterskin into my pack and throw the bag over my shoulder.

"You mustn't say those words ever again. If any clansman heard you, it would be far worse than what you've suffered already . . . and for me, too. They would think I told you. Damnation! Forget them." I started down the path again. If I could have run from him, I would have done it.

He caught up with me quickly. "You've not said them. Keldar did, and I have, and if you tell me what they mean,

I won't have to say them again. If you don't tell me, then all this is wasted."

"You don't understand."

"I think I do."

"It's part of a ritual—the most sacred, the most secret of all the Ridemark rituals. It's worse than death to betray the words. I can't do it. I won't."

He stopped me, forcing me to look at him, at his dark eyes that had once been filled with holy visions . . . at the mangled hands that rested so heavily on my shoulder. "I have lived worse than death, and my feet still walk the earth. You've done the same. You've forsworn your vengeance . . . and I know what that means to one of the Ridemark. You've saved my life at the cost of your own redemption and your everlasting guilt, because you've sworn to do as Narim asks. You know he would insist that you tell me."

Had Narim been with us, I would have broken his neck. I wanted to spit out the gall in my mouth. "It is the rite performed after a Rider dies, when a new Rider is mated to the kai and its bloodstone."

"And the words?"

"The kai is surrounded by Riders with bloodstones. It is controlled and goaded to fury until it spews out its deadliest fire, white-hot fire that can melt stone and incinerate an entire forest in one breath. The words—the seven invocations—are said when the chosen Rider takes the dekai'cet—the bloodstone that has been forever bound to that dragon—and he walks into the fire, taking control of the kai, becoming one with it so that his will becomes the will of the beast, and his body burns with the inner fire of the beast, and the beast will bow down when he steps close and allow him to ride. Does that please you? Are you satisfied?"

Understanding dawned on his face . . . and resignation. I wanted to hit him, curse him, anything to make that expression go away. He hitched his pack higher on his back and walked down the trail. I followed after, sick at heart, wanting to forget the conversation, to pretend I had never spoken. But I could not.

"You must understand that it's impossible. You don't have Roelan's dekai'cet, and there's no possibility, absolutely no possible way, for you to get it. You can command a dragon with any bloodstone, but to join with it, to step into its fire, you must have the dekai'cet, the one that has been bound to it since the beginning, since the Elhim first controlled them. We've never been able to bind a second stone to a dragon, whether we have its dekai'cet or not. The rite never works for a second stone. So you can't do it."

"I won't need a bloodstone."

"Of course you need a bloodstone. Without its protection, you'd burn. You'd—"

"The absence of the bloodstone must be the key to setting them free. To create the bond . . . to become one . . . without the stone. He said I must go as a youngling. In nakedness, he said, but I knew he wasn't referring to clothes. He doesn't understand clothes."

By the time I recovered enough wit to close my mouth and follow him, his long legs had reached the bottom of the slope, and he had disappeared through a rocky tunnel that led into the wild western lands of Catania, toward Cor Neuill and the other dragon camps in Elyria and beyond, in search of the beast he had believed was his god.

Chapter 22

"Why don't the blasted twits come back?" I threw my sword onto the dirt floor and it skidded into the stone firepit, no doubt nicking the exquisitely perfect edge I'd just spent most of a day giving it. "How long can it take to get a look at four dragons?"

"I don't particularly like the waiting," said the singer quietly, "but I can't say I'd rather be poking around a dragon camp myself just now."

"You—"

"I know. I'm a sniveling coward not worthy of being called a man." Aidan MacAllister sat in the corner of the grimy hovel, his face expressionless, his hands quiet in his lap, exactly where he'd put himself that morning.

"How can you sit there and do nothing for eight hours on end? You're driving me mad."

He'd said not a word until I'd spoken to him. He'd not moved, not occupied himself with anything I could see, yet his eyes had stayed open, staring into nothing. It was infuriating. While I could think of nothing but climbing to the top of the sod roof and screaming at every Ride-mark clansman in Elyria to come and fight me, the Senai sat on the damp, filthy floor as calm as an old granny.

"Practice," he said. "I wouldn't recommend the schooling though."

"Pitiful," I snapped, and for the fiftieth time that day I stepped outside the door of the hut into the rutted dung pit that passed for a road. I peered into the distance, watching for any Elhim approaching the cluster of hovels the locals called the village of Wyefedd. It was far too much of a name for the five filthy shacks and the half-burned "stable"—a lean-to that had housed no beast but rats for at least ten years. For one who had been born in a palace, MacAllister certainly knew more about the nastiest places in the kingdom to bed down than any Rider would ever guess.

Wyefedd lay just north of Vallior, outside the small dragon camp of Fandine, which housed dragons and Riders who had been injured in battle. Since leaving the mountains of the Carag Huim, we had been working our way toward Vallior and the large dragon camps of central Elyria, staying on back roads, avoiding cities and people and the persistent Ridemark patrols. Since there was no reason to believe "his" kai, the one he named Roelan, was any more likely to be there than at Cor Marag, or L'Clavor, or Aberthain, or in any of the twenty other dragon camps throughout the kingdom, MacAllister decided that we would visit Cor Neuill last. Though it was the first Ridemark encampment we passed, the singer's sneaking visit with the leather merchant would ensure that it was closely watched.

We traveled at night. During the day we slept out in stables or sheds or sometimes in sleazy inns where a whisper to the landlord would get you a room that no royal guardsman or Ridemark officer would ever be allowed to find.

"I thought you were welcomed everywhere, fed and lodged without having to pay," I'd said to MacAllister one morning as we lay down in a deserted, sod-roofed shack next to an abandoned coal pit. "How do you know about these vile places?"

"Because those who lived in these circumstances had the same claim on me as the high commander of the Ridemark."

The Senai would answer whatever I asked of him, but no longer anything beyond it. Everything had changed since the cursed Iskendar had planted his vile seeds. Though no less gently spoken, Aidan MacAllister had closed himself up again. I believed he would name me his ally, but it was clear he no longer trusted me. Fair enough.

We had found Davyn and Tarwyl on the Vallior road ten days after leaving Cor Talaith. Or perhaps it is more accurate to say they found us. On a sultry dawn as we approached the turnoff to Grimroth Lair, our first dragon camp, we narrowly escaped running into a roadblock that had sprung up in the night. As we lay panting in a dry hedgerow, caked with dust and sweat after a half-league sprint down a wagon road, I told the Senai for the hundredth time that we needed to find Narim. "He'll know what to do. He's had enough years to think about every possibility. Even if we get to a camp with our heads intact, how do you propose to get inside? One slip will have you back in your cell."

MacAllister shook his head. "I can't wait for Narim to decide what bit of his plan to reveal to me today. He started me on this venture, but I'm the one who has to finish it."

"Then why am I here? I've no intention of risking my neck for your private adventure. It's only my swearing to Narim that keeps me with you. If you're not interested in his plan, I'll be off in a heartbeat. But what would you do then? Once you get inside a camp, how do you think to keep the dragons from cooking you while you figure out what to do? Will you sing to them?"

We were both tired from constant hiding and running, and we hadn't even begun the search. He just didn't see the impossibility of it, and I couldn't make my tongue keep still. I wanted him to lash out, to explode in anger at the cruel things I said to him, to demand to know what I was hiding, so perhaps I would have no excuse to hide it anymore. But all he did was bury his anger. "Of course you're right. Send him whatever message you want. But I'm going ahead." I wanted to kick him.

We backtracked half a day's walk to a wretched little market town called Durvan. Half the houses and shops were burned rubble, and the other half were worse: dark little hovels with sagging sod roofs, rotting timbers, and filthy rugs hung over the doors to keep out the rain and wind. Pigs rooted in the lanes, and people emptied slops jars right outside their doors. I never could see why people would think such places were better than tents. No one in the town would look you in the eye, and no one looked as if they'd had a decent meal in a year.

Just at the edge of the houses sat the Bone and Thistle, the inn where Davyn had been working at the time MacAllister was released from prison. We found two Elhim working there, a groom and a pot boy, neither of them familiar to me. They claimed not to know our friends and didn't want anything to do with us. They just about chewed their boots when we made a sideways mention of Cor Talaith. But just before nightfall, when we slipped into the local market to restock our food supplies, we saw Davyn and Tarwyl playing draughts on an upended barrel.

They continued their game as we strolled past, and showed no sign that they knew us. I thought for a moment we must be wrong. One Elhim looks very much like another. But MacAllister said he could not mistake the hair that always fell over Davyn's left eye nor Tarwyl's nose that had been broken and healed crooked, so he assumed they were being cautious. We followed their lead and did not search them out, but took our time leaving the town. Sure enough, at nightfall, just as we left the last straggling shacks behind, two Elhim drifted onto the roadway two hundred paces ahead of us. We kept our distance and made sure no other travelers were watching as we followed the two down a narrow track into a thickly wooded glade. They were waiting with a lantern and outstretched hands.

"By the One!" said Davyn. "We'd almost given up on you. Not a word, not a glimpse, not a hint of your whereabouts until Greck and Salvor sent the news. You'll probably hear a great sigh of relief go up through the land. We've set watchers everywhere."

"It seemed prudent to stay hidden," said the Senai. "We've had a wicked time avoiding Ridemark patrols. I would as soon have kept it that way, but Lara seems to think we'll never accomplish anything without Narim. I have less faith in his plans. I can get people killed well enough on my own."

"We've known the risk ever since we took Lara in," said Davyn. "You must understand that it could have happened anytime. And Iskendar and his followers agreed to that risk. They never regretted helping her, no matter what the consequences would be. And they never regretted helping you either. You could have stayed there in peace forever if—"

"If I hadn't given them reason to believe I was still interested in gods and dragons."

"Yes. I see you've come to some understanding of the attempt on your life. When we saw your beacon, all knew what it could mean. Narim . . . all of us . . . tried to make Iskendar listen to reason. He didn't have to agree with us; all he had to do was get out and live. But he wouldn't. It's not your fault." Davyn laid his hand on MacAllister's arm.

The Senai didn't welcome it, but he didn't shake it off either. "Perhaps if I had known some of this earlier, we might have been able to avoid the event as well as the guilt. So where is Narim?"

"He's helping the survivors find a place to settle until we can find a new sanctuary. With your permission, we'll send him news right away. He is most concerned . . . most anxious, as you can imagine, to find out what's happened with you . . . what happened with Keldar. We've all wondered. . . ."

"We need to keep moving. I'll tell you about Keldar as we go."

As we set out again on the darkening road, MacAllister was gloomy and untalkative. The Elhim enjoyed them-

selves as always. Davyn clapped Tarwyl on the back.
"Never will I go plotting without you, friend. 'Sit in the
market,' you said. 'After thirteen days of hiding, they'll
need supplies.' "

Tarwyl laughed his deep-throated laugh, always unexpected from a soft-faced Elhim. "At least you remembered to bring your kit. I'll have to share your cup and dig
into my purse to buy a change of shirt!"

I brought up the rear and watched for pursuit. Someone had to keep a mind on danger.

In the three weeks since that day, we had visited three
dragon camps. Tarwyl and Davyn would work their way
into the lair, posing as an ironmonger's assistants looking
for custom from the Ridemark, or supply clerks hunting
work. MacAllister instructed them to watch for any
dragon that looked older than average and had either an
oddly formed shoulder or back, or one that seemed to
draw an unusual number of birds about it. Idiot. He might
as well have told them to look for Grimaldi the dwarf
king, the enchanted swan Ludmilla, or any other creature
from his myth songs. But the Elhim took the Senai's
word as god-spoken. At the first three camps they had
found no possibilities, and now we sat in the hovel near
Fandine, waiting, waiting, waiting—interminably waiting.

"At last!" The sun was low when I saw the two slight
figures coming over the rise in the road at the edge of
Wyefedd. I yelled at the two as they strolled casually
toward our hiding place. "Can you lift your feet any
slower?" I said. "We've had such an exciting day waiting
for you, I can't bear it to end."

"We're saving something for the journey back," said Davyn.

I felt MacAllister jump up in the darkness behind me. "You found something?"

"There are four dragons in Fandine. One of them has a 'bad wing.' We didn't see it, but the smith told us of it. We could see flocks of birds over the place where it lay. It seems the first possibility."

"We'll go in tonight," said MacAllister. "Show me how to find him."

With a burned stick Tarwyl drew a map on a scrap of wood, showing a little-used path into the lair, the guard posts, the outbuildings, the Riders' huts, and the approximate position of the kai.

"How will you know if he's the one, Aidan?" asked Davyn. "You've never told us what you plan. Perhaps we should wait for Narim. He should catch up with us any day now."

"Lara must command it to say its name, just as she did with Keldar that first time," said the Senai, pulling his cloak about his shoulders.

Davyn was horrified. "But you said you almost—"

"I wasn't dying; Keldar was. I felt it from him. This time I'll be ready. Let's go."

"Wait!" I said as the Elhim followed the Senai out the door. "You might ask me—" But by the time I shouldered my armor bag, they were already halfway through the village. I had to shove my way through a clot of five nagging beggar children to catch them before they disappeared.

MacAllister strode the half league through the stickery brush and stunted trees to the boundary of the lair as if the legions of the Ridemark were on his heels. While Davyn and Tarwyl scouted the path into the lair, the two of us crouched behind a wall of crumbling red sandstone and looked down on Fandine. Short bursts of sharp-tongued, blue-orange fire streaked across the darkening sky. Balefire, my clan called it, for its color and intensity told us that the kai was in pain—and thus likely to blast anything that wandered within a thousand paces of its snout. Wounded kai were exceedingly dangerous.

"I'm sorry you have to go," said MacAllister softly, breaking his long silence as if he had read my thoughts. "If I could spare you, I would."

A kai screamed in the distance, the cry echoing from the red cliffs behind us and before us, and the Senai shuddered at the sound.

"We can stop now," I said. "Even if they were once as you believe, they are no longer. They're killers. They have no minds. You've been deceived. Narim has—"

"Has what?" His dark eyes flared, reflecting the blue-orange fire of the wounded kai.

I couldn't answer. "Wait and talk to him."

"No." He pointed toward the spot at the cliff edge where Davyn had just reappeared and was beckoning us to hurry.

We used the last of the daylight to creep down the steep path—if one could call a crumbling, boot-wide seam in the cliff face a path. At every step more of the red stone dissolved to powder under our feet or split into tiny pebbles that skittered down the sheer drop beside us. By the time we wedged ourselves into the too-small crack in the base of the path where Tarwyl waited, the only light was a fading red glow in the west. The lair itself lay in darkness.

"A quarter of the way around the lair to your right, just below that cone-shaped spire," said Tarwyl. "Just as I drew it. There are three Rider huts along the way; only the first two are occupied."

A thunderous bellow split the night, and the spout of fire lit the valley. MacAllister's face grew so rigid that I thought his skin must split and show the iron beneath it.

"They don't wander . . . the wounded ones?" said MacAllister, his eyes fixed on the bilious streaks fading in the sky.

"No. Only if its Rider commands it. If it is not allowed to go to ground where it chooses, it will stay in one place until it heals or dies."

I was donning my armor as I answered him. MacAllister had, of course, not brought his. A worried Davyn started to speak, but another bellow—grinding, shrill, murderous—cut him off. By the time the echoes had died away, I had finished lacing my boots, and Tarwyl had given a small lantern to MacAllister.

"I'll carry that," I said, jamming my helm over my hair to mask the last evidence that I was a woman. "You stay behind me, just out of the light." I hung my coiled whip on my belt and patted my belt pouch to make sure my emergency gear was still in it. I didn't want MacAllister to see what I'd brought. It might worry him. It might make him leave me behind.

"The blessings of the One Who Guides go with you," said Davyn. "We'll be waiting for you right here."

MacAllister pressed his hand and Tarwyl's, and then turned to me with a mocking bow. "To our doom, Mistress Lara," he said, raising his dark eyebrows to pull his eyes wide open. "Shall we be the dragon's saviors or its supper?" Then he motioned me to lead.

A hot, stinking wind gusted through the narrow, steep-sided valley. Because the only kai in the lair were wounded, they could be held in tighter quarters. The tighter, the better, clan lore said. Perhaps because it was more like the caves to which the dragons would go to heal or die if they were allowed.

We crept past vast pens crammed with goats that surged against the stout fences in waves of bawling terror at every blast of balefire. Beyond the herd pens were a few wooden sheds built up against the cliff walls: a cook-shed, a smithy, a storehouse, a granary, a shelter for the women who cooked and served the Riders, and one for the drovers who kept the herd pens filled. A hospice for wounded Riders sat at the far end of the valley, far from the noisy, stinking pens. Lantern lights flickered in several of the buildings, and two slaves were hauling a heavy slops wagon slowly toward the pigsties.

We held up for a moment in the shelter of a wood cart until the wagon had passed. A heavyset man took a piss outside the smithy and then went back inside, shutting off the orange glare flooding out of his door. A short distance beyond our position, a dry, rutted wagon road angled to the right into a narrow cleft in the cliff wall—the main entrance to the lair. The guard posts would be at the far end of it. Unless you were holding hostages, you didn't need guard posts inside a dragon lair. To our left we could see the first Rider hut, its back to us. It faced the center of the lair where the kai were held captive by the ring of bloodstones. We would either have to cross the open ex-

panse of the road behind the Rider's hut, or risk the
Rider—or a dragon—spotting us as we went on the
darker, more dangerous front side of the hut.

I chose the road. A mistake. No sooner had we stepped
onto it than a party of horsemen came galloping out of the
cleft—on us too quickly for us to dive back into our shelter. Two of them were Riders, very drunk from the sounds
of their bawdy singing; two more were other clansmen
equally drunk, each with a woman astride behind him.
One horse carried two more women—drunk enough or
stupid enough that they didn't know how difficult it was
for a drunken Rider to control his inner fire when he was
mating. They would likely be dead before morning. The
other two horsemen were servants carrying torches. The
Riders' horses reared as the party pulled into a milling
knot no more than fifty paces from MacAllister and me,
the women laughing and squealing like pigs. The men
dismounted and turned the horses over to the servants. I
thought we might escape notice in the confusion. But one
of the servants lifted his torch high and called out,
"Who's there?"

No time to think. No time to delay. I had to keep them
away from us. I pulled out my whip and whirled about to
face MacAllister, keeping my back to the Riders' party.
"On your knees," I said quietly, "and do exactly as I say."
I cracked the whip on either side of him to drown out any
protest he might make. Voices carried exceedingly well in
a lair. Unfortunately mine was a woman's voice—entirely inappropriate for one in Rider's armor. "You must
be my voice," I whispered. "Tell them your name is Ger,
and you've brought in an injured kai from Gondar and a
Senai card cheat from Vallior. Say it like a Rider."

As I cracked the whip again, raising spouts of dust and dried mud, MacAllister dropped to his knees with a steel-eyed glare. "Stay away!" He screamed out the words I'd told him—remembering to use the old tongue and the very voice of besotted arrogance that would be expected. "I'll take my pleasure with the Senai vermin undisturbed; then I'll join you and see what revels can be found in this pitiful excuse for a camp."

Blast them, I thought. The clansmen stood watching, swilling from bloated wineskins while the women wrapped themselves obscenely around their waists.

"We're going to have to play it out," I whispered as I kicked MacAllister sprawling and wrapped a thong of my whip about his wrists.

He screamed out, "Never again, Senai. Never will you think to cheat a clansman of the Ridemark!" Then he struggled to get up, whispering back to me with the slightest edge of anxiety behind his smile, "As long as you don't get to like this."

I kicked him again and stuck the point of my rapier under his chin.

"Now what to do with you," he snarled, then followed with a string of curses that I wouldn't have imagined he knew. "Something fitting for a Senai donkey."

I coached him, and he played it well. Sheathing my sword and yanking on the whip, I stretched his hands over his head and dragged him away from the drunken party toward the wood cart. He helped by digging in his feet as if to get up and fight, but would propel himself forward so that it wouldn't be too obvious that it wasn't easy for me to drag him. Several times he stumbled onto his back, and I had to drag him on it until he could get purchase with his feet again. I dared show no mercy. When we had covered the distance to the wood cart, he dragged himself slowly to all fours, working to get his breath, while I pulled manacles and chain from my pack and dangled them high in the torchlight. The onlookers laughed and cheered and whistled.

"Ask them if they approve," I said. "Hurry. Keep them amused, and they won't get involved."

"One moment." He gasped; then he looked up and saw what I held. "Oh, gods . . ."

"Say it."

"So you approve?" he screamed, all the while shaking his head. Then, quietly, "No . . . no . . . I most certainly do not."

As the drunkards cheered, I kicked him flat again, stepped on his chest, and loosened the whip enough that I could lock the iron bands about his scarred wrists. "I don't know any other way," I said. Then, without looking at his face, I attached the length of chain to the rings bolted to the wood wagon. "We'll go between them and the Rider's huts, just like I'm planning to take possession of the empty one. It's the only way."

It seemed to take two hours for MacAllister to drag the wood cart the fifteen hundred paces to the deserted Rider hut. The wagon was three-quarters loaded, heavy and cumbersome. Our audience cheered as we passed them by. I saluted with my sword and repeatedly laid the whip as close as I dared to the Senai. Once I grazed him on his cheek, and another time on his shoulder, ripping his tunic and drawing a smothered curse from him. He flinched dutifully with each crack, and I believed there was more truth to his groaning effort than he would care for anyone to know.

Once we were past them, the onlookers seemed to remember their own plans and staggered toward the occupied Rider's huts, calling out that I should come join them when I'd had enough of my vengeance.

"Tell them to save you a woman," I told MacAllister.

But he was panting and heaving, and shook his head. "Can't."

So instead I raised my sword again and whirled it in circles above my head. I didn't let him stop until we reached the third hut, and even then I scouted the area thoroughly before I unlocked his bonds.

He bent over, resting his head and arms on the side of the cart. "Thank the Seven, it wasn't fully loaded," he said.

"We've got to get moving. The Riders and their friends were drunk enough to forget us, but the servants weren't. They'll ask about the new arrival."

"You're very resourceful and your plan worked, but next time you might warn me." MacAllister straightened, stretching his shoulders and back, wincing as he rubbed his wrists. "I could at least practice my name-calling."

Trying to ignore his eyes on me, I took the kai'cet from its case, slipped it into its leather collar, and tied it about my neck so I could have both hands free. Then I pulled on my gauntlets, stowed the manacles and chain in my pouch, and coiled my whip. I didn't need to see MacAllister's expression to sense how he was revolted. "If you weren't such a sniveling fool, you might give our safety a bit more consideration," I blurted out. "I, for one, have no wish to die, so I don't walk naked into the most dangerous places in the universe."

Without letting him speak any more teasing foolishness, I tramped into the darkness, aiming for the cone-shaped spire Tarwyl had described. MacAllister trailed silently behind as I picked my way around the pits and cracks in the iron-hard earth. Though there was a small risk of the yellow lantern glow being spotted by one of the Riders ringing the lair, I wasn't about to fall into some blast fissure and break a leg. I picked up the pace. We needed to hurry.

A thousand paces from the Rider hut we began to feel rumbling beneath our feet and hear the muted, angry grumbling of the kai. A blast of blue-orange fire to our left caused me to stop for a moment while I considered which way was shorter to get around a monstrous heap of rubble. MacAllister caught up with me as I moved off again to the left. "You'll command him to speak his name, just like the first time with Keldar?"

"If that's what you want."

"Whatever happens after . . . you must get away as quickly as you can. If it's not Roelan, I'll be right on your heels."

"And how will you manage that? It seems like you had to be carried before. I've dragged you far enough tonight."

"I can do what I have to do. I've no wish to die."

I didn't say anything. He caught my shoulder and made me stop and look at him—the last thing I wanted to do with the balefire glaring in the sky just beyond the next rise. "Promise me you'll keep yourself safe," he said. "Please. It will help a great deal to know you've sworn it, because anything you've sworn to, I know you'll do, no matter how much you hate it. Then I won't have to worry about you."

He didn't know just how good I was at compromising my swearing. "I promise," I said. "Now can we get this done?"

The kai lay buried in carrion. It had blasted a deep hole in the earth in a vain attempt to go to ground. Herd beasts had been driven in to feed it, and many of them had fallen into the pit where the kai could not reach them with either its fire or its jaws. So they lay uneaten, bloated and rotting, while the injured dragon roared its fury and pounded its tail. A charnel pit, the smell so foul that I came near vomiting up my last week's food.

Blue flame spewed into the air as we lay on the ground at the top of the rise. MacAllister had pulled his shirt over his nose and mouth, his face the sick blue of the balefire.

I knew from the first it was the wrong dragon. It was not old enough. The brow ridges were not the most reliable indicators, but I had seen fifty dragons older than this one. And the left wing that lay partially unfurled, twitching so awkwardly, had clearly been broken in battle. The Elhim said that Roelan was one of the seven eldest dragons, and that the legend that named him hunchback was as old as his name. Any gathering of birds about this kai would be only the hardiest of vultures, desiring the rotting meat the kai could not reach.

"It's not the one," I said to the Senai, trying to explain, trying to make him give it up.

But MacAllister shook his head. "We've come this far; we must be sure."

And he dared call me stubborn! I drew out my whip,

in case the beast could get about on one wing better than it looked, and with a certainty that I was wasting what remained of my life, I scrambled and slid down the rocky slope until I was standing much too close to the kai.

"Teng zha nav wyvyr," I cried, drawing its attention, its hatred, and its fire all at once. It bellowed so horrifically that I feared that Aidan's skull would shatter. My own came near it. I called on the bloodstone and fought for control, laboring to build a cocoon of safety about MacAllister and me. If I let go, if I showed any weakness, the fire would creep closer and destroy us. This was a very different beast from the one they called Keldar.

"Speak your name, beast," I shouted. "Speak the name your brothers cry out; speak the name your sisters call, the name your younglings heed."

It just did not want to obey me. It writhed in its pit until the stench of the churned-up carrion made me gag. It screeched and bellowed and grumbled like a live volcano. It slapped its tail so hard I could scarcely keep my balance. The monstrous head hung above me, the flaming red eyes like twin suns from my worst nightmares—murderous, damned eyes. I commanded it again. "Speak your name!"

A ferocious bellow, louder and more violent than any so far, slammed me to my knees. My whip slipped from my fingers that were suddenly unable to grasp. I could not rise, could not think, could not hear anything but the roaring, twenty paces from my head. The noise wouldn't stop, though the kai's mouth was closed, and it was searching, searching with its hellish eyes. Its nostrils flared, and its head dipped. *Control.* I had to maintain control. I screamed at the kai to hold its burning—but I

could not hear my own words, only the roar in my ears. I
screamed at it again and commanded my muscles to
work. Never had I been laid so flat by a dragon's cry.
Now perhaps I understood what Aidan felt. *Aidan* . . .

I scrambled to my feet, grabbing my whip and loosing
it at the slavering jaws gaping all too near my head. The
head jerked away. The kai unfurled its uninjured wing
and strained with it, while drumming the broken one on
the ground, desperate to fly. Pain and anger were driving
it into frenzy. Searing blasts of heat passed to each side of
me. I could hear nothing but the roaring in my ears.

The dragon lurched halfway out of its pit, blasting
constant fire. I tried to remember the lie of the rocky hillside as I backed away up the slope. I dared not turn my
back. *Careful, careful. Make sure the snout comes no
closer. Make sure the head stays up and the angle of the
fire stream stays steep or you'll be ash. . . .* But I had only
two eyes and too little practice. I didn't see the undamaged wing sweep around behind and graze my left leg
with its poisonous edge, slicing through my leather
greave as if it were paper and through the flesh underneath as if it were air. I staggered backward, trying to stay
upright, for a fall was sure death. But my boot found no
purchase, and the side of my foot hit the side of a hole,
bending my ankle sideways much farther that it should.
My leg was already in agony from the long, deep cut and
the sticky yellow dragon venom eating away the tissue.
My ankle refused to hold me up, and with curses I could
not hear over the roaring in my ears, I fell. I might have
fallen all the way down the slope into the kai's pit, except
that I landed right in Aidan MacAllister's lap.

Chapter 23

I could not stand alone when the Senai got me back upright, for my ripped leg kept folding up underneath me as if it had forgotten its purpose. The only thing I could hear was the torrent of noise from the dragon behind and below us. MacAllister's chest was rumbling as he held me, so I knew that he was saying something, but I tried to make him understand that the bellowing was just too loud. Damnably awkward. Drops of blood rolled down his face like tears, joining the dribble from the lash mark on his cheek.

Fire exploded below us, and MacAllister dragged me up the slope, motioning that we'd best hurry. It was annoying the way he kept waving at me instead of speaking louder. Once over the rise he put his arm around my waist, I gripped his shoulder, and we started back the way we'd come. At first we couldn't go three steps without getting our feet tangled, and I yelled at him to follow my lead, but I couldn't even hear myself. He held up his fingers, one and then two, one and then two, telling me with gestures how we would proceed. On the count of one, we would step with our outer legs. On two he would step with his inner leg, and I would most certainly not step on mine. He tapped the rhythm on my ribs as we went. We got faster and smoother, and soon we were back to the herd pens. A dark shape stumbled out of the first Rider hut and hurried into the wilderness toward the blaze of orange fire.

Though we had moved a considerable distance from the raging kai, the noise was as loud as ever. But kai never screamed so long at once, and at last the thought penetrated my thick head that something was wrong with my hearing. I pounded and dug at my ears, trying to un-clog them, to let the roaring out, anything to make them work right again. Locked inside myself with the fire in my leg and the terrible noise, I was sure I was losing my mind. MacAllister grasped my hands and pulled them away, then pressed his gloved fingers on my chin and forced me to look at him. He was not smiling, but his look was telling me that everything would be all right if I just wouldn't panic. Easy for him to say.

"Too loud," he said. I could clearly see the words he formed, though I couldn't hear them. "Too close. It will take time." Then he put his arm around me again, and helped me across the endless wasteland to the base of the path. The Elhim were waiting. How in the cursed world were they going to get me up the path? It wasn't even wide enough for one.

They sat me on the dirt leaning against the cliff. Tar-wyl brought down my bag to stow my armor and whip, ready to haul it up the track. MacAllister looped my sword belt about his neck and hung my belt pouch from his bleeding shoulder. But it was Davyn's sturdy shoul-ders across which they draped me like a sack of grain for the most terrifying ascent I had ever made without leav-ing the earth.

By the time we got back to Wyefedd, my face and fingers were numb, and I was seeing two or five of everything—clear signs of dragon poisoning. They laid me on the dirt floor of the stable, and a blur of faces—some of them pale, some of them blood-streaked—hovered over me, mouthing things I could not hear. I tried to speak calmly, determined not to lie there sobbing like a Udema milkmaid. I needed to tell them where to find the gillia in my pack, the leaves that could draw the dragon venom from the wound before it ate through the muscle and bone. But my tongue refused to work, and the yellow light wavered, and everything was lost in the roaring of my ears. Someone must have touched my leg then, because it felt like a dragon had bitten it off. I screamed, but no sound came out.

Torchlight. Jostling. What were they doing? Vague impressions of being imprisoned with a flock of sheep while being battered with wooden planks, of begging them to cut off my limb before I lost my mind, of cool water dripped on my lips, sun-dappled greenery, and a resting place so soft I believed I had fallen from a dragon and landed in the clouds. The clouds would have been a peaceful ending but for the ever-present roaring in my head and the waves of fire that consumed my left side over and over again so that I knew I was falling . . . burning . . . falling from the sky. . . .

I must be dead. Nothing hurt anymore. Was it the heavy earth that held my eyes closed or gold coins laid on them by clan brothers at my funeral rites? If only the roaring noise would stop, I might figure out the truth. At least I was not alone in the realm of death. Spirits tended

*me, and their touch was gentle, but nothing of flesh, so I
wept beneath the cold weight on my eyes. It was fearful
to be dead. "Oh, please, good spirit, speak to me," I
begged, as I sank further into darkness. "Touch me with
a hand of blood and bone, not these fleshless things."*

*And the spirit heeded me, for in my next half waking
the hands that eased my fears were made of flesh. They
were not human hands, though, for their shape was
wrong and they were so very cold. But I was not afraid. I
recognized their kindness.*

*A weight lay on my chest like that on my eyes, and it
grew heavier with passing time. The darkness crept into
me and around me, and I felt myself melting into it, becoming part of it, losing all memory and feeling. Drowning. I hungered so for life.*

*I clasped the spirit's hands with my own and said, "If
I warm your hands, kind spirit, will you speak to me? Will
you send me back to the living? I can't be dead. I have
things I need to do, but I can't find my way back."*

*And into the grinding bedlam intruded a sound so
magical it might have been the speech of stars, a brief,
haunting breath of music . . . no words that I could understand, yet the melody penetrated the chaos and settled
in my soul, bringing peace and clarity to order my confusion. I was no longer afraid, but neither would I yield my
last breath if I could help it. I could see the path that lay
before me, and slowly I began to climb out of the darkness.*

The smell of rain and green grass. Somewhere bacon
was cooking. The roaring had fallen silent. I heard only
random snapping against a background of insect sounds—

swarming locusts perhaps. The cold weight had been lifted, and I carefully cracked my eyes open, shoving aside the fearful thought that I was about to look upon the world beyond the last crossing. My clan loremaster had never taught that one might find bacon in the warrior's encampment of the afterlife.

I was confused at first. I saw clouds and blue sky and birds high above my head, but the birds were not moving and the clouds did not change shape as I watched. No sun beat down on my face though the sky was bright like noonday. I glanced to the left and was startled to see walls. And I was on the inside of them, so the sky—I looked up again—was painted on a ceiling. A very high ceiling. Between me and the wall lay an endless spread of dark green carpet. The room was as big as a kai's cavern, brightly colored and strangely furnished. A long yellow couch with a gray wool blanket thrown on it, two lumpy shapes—chairs?—shrouded in white. More shrouded shapes sitting on the floor or hung on the pale yellow walls. I was tucked up in what must be a bed, though it was far too large, and I had felt nothing so soft in all my life. I shifted my head very slightly. A dark-haired man in a blue shirt and black vest was sitting in front of a white marble hearth, poking at something inside it. The insect sounds were only raindrops, falling on a flagstone terrace beyond two doors thrown open to a gray day.

"Am I dead?" The very asking was a comfort, for I could hear my own words through my ears and not just inside my head. And what dead woman is unsure enough to ask?

The dark-haired man whirled about, wielding a long-tined fork with a thin slab of half-cooked bacon skewered

on it. On his lean face blossomed a smile to win a kingdom. "You tried," he said, "but you weren't very good at
it." He propped the bacon fork on the fire grate and came
to help me sit up on a bed as large as the tent where I was
born, supported by more pillows than I thought existed in
the world. The bedsheets were fine linen, and clean. I'd
never been in a room so grand.

MacAllister poured wine into a crystal goblet and
pressed it into my hands. "Until I can get you something
more substantial." He wore no gloves. "How are you
feeling? Limp as plucked weeds, I'd guess. Can you really hear me?"

I shifted my position and got a mild but reassuring
twinge from my left leg. I'd seen many warriors left
limbless by dragon venom, and I remembered my maddened begging. My cheeks grew hot. "Of course I can
hear you. What are we doing in a place like this?" I tried
to focus on the present. He must have done something
stupid; this was not some abandoned hovel by the side of
the road. "What if someone finds us here? We'll have our
hands cut off for thieving if the owner catches us."

"No need to worry. The owner hasn't been home in a
very long time"—he didn't look at me—"and he doesn't
mind."

"Yours . . ." Though I knew of his childhood, I'd never
actually connected him with a place . . . a house . . . such
a grand house.

"Mmm." He returned to the hearth, dipped a cup of
something from a copper pot, then set it beside the bed on
a table that had legs carved in the shape of birds. Seating
himself on the edge of the bed and biting his lip like a
five-year-old child, he slowly and awkwardly lifted a

spoon to my mouth. When the spoon slipped a little and he spilled half the contents on the sheets, he sighed, then laughed in exasperation. "This was easier when no one was watching."

I took the spoon from his gnarled fist. "How about if I do this, and you tell me what in the name of Vellya we're doing here?"

"If you're sure . . ."

I showed him that I could hold the cup with a steady grip and maneuver the spoon much better than he, and he relaxed a bit.

"Well, our activities in Fandine set up quite a noisy party, and we had to get out of the way pretty fast. One of Tarwyl's cousins found us a wool cart, but we needed someplace to take you. We were only half a league from here, but I wasn't sure . . . Well, it seems my cousin hasn't given the place away even after all this time."

His cousin. The king of Elyria. I had never really believed it.

"Tarwyl found caretakers about the main house, but I knew they wouldn't bother to come back here. It's pretty deep in the park. No one's lived here since my mother died." He poked one of his horrid fingers through a tiny hole in the sheet. "This is a guesthouse—the place where she would stow discreet friends and unpleasant relatives. She'd be horrified to see it so dusty, insect holes in the linen. . . . She always wanted it comfortable and welcoming."

All my life I had scorned those like Aidan MacAllister. I knew more of life; I was stronger, harder, closer to the world. I understood their soft, decadent lives, but they could have no concept of mine. But in an instant I saw how impossible it was that I could understand anyone who had grown up in a place like this. I had never thought of Senai as people with bacon forks and insects and unpleasant kin, with beds and couches and hospitable mothers. Perhaps there were reasons beyond his own nature that Aidan MacAllister did not belch and throw his cups on the floor or strike me when I said something to hurt him. What was I, who had considered the Elhim cavern a palace, doing in such a place? I looked down at my clothes, expecting to see the shabby reminders of my own life. But I was clad in a soft white shift, high-necked and plain, made of embroidered linen so fine it felt like silk. Nothing underneath it. I glanced up quickly.

MacAllister's fiery red face was averted. "The Elhim . . . Davyn took . . . takes care of those things . . . private things." He was about to break into a sweat.

Carefully I set down my cup and pulled a pillow to my mouth, trying to smother the sounds that burst forth unbidden. I needed to hide, lest I reveal the truth about testy, vicious Lara the Dragon Rider, who chewed up men with her fangs and spit them at the world. MacAllister's embarrassment shifted to worry. Frowning, he dragged the pillow away. "What's the mat—"

But I was not in pain, only laughing as I had never laughed in my life. He turned red all over again, then exploded into hilarity of his own. Did he know there was music in his laughter?

"Where are the little twits?" I said when I could speak again, knowing full well whose hands it was that had bathed me and combed my hair and drained my festering wound ten times a day for uncountable days. "And how long have I been here?"

"Ten days."

"Ten days! And no one's recognized you? In a place you're so well known?"

"No one's likely to know me anymore. Who would come looking for a singer presumed dead for seventeen years? Not much profit in that. But the Elhim bring supplies when they come back from a scout, so I've no need to go near the main house or the village."

Back from a scout . . . My laughter fell dead. "You're not still hunting this phantom dragon?"

His sobered expression was answer enough.

"You can't mean to go on. We'll not get ten steps into any dragon camp. The guards will be tripled. It's madness even to think of it." I could not bear to hear his answer. I begged the roaring deafness to return before he spoke it.

"I've no choice. But you—"

"Of course you have a choice. There's always a choice. You had chains on your wrists in Fandine, and I had dragon poison in my veins. We could have died, or you could have ended up with your friend Goryx for the rest of your miserable life. And for what? For nothing. We learned nothing. Accomplished nothing."

MacAllister looked stricken—as if I'd chained his hands again and left him naked for the wolves of winter. "Gods, Lara . . . I thought you knew . . . I thought you heard . . . ." He sat on the edge of the bed beside me. "The dragon in Fandine . . . her name was Methys, which means 'daughter of the summer wind.' She had almost forgotten it. There at the end she sang to me, and it waked . . . a spark. I don't know. Just for a moment. And then you were hurt, and we brought you here. I thought you were going to die, and I . . . I tried . . . I can't seem to do it again, but I believed you heard and that it made a difference." His face was like those of the starving villagers who came begging at Ridemark camps.

He was mad. There was no other answer. I'd heard the "song" of the injured dragon in Fandine, and it was not the glorious melody Aidan had sung to me in my dying. There could be no connection between such horror and such beauty. But if I told him I'd heard his singing and that it had taken away my fear and made me choose to live, it would lead him nowhere but to the dragons. So I couldn't tell him. I cursed Narim, then, and I cursed the Elhim and my own people and King Devlin, and I cursed the dragons and the universe that had created such monsters. They had robbed a good and innocent man of his life and his reason, and I could not tell him the truth he yearned to hear lest I be a party to their cruelty.

"I heard nothing. You're a fool. You can't go on with this, or you're going to be dead."

The silence was long. I could not meet his gaze while he sat so close. To my relief he moved away to stand quietly by the hearth. "Ah, well. Foolish. I'm sorry," he said at last. He picked up a polished oak stick that was standing next to the hearth and twirled it idly for a moment. "The Elhim say your ankle was only sprained, not broken, so you can get up whenever you feel like it."

"Now would be none too soon," I said.

He forced lightness into his words. "You hate being down. I can tell that. Even worse than being dragged around by mad Senai." The mockery in his smile was not for me but for himself. "Tarwyl even brought you a cane to start. From another cousin." He tossed me the stick and grinned. "I'll help if you need it, but I'm going to make you ask for it. I figure I can get myself comfortable for a long wait." He flopped onto the yellow couch, stretched his long body, and closed his eyes.

Before I had made three circuits of the room leaning on Tarwyl's cane, two soggy Elhim burst through the door from the terrace, dropping an armload of parcels on the carpet. "Lara!" shouted Tarwyl. "You're awake!"

"I can hear very well, thank you," I said. "Unless you keep up the yelling."

"And ready to hike the Carag Huim, it seems," said Davyn, smiling as he joined me on the far side of the room. "Healing well?"

"I'll be ready when I need to be," I said, "for whatever stupidity comes next."

Davyn laughed uproariously. "I expected no other answer."

Foolish Elhim. He offered his arm to escort me back to my bed, for which I was sorely grateful. I would have crawled on the floor on my belly before asking the Senai.

"What did you find?" said MacAllister. He had popped up the moment the Elhim came in and sat poised on the edge of the yellow couch like a skittish cat.

Davyn's cheerfulness dropped away with his wet jacket. "Nothing likely. Precious few dragons about any of the camps in northern or central Elyria. We've covered them all. We did drag back something interesting, though he lags behind so pitifully he may never arrive to show himself."

"Patience, you sprout of a nocre-weed," said the Elhim just stepping through the doorway. "Ah, Lara, you must find a new way of making friends. Wrestling with dragons is the hard way."

"Narim." Not since the worst days of my burning had I so hated the sight of him.

He came to my bedside, took my hand, and smiled. "You are blooming, my lovely Lara. Aidan has done well by you." Sympathy welled up behind his kind and cheerful face, as if he could read every thought in my head. "Did I not tell you that this one would change your opinion of Senai?"

"He has his uses," I said, averting my eyes. I did not want to acknowledge the bond between Narim and me until I could avoid it no longer.

Davyn took up MacAllister's abandoned bacon fork and was soon busy melting cheese on hot bread and cooked barley. Tarwyl presented me with my own boot, the slit down its side skillfully repaired by yet another Elhim "cousin." Narim and the Senai sat on either side of the bed making conversation across me about less than nothing: where the Elhim thought to make their new sanctuary, the futile attempts to convince Iskendar to leave Cor Talaith before the assault, our hunt for Roelan, and our adventure in Fandine. Nothing of importance. Nothing of the essence—the unyielding, unforgivable truth.

Davyn served up supper and gossip. "In Lepan we heard a rumor that the host of the Ridemark is gathered on the Gondari border. The Gondari king has been getting bolder with his raids into the southern kingdoms. Ten villages destroyed. Two thousand people burned out of their homes."

"Burned half of Grenatte before the southern legion chased him back across the border," said Tarwyl around a mouthful of bread. "The Riders grumble that King De-

SONG OF THE BEAST 309

vlin has lost his spine, as he's still not crushed these
Gondari upstarts or even pursued them with a will."

"They say MacEachern has started shifting the legions
himself," said Davyn. "Always closer to the border. Always in more vulnerable positions."

MacAllister propped his chin on his hands. "He's trying to force Devlin into an assault."

"I've heard that too," said Davyn.

"He'll push and provoke the Gondari until there's no
going back, never understanding why Devlin hasn't done
it yet."

"Why hasn't he?" asked Narim, his spoon poised in
midair.

But MacAllister's mind was far away, and he didn't
answer for a long while. And when his outburst came, it
answered a different question altogether. "Aberthain!"
MacAllister leaped up from the table, slamming the heel
of his fist onto the table. "Stupid. Stupid. Why didn't I
think of it before?"

Narim voiced our question. "Think of what?" Aberthain
was a vassal kingdom in the southwestern mountains. Forever embroiled in local disputes. Unimportant.

The Senai was twitching with excitement. "Eighteen
years ago I visited Aberthain. I couldn't sleep for the music
pounding in my head, so I went out to the lair. I'd never felt
Roelan so clearly, so close, and—prideful, insupportable
stupidity—I thought it was something in me that made it
so different that night. Within days the dragons in
Aberthain Lair allowed hostages to go free, and within a
week I was arrested. All this time we've spent hunting in
Elyria, but Roelan is in Aberthain. I'm sure of it."

Chapter 24

Davyn, Tarwyl, and Aidan left for Aberthain the next morning. Narim and I were to follow more slowly, allowing me time to regain strength and mobility before making any attempt to command a dragon. I dreaded the moment Narim and I would be left alone, so I leaned on the cane and trailed Aidan across the terrace into the lane where the horses were waiting. The damp terrace steamed in the morning sunlight.

"The lair at Aberthain is near impossible to get in," I said, as he loaded his pack on his horse. "The surrounding cliffs are a sheer drop, and there's only one gate. The road to the lair leads right through the city."

"I remember. I saw it."

"You heard Davyn. They've got every lair heavily guarded. There will be signs, passwords, inspections. No Senai will be able to get into Aberthain Lair. None."

Aidan cast a solemn glance over his shoulder. "I promise I won't go without you, if that's what you're afraid of."

"I'm not afraid of—"

"You're not afraid of anything. I know." Only after he'd turned away did I recognize the teasing glint in his eyes. He fumbled with his straps for an interminable time and faced me again only when he was finished with them. "The Elhim say that when you save someone's life, that life belongs in part to you. You're obligated to participate in its future course—delight in its pleasures, grieve at its sorrows. Davyn will tell you. So we are inextricably bound together, I think—you, me, and the others. No matter how much we dislike it." Perhaps he thought his smile could soothe the sting of his words.

"And what do the Elhim say if you destroy someone's life?" I gave him no smile to ease my words. But as ever, I could not seem to make him angry—only melancholy.

"Ah . . . that I don't know. Perhaps it doubles the requirement. Fitting punishment to know you can give them no comfort, to be unable to heal the wounds you've caused. I've given it a lot of thought these past days."

I was ready to tell him that I was not referring to *his* crime, when Davyn and Tarwyl walked out of the house with Narim in tow. "Time to be off," said Davyn. "We've got a plan. We'll meet seven days from this at the Red Crown, just outside of Aberswyl. Turns out the cook is—"

"Tarwyl's cousin." MacAllister and I said it at the same time. The three Elhim chortled and embraced each other, and with no more than that, MacAllister, Davyn, and Tarwyl were off.

The hoofbeats had scarcely faded, and I'd not yet taken my eyes from the leafy lane where the three had disappeared, when Narim voiced the thought I would have died to keep my own. "You love him."

I did not speak. Instead I returned to Aidan's house, stripped off the fine linen shift, and pulled on my own threadbare russet breeches and coarse brown shirt, my vest of cracked leather, and the repaired leather boots.

Only as I twisted my hair into a braid that would keep it out of my face as we rode . . . only then did I trust myself to speak to Narim. He had followed me. "I've sworn to do whatever you ask of me. I keep my oaths."

The Elhim who had exhausted himself for two years to make me live stood in the doorway, his face left in shadow by the bright morning behind him. "It was never my plan to hurt you, Lara. And you must believe that I value Aidan MacAllister even as you do. I hope to give each of you the single thing you most desire, but this . . . it cannot be. You know that."

"I know far better than you. Have no fear. I'll do exactly as you've told me. But I'll never forgive you, and I'll never forgive myself, and don't tell me of dragon souls and the Elhim's sin and the changing of the world. You were wrong."

"He could not have sustained his life as it was. The dragons were getting wilder. He was at the peak of his talent. He would have lost their voices and died inside, never knowing the truth. Would that have been better?"

"You never asked him, Narim. You thought you understood what was happening. You plotted and schemed and scribbled in your journal. But you were wrong. It was never the dragons. It was his own heart that made his music, and you ripped it out. And now he's going to die. He will either step into a dragon's fire unprotected or he'll be captured. I'll kill him myself before I allow him to be taken prisoner again."

I did not give Narim the chance to answer. I had listened to him too often . . . like the night he first told me that terrible deeds were sometimes necessary to save the world. I hadn't been interested in saving the world. I didn't believe in Narim's legends of Dragon Speakers. I had done as he asked because I was twisted with hate and craving vengeance, and now I was locked into his schemes by my honor as a warrior. To refuse him would complete my own corruption, violate my only remaining link to my clan. I could not do it. But I believed it was going to destroy my life as surely as it was going to destroy Aidan MacAllister's.

We left the green and beautiful place called Devonhill and rode slowly southward in the garish spring weather. I would have preferred rain and gloom. In the first days I had to stop every hour and walk to loosen up my leg, and after only a few hours of riding I was so tired I would drop off to sleep on whatever piece of ground was closest.

Narim reviewed his plan, insisting that the impossible would happen and the Senai would learn what was necessary to free the dragons. I mouthed the answers he wanted from me. Yes, I would see the dragons brought to Cir Nakai right away. They would not come to the lake on their own, for they would surely remember the poison, the jenica in the water that had caused all their trouble. MacAllister must convince Roelan to lead the others to the water. It was the only way. And yes, there must be no delays. Once the hold of the Ridemark was broken, there would come a storm of vengeance such as the world had never seen. The dragons must be secure before the storm could break. I would not think of what was to come after. It would never get that far.

Narim was as mad as MacAllister. Was this the punishment for my childish rage at the future life had parceled out to me? Because I was not content with my own people, I must live out my days with lunatics of other races?

By the fifth day we were making good speed through the rolling forestland of southern Elyria, stopping only to rest the horses and to eat. On the sixth morning, as the land began to rise toward the rainswept hills of Aberthain, I could not spur my mount fast enough. I felt like wolves were nipping at my feet. When Narim called a midday halt at a deserted crossroads, I wanted to scream.

"One moment only, Lara, love," he said, "and you can be off at your own pace to find our friends. Our paths must diverge here, for my instinct is the same as Aidan's. I believe he will find Roelan in Aberthain, so I've got to set things in motion. I'll come find you the moment I get word you've made the attempt."

Mad. They were both mad. "So you'll not be there to watch him die?"

"I'll not be there to see him reap the joy he so deserves. No. Sadly not." Tenderly he brushed away the hair that straggled across my ugly face as he had done so often when I was healing from my burns. "But I will see him after, and I will see the fulfillment of your destiny, Lara. You will soar across the sky, and your beauty and courage and honor will be visible for the world to see."

I spurred my horse as hard as I dared and left Narim, hand outstretched, in the middle of the crossroads.

By nightfall I rode into the stableyard of a small, tidy inn tucked away in the forest half a league from Aberswyl, the royal city of Aberthain. Lanterns sparkled in the clear darkness, and laughter and the music of pipes and whistles spilled out doors and windows opened to the warm, humid night. I left my horse with a stable lad—a sleepy Florin boy with a slave brand burned into his cheek.

I headed across the yard toward the inn, but the boy's scarred cheek reminded me too closely of my own. The thought of stepping into a brightly lit common room was so repulsive that I walked right past the door and into the dark cluster of sheds, storehouses, and refuse heaps crowded between the inn and the surrounding trees. Crouching beside a stack of bricks, I waited for the party to be over and the lamps to be turned down. From the number of revelers who staggered into the yard to vomit, and the tittering flower-decked couples who stumbled into the trees only to emerge panting and rearranging clothing a quarter of an hour later, I gathered it was a Udema wedding party. If so, it could go on all night.

I settled down for a long wait and slept a bit, only to be waked about moonset when a wagon decorated with flowers, wheat sheaves, and cowbells carried the happy couple to their bed. The remaining guests returned to the inn for another hour of serious drinking before heading home.

It was in the quiet that followed that I heard the call of the teylark from the woods. Only those who had grown up in the tents of the Twelve Families would remark the nasal, yipping cry of the most common bird in Elyria. And no one else would recognize the code: one chirp, then two rising, then one again, and a trill. *All is ready.* A double whistle, then a single. *Hold until the command.* In a ring around that forest glade the calls repeated, blending in with the humming insects, the rustling of new

green leaves, and the occasional bark of a dog who'd had
good luck in its night's hunting. Inside the inn a sentimental piper squalled on his pipes.

Ridemark discipline would permit no further breaking
of the silence, so I would learn nothing more of their
plan. But it was easy enough to guess. Somehow they had
learned that MacAllister was inside. As soon as the wedding guests were gone, they would take him as easily as
boys stealing blackberries. The question was whether
they had a man inside keeping watch on the Senai. If so,
the problem was far more difficult. My instinct said not.
Best test it quickly. More guests were straggling away
down the road, and soon the teylark would cry again with
a far deadlier message.

How was I to get to the door? If the watchers were
counting who came out and who returned, my unexpected appearance could set off the very attack I feared.
Amid the cheers and laughter of the company, another
flower-draped couple darted out the front door into a rose
arbor to express their fervent hopes as to the newlyweds'
fertility. Before I could figure out how to take the girl's
place, they were strolling back to the inn.

An unendurable quarter of an hour until someone else
staggered out of the doorway. The pudgy man relieved
himself against my pile of bricks, happily singing mournful songs of youth and love along with the piper's tune.
Clearly the fellow had drunk a barrel of ale. I plowed a
foot straight into his belly before he could get himself
tucked up again. It knocked the wind right out of him. I
dragged him into a stinking slaughtering shed, trussed
him up with my belt and a scrap of rope, then patted his
cheeks and his exposed bit of Udema manhood. "We're

setting up a surprise for the groom," I whispered in his ear, counting him too drunk to remember that the groom had already gone. "Hold quiet here until he comes, and we'll have a good laugh." Udema love bawdy jokes.

My victim giggled, then shushed himself, spluttering. "Shhh . . . no noise . . . good joke . . . shhh . . ." He would most likely fall asleep and dream a hilarious outcome. I borrowed his cloak and stumbled across the yard toward the inn, growling a note or two as I went.

Perhaps twenty people occupied the lamplit common room. Most of them were gathered about two long tables littered with empty tankards, baskets of flowers, pools of ale, and the bones, crumbs, and rinds of a farmer's feasting. They were singing at least three different songs at once and drinking prodigiously. A fat man snored from one corner of the room, while an exhausted serving girl carried a heavy tray of filled mugs to replenish the table, and a drowsy Elhim turned a goose on a spit. No one in the group had the air of a Rider.

MacAllister and the two Elhim huddled over a small table to one side of the party, not looking at anyone. I shed my stolen cloak and startled the three of them out of a year's peace when I dropped onto the bench beside MacAllister. "You've got to get out of here right now . . ." I said, forestalling the Elhim's greetings as I told them of the circle of Riders posed at the edge of the forest. "We can pretend we're wedding guests. Head down the road with some of these others." Even as I said it, three young men fell weeping on each other's shoulders and waved farewell to the others, holding each other upright as they staggered out the door.

"They're sure to have a checkpoint on the road," said Tarwyl.

"Through the woods might be better, then," said MacAllister. "We could slip between the watchers."

"You don't understand," I said. "These will be experienced Ridemark scouts, and the moon's full. You couldn't do anything in the woods they wouldn't notice."

"Well," said Davyn. "There's one thing they wouldn't notice." He nodded his head toward a burly man who had his hand down a blond woman's bodice while she slathered his mooning face with kisses. The other party-goers began cheering and garlanding the two with flowers. A fiddler took up the piper's tune.

"Tjasse's gift!" toasted a red-haired farmer with a feathered hat. "May Ule sire fifty sons!"

"May Norla birth healthy babes!" cried a wizened woman, who then sucked down a tankard of ale without taking a breath. The group laughed and applauded when the burly man and the blond woman, draped in flowers and already half-undressed, ran out into the night bearing the blessings of Tjasse. The more matings at this celebration, the more pleased Tjasse would be and thus the more likely to bless the newlyweds with children. Two more fawning pairs were close to bolting.

"Offer to buy a round for the party," said Davyn, placing a silver coin on the table. "Make your good wishes. And . . . demonstrate your sincerity." He jerked his head at me. He had to be joking. MacAllister flushed, his gaze riveted on his mug.

"We'll take the road and kill the sentry if we get stopped," I said. "Attach ourselves to the other guests here. Or do something else . . . set fire to the place to cause a commotion."

Tarwyl ignored me, wrinkling his brow. "You could each approach one of the guests. At a Udema wedding party anyone is fair game—well, I don't think they'd take me or Davyn." He grinned. "But of course if you two were together it would be easier. Once you were sure the watchers had lost interest—a convincing few moments at most—you could be away. We'll come along later. Meet you at the shop in Aberswyl. Aidan knows where it is. Are you game?"

MacAllister glanced over at me bleakly. "We'll think of something else."

The Elhim were right, and we had to be quick. "I can do what's necessary. You keep saying the same of yourself. Prove it."

Davyn was sympathetic. "I understand that customs differ widely in these particular matters—"

"Stop talking and do it," I said, fighting not to scream at them. Every time the music fell quiet, I feared I would hear the teylark's hunting call that meant *now*.

"Begin here," said Davyn, laying a hand firmly on Aidan's arm as the Senai started to stand up. "Do not these activities take fire in small ways?"

A grinning Tarwyl raised his cup and proclaimed loudly in his deep voice, "To our human friends who have developed such affection for each other—an uncommon bond, unrivaled in all of history."

If we were not so desperate, I might have laughed at Tarwyl. MacAllister closed his eyes and murmured, "Vellya, god of fools, defend us." Then he raised his mug to Tarwyl, drank deep, and laid his arm around my shoulders as if trying to do it without touching me.

"Your turn, Lara," said Davyn. "We're trying to attract attention here, if you recall. From your current aspect you might well be mistaken for a part of this bench." The two Elhim were having more fun than the Udema.

"Put your hands on him, Lara," whispered Tarwyl, unable to smother his grin. "I'm sure hands are important." I gritted my teeth and clasped the gloved hand that rested so lightly on my shoulder, and I put my other hand on Aidan's cheek, pulling it close to mine.

"This isn't going to work," I said. "I can't—"

"Perhaps it would help to think of something else." Aidan's head was resting on mine. He whispered in my ear, "Did I ever tell you about the time I was chasing bats out of a cave and set my hair on fire?"

I turned my head and stared at him, sure he'd gone mad.

"Oh, gods, don't look at me," he whispered, ducking his head so that I could only feel the heat from his rush of embarrassment. "Do you think these people will notice if we take the Elhim with us for tutors? Were ever two players so woefully miscast?"

From such a close view, I could not miss the nervous terror behind his merry humor. Suddenly I understood a great deal about him that I had never imagined. "You've never . . . in all your youth . . . all the people you met . . . the women and girls fawning over you . . ."

"I never had time. Always traveling. Preoccupied. Tangled with gods and music. And I'd been brought up so strictly. You just didn't . . . not even to look . . . until you'd known someone a long— Until you married. And I never learned— Damn! Am I red enough now?"

To Davyn's and Tarwyl's immense satisfaction, I burst out laughing. Was nothing ever easy? I'd thought he was only excessively modest or disgusted by my common manner or revolted by my ugliness. I had never imagined that a Senai noble who had grown to manhood in the world could be a virgin.

"Laugh as you will," he growled quietly. "But you're perhaps not so worldly as all that. You were only thirteen when you took up with Elhim!"

"I grew up in a tent smaller than this room with my parents, two grandmothers, two uncles, one aunt, three cousins, and an older brother with many friends. Modesty is not a value the clan prizes, nor is celibacy. There is nothing that you don't see and nothing that you don't hear, and a Ridemark girl is available to her father's friends and her brother's friends and any Dragon Rider when she is eleven." I said it lightly, but it had been yet another teaching of my true place in the clan. There was nothing of pleasure in the remembrance of ale-sotted men and groping boys in the dark corners of the family tent.

"Ah . . . Well." He didn't know quite what to say. "I'll do as you command me, then."

"The couple at the end of the table are the bride's parents," whispered Davyn, who had been observing the Udema while we were babbling. "And they've sent a boy to light their lantern."

"Time for the second chorus," said MacAllister. "Perhaps I can do better at this part. I suppose you'll have to bear with me." His grin chased away a shadow from his face. I had most likely revolted him with my unclean past. He looped my hands over one of his arms so he could grip his ale mug securely with both hands; then he approached the wedding party, wobbling a little as if he'd drunk as much as they.

"Greetings, good friends," he said, slurring his words ever so slightly and bowing to the stocky blond pair at the end of the table. "Please excuse my intrusion on this happy occasion, but I could not hold back my congratulations and best wishes for the bride and groom—not when I am so blessed myself." He pulled his elbow inward. I took the hint and clung to him. "Innkeeper! A round for these good Udema. And a toast"—he drained his mug with a flourish and tossed it onto the pile of empty ones littering the table—"to the happy union. May Tjasse bless them with . . . all her blessings!" To my astonishment he threw his arms around me and, with tenderness quite at odds with his performance, he kissed me on the left side—the scarred side—of my face. "I am reminded of a verse from one of your great poets. . . ." Softly he pressed my horrid cheek to his chest as he began speaking in the tongue of the Udema rather than the common speech. I did not know the words, but he did not slur them; rather he caressed them with his beautiful voice as gently as his hands were unbinding my hair. Before he was finished every eye among the Udema was swimming with tears. I was on the verge of panic.

As the wedding guests wiped their eyes and murmured their thanks, Aidan leaned over and buried his face fiercely in my neck. I had to wrench myself to pay attention to his whispered words. "What about the time I was practicing on my flute while riding my horse and knocked myself silly on a tree branch?"

I buried my disbelieving laughter in his chest, while a large, soggy Udema woman next to me snuffled and said, "Tjasse's gift . . . you lucky, lucky girl." In an instant we were blanketed with daisies and milkweed, and amid sentimental blathering about Ule's seed and Norla's womb, we ran out the door.

"To the left of the road," I said, trying to recapture my wits. There were fewer trees to the left, which meant the watchers were farther apart. And it was hillier, which meant it would be easier to get out of sight. "And make likely noises." With as many sighs and moans and giggles as we could muster, we hurried into the trees. At about the right distance for the Ridemark perimeter, I yanked MacAllister toward a broad-trunked oak, pushing him down on his knees to mask his height. I pulled his head up against my belly and draped my unbound hair over his head. "We're going to push farther into the woods," I said. He did not answer. His breath came fast, and he must have felt the Riders close, for he was trembling. After a moment we ran on, stopping twice more as if we could not contain our desire, until we found a dark, grassy hollow sheltered with monkberry bushes. We rolled onto the ground, and I draped his long cloak over us, making sure that no observer would hear or see anything to question.

I tried to keep my mind on the deception, on the mockery we made rather than the living man who knelt beside me doing his best not to touch me again. But after only a few moments more we stopped. Just as if we had done the thing we mimed, we suddenly lay still and quiet in the darkness under his cloak, all merriment fled, all cleverness exhausted. No satisfaction, though. Only the linger-

ing kiss on my scarred cheek was left of our playacting. I
had never felt anything like it. *Lucky, lucky girl.* Foolish,
stupid girl.

I shifted to sit up, and, when my arm brushed his,
Aidan jerked away as if it scalded him. Disgusted with
myself, I threw off the cloak. "We've got to hurry. If
we're lucky, they'll think we've fallen asleep. Davyn said
to go south and that you'd know the path. Is that right?"

"I'll know it." His voice was husky, and he wrapped
his cloak tight, strange for a warm night, as we scrambled
through the woods toward the southern guide star just
visible through the trees.

When we reached a narrow, rutted track, he pointed to
the right, still without words. Too much hung between us,
like the sultry nights of summer when you need a thunderstorm to clear the air. "A good ruse," I said. "Better
than chains and whips, at least." He didn't answer even
then, and I dismissed the remembrance I carried on my
face. We hurried through the night, ready to bolt into the
trees when the inevitable pursuit would catch us up.

Chapter 25

Three times we were forced to duck into the trees to avoid Ridemark search parties or messengers racing down the road toward Aberswyl. We had to hide a fourth time when a party passed us from the other direction and set up a checkpoint two hundred paces behind us. Their commander gave them the order to spread out and search the woods, and we took our chance and ran, keeping to the edge of the trees, hoping their noise would mask our own. Just about the time we thought it was safe to get back out on the road instead of clambering through gullies and over fallen trees, we came on a second checkpoint. Torches blazed to either side of the road, but only three men stood guard. We dared not proceed through the woods lest the rest of their party be waiting for us, yet we could not fight three. Trapped. If the two search parties converged we'd be caught.

But as we crouched low in the scrub, debating how to proceed, two horsemen passed by very slowly . . . slight, with blond, curly hair . . . Elhim. "Hsst, Davyn," I called softly. They were listening for us. Tarwyl slid off his mount and stepped into our hiding place, proclaiming loudly that he had to relieve himself—though Elhim truly

had very different habits than humans and were far better
at controlling such urges.

"You two take the horses," said Tarwyl. "They'll not
expect you mounted, and they'll assume you've already
passed through the first checkpoints if you've made it
thus far."

We had no time for planning or deception. The longer
we delayed, the more likely the searchers would stumble
on us. "Ride hard and don't stop," I whispered to MacAllister. Our only advantage would be surprise. We could
not risk stopping for the checkpoint in some vain hope to
convince the clansmen that we weren't who they thought.
So Davyn dismounted as if to take his turn in the trees,
and Aidan and I mounted up. The Elhim spoke to their
clever horses, slapped them hard on their rumps, and
Aidan and I shot forward between the two guards like
bolts from a crossbow. We left the warriors scrambling
for their horses and screaming for their comrades. I
would have sworn I heard the Elhim laughing from the
forest.

The little horses from Cor Talaith raced through the
night, up and down the rolling ribbon of road, and in no
more than half an hour we were slipping through the
quiet lanes of Aberswyl. MacAllister led me into a small,
muddy stableyard behind a dark shop labeled, *Mervil,
Tailor*.

"We've been staying here," said the Senai, pointing
me up a wooden staircase stuck onto the back of the tall,
narrow building. "There are beds in the room upstairs. If
you're as tired as I am, you won't mind the clutter. We've
been preparing . . . Ah, well, you'll see in the morning."

"And what of you?"

"I . . . think I'll stay down here. Unsaddle the horses. Wait for the Elhim."

"I'll help."

I reached for the buckles, but MacAllister tugged on the reins to move the beast away from me. "Please go. I'll do it. I need— Please." His voice was tight, his eyes averted. I was too tired to argue or question. If he preferred to sleep with the horses rather than in the same room with me, that was his affair. Perhaps he thought I would ravish him. Or perhaps he had finally realized how close he was to being dead. *He's a madman. Who cares what he thinks?*

The hot little room over the tailor shop had five pallets on the floor. Every other bit of space was crammed with gaudy, useless junk: piles and rolls of silk and satin, boxes of thread and lace and beads, a long worktable littered with scraps of silver wire, fabric, and thread. Various articles of clothing, fit for no one but whores and princes, hung about the walls. I saw no evidence of my companions' preparations for our assault on Aberthain Lair, but I was too tired to be curious, even when I laid down my head and stared into the empty eyeholes of a silver mask.

I woke up in early afternoon and found Davyn and Tarwyl occupying two of the pallets. Davyn's eyes opened just after mine, and he sprang off of the floor as if he'd slept fifteen hours instead of five. "Ah, Lara, it was good to find you safe last night." He yawned, peered out the tiny window, yelled, "Sausage!" to someone in the yard below, and then kicked Tarwyl, who was sprawled on the pallet next to the door. "Up, lazy wretch.

We've slept away the morning, which leaves us less than ten hours to finish this."

Tarwyl groaned and pulled a blanket over his head. In Cor Talaith Tarwyl had been well known for sleeping like the dead and never speaking a word until he'd been awake for an hour. Davyn started to kick him again, but thought better of it. Instead, he poured water from a flowered pitcher onto his friend's head, blanket and all. While Tarwyl leaped up, cursing and rubbing his dripping hair, Davyn grabbed a biscuit from a plate of them on the worktable. He grinned at my curiosity and waved his biscuit about the room. "Have you guessed how we're going to get you into Aberthain Lair?"

"If you think to put us in a delivery wagon or play some stupid impersonation like MacAllister tried in Cor Neuill, give it up," I said. "They'll be waiting for just such a thing now they know we're here. The warriors of the Twelve Families are not idiots."

"Well, one might argue that," said Davyn, "but they certainly almost had us last night, and this will be far trickier."

"What, then? Are you planning to weave us into a bolt of cloth?"

"Actually . . . Here, let MacAllister explain." The Senai, a sword belt draped over his arm, topped the last stair carrying a plate of sausage.

"Explain what? Oh, all this?" He jerked his head about the room as he set down the plate and dropped the sword belt onto the table. "We've another bit of playacting to do. Easier"—he was concentrating on the soupy porridge he was scooping into a painted mug—"easier than the last time, I think." He filled three more mugs, and we settled down to the fine-smelling breakfast. "You said there was only one entry to Aberthain Lair, Lara, but in fact there is a second. The Aberthani purposely installed their dragons close to the palace. They see it as a measure of their wealth and privilege to have dragons, and they like to show them off. Makes them feel strong and safe. In fact, whenever King Renald entertains, he takes his guests to view his little flock. At midnight his servants open the gate onto a balcony that overlooks the lair. Though they're rarely used, steps lead from the balcony straight down to the dragons."

"And you think to sneak into the palace and broach this gate?" I could not hide my contempt.

"Not at all. We're going to let King Renald open it for us." He picked up something from the table and whipped it across his face as he gave me a sweeping bow. The silver mask. "Madam, may I request the honor of your presence at a masked ball given by King Renald of Aberthain in honor of his daughter's birthday? I've managed to come by an invitation, and I would very much regret going alone."

A ball! At the royal palace of Aberthain! I had to force my mouth to speak instead of gape in disbelief. "You're mad. Absolutely mad. You couldn't possibly get in, and even if you could . . . With me? No mask has ever been crafted that could pass me off as so much as a servant."

Tarwyl bustled into a corner and returned holding a long gown of dark green silk, sewn with silver thread. "Mervil has only to finish the hem."

"I can't wear anything like that." It was a ridiculous garment. A ridiculous plan. "I won't." In his other hand

Tarwyl held a second silver mask, one designed to cover the eyes and the left side of the face.

"We won't be there long," said MacAllister, tossing his mask to the table. "We'll arrive about eleven. The king always opens the gate at midnight. We'll go through with the rest of the guests, but we won't return with them. The Elhim believe they can hide your gear in the lair. Only an hour and we'll be in. They'll never think of us walking in the front door."

"And how do we get out?"

The Senai hesitated only briefly. "I suppose Roelan will take us."

Madness. "And if your dragon friend isn't there or you can't get its cooperation?"

"He's there," Davyn broke in eagerly. "I've seen him— a dragon the age of Keldar with a malformed shoulder."

"And you'll go whether I agree or not," I said to MacAllister. "Whether you can get out or not. Whether you will be captured or go mad—or whether I will."

"I have to go."

How in the name of heaven was I going to stop it? "When is this ball? I don't even know how to dance."

MacAllister grinned like a fool. "Tonight. So you've no time to figure out how to talk me out of it. As for dancing . . . I'll teach you."

Twice that day Ridemark search parties swept the Elhim districts of Aberswyl looking for a Senai murderer and an abducted woman of the Ridemark. Mervil's front door was kicked in by angry clansmen, and MacAllister and I had to hide in a cupboard with a false back. As soon as the searchers were gone, Mervil packed his family and his assistants off with friends who planned to take refuge in the new Elhim sanctuary in the hills south of Aberthain. "Bad times coming," he said.

MacAllister disappeared in midafternoon, and Tarwyl left with my armor bag to deliver it to Aberthain Lair. Davyn attended to me, seeing me bathed and combed and measured so that Mervil could finish the hem of my gown. Ten times I gave it up. "Narim never made me promise to wear silk gowns, nor to scrub my fingernails with stiff brushes, nor to allow some filthy Elhim to wash my hair with stuff that smells of whorehouses." When Davyn smiled and began scrubbing my feet, I kicked him and said I would wear my own boots or they could all be damned. "This tent of a garment will cover my feet well enough, and I'll not step into any dragon lair without my boots."

As he had all afternoon, Davyn gazed at me with his soulful gray eyes. "Your boots are already gone with Tarwyl and will be dutifully awaiting you behind the cookshed in the lair. I'll confess that shoes have been our greatest dilemma. Mervil has none to fit you, and there's no time to get any made. Aidan has promised to come up with something."

Aidan. "He's enjoying this, isn't he? Making me look ridiculous in this Senai finery."

"Ah, Lara, when will you understand that you could never be ridiculous in his eyes?"

"Repulsive, then. Hideous."

Davyn shook his head. "Do this for me. Watch his face as he sees you come down the stair tonight and judge how repulsive he finds you. As for now, we must practice your curtsy."

"I will not."

"You will be presented to the king of Aberthain. If you don't curtsy, you'll be arrested. Now do it."

My leg did not enjoy curtsying. That gave me even more reason to curse the Senai, and the Elhim, and every male or sexless being that ever walked the earth.

Tarwyl staggered in at sunset with his left arm broken, his clothes in bloody shreds, and his face battered beyond recognition. As Davyn tended his injuries, Tarwyl kept trying to talk. "Have great care, Lara. They know you're here. They've guards everywhere, primed to kill. I did no more than look at a Rider, and they were on me. They said I smelled of vigar. I don't even know what that is."

"The grease," I said. "The fireproofing. Did they find—"

"Your armor is safely stowed. But you and Aidan must take care."

"We'll be all right," I said. "Now let Davyn take care of you."

"Then I'll see you next at Cir Nakai," he said. He smiled through the wreck of his face and let his eyelids sag.

"At the lake," I said, though I did not believe it in the least. "Where is the blasted Senai?" I asked Davyn.

"Out procuring transport, I believe." His kind face was grim and colorless as he dressed Tarwyl's wounds with soft cloths and herbs and ointments.

"The fool will be recognized."

"He promised to be careful."

Two hours after Tarwyl's return, when I was about ready to rip off the green silk gown, I heard a horse and carriage in the cobbled lane. From the window I watched them pull up just outside the tailor's shop. A light-haired

man was driving, and a dark-haired one—MacAllister—
jumped down from the box beside him and disappeared
into the shop. Moments later Davyn burst through the
door. "Time, Lara. The carriage is borrowed and may be
wanted."

The Elhim gave a last touch to my hair that he had
piled up on the top of my head like a Florin pudding. I
slapped his hand away. "Do you remember that I still
have no shoes? I can't go. I look like a whore."

"Aidan has them. Come, Lara, you are beautiful
enough for any king."

"Madness." I grumbled and tried to think of some
other reason not to go down. But eventually I gave it up
and crept down the tailor's narrow stair, trying not to trip
on my skirts. I hadn't worn skirts since I was thirteen. I
felt naked. In the front the gown fell from a narrow band
at my neck to a band at my waist, but it had no back at
all. I had been ready to call off the whole thing when I
saw it had no sleeves. My left arm was as scarred as my
face and my legs, but Davyn had shown me the long silk
arm coverings favored by Senai ladies. The sleeves, made
separate from the dress and fastened tight about each arm
with thirty tiny buttons, left only a narrow band of my
shoulder bare, successfully hiding the telltales of fire.

When I turned the corner of the stair, I caught sight of
Aidan head-to-head with Mervil. Good. I wouldn't have
to see him laugh at my ridiculous clothes. But at the same
time I couldn't help but notice how fine he looked, as natural in his dark jacket, waistcoat, and breeches, white ruf-
fled shirt with a high collar, black hose, and low black
boots, as he had been in the coarse shirts and breeches the
Elhim had given him. He wore white gloves, and his dark

hair was held back by a green ribbon. Tomorrow he would be dead. I could not imagine any woman in the world who would not walk into the fires of death alongside him.

"I can't do this," I murmured and began backing up the stairs. He turned just then, and I closed my eyes quickly so I would not see.

"My lady, you are a vision indeed." His voice was polite and even.

When I peeked again he was expressionless. Clearly he was forcing himself sober. Well done, though. If his lip had so much as quivered, I would have killed him. He held out his hand for mine, but I stuck out my foot instead. "Tell me, Lord Aidan, how many ladies of your acquaintance go shoeless to royal balls?"

"I've only now received the remedy from Master Mervil—and a wonder he's done with it. Please be seated." This time I took his outstretched hand so I wouldn't rip the cursed skirt as I sat down on the stair. He knelt in front of me and lifted my foot onto his knee. I thought it was a necklace that he held, but he twined the simple band of pearls around my ankle and great toe. A narrow strand of fabric stretched beneath my bare foot to hold the loops together snugly, leaving all the pearls exposed on the top of my foot—the most elegant sandal one could imagine. I'd never worn anything so beautiful. His awkward hands rebelled at fastening the gold clasp on the side of my foot, but he set his jaw and accomplished it in only four tries. "This is a fashion that was popular in my mother's day," he said as he worked at my other foot. "She would come to my room to tell me good night before going off to a ball, and she would show off her feet.

She'd say, 'Silly, is it not, that we scorn peasants for having holes in their boots, when ladies of fashion have decided it elegant to go dancing barefoot?' "

"These are worth a city's ransom. Where in the name of sense did you get them?" I said.

He finished the second clasp and nodded in satisfaction. "When we were at Devonhill, I retrieved a few things of my mother's. One was a pearl necklace I'd sent her from Eskonia."

"Your mother's pearls! I can't. Not on my feet." I'd heard his voice when he spoke of his mother.

He shook his head. "She would think it a terrific adventure. This whole thing." He stood up and offered me his arm. His dark eyes sparkled with the smile he knew better than to display. "She would be honored to have you wear them. As am I."

I wanted to say something horrid, to break the spell he laid upon me with his voice and his manner and his teasing. If I could shock him enough, remind him of my origins, of my hatred . . . But Mervil bustled over with a lightweight cloak of black, lined with green, while Aidan bounded up the stairs to see Tarwyl. The singer was back in time to hand me into the carriage. I spit on the ground when he offered a quiet suggestion on how to lift my skirt the proper way. Aidan shook hands with Mervil and embraced Davyn.

"Thank you, my true and honest friend," he said to Davyn, whose eyes glistened in the torchlight. "Regret nothing, whatever comes."

"The blessings of the One go with you, Aidan MacAllister, and the hopes of the world."

MacAllister jumped into the carriage and rapped twice

on the roof. We started off, rocking gently on the cobbles. The Senai sat opposite me. He propped an elbow on the window and leaned his chin on his hand. After a moment he spoke softly. "The hopes of the world . . . It would be a great deal simpler if everyone believed as you do."

"The only hopes you carry are those of three lunatic Elhim," I said.

"Then why is everyone so devilish determined to get their hands on me?"

"And what do you do but walk right into their hands? There's proof of madness."

He leaned his head back against the cushioned seat and laughed. "Ah, but what else would you be doing on this beautiful summer evening? We are elegantly dressed, riding in a duke's carriage, and on our way to a royal birthday party—an adventure to be sure for a woman who seems perfectly suited for adventure."

"I can think of only a thousand things I'd rather be doing. Almost anything."

As the carriage turned slowly out of the lane, we were passed by three horsemen riding furiously back the way we'd come. Even in the feeble light of our carriage lamps I recognized the leader. "Desmond!"

Aidan rapped once on the carriage roof, and we rolled to a stop. We crowded together to peer through the window back down the dark lane toward Mervil's shop. Torchlight blossomed in the quiet night. Loud hammering and shouts echoed in the lane, drawing curious heads from every window and door.

"I've got to go back," said the Senai, his easy humor vanished.

He shifted to open the carriage door, but I moved

quicker, shoving him back onto the seat and rapping twice on the roof. "We've left nothing behind to connect us to Mervil or the others. You'll do them no service by showing up at their door." I fell into the seat opposite him as the carriage jogged forward again. "And Desmond will never think to look for me dressed in silk and riding in a Senai duke's carriage. Wherever did you come by such a thing?"

He kept glancing back uneasily, but I nagged at him until he paid attention to me. "I would rather not have done it," he said, "but you can't just walk into a palace ball. So I remembered a man from Aberswyl who once told me he'd do any favor I asked. He's got no family to reap the consequences, and he happens to drive for the Duke of Tenzilan. He believes I'm a ghost."

"What did you do for him to earn such a gift?"

MacAllister shook his head. "He owed me nothing. It is I . . . I who owe everyone." He sank into grim silence as we rode through the streets of Aberswyl.

All too soon the carriage slowed, then rolled to a stop, only to creep forward a few paces before stopping again. From the carriage windows I could see nothing but trees and blazing lights. There were voices ahead of us. Roadblock. I felt for the knife I had secured in the waistband of my gown and cursed the lack of a sword. "We need to get out before they search the carriage," I said.

MacAllister shook off his preoccupation and laid a hand on my knee. "No, no. We're in the carriage line to be left off at the palace. Dougal will open the door when we reach the front portico." He searched my face, his brow wrinkled with concern. "Are you all right with this? I'll tell you whatever you need to know."

"I feel like a fool."

He leaned over and took my hands in his, and in his dark eyes I saw the reflection of a woman I did not recognize. "You are the most beautiful, the most glorious fool I have ever laid my eyes on," he said. He gave me my silver mask and donned his own, as the carriage door opened and a flood of music and light welcomed us to our doom.

Chapter 26

The royal palace of Aberthain made Aidan's guesthouse at Devonhill look as plain as a Ridemark tent. I never knew there was so much gold in the world or so many candles, or rooms so large a forest of marble was required to support the roof. I had never seen walls painted with scenes of dancers so like to life you felt the brush of their skirts or warriors so real you heard the clash of their swords.

Surely a thousand people crowded the room, all of them wearing diamonds and emeralds, silk, brocade, and satin, and every kind of mask: some simple like ours, some elaborate concoctions of paint and feathers, jewels or ivory. I would have stood gawking until the world ended had not Aidan taken me on his arm and propelled me through the mob. He spoke to the footman at the door, who passed along the whispering to a line of ten others in gold-crusted livery, ending with a haughty man in blue satin. The haughty man cried out, "Lord Fool and Lady Fire" as we descended a long flight of steps into the room.

"Lord Fool?" I scoffed, thinking I had mistaken MacAllister's ease in these surroundings for some small talent at intrigue. "You think no one will question such a ridiculous name?"

"Our masque names," the Senai murmured as he led me through the crowd. "I gave my father's title as our true identity—it will appear on the Elyrian Peers' List when they check. But at a masque they'll not announce it, and by the time anyone makes the connection with me, we'll be gone."

I felt like an ignorant beggar. I would rather have walked into a lair undefended than take one step into that ballroom. The air was thick with sickly perfumes and the smells of wine and roasting meat. The lamps—huge, garish things made of bits of glass—hung over our heads, blazing, brilliant, threatening to expose our true identities. People swarmed everywhere, bumping into us. Women glared at me through their masks. Men bowed and grinned, and glanced over their shoulders as we passed. What were they looking at? Everyone talked at once. Though they used the common speech, it might as well have been the tongue of frogs for all I could understand of it. Everything was light, noise, and danger. My stomach curled into a knot, and I thought I would suffocate.

But then an odd thing happened. I stepped on a sharp pebble tracked in on somebody's boots. I winced and kicked it away, but somehow when I felt only the cool marble beneath my bare feet, I was able to breathe again. It was a touch of reality, a steadiness beneath my feet in a strange and unreal place. Whether he knew it or not, MacAllister had done me a great service, leaving me shoeless.

At the far side of the room were two huge doors,

flanked by tall trees that had every leaf and twig painted silver. Between us and the doors, a line of guests moved slowly. I couldn't see what they were doing, but Aidan steered me to the end of the line, murmuring in my ear. "Once we're received by Renald, the queen, and the princess, we'll be on our own. You must curtsy to each one, and for the king you stay down until he gestures you up. No need to say anything unless they speak to you. Take it slow and don't fall over, and you'll do fine."

"But . . ." Before I could ask him what kind of gesture the king might make or what in the world to say if he did speak to me, MacAllister started talking to a man wearing a bird mask. It sounded as if he knew the man. Aidan was making some idiot's joke about "did we not fly together at the Duke of Folwys's hunt last year?" How could he be so stupid as to speak to someone he knew? I tried to pull him away, but he wouldn't budge.

The bird man laughed and presented his wife, who wore a mask of swan feathers and diamonds. "Countess Cygne," he said.

"Lady Fire," said Aidan as he bowed, tugging slightly at my elbow to remind me to dip my knee at the swan countess. The lady looked down her nose and nodded so slightly, you'd think she believed her head would break off if she moved it. The line crept forward like a snake. Aidan kept talking about nothing, and I listened to the others near us in the line. They all talked like that, as if they knew each other even when they didn't.

The princess was a cold-eyed, dull-looking girl of ten or twelve, her plump child's body stuffed into a silver gown that was much too tight for her. Little rolls of pink fat peeped out around the armholes of her gown, above her long sleeves. The queen was tall and slender and wore a ruby-studded gold mask that curled into her dark hair like a devil's horns. She was too proud to notice us, but greeted the swan countess over our heads and began talking about "the princess's fine health." Aidan bowed gracefully, but I wobbled a bit on my curtsy, saved from falling by his hand under my elbow.

"Lord Fool and Lady Fire," announced another man in blue satin who stood just behind the dark-haired, heavy-jowled man of thirty-some years—King Renald of Aberthain.

The king wore no mask and scowled impatiently at the room while speaking to someone over his shoulder. The aide standing behind him was also unmasked, dressed more for war than a ball. "They know we'll fight," said the king. "They don't have to ensure our alliance by trumping up some story about murdering madmen. Clear them out of here. I don't care what they say. I don't want them ruining Raniella's birthday."

"They refuse, sire," said the aide. "They'll not leave without bloodshed."

MacAllister sank to one knee and pulled me down beside him. It boiled my blood to do it. A daughter of the Ridemark making obeisance to a Senai king—it was humiliating, obscene. I tried to make it as brief as possible, but Aidan dug a finger into my arm so hard I almost struck him. The king dismissed his aide, then waggled a finger, which must have been the "gesture," for the singer finally allowed me to get up.

"Is that you, Gaelen?" The king cocked his head at MacAllister as he actually looked at us for the first time. "I've not seen you since winter."

"No, Your Majesty, the good Earl of Sennat does not lurk behind this Fool's mask. And it is a very long time indeed since I was fortunate enough to visit Aberswyl. It was your late father—all honor to his memory—who last received me here."

"Ah, well, then." The king lost interest and shifted his attention to the bird-masked man.

We had to greet fifty other nameless people in the line, all of them soft and proud and garbed with outlandish extravagance. Only then were we able to pass through the double doors into an even larger hall. Musicians were playing all sorts of harps and flutes and horns. Long tables were piled with food enough for a small city. I couldn't even say what most of it was. A few guests were dancing, and some were drinking and making loud, boisterous conversation. But more of them were standing about in small groups, speaking in furtive voices with sidelong glances. Perhaps that had something to do with the soldiers who stood alert at every doorway, and the proud strangers clad in red and black who stood with them.

"Clansmen!" I said. "We've—"

Aidan quickly swept me around to face him and stuffed a pastry in my mouth before I could say anything more. "Don't notice them," he said, smiling. "Pretend they are furniture." He guided me through the crowd and between the silent watchers onto a flagstone terrace.

Tall poles at every corner of the terrace were hung with garlands and topped with flaming torches. Fountains splashed, and flowering shrubs grew right out of the paving. Only a few people stood on the terrace, so it wasn't a good place for us to hide. I tried to drag Aidan

back toward the ballroom, but he placed his left arm behind my shoulders, catching my left hand in his, then
clasped my right hand with his right, just in front of us. I
growled and tried to pull away, but there was steel beneath his soft manner. I could not get loose without drawing attention. "We need to be dancing," he said. "Too
many curious eyes about tonight. Follow my steps, and
we'll practice." He moved me forward three steps, then
stepped behind me, coming out on the other side. Forward three steps more.

"I don't need—"

He spun me about until we were facing each other,
then bowed and caught my hands again. "This is a ron-
delle . . . the most romantic of dances. Hear the rhythm:
one, two, three, one, two. One, two, three, one two.
One . . ." As he had when he led me across Fandine, he
tapped the rhythm with his fingers and willed my feet to
move in harmony with his. I fretted about my bare toes
and his mother's pearls, about tripping over his feet and
falling into the fountains, or tumbling into the beds of
roses and entangling us with mud and thorns. But after
my first stumbling steps, I felt the music flowing through
him and into me, a clumsy warrior who had never lifted
a foot to dance. The torchlight blurred. The other people
disappeared. For one moment Aidan took me away from
that place, made me into something I never thought I
could be. All I saw was the torchlight and the spinning
garden and the white ruffle of his shirt in front of my
nose, and all I heard and all I felt was music. . . .

"Are you sure you've never done this, Lady Fire?"
came the question from above my head.

Startled, I stumbled. He caught me, never missing a

step. But the world came back into focus, and I yanked my arm away, unable to contain myself. Anger, I called it. Humiliation. "A curse on you and your Senai ways. No oath can make me do this."

He smiled his infuriating smile beneath the silver mask. "Then don't do it. I'll walk you to the door, we'll call for the carriage, and Dougal will take you anywhere you like. I'd like nothing better than for you to walk out of here safely." I started to answer him, but he laid his white-gloved finger on my lips. "You believe I'll die anyway, so what use is there for you to take these risks?" He took my hands again, and we drifted with the music. The scent of flowers lay heavy on the garden air. "Shall I tell you—since we are masked and not ourselves at all, Lord Fool can speak as a fool at last—shall I tell you what Aidan MacAllister would wish to be the reason that you stay?"

"No." My answer came out weakly. Not at all as I wanted. "You should not tell me anything."

"Should not. Mmm . . . not enough to prevent a fool. He—this Aidan who is the greatest of fools, a mad fool— would wish that perhaps you did not want him to die. And if his death were to be the result of his madness, then at least he would have spent his last hour in your company, regretting nothing . . . nothing . . . that had brought him to it."

For that single moment, everything I never knew I wanted lay in my hand. All I had to do was pretend that the past had never happened and the future was unknown. The music soared. The lights shimmered. The night whispered a promise of joy. But I could not do it. I had abandoned the teachings of my people, betrayed every tradition, every code, every rule, but I would not permit my desire to destroy the remnants of my honor.

Yet neither did I do what I ought. I needed to tell him he was wrong, that I despised him, that I would be happy to let him die in a dragon's fire or in the torment of Mazadine. I wanted to say that only my oath would force me to go into Aberthain Lair with him and aid his futile purpose. But I could not do that either. I held mute, and Aidan laughed with delight. We danced through the glass doors into the whirling crowd, and I would have slain the gods themselves to make time stop.

"My lords and ladies!" A trumpet fanfare and a shouting fat man in blue satin brought me back to my senses. The music fell silent, and a hush fell over the crowd. "His Majesty King Renald welcomes all to this joyous celebration of Her Royal Highness Princess Raniella's natal day. May King Renald reign in glory, and Aberthain ever triumph o'er all that seek her downfall. Let the gates be opened so that all may witness the power of Aberthain!"

The trumpets shrilled again, and Aidan's arm urged me toward the glass-paned doors at the farthest end of the ballroom and the iron gates just beyond. I refused to move. Two Ridemark warriors had moved swiftly into position beside each of the three doorways. "Vanir's fire, do you see who's in command?" I whispered, nodding to the tall warrior who stood to the side watching all three doors. "It's Duren Driscoll, the high commander's adjutant. He saw you in Cor Neuill."

MacAllister paled beneath his mask. "This way," he said, and he began to work us sideways through the press. I could not see our objective above the heads of the crowd, until we came upon the man in the bird mask and his swan wife.

"Countess Cygne," said Aidan, bowing and sidling up close to the lady. "I had a delightful story from King Devlin when last I saw him. One could hardly believe it true. I've never known him a great joker. Before I pass the story along, I thought I should confirm it with someone who knows His Majesty better than I. What do you think?"

The simpering countess hung herself on Aidan's arm as if he had offered her the Elyrian crown, and the bird count took my arm as the crowd flowed toward the doors and the Ridemark commander. At Driscoll's direction, the warriors in red and black were forcing some of the guests to remove their masks or . . . curse it all . . . their gloves. Surely MacAllister could not see what was happening or he'd never be prattling so calmly.

A sudden silence from beside me made me realize that the count was waiting for me to answer him.

"What? Pardon, my lord, I didn't hear you. The noise . . ."

"What think you of the ball, my lady?" He spoke as if taking care that his words did not fall so low as the floor.

Aidan had smoothly arranged himself between the count and his wife so there was no possibility of getting his attention. How did these people talk?

"Delightful, a delightful ball"—only two people remaining between the warriors and us—"except for these ruffians. What business have Ridemark scum at King Renald's palace?"

"Intolerable, I agree," said the count, his lip curling and his eyes glittering fiercely through his ivory and feathers. "They're pretending to hunt a criminal. Likely they only want to spy on their betters. Barbarians."

I dearly wanted to pull my dagger on the sneering count and introduce him to a barbarian.

A red-cloaked young man in front of us was commanded to remove his mask and gloves, and he put up a great fuss. Aidan was still babbling with the countess. I fingered the knife hidden at my waist. I would not allow Aidan to be taken.

"How dare they touch King Renald's guests?" I said to the count, slowing my steps. "I'll scream if their foul hands come near me."

Driscoll—cold and hateful as I knew him—addressed the young nobleman's complaint by stuffing the gloves in his mouth and twisting his arm behind him as if to break it. Heads turned away, choosing not to see as the choking guest was dragged to the side.

The young clansman just ahead of us forced another man to remove his gloves before allowing him to pass through the doors. Then it was our turn. Aidan was laughing, his head close together with the countess, their arms entwined. I clung to the count and shrank from the clansman, while using my left hand to ready my knife.

The warrior motioned to Aidan. "Show your hands before you pass. Take off those gloves."

But before Aidan could turn his head, the count laid his hand on the jeweled hilt of his sword. "Touch anyone in my party, and I will remove your nose and ears."

"I have orders—"

"You have no orders that pertain to the Count de'Journay. I will pass here as I choose, or we will settle it with blood. However skilled you may deem yourself, consider that I have forty years' experience in my arm. You will not prevail."

The warrior looked helplessly at Driscoll's averted back, but the commander was still occupied with the rebellious young nobleman. Evidently the count's name carried weight, for the Rider gritted his teeth and jerked his head toward the gate. "Pass. I'll inform my commander of your refusal."

"Tell your mongrel commander that my challenge extends to him also, beast rider."

The count escorted me and his wife and Aidan, who had scarcely paused in his chatter, through the iron gates. We came onto a broad terrace that hung out over the night like a dead limb of the brightly lit palace. Servants passed through the crowd with trays of wineglasses, and Aidan carefully handed them around. He lifted his own in a toast to the count and his lady. "Though it is proper to toast Aberthain and its king when on this terrace, I will offer my first to the noble and gallant Count de'Journay, the hero who turned back the barbarians at Desmarniers as well as in this latest minor skirmish, and to his ravishing wife—may you continue to grace Aberthain and Elyria with honor and beauty."

The count nodded an acknowledgment, then responded with a toast to the king. I only pretended to drink. I needed all of my wit to keep the fool of a Senai alive.

The swan countess put her hand on Aidan's arm. "Tell us your identity, Lord Fool. I'm sure I know you, such a charming young gentleman. Your voice is so familiar."

"Ah, my lady, now is not the time to show ourselves. Allow us lesser lights to glow for a while longer in your brilliance. When the moment comes to unmask, all shall be revealed. But if I am not to be found, you must ask King Devlin, when next you meet him, who it was knew the story of his father's missing crossbow. For now I must beg your indulgence. My Lady Fire has never seen the dread glory of Aberthain, and I would show her before the trumpets recall us to our dancing."

As he kissed her hand, the swan lady laughed at his foolishness. Then she took her husband's arm and moved away to greet someone else.

Though his voice had been light and even, Aidan was trembling as he guided me to the outer wall of the terrace. A gout of fire arced across the sky, and the crowd cheered along with a distant bellow. "To the western edge," he said. "The wall is lower there."

From the pit of blackness before us came an answering bellow, closer this time, furious, tormented. MacAllister faltered, losing what color remained in his face. I draped my arms around him and laughed as if we were flirting, but I kept him moving toward the wall. "How long until they go back inside?" I said. "Is there any place to hide? No one bothered to tell me your plan." Anything to draw him from his distraction. "Tell me what to do, or I might as well put this knife in you right now."

"Over the wall." He forced the words out. "Around the outside to the steps. We've only a few moments, no more, until everyone goes inside again."

The crowd was thinner near the waist-high wall on the west end of the terrace. Most of the guests remained well away from the wall, chattering and laughing as if they had no idea what horror lay so close by in the darkness; several couples, who seemed to enjoy being alone among so many, drifted toward the outer edges of the crowd. Three men and one woman stood singly, gazing out over the dark lair. Those four were the dangerous ones—lone observers who might notice something unusual.

"We're going over the wall?" I said. Aidan nodded, drawing breath sharply as another cry echoed from the towering cliffs to our right and left. I put my hands around his neck and drew his head down close to mine. His eyes were squeezed shut, and his breath came shallowly. He was not going to be able to think of his plan, much less tell me of it. "I'm going to sit on the wall," I said, "and you must examine my ankle as if I've hurt it. Do you understand me?"

"Ankle . . . yes . . ."

"You'll have to help me get up." I stumbled and grabbed onto his arm. He put his arm around me and half dragged, half carried me across the terrace, then awkwardly supported my waist as I lifted myself onto the wall. "Sorry," he said. "I can't—"

"It's all right. Now examine my ankle however a Senai gentleman would think proper."

He knelt in front of me, murmuring so softly I had to bend over to hear him. "Lara, I've got to tell you—"

He was interrupted by another trumpet fanfare. Dancing music started up inside the palace, and laughing guests began to stroll inside. One of the lone observers walked away.

"When I tell you, dive headfirst over the wall . . ." I peered over my shoulder to make sure of the terrain. It was as bad as I expected—a narrow, outsloping strip of rock and turf, verging on nothing. ". . . instantly."

The terrace was emptying rapidly. We couldn't wait

too long or we'd be too conspicuous. The clansmen might check for stragglers. The count was arguing with the Ridemark warrior again. The second man of the four single stragglers called out to a friend and moved toward the gates, and the woman hurried away.

Aidan pretended to adjust my nonexistent shoe. I reached down and removed the pearls from my feet, dropping them into his gloved hand. He stared at them for a moment, and then stuffed them into the pocket of his cloak. The last lone man glanced toward the doors, where Duren Driscoll was gesturing violently at the Count de'Journay.

"Now," I said, and rolled backward off the wall. Aidan came headfirst after me, and we tumbled and slid down the small weedy slope much too fast. I dug in my fingers and toes to stop us. None too soon. My head dangled over the edge of the cliff, looking down upon the fire-streaked desolation of Aberthain Lair.

Trumpets blared from behind the wall, and a voice cried out, "All hail the glory of Aberthain!" We heard a clash of iron as the gates were closed and locked. MacAllister and I lay paralyzed, waiting to hear the alarm raised, but no cry interrupted the noise of the ballroom, now muffled by the palace walls. No head peered over the wall. No sword jabbed our necks. We gave it a few agonizing moments, then crept along the narrowing gap between the wall to our right and the sheer drop to our left. But just as we reached the steep flight of steps that dropped from the terrace into the black pit, the iron gates rolled back again. We crowded into the dark gully where our little shelf of rock and dirt met the stone steps.

". . . fools not to get the attendance list. He mocks us

by putting it there for all to see." The voice floated over the terrace wall just above our heads.

"Who could expect he'd use his father's title?"

"Not the cretins I sent here to watch, obviously. Two of you check the walls. The rest of you into the lair. The vermin will not escape us this time."

"Hurry," I whispered to MacAllister as I yanked the small knife from my skirt and the longer one from the strap on my leg. "Go on down. I'll take care of these bastards from behind and catch up with you."

"No." He laid his hand on my wrist. "No one is going to die tonight."

"Except you. Is that it?"

"If that's the way of it. But I have no wish to be excepted. Wait for them to pass."

Three clansmen clattered down the steps just above our heads. We climbed up onto the stair and ran recklessly downward after them. My back crawled with the certainty that Driscoll would glimpse us from the terrace wall above, but we reached the lower stair without discovery. A glimmer of lantern light told me we were nearing the bottom of the steps, a likely place for a guard posting. At this point one side of the stair hugged the cliff wall, and the other side dropped off into the pit.

I grabbed MacAllister's coat and his attention, pointing down off the side. He nodded and went first, supporting himself with his forearms and stretching his long legs into the sheer darkness, craning his head to see how far was the drop. One muffled groan as his foot slipped and his damaged shoulders bore his full weight. I dropped to my knees and locked my arms with his as he fought to find a foothold. Lying down on the step, I stretched my arms and lowered him over the edge to give him a little more extension; then I felt his fingers tapping rapidly on my arm. I let go. A quiet thud, not too far away. Then a soft whistle. As I scrambled over the edge, preparing to let go of the warm stone and drop through the darkness, a wave of dizziness and terror almost stopped my heart. Stupid. We weren't yet in the fire.

Aidan kept me from hitting the ground, though rather more in the way of allowing me to fall on him than catching me. We ended up in a ridiculous heap of silk and satin, dirt and rocks. My bare back was on his face, and his arms were wrapped about me. While grunting to catch his breath, he murmured, "We'd better find your armor or I'm going to have the devil of a time keeping my mind on business." I shoved his arms away and stood up, digging my elbow into his gut hard enough to make him clamp off a groan. We had no more time for teasing nonsense.

Tarwyl had told us that the cookshed was fifty paces left from the bottom of the stair, and without checking to see if MacAllister was behind me, I set off, creeping along the cliff wall. Three men rushed past us, their torchlight flattening us against the rocks for a terrifying moment. But their eyes were straight ahead of them, and they didn't see us.

We ran the rest of the way to Tarwyl's hiding place, a waist-high shelf where the broad, outsloping cliff wall broke away from the back wall of a ramshackle shed. My bag was stuffed in the corner of the niche, which was littered with bones and rotting scraps from predators who preyed on stray herd beasts. We dared not stay long enough for me to change into my armor, for the Elhim might have been forced to reveal our plan. I grabbed the bag, and we hurried away from the herd pens and the lamplit sheds toward the center of the lair.

Unlike Fandine and Cor Neuill, the floor of this valley was not flat. At the base of the cliffs was a broad shelf ring on which they had built the herd pens and barracks, the serving women's shelter, and the smithy. At the inner edge of the shelf ring was a steep, rocky border where the land dropped away into the heart of the lair. The Riders' huts would be down below, butted against the rocky slope.

The farther we went, the worse I wanted my boots. An afternoon rain had turned the blasted wastes into thick, black muck, and every step was a small panic lest I slice my bare foot on a stray dragon scale. Shouts rang from every direction, and twice we had to cram ourselves into some narrow shadow to avoid Ridemark patrols. There seemed to be five hundred clansmen in the lair to guard the three dragons of Aberthain.

After a third close call with a search party and a moment's pause to let MacAllister recover from a dragon's bellow that had him staggering, we streaked across a deserted area of the shelf and scrambled into the rocky perimeter of the inner lair. From a sheltered niche in the rocks we peered into the vast pit, and just below us, not five hundred paces away, was the kai we'd come to find.

The beast was immeasurably old: the brow ridges as gnarled and thick as old oak trees, the neck folds so deep you could hide an army in them, layer upon layer of jibari encrusted on its scales. And its right shoulder was not a long, smooth taper into the bulging haunch, but sharp and angular, as if a giant had broken it and set it improperly. The right wing sat higher than the left, yet the twisting deformity was not a new thing. Jibari grew thick in the shoulder crease, and there was no slackening of the beating fury of the wings when it tried to escape the binding that kept it earthbound.

"The birds," whispered MacAllister in awe, his hand on my shoulder. "Look at the birds."

Indeed there must have been five thousand small, dark shapes hovering about the kai, picking its leavings from the blasted earth, settling on its back and shoulders, twittering and chirping, yet never getting caught in the streams of fire that poured from the beast's mouth. But this beast was no gentle companion. The kai lurched in its half-walking, half-flying way toward a penned cluster of no less than fifty bawling sheep. An arc of orange fire shot from its mouth as it let forth a raging bellow loud enough to split one's skull. Its eyes were windows on the netherworld, and its massive tail whipped and pounded until the very earth shuddered. With little more than a flick of one taloned foot, the kai left the sheep a bloody, writhing wreckage. After another blaring trumpet, its jaws closed around the gory mess, slavering blood and spitting fire.

Aidan drew back and sank to the ground, leaning against the rocks in shadows neither the growing moonlight nor the sallow glow of dragon fire could reach. I could feel his eyes on me, the dark eyes welling with tears of blood for his lost god. "Lara, how am I to do this?" His voice was filled with anguish and fear, and I was on the verge of such weakness as I had never imagined. But any answer was precluded by another blaring wail from the dragon, and like the herald summoning me to battle, it reminded me of where and who and what I was.

I dumped out the contents of my bag—the articles that were the proper focus of my life. "You will be silent," I hissed, as the flesh-tearing screech died away. With no heed to his shyness, I stripped off my false skin of mud-fouled silk and pulled on my own life: coarse wool and leather and russet, the stinking armor of my clan. I twisted my hair until my scalp ached and jammed the stiffened helm on it, and I arranged the coils of my whip and snugged its sharp steel tips without regard to the watching eyes that were revolted by it.

The treacherous moon had crept over the cliff wall and invaded our hiding place, throwing MacAllister into deeper shadow and glinting off the tin box that lay at my feet, where it had fallen from the armor bag. It was time. The singer was going to die, and he deserved to know the truth before he screamed his mind away in a dragon's breath. I wished that hatred and revenge might deter him from his course, but I knew better, so I would not dally while he read what I would show him.

"This is how we shall proceed," I told him. "I'll say all the words as they are spoken for the binding rite in the clan—the seven invocations that I should be damned forever for revealing. When the kai is ready, at the moment the Rider would step forth with the kai's bloodstone, I will raise my left hand. You'll have perhaps half a minute to do whatever you imagine will save your life."

He tried to speak, but I would not permit it. One word and I would crumble.

"Before you address this creature, you should review a few bits of dragon lore," I said, pulling Narim's journal from the box and opening it to a page written almost eighteen years in the past. I thrust it into the white-gloved hands, then strapped the bloodstone about my neck and left him sitting in the cleft of the rocks, reading the account of how I had stolen his life.

Chapter 27

Day 26 in the month of Vellya
Year 497 of our shame
Year 4 in the reign of the human King Devlin
Journal entry:

What satisfaction is in my heart tonight! There is no doubt that this Aidan MacAllister is the one for whom we have waited, the Dragon Speaker that Jodar described to me over five hundred years ago. He sings their visions and follows them about the land without understanding why, completely unaware of the trail of chaos he leaves behind him. Never in my long life have I heard such beauty and clarity and truth. And the youth himself is all that is good.

Even such a magnificent discovery leaves a trail of complications, though—however small in comparison to the finding. How am I to tell him he is unfinished—a boy who has no idea of what he is and what he is capable of doing? How can I convince him that he must leave his life behind for seven years? In ancient days Jodar told us of the seasoning time of silence needed for a true

Dragon Speaker, and though it is beyond our understanding, we dare not proceed without it. What if MacAllister is not strong enough to do what we need? He is human. He is so young. Humans are so easily distracted—a penalty of short-lived races. Humans need answers for all mysteries.

Even if I could convince him, where could I send him to live out seven years safely, now that the Twelve know such a one exists and hunt him? If they discover him, we are lost.

Lara says she was able to hide her bloodstone for four years, that the Twelve cannot see what is right under their noses. The child is filled with bitterness, but her perceptions are acute. If only I could believe her.

Yet if she is correct, there could be a plan here, now I think of it. Under their noses . . .

By the One, the thought that comes to my head appalls me. Yet the more I consider it, the more reasonable it seems. The Ridemark will not rest until they discover who is inciting insurrection among their dragons, and if he continues, they'll likely kill him in their rage. But what if I were to solve their problem for them? MacAllister must live in silence for seven years to perfect his gift, and I have no doubt that he will need to be coerced to do it. Those of the Ridemark clan are experts at coercion of a cruel and deadly sort, but they would never dare truly harm MacAllister, for he is cousin to the king and known across the world. And I have the perfect resource to reveal

*his identity to the Twelve. Lara will tell her
brother the name of the one who torments their
dragons, and that Narim's secret journal says that
the only way to cure him of it is to force him silent
for seven years. MacAllister will do as he is told,
for he is human and will be afraid. Once he sees
the Ridemark is sincere—a scratch or two
perhaps—no other course will be open to him. He
will obey and be silent, and in seven short years
we will all of us be free.*

Chapter 28

I picked a position perhaps fifty paces left of MacAllister and halfway down the steep ring wall, among the largest boulders I could find. The boulders might shelter me briefly, though no venue so close to a kai was safe for long. It didn't matter that I was still outside the Riders' perimeter, for the purpose of the rite was to drive the beast into madness so that its fire burned sheer white, the hottest it could possibly be. When I took up my stance on the top of an angular boulder, a new risk presented itself. Just below me was a stone-and-leather hut—a Rider's hut. Bad luck if it belonged to the Rider who controlled this kai. I wasn't sure I could prevail in a direct contest of wills with the bound master of the beast. But there was nothing for it but to begin.

I dismissed every thought of Aidan, of love and guilt, of doubt and fear. There could be no place inside me for anything but will. Already the kai's nostrils flared wider, and the red eyes blazed hotter, and from the monstrous head came a low rumbling that made my teeth hurt. I uncoiled my whip and unsheathed my dagger.

"Teng zha nav wyvyr," I cried out.

Thus began the most difficult battle of my life—harder even than the disastrous venture of my childhood. On this night I had not only to control the kai, but, at the same time, purposely drive it into uttermost frenzy. It wasn't going to take long. By the time I was through the initial summons and the first of the seven invocations, the beast screamed so powerfully that I lost my balance and fell backward on the rock. Without releasing my control I got back to my feet and found a steadier foothold on a narrow ledge with my back to the angular boulder. Then I pronounced the second invocation.

I had reviewed Narim's journal where he had written all he knew of the Rite of the Third Wing—of the day the Elhim had enslaved the dragons using the songs the dragons sang to calm their restless younglings, of the day the dragons had seen those younglings dead and breathed white fire upon the Elhim, somehow binding dragon and Elhim to the vile bloodstones. I had racked my childhood memories for tone and position and every slight variation that could influence the outcome. But in the rites I had witnessed, the Rider had carried a bloodstone and worn armor to protect him from the dragon's wrath. And the only Elhim to survive the long-ago debacle beside the lake of fire had worn bloodstones. Aidan planned to go defenseless, thinking . . . what? That he could himself become some living bloodstone? That his talent . . . his heart . . . his compassion would bind him to some scrap of sentience buried in this horror and allow him to control it?

Concentrate, fool, or you'll be dead before him.

I spoke the third invocation—a verse about gathering with brothers and sisters in the realm of the wind. The kai thrashed its tail and unfurled its wings, an ocean of flailing green and copper that seemed to cover half the valley.

Forbidden by its bound Rider to fly from the lair, the kai set up such a screaming that I thought I would be deaf again. It lurched closer, half the distance between us in the space of a heartbeat. I pressed my back against the rock, wishing the kai were blind like Keldar or crippled like the beast in Fandine.

From before and below me came a glimmer of red light, and as I screamed out the fourth invocation, the Rider stepped out of his hut. The kai's hatred was made more vicious and more direct by the command of its Rider. The beast lurched forward again, and the snout waved back and forth, searching . . . listening . . . closer. My eyes burned with the acrid smoke. Too close. I ducked and shifted right along the ledge, trying to find a place where I could retreat, then threw myself onto the ground again when a wing swept past my head. I was coughing and choking, buffeted by the stinking wind of its passing. Raging malevolence blazed in the red eyes as I struggled to speak the fifth invocation. I lay on my back, pressed to the rock by the weight of hatred from the devil kai.

"Lara! What madness is this?" The voice came from behind and above me. My brother's voice.

"Get her out of here!"

"She'll have us all baked."

"Holy Jodar! Treachery! She wears a bloodstone!"

"Slay her now and be done with this. Gruesin, get up here!"

"Let it go, Lara," Desmond yelled. "Gruesin will control the kai if you but let it go." Four men in Rider's armor moved toward me from the left. A fifth, the Rider from the hut, climbed up from the valley floor to my right.

I lashed out to each side with my whip, as much to keep Desmond and his cohorts away as to deter the monstrous head that swayed toward me. I screamed the sixth invocation, and the dragon reared backward, spewing fire straight up—white flames only slightly tinged with orange. My helm had been knocked off when I fell, so the skin of my face blistered in the heat.

Hands clutched at my armor, and I slashed at them with my dagger while I struggled to get out the last verse. I had never listened to the words before. "Take this youngling, child of fire and wind. Lift its wings with your breath and your power. Be its third wing until it masters the upper airs. This fledgling is yours and not yours. It lives by your grace and dies by your command, and its service shall ever be your pleasure. In the sun shall you fly as one; in the cold moonlight shall you together devour the night. Inseparable. Unchanging. Eternal."

The Riders dragged me across the rocks and up the slope, away from the raging kai. My dagger was snatched from my hand, and my whip snagged in the rocks. Five whips slashed around me and at least two bloodstones flickered, fighting to keep the maddened beast at bay. But as the screeching kai stretched its neck high above us and belched forth a trailer of pure white flame, I pulled loose my left hand and raised it high. Abruptly I was dropped onto the hard, hot ground, while my captors pointed and yelled in dismay at a dark figure scrambling down the steep rocks on our right. I began kicking and screaming, laying my hand on the spare knife hidden in my boot and embedding it in at least one leather-clad leg so they had no chance to give chase until it was too late. For, of course, the kai had seen him, too.

He stopped no more than twenty paces from the mad dragon and raised his arms in supplication. So tiny, so fragile a being beside the monster. I could not hear if he said anything before he began screaming, for the dragon knocked him instantly to his knees with a bone-shattering bellow and bathed Aidan MacAllister in eye-searing white fire. "Aidan, beloved!" I sobbed. His hair and clothes were burning when I closed my eyes, and covered my head, and sank to the hot, stony earth. I could not weep. All my tears had burned away with my heart.

Chapter 29

Chaos. The red claw shatters wholeness. Rends.
Grinding discord rules.
The hglar—our masters whose stink is unlife,
whose claw is red that scrapes, wrenches, tears—
the hglar torments me ever.
Fly . . . fly to seek wholeness,
but the biting red claw will not loose me.
I who once . . . what was I? Lost am I.

These noises . . . the hglar makes words of remembering:
of flight, of youngling wings so tender, of the upper airs.
Ahhhh . . . to remember! To fly!
Yet not. Crushing horror,
Bound to this hard, unyielding plane.
Heaviness. Vileness.
The taste ever in my mouth—
red, warm, stinking human blood and human flesh.
Despised taste.
Bitter taste of wretchedness, yet become an unstoppable
*   craving.*
Take the human blood and flesh the hglar offers,
It numbs pain, silences remembering, and there is
*   nothing else.*

Nothing.
I am become chaos. Chaos ever.

Again come the words of remembering.
I would sear the younglings to bear them up.
Not yet, for the red claw tears and binds.
Captive ever. No joining. No sisters. No brothers. Chaos.

Remember! Ever again come the words.
Burn them, gently burn them
to guide and nurture to eternal wholeness.
Come, my youngling . . . fly!
I will lift thee to the upper airs, to the cold lights,
to the glorious burning of the greatest fire.
Fly with me and thy wings will not falter.
No.
No younglings. Only pain that crushes.
Chaos ever.

But here, what creature comes to join with me?
Hglar? No. This one is clawless. Scaleless.
Is it human flesh . . . blood . . . sent to ease my vile
*   cravings?*
No. It comes willing.
Is it beast flesh sent to fill my belly?
No. Not beast.
Nor a flying one . . . the blank, empty flying ones,
younglings yet unborn, not bound to the cruel hard nest.
They sweeten the passing winds of binding horror with
*   their singing.*
But this not-hglar, not-beast, not–flying one . . . a
*   youngling?*

It cannot be.
The creature's air is storm-driven. Discord.
Human flesh. Human blood.
Smash it. Devour it. Soothe this unwhole craving.
Yet . . . hold . . . a word it speaks of wholeness.

"Roelan, remember!"

What voice is this?
Wholeness? No.
Another bound with sorrow . . . bound to pain.
Younglings know not of pain and horror,
nor do the bleating beasts who sate my hunger.
This one is other.
Release this creature from its cruel nest.
Loose its flight into the airs we know not.
Burn it with unlife to free it from its pain.

Yet again, hear. A voice names this not-youngling,
not-beast, not-hglar.

"Aidan, beloved!"

Aidan . . . Aidan, beloved . . . ? Remember . . .
Who calls me to remember?
Can it be my own, my lost one?

Burn, my youngling! Transform me.
Soothe my uttermost sorrows.
Burn with all of my life and make me remember!

AIDAN

Chapter 30

What is the shape of time? Humans speak as if time takes the form of those things that occupy it: pleasurable things gone too quickly or dull things that linger long past their welcome. Yet in my years of silence, when life was emptiness, the hours did not collapse upon themselves like empty grain sacks. Every moment had depth, breadth, and length; every hour had its immutable volume and built one upon the other until time's edifice was tall enough that I could be free. Yet from the moment I gave myself to Roelan in Aberthain Lair, the shape of time was altered, so that I could not say what was a moment or an hour or a day.

Half a minute, Lara had told me. Half a minute from the time she would raise her left hand until the dragon would let loose its fire that could melt stone. And I would need half of that to ensure I stood directly in its path. Mad fool. How did I ever expect to deliver the message I had worked on so painstakingly in the past weeks, the words so carefully chosen from my memories of joy?

It was not that I was unwilling. My intent was clear. My resolution firm. Whatever were Narim's secrets—and I had come to the conclusion that his secrets were monumental—I believed they were beyond my purpose. I had to reach for truth. But I had not counted on being half-crazed with Lara. Mazadine had presented no torment so refined as had these last two days with her, playing at the intimacy I desired above all things, forbidden by her spoken hatred from making it real, yet tantalized with words and deeds that lured me into thinking she cared what happened to me. And I had not counted on my rage at learning that Narim had sent me to the netherworld to keep me "safe," because he believed no human capable of faith. Yet even from that horrific revelation had sprung a hope to feed my love-struck lunacy. Lara must have thought her revelation would make me despise her, but all I could see was that she refused to leave untruth between us. And even as I wrestled with all of this, the dragon threatened to crack my head with its trumpeting madness.

What rational words can form themselves from such chaos in a quarter of a minute? What instant's communication can penetrate the awesome, terrifying, majestic horror of a dragon in wildest frenzy?

So when the time came and I ran to embrace the world's worst nightmare, all I could come out with was "Roelan, remember!" And it was clearly not enough. The red-slimed nostrils flared and the monstrous head dipped toward me; then came the ear-shattering bellow and blinding holocaust that knocked me to my knees. One fleeting instant of grief for Lara, for music, for dragons, and for glorious, decadent, holy life, and I was consumed by pain so horrific it made everything I had ever experienced a mere pinprick.

Across my mind skittered the word *hurry*, which was odd in itself because I was expecting death to be quick at least. But time had begun to play its unsettling tricks, and

the pain and the earth-splitting noise did not end. Somewhere amidst the cacophony of raging white flames and
dragon's madness, I heard my own screaming, and
thought, "Why isn't that miserable soul dead? Why
doesn't he shut up?"

Remember . . .

Was it my own word echoing in my dying ears?

"Aidan, beloved!" From outside the fire came Lara's
cry . . . so dear, so poignant, penetrating my agony with
sweet revelation and piercing regret.

Then from somewhere so remote as to be beyond the
moon and stars, drifted the same call, so faint that the
flutter of a moth's wing would mute it, or the whisper of
a cloud's passing, or the landing of a snowflake on a
knee-high drift. Not words, for the speaker could no
longer shape words, not even the subtle vocalizations
Keldar had used. An image. A questioning image.
Aidan . . . Aidan, beloved?

In the formless, shapeless moment that I heard it, I resolved to postpone death. I could not ignore the voice that
had been the foundation of my life, but chaos, pain, and
horror deafened me to his faint call. I had to seek some
inner quiet where I could hear him and make answer. To
find that place I made a journey beset with visions,
pushed through all those things that crowded into my
mind, demanding to stand as my last grief or my last
pleasure. Beyond the fire and present anguish floated the
image of Lara, not dancing with the grace and beauty she
denied, but dressed in leather and pride, bending terror to
her will. More images: a laughing Davyn slapping me on
the shoulder, a wine-soaked kiss from Callia, a hurt and
angry Alfrigg bleeding with my betrayal. I forced them

all to give way: Goryx and Garn MacEachern and their whips and chains and despair, the charred bitterness of Iskendar, the enigma that was Narim. I delved deeper and grieved again for Gerald and Alys and Gwaithir, and I heard my father's mindless wailing and my mother's loving laughter. As I had learned in Mazadine, I left them all behind. And somehow in the midst of chaos, I reached the silent darkness, the cool and quiet ocean of my soul's peace.

"Remember," I said with blistering tongue and cracking lips. "It is thy servant . . . thy brother . . . Aidan come to set you free." Then I settled myself to wait and listen for as long as time might let me live.

Aidan, beloved . . . The image came so much clearer.

"I am here," I answered.

My own. My lost one. I remember thee . . . broken, sorrowing, alone.

"No longer sorrowing," I said. "No longer alone. Thy voice is my comfort and my delight."

He was with me. The voice I perceived—hearing is not at all an accurate description of what I did—was indeed the voice I had called a god. I'd had no other name for such a being. As in our first days together when I was a child, he was buried so deep in wildness that I could scarcely comprehend the images he poured into me— only their undying beauty, and the love and joy with which he created them.

I could have drunk in his wild visions forever, but the darkness began to waver before my eyes, and my lungs labored as if bands of molten steel were tightening around my chest. I was burning . . . dying. . . . "Roelan, remember! Fly free and live with joy!" The strange interval of peace that time had granted me was past, and I opened my eyes to see my outstretched arms ablaze. My clothes charred to ash and fell away, yet to my wonder, my flesh did not. The hair on my arms and body flared into glowing cinders, and the blood in my veins surged boiling against my skin. but I knelt on blackened earth and did not die. And at some boundary just short of madness, pain was transformed into near-unbearable ecstasy.

Burn with all of my life, beloved. Make me remember.

For a moment or an hour or a day I was consumed by dragon's fire. Like a youngling dragon my childish scales were burned away, and I was joined with my elder, each of us giving freely of the gifts the gods had left us. So simple an answer. The song set him free. The words Lara had spoken, perverted for so long by the will-destroying bloodstones, now returned to purity and grace. The music we made together. Roelan was my third wing, lifting me out of mortal existence for those few moments, teaching me of life and wonder, now I had reminded him of his soul.

The fire faded and was gone. The dragon straightened its neck and trumpeted in triumph and exhilaration, showering me with a fountain of cold blue sparks that fell with the blessedness of drought-relieving rain. Limp, spent, incapable of thought, I raised my arms and laughed mindlessly with him, for my every sense, every pore, every bone understood that Roelan was free. I could have been deaf—perhaps I was—yet I could have heard the joy in his cry. I could have been blind—that might yet come from the brilliance of his flames—yet through his eyes I could see the world changed, as if a charred gray curtain had been torn away. The stars shone like shattered diamonds on the velvet sky; the summer lightning sparked pink and orange over snow-tinged pinnacles to the south. As the sun unveils its splendor in the coming of the dawn, so did Roelan unfurl his wings of luminous red-gold and green and, in a hurricane of glory, soar into the night sky, splitting the heavens with a rainbow arc of flame as he disappeared beyond the horizon. Tears scalded my cheeks as I huddled, naked and alone, to the black, unyielding earth.

For the moment or hour that it took me to regain some semblance of reason, I was not yet able to consider my position or my future or even whether there was anyone to observe the oddity of my continued life. I could think only of Roelan. Was he gone to wreak vengeance on the Riders or King Renald and his soldiers? Was he already winging his way to the lake of fire? I craved knowledge of his purpose and what the result of our night's mystery might be. While I had burned in his fire I had felt my heart reborn, sensing a stirring of words and harmonies long dead. But as time creaked slowly on its way and I gazed upon the empty sky, the darkness came creeping back, and my bones that had felt young and whole in his warmth began to ache again.

I glanced over my scarred shoulders uneasily. There was no one about. The Rider's hut stood empty, the rocky slope devoid of life. The wilderness of the lair spread out before me was dark and silent. I supposed they all believed me dead, and I began to wonder about it myself. Perhaps I was rooted to the spot, a naked phantom to haunt the lair of Aberthain. Where did ghosts find their filmy draperies? I could use one, I thought, as the dawn wind blew cool on my raw bare skin.

I struggled to my feet, and while I tried to decide what in the name of the Seven to do with myself, the petty, prideful insignificance of Narim's plans left me laughing weakly. The thought that any human or Elhim could foresee what a dragon would do when freed from five hundred years of torment was as ludicrous as a naked, hairless man wandering a dragon lair in the hour before sunrise. Somehow I had accomplished what I'd come to do, but the aftermath was not at all as predicted.

Narim had been sure I would control Roelan after it, that I would ride him across the sky to free the rest of the dragons and lead them all to the lake of fire to regain their minds and voices. But Roelan was no more my slave than I was his. Someday he might answer my need as I had chosen to answer his, but then again he might not. I had offered him my service, but could expect nothing in return. And I would never ride him. He was not a beast.

Lara was not going to like that. Lara . . . Slowly I began to remember how all this had come about. There had been Riders . . . grabbing Lara as she raised her hand to send me into the fire. Vanir's fires! What would they do to her when they realized Roelan was free?

Throwing off my weakness, willing my shaking legs to hold me up, I climbed up the rocky slope to the place I'd last seen her. The angular boulders where she had stood so proudly were splashed with blood, as was her dagger that I found wedged in a crevice in the rocks. The blood was dark and dried and cold. Her dragon whip was tangled in the rocks. I had to find her.

Clothes. The Elhim had sent a change of clothes for me; I just hadn't had time to get them on before Lara began the rite. If the Riders had not found the niche where we had made ready . . .

They hadn't. I crawled back over the boulders and found breeches, shirt, tunic, and boots spilled out of Lara's bag. I pulled on my discarded cloak over all, trying to quiet my incessant shivering. Narim's journal lay open in the dirt where I had thrown it, its pages fluttering idly in the breeze. I snatched it up and thrust it in the pocket of my cloak. I would learn more of Narim's plot after I found Lara.

Behind me exploded a mighty bellowing from the far reaches of the lair. I flattened myself against the sheltering rocks. When I dared peer out again, I could not help smiling. A hot, white glow suffused the lower sky. For a moment it looked as though the sun were rising on the western boundary of the lair. But from the fire rose, not the sun, but one, then two, then three wing-spread dragons. Their massive bodies wheeled and reeled about each other like playful children, their cries rattled my bones like joyous thunder, and in my heart I felt the whispered torrent of their gratitude. The deluge of their speaking was so monumental that it was a struggle to keep breathing or maintain the beating of my heart. Only after they disappeared beyond the horizon could I summon wit enough to answer. "It was my pleasure," I said.

They seemed to hear me, for I felt and heard them trumpet their delight. Roelan could free the others. Lara and I had given him the words. The music was their own.

Shouts of dismay, curses, and barking of orders from every side sent me diving back into my rocky niche. It seemed the clan had at last begun to glimpse their undoing.

"Gruesin? Is that you? I saw your—"

"Damn and blast, what's happening here? Who dares command my kai? The beast was screeching over its kill half the night, but now someone's sent it up. Where's the captain?" The Rider bellowed at a pitch worthy of a dragon.

"Didn't you hear? It's the singer, the black-tongued bastard—"

"He's dead. I saw it. I heard his death song and never have screams been so sweet."

"Maybe he did something before he died. You know . . . like he's done . . ."

"He never did nothing. Never! The turncoat female had a stolen kai'cet. She was trying to save the singer with it, but I watched the kai roast him. This is something else."

"But then who's sent it up, Gruesin? All three of them are flying. Are Dyker and Jag giving chase?"

"All three?" The Rider was near strangling on his words. "But that's Dyker and Jag running this way."

"Blast and thunder! All three! We'd best get to the commander!"

"I'll flay the traitorous bitch myself!"

Boots pounded and harsh cries and curses echoed through the lair as the other two Riders joined Gruesin and his friend. As soon as they moved away and a cautious glance assured me that the way was clear, I hurried after them. Lara would be taken to MacEachern. Whatever these Riders said, the high commander would allow no one else to wreak the clan's vengeance on her. I prayed he would try to learn what had happened before he did so, for I needed time to save her. Otherwise, she had done the unpardonable, and she would die for it . . . slowly, painfully, as only the Ridemark could manage it.

After a close call that sent me headfirst into a herd pen full of sheep and another that flattened me into a far too shallow slot in the cliff wall, I reached the narrow road that led out of the lair. No one was left to guard it. As I followed the four clansmen into the city and merged into the sleepy streams of people heading out on their day's business, time took up its familiar course again, and the dawn broke on a world forever changed.

Chapter 31

I could get nowhere near Lara. By the time I threaded my way through the busy streets of Aberswyl to the Ride-mark encampment outside the city gates, the clan had closed in upon itself. Grim-faced, heavily armed Ride-mark guards encircled the camp that was already being dismantled, turning away puzzled carters and laborers with no explanation. Men and older children were haul-ing down tents and loading mules and wagons. Women were stuffing smaller children in with the baggage or strapping them on their backs. There were no shouts, no disorder, only instant obedience to their commander's or-ders. No dragons lived in Aberthain any longer, and the Riders would be gone before anyone else discovered it.

What would the people of Aberthain do when they re-alized that their pride, the bulwark of their kingdom's de-fense, was no more? What would happen when the Maldovans, the traditional enemies of the Aberthani, dis-covered that Renald was bereft of dragons? As I hurried toward Mervil's shop to retrieve a horse to follow the clan, I watched people going innocently about their busi-ness, oblivious of what was to come. The safety of one race could not be built upon the enslavement of another, yet the change was going to be dreadful. Civil war. Revenge. Chaos. Invasion. What had I done?

Lost in such uncomfortable musings, I entered a morning market just coming alive, noisy with fishmongers and farmers hawking their wares, with the bleating, grunting, and squawking of beasts, with strident voices of women and traders hunting bargains. A cloth merchant was hanging colorful lengths of silk and linen that flapped in the breeze. A tinker banged his pots to attract commerce. I was perhaps halfway across the marketplace when the glaring sunshine of the day winked out like a great eyelid had shut upon it. People, buildings, merchandise, noise—all vanished, and I was caught up in a blaze of white light and a flood of sensations akin to the relief of the first water after a desert march or the exaltation of a mountaintop after a day's long climb.

> *To the morning lands where the fires of day take*
>   *flight,*
> *where the cries of brothers tear.*
> *Sisters, bound to torment, rage.*
> *Lift them, unbind them, sing them upward.*
> *Thy giving is ever, beloved. Glory to you ever.*

Roelan. My perception of his towering anger and his indescribable joy and gratitude vanished almost as quickly as it had come, a hammer blow that left me a dizzy island in the sea of unknowing Aberthani. The daylight seemed pale and insubstantial after the dragon's touch, the colors of the marketplace washed-out, the noises thin and meaningless. Passersby cast curious glances my way, and I realized how odd I must look

standing stupidly in the middle of the marketplace with
no hair, no eyebrows, no eyelashes. And I had no gloves
to hide my hands. I pulled up the hood of my cloak and
hid my hands in the pockets of the cloak alongside
Narim's journal and my mother's pearls. I hurried
through the square and into narrower streets.

The clamor of hammers and saws greeted me as I
turned into Mervil's lane. At least five Elhim were making repairs to the front of the tailor's shop. The splintered
wall looked as if it had been kicked in by a dragon. None
of the Elhim seemed at all familiar—or rather all of them
did, but in no particular way. Though there were only a
few other people abroad in the lane, I was cautious,
strolling past the shop, then slipping through the alleyway that would take me to the back of it. I considered
simply riding off with one of the horses in Mervil's stable. I knew the kindly tailor would not grudge it. Yet, in
view of the heavy damage to the shop, I could not leave
without inquiring after my friends.

An Elhim came out of the house and was picking over
a stack of thin wood strips when he caught sight of me
and straightened up again. "Who are you? What are you
doing sneaking around?"

"Is Mervil here?" I said. "I've a job for him."

The Elhim examined me carefully as he started gathering up a load of strips. "Mervil is dead. His cousin Finaldo has inherited the business, but he won't be taking
on work for a few days until these repairs are done."

"Mervil dead? Vanir's fires, no!"

"What do you care as long as there's another tailor to
serve you?"

Something about the Elhim's tone held my dismay and anger at bay.

"I care a great deal. Mervil was my friend," I said.

"A friend of yours?" The gray eyes looked skeptical as he took in my odd appearance. "How so? Finaldo would be interested to hear it."

Interesting. He was not grieving. He was listening and watching . . . for Finaldo, Mervil's cousin and a tailor, too. The Elhim were very good at losing themselves when times grew difficult. I decided to test my theory before I shouldered a new guilt.

"A good friend. Would you tell Finaldo or whoever in the house might be taking an interest that I'd like to pay what I owe, then? It looks like he needs the income." Into the astonished Elhim's hand, I dropped my mother's pearls. He dropped his wood strips and stared at the jewels and my hands. "I'll wait here by the stable," I said.

In no more than three heartbeats Davyn ran out of the door holding the pearls, only to stop short at the sight of me, the eager smile falling off his face. "Who are you?" he demanded harshly. "Where did you get these?" An Elhim who looked remarkably like Mervil, but probably answered to the name Finaldo, was at his shoulder, and a bandaged Tarwyl hobbled out slowly after.

I hadn't imagined they wouldn't recognize me. "Eskonia, the first time," I said. "My mother's jewel safe, the second. Then a lady's feet. My pocket, this last."

"Aidan?" Davyn's face blossomed into delight tempered with wonder; then he laughed and hurried over to grab my hands. But to our mutual discomfiting, sparks crackled and flew upward from our touch. The Elhim cried out and fell back, his outstretched hands red and blistered, his face stunned. "By the One!"

"I'm sorry," I said. "I had no idea. . . ." My hands tingled strangely, and thin, blue smoke drifted away on the morning air. "Are you all right?"

I stepped closer to see the damage, but the Elhim backed away from me, glancing upward nervously as if expecting a dragon to be perched on Mervil's chimney like a pigeon. "Only singed," he said. Then his voice dropped to a whisper. "What's happened to you? Are you a Rider, then?"

It grieved me beyond all expectations to see Davyn step away. Awe and mystery can place an untenable burden on friendship. "I don't know," I said. "I ought to be dead."

I tried to tell them everything at once, in the pitifully inadequate words that I could muster to describe such extraordinary events. Once I was inside the shop with a mug of wine in my hand, exhaustion muddled my telling, so that I wasn't sure I made anything clear except that Roelan was free and Lara in danger. "They'll be taking her to Garn MacEachern—they'll not dare do otherwise—but I don't know where he is. So I need to follow the clan as they move out."

Davyn spoke softly, his eyes wide. "Will you call down the dragons to make them free her?" He really believed it might be so. After all of it even Davyn didn't understand.

"No." I tried to explain that I had no idea if I would ever hear Roelan again. What I did know was that the clan would not relinquish Lara while one Rider yet lived, and no matter what befell in our strange relationship, never could I ask Roelan to kill for me. Even for Lara I could not ask it. ". . . so I can't."

"Then there's nothing to be done as yet," he said. "The clan won't exchange her for you—I see in your face that you intend it. They'd only kill you, too. From their point of view, you've done your worst, and unless you can undo it, vengeance will be their only satisfaction."

I closed my eyes, wishing desperately that I could disagree with him.

"Come, my friend." Davyn's kindness transcended awe, and gingerly he laid a hand on my shoulder. No sparks flew. "It takes no holy gift to see that you need food and rest. I'll send out word, and we'll find out where the high commander lies. Until then, take this comfort: She believes you dead, so she'll feel free to tell them everything they want to know. And when she hears that the dragons are free, she'll know you won. That will sustain her."

I was not eased. Not even a god could sustain one through Ridemark vengeance.

While the Elhim dispatched an unending stream of blond, gray-eyed messengers to track the movements of the clan, I sat by Mervil's hearth and ate what food was put before me. I did not feel connected to any of it, no matter how much I tried to listen. I pulled out Narim's journal, anxious to unravel his plotting, but my head ached and the fine scrawling blurred in front of my eyes. All I could see was Lara at the Udema wedding party, her hair unbound, laughing at my foolishness. All I could feel was the weight of her head on my chest.

Even as I held that image and cherished it, the world flicked out again. The talk and the incessant hammering, the shop and the gathering clouds of noonday outside its windows disappeared in the space of a heartbeat. My vision was filled with sky and brilliant sunlight and rolling clouds beneath me like a gray ocean. The voice of Roelan pounded in me like my own blood gone wild.

What sorrowing is there when Jodar flies?

When Rhyodan, Noth, Lypho, and Vanim soar through the dawning airs?

When Phellar, Nanda, Melliar tread the winds and sing their waking?

I would lift thee to the heights, Aidan, beloved, where the cold burning of the night meets the colors of the day fire.

Thy sorrowing lies heavy on my wings.

Of all beings in the universe, Roelan understood helplessness. He grieved with me as I shaped the words, of how the one I cared for most in the world, the one who had opened the way for me to wake him, was taken into captivity very like that he had known.

Cruel is the hand that harms the one who completes thy being.

Tell us how to unbind her.

If ought of my working might free her from this harm, but speak the word to set my course.

I was humbled and overwhelmed with his offer. But there was nothing to be done. The clan would be waiting with bloodstones, dragon whips, and poison-tipped spears for just such a move. I could not ask it. And even if they could not harm Roelan, they would kill Lara. I shared Roelan's rejoicing that more of his brothers and sisters flew free, and soon afterward his vision faded into

the light of Mervil's hearth fire and the untidy mess of the
tailor shop.

The Elhim were silent, staring at me and at Narim's
journal that had fallen from my hand, its pages intact, but
its leather cover brown and curled, a wisp of stinking
smoke rising from it. They were bursting with unspoken
questions, but I could form no human words to tell what
I had seen and heard, so I just shook my head. I was desperate for sleep. They led me to a pallet on the floor. My
sleep was plagued with dreams of Goryx, licking his lips
and blinking his bright eyes as he was given Lara.

The house was dark and silent. I was perishingly
thirsty and sat up on the pallet rubbing my head until I
could think where I was and where I might find something to drink. Waking and sense were accompanied by a
dream-wrought conviction that I must be on my way with
the daylight to find Devlin and warn him. Only he among
all the kings and princes in Elyria and her neighboring
kingdoms had the strength and resources to hold order
once the dragons were free. And that would be the case
only if he were ready. I had to make him listen and understand what was coming, lest the havoc I had wrought
come down too hard on the people who had least to do
with it—the very ones who had suffered most from the
savage dragon wars. Once the news spread throughout
the land, the wars of vengeance would begin. Once the
word spread outside our borders, the wild men would
come.

And another idea had emerged from my dreaming. If I
gave Devlin warning, he might be grateful enough to help
me. . . .

Someone had kindly removed my boots, so I moved silently through the house. I could not stomach the thought of wine or ale, and thought to go out to the cider barrel Mervil kept cool in a shed near the stable. But the door to the stableyard was jammed or locked. I could find no way to get it open without creating a commotion. Too parched to be discouraged, I padded through the tailor's workroom to the newly rebuilt front door, only to find Davyn sitting propped against it, reading Narim's scorched journal in the light of a single candle.

"Learning anything interesting?" I said quietly. I had no idea where Mervil's helpful friends might be sleeping.

Davyn started and whipped the book behind him, peering into the midnight to see who I was. "Aidan!" He dropped his voice immediately. "Are you all right? What are you doing awake?" I assumed it was his possession of the private journal that gave him such an aura of guilt . . . or perhaps knowledge of the journal's secrets.

"I was considering going out," I said. "But the back door is jammed."

"Go where? It's the middle of the night."

"Does it matter?"

"You shouldn't— I wouldn't— Of course it matters." His voice limped off like a lame dog. "You can't."

"What do you mean I can't?"

Davyn glanced about, then pressed his finger to his lips and motioned me to the floor beside him. Exquisitely nervous, I sat down. "What's going on?"

"I don't know. Not at all." His slender forefinger tapped rapidly on the journal.

I waited, thinking I'd get a clearer answer once Davyn

had settled whatever argument he was waging with himself.

"Narim's come. While you were asleep."

"Ah." I settled back against a mountain of rolls of cloth. "And Narim doesn't want me out getting a drink of cider?"

"Cider? Oh." Davyn rubbed his gray eyes and shook his head. "When Narim got word that you and Lara were making the attempt, he'd already been awake for more than a day. Then he rode fourteen hours straight to get here. He had to sleep, but he wanted to make sure you didn't leave the house before he talked to you." The Elhim ran his slender fingers through his blond curls, clearly troubled. "I thought nothing of it. But then he sent Mervil, Tarwyl, and Jaque to another house, and wanted me to go with them. I said I'd rather stay here in case you needed me. He agreed, but certainly wasn't happy about it. Then I saw him remove the keys from the rear door and bar the windows. There's no one here save him and you and me. But Rorick and Kells are watching the street. Watching for you . . ."

"And these things bother you?" They certainly bothered me.

"Narim has been my dearest friend since I was young—two hundred years, Aidan. He is everything of goodness. Devotion. Friendship. Honor. Whatever of decency you see in me, he has nurtured. He—"

"I disagree."

The lock of blond hair hung over gray eyes filled with distress, but not shock. "So you read this?" He turned the journal over in his hands and stared at it as if it were a poisonous spider.

"Only enough to know who murdered my friends and stole my life."

"I didn't know, Aidan. On the name of the One I'll swear, neither Tarwyl nor Mervil nor I—"

"I never thought it. So what bothers Narim now? I've done what he wanted. The dragons fly free."

"When Narim arrived, we told him everything you'd said and about the changes we saw in you. Though I knew he'd be heartsick about Lara, I thought he would take satisfaction in your accomplishment. But he was frantic when he heard that you weren't in control of the dragons and sending them on to the lake. He's afraid, Aidan. He believes they're going to destroy the Elhim."

"They won't."

"He says he can't be sure until they go to the lake and drink the water, so he can talk to them himself."

"They'll go to the lake when it's time, and they'll speak when they're ready, and maybe humans and Elhim will be able to understand their words and maybe we won't, but killing intelligent beings is the last thing they want. They despise it. They don't understand it. They never have."

Davyn frowned and fluttered the pages of the journal nervously. "Maybe you can convince him." He didn't sound confident. "He wants you to go to the lake with him and make the dragons come there. That's why he didn't want you to leave. He's crazed with it. I've never seen him like this."

"He's got to understand that I can't force them to do anything. But he doesn't need to worry. If Roelan speaks to me again, I'll find out if they're coming to the lake.

And I'll come myself. Willingly. Just not yet. I've some things to do first. Critical things . . ."

The Elhim looked up curiously. "What things?"

I told him of my certainty that I had to warn Devlin, and of the fragile possibility that had emerged from the consideration. I hoped to persuade my cousin to save Lara.

The Ridemark produced powerful warriors, but without their dragons they would be no match for Devlin or any of his stronger allies. If the clansmen were to survive, they would have to seek an alliance, and from that need might come the leverage to pry Lara from their hands. MacEachern would never turn Lara over to the Elhim, and his hatred would allow no accommodation with me, but he might exchange her for Devlin's protection.

"Holy fire, Aidan, to speak to the king is suicide! He'll have your head for treason."

"He may very well, but I don't think so. Devlin takes his responsibilities very seriously. He'll be furious and horrified, but he'll come to see that I've given him a chance to control his own power . . . and to prepare. It's all I can do. If I can make everything happen as I want, I don't think he'll refuse. The first thing I have to do is convince him to meet with me."

I had come up with the scheme in my sleep. Nightmares of prisons, of Devlin and Lara and all those who were going to die because the dragons flew free, had led my thoughts inevitably to the youth who lay captive in the dragon lair of Gondar. Devlin's son. The moment the Gondari dragons were released, Donal would be dead, for the Gondari would think it Devlin's doing. With Roelan's help I was going to get Donal out. "Can I depend on you and Tarwyl to help?"

"We'll do anything you ask. Count on it. But there's something else going on. . . ." His voice trailed away, and his fingers drummed insistently on Narim's journal. He was wrestling with himself again, and only with difficulty did he come out with anything. "Aidan, you've got to convince Narim about the dragons. He's been poking around in Nien'hak. I—"

Footsteps in the lane in front of the shop and a soft knocking interrupted Davyn, and he jumped up to answer. I stood behind him while he unlatched the door. As he pulled it open he stepped backward, bumping into me. I felt the journal being pressed into my hands. Once I had it, he guided my fingers to a place he had marked.

"Kells! I didn't expect to see you before daylight," he said to the Elhim who walked in. "Is everything all right?"

"Just came for my cloak," said the new arrival, eyeing me with interest. "Summer never feels warm enough in Aberthain."

The journal was stuffed in the waist of my breeches underneath my rumpled shirt. Davyn introduced me as the Dragon Speaker, then offered to get me cider from Mervil's barrel.

"I think I just need to get a bit more sleep. I promise I'll talk to Narim before I go." I padded back into the living quarters of the house, sat on my blankets, and pulled out the journal. Davyn had marked a maplike drawing labeled Nien'hak and a number of lists: one of Elhim names, one of various equipment like barrows, shovels, and hammers, and another that looked to be a record of place names—Vallior, Aberswyl, Camarthan among them—each with a number beside it. None of it made sense. I needed better light to decipher the fine handwriting, so I slipped the journal under the tangle of blankets. I wanted to set my own plan in motion first.

For an hour I lay on my pallet collecting words. They had to be right for each of the three listeners. By the time I was satisfied, the house was still again, and I went prowling for pen and paper and light.

A frustrating half hour in Mervil's larder with my finds and I had produced two barely readable notes. One was for Devlin, entreating him to meet me alone on the Gondari border at sundown two days hence. I called on his promise to do me any service in his power and did everything I could to assure him of my good intentions. I would ask Davyn to carry it to my cousin.

The second note was for Lara. I could not face death again without leaving some trace of what she had meant to me. I smoothed the paper folds and imagined her strong, capable hands opening it and her clear blue eyes reading it. The imagining eased the dull ache in my gut just a little. I would entrust that one to the dogged Tarwyl, who, through some cousin or friend, would find a way for Lara to read it if she yet breathed the air of the world. For the moment both letters went into my pocket.

The third message was going to be more difficult to deliver. But I sat in the earth-walled room off Mervil's kitchen among his turnips and onions, his bags of flour and dangling sausages, closed my eyes, and banished the world. With every skill I could muster, with every sense at my command, I called Roelan. To my astonishment, his voice was with me faster than my mind could comprehend it, as if he had been sitting on a shelf above my head awaiting my call.

It is an interesting challenge to discuss geography with a dragon. Twenty years had passed since I'd visited Gondar. Translating everything I remembered into a flyer's view twisted my mind into knots. After a great deal of image shifting and word exploration, I concluded that Roelan had not yet freed his brothers and sisters in Gondar—a relief, since it meant that Donal was likely still alive. Once we had settled on the place, the rest was easy. Roelan would find the human held captive with his kin and "bear him gently to the smooth-complected hill beside the roving water"—Za'Fidiel on the Gondari border, perhaps three leagues from where Devlin was encamped.

"I would not lead thee into harm, my brother," I said, trying to express my fear and thanks and caution. "Never will I ask it."

Through pain and crushing horror hast thou served my need.

Giving ever.

Thou art my heart, Aidan, beloved, and I will hear thy songs again.

"Would that I could sing for you. . . ." Even as I spoke, our contact was broken, but I knelt on the earthen floor trembling with its lingering power.

"So it has come to pass," said a voice much closer than the dragon's. "You have found your heart again, and your dragon has found his. Did I not tell you it would be so?"

"Narim."

"Do you realize that your body burns white as you speak to him? A longer conversation and Mervil's turnips would be cooked. You must be quite a sight at night." The Elhim stood in the doorway, leaning against the wooden frame, almost quivering with his edgy humor.

"The dragons will not harm the Elhim."

"How do you know?"

"Think of how you know you need sleep, or how you know when a storm is coming, or how you know when Davyn is troubled. I wish I could explain all this better, show you how it is with them. The dragons have no concept of vengeance. They won't touch any Elhim . . . nor will I."

Narim relaxed into a more thoughtful wariness, his eyes flicking to my face and away again. "Ah, I see." He leaned against the doorframe, fidgeting idly with something he'd pulled from his pocket. "So perhaps the answer is not that you are *incapable* of commanding the dragons to the lake, but that you choose not . . . because of things you have learned, deeds long past and terrible in their appearance."

"No. I meant what I told Davyn and Tarwyl. This joining, this mystery that's happened to me, I understand it no better than I understand why the moon hangs in the sky or what it is made of. I don't know what I've become, but I know what I am not. I am not a living bloodstone. I cannot command him."

"Not even to save Lara? You know what they'll—"

"If dragons were guarding her, I would beg Roelan to set her free. But the clan won't trust the dragons now. They'll have ten Riders around her every moment, and Roelan would have to kill them all to get her away. I cannot ask him to kill, Narim. Even then, she'd likely be dead at the clan's first glimpse of an uncontrolled dragon.

In the best case, negotiation will get her back. If that fails, then it must be stealth and hand-to-hand fighting."

He was only testing. He had known what I would answer. Nodding his head slightly and blowing a long, silent sigh through pursed lips, he stopped fidgeting with the object in his hand and folded his arms. "Then I suppose you must help me fill out the last pages of my journal. Tell me, in these times when you are 'linked' to Roelan . . . he feels your joy and sorrows as you feel his. Is that right?"

"Yes."

"And does he know where you are when he speaks to you—your physical location?"

It was an odd question. Intriguing. "I'm not sure. The visions show me where *he* is. But his voice is so strong, and mine . . . I don't know. Distance plays no part. It's always very quick. . . ." I thought back to the experiences of my youth, and smiled as I recalled the songs Roelan and I had created together, always reflecting the place where I was. "Yes. I think he does know. He sees where I am before I tell him."

That was the wrong answer.

I was still on my knees on the dirt floor of the larder, and as Narim gazed down at me with sorrow, he flicked his hand behind him. Before I could comprehend the meaning of his gesture, Kells and two more Elhim I didn't know grabbed my arms and head, holding me immobile while Narim emptied a vial of bitter, oily liquid down my throat. Sparks flew as I fought to spit it out, but Narim held my mouth and nose closed until I could do nothing but swallow it. It gave me some momentary satisfaction that all four of them nursed scorched fingers afterward. They left me in a heap on the floor.   •

"Was half my life not enough?" I said when I'd done with coughing and choking and gotten up again as far as my knees. "And don't tell me how sorry you are."

"Ah, Aidan, but I am. If there were any other way . . . For Lara's sake if naught else. But you're too good at what you do, and too naive. You've one more service to perform, and then—"

"—you'll finish what you started." The room was starting to weave in and out of focus. The candlelight grew bright, then receded to a pinpoint so fast I fell over trying to keep it in view.

"Yes, I will. I started this long before you were born. I cannot risk history repeating itself for some simplistic, misguided notion of justice. There's too much treachery in the world. Too much hatred. Too much vengeance. Did you see what the Riders did to Tarwyl? What is to stop them doing the same thing to the rest of us?" He crouched down in front of me and his pale aspect reflected such single-minded determination that his words disturbed me far beyond the matter of my own death. "No human will ever again control a dragon. And not one more Elhim will die for a five-hundred-year-old sin. We are on the verge of annihilation, Aidan. I'll not permit it."

My tongue was already thick. "You sent me to prison for seventeen years, and I never knew why. Now you say I have to die when I've done everything you want. This time you've got to give me a reason. You misjudged so many things then. You might be doing it again. I need"— a wave of nausea left my skin clammy, but with no strength to heave up whatever poison he'd given me—"I need to know."

"I was *not* wrong. You would never have heard Keldar or Roelan or been able to speak with them if you had not lived the seven years of silence. And I'm not wrong now. You just wouldn't understand."

"Try me. For once. For the gods' sake, try me."

"I promise you'll know before you die. Now, Aidan, show me what you've written while you were hiding in here. I can't have you giving anyone a head start on us. Spreading chaos is our only protection right now."

One of the Elhim started digging in my pockets, but I slapped his hand away—or rather slapped the air where his hand seemed to be—and clumsily scrambled backward through the dirt until I was slumped in the corner. "I'll have no stranger's eyes on it," I mumbled. "Narim, at least you care . . . for one human . . ." Speaking was becoming difficult, especially when I had to concentrate on my pocket, trying to persuade my awkward fingers to detect which note was which. I prayed I'd chosen correctly, as I drew out the folded paper and threw it onto the dirt a hand's breadth—or was it half a league?—from my foot.

Narim snatched up the note, read it, and folded it again with a great sigh. "By the One, Aidan, I do wish things could be different. We will save her. And I'll see she gets this."

I would have to be happy with his assurance, for my tongue would no longer function to ask him how he planned to rescue Lara. By the time the three Elhim carried my limp body to my bed—Narim was kind enough to have them roll me onto my stomach—my thoughts were as hard to catch as minnows in a stream. The poison burning in my belly demanded I sleep, but I dared not. Surely whatever sense I yet claimed would be lost if I succumbed.

"Saddle the horses," Narim told his henchmen. "We need to get away before Davyn wakes."

"Davyn can't stop it, Narim," said Kells. "Why don't you just tell him?"

"No. Not until it's done, and he can see the rightness of it."

So Narim had enough of a conscience that he couldn't explain himself to his dearest friend, his decent, honorable friend who would most certainly disapprove of killing me. But Davyn would never see the rightness in killing me, so they must be talking about something else. Curse all conspirators, what were they planning?

The minnows swam around in my head, a particularly large one reminding me that the annoying rectangular lump poking into my stomach most likely contained the very clues that might help me understand it. Why hadn't I taken the time to read the damnable journal? Nien'hak . . . what was it? Where had I heard the word before? And why did it bother Davyn so? I couldn't concentrate. The minnows teased at the murky edges of my mind. One kept reminding me that I had to warn Devlin. Whatever happened to me was no matter. Davyn could tell Devlin our story, but the Elhim would need my letter to get a hearing from my cousin.

As the night slowly shifted into gray morning, I began the monumental task of moving my right hand—the one that lay somewhere in the same distant realm as my thigh—toward my pocket. It seemed to take two hours. I kept forgetting what I was doing, losing control of my hand so that it lay on the blanket like dead meat. When at last it reached my pocket, I had to convince it to extract the letter and . . . do what? I was as tired as if I'd moved Amrhyn from the Carag Huim to an entirely different mountain range.

Wake up, Davyn! I wanted to scream it out. But my tongue was dead, and Kells and Narim returned before I saw any sign of my friend.

Narim crouched over me and put a hand on my shoulder. "I've had word from one of Davyn's runners. Lara is as yet untouched," he said, somehow sure that I would hear him. "MacEachern is at Cor Neuill, so they've taken her to meet him. If we're quick and you help me, we'll have her back before they can harm her."

I had no time to take comfort in his assurance. Desperately I crumpled the letter in my hand as they stood me up—my knees about as useful as soggy dumplings— and half walked, half dragged me into the stableyard. The motion got me all jumbled up again, and I wasn't even sure who was who.

"By the gods, Narim, what's going on? What's happened to Aidan?" Someone was standing across the gulf of the stableyard.

A minnow swam by my eyes in the circling world. It mouthed words at me and insisted I repeat them, but I couldn't do it. Just felt seasick.

"He's been in contact with the dragon again, and it's about done him in. He almost set fire to the house. Says he doesn't dare speak with Roelan in that fashion again, but he'll come to the lake and try it the easier way. So I didn't have to do much convincing after all."

"But what about—" The speaker stopped himself abruptly, and a face that was not a minnow appeared in front of my own. It had blond hair falling over one of its unfishy gray eyes. "Aidan, are you all right? Are you sure? What about the things you wanted to do before going to the lake?"

Narim urged Kells and me toward the horses. "I don't think he can answer you. We'll take—"

I lurched forward out of Kells's hands and lunged for the worried face, mustering all the words I could find and willing them to my useless tongue, trying to make them loud enough that someone could hear. "Roelan . . . understands. Elhim always do . . . everything . . . I ask. I count . . . on it."

Hands dragged me off of him.

"Don't worry, Davyn. We'll take good care of him."

While Kells and his cohorts draped me on a horse, I caught a glimpse of a puzzled Davyn standing alone in the stableyard. I squinted to see if he held a crumpled paper in his hand, but he swam out of sight too quickly. But my hands were empty when they tied them around the horse's neck so I wouldn't fall off, and with only such precarious security did I set out on the journey to the lake of fire.

DONAL

Chapter 32

As I was growing up, I never thought it strange that my best friend was a legend. An heir to a throne is never sure of his friends—a lesson learned when I was five and a playmate stabbed me with a poisoned dagger. It was in the three weeks I was confined to bed recovering, alone because all my playmates were banished or executed, that I was introduced to my father's cousin—my cousin—Aidan MacAllister.

My nurse first spoke of him as I continued to make her life miserable with my incessant complaining: my stomach hurt, my head hurt, my bandages itched, I was bored, I hated broth, I wanted to go riding, why wouldn't anyone come to play with me, and why couldn't I do whatever I wanted. "It's the gods' own wrath on my poor head that they took Aidan MacAllister from the world," she said, after threatening to tie me to the bed if I would not be still, as my father's physicians had commanded. "He's the only one ever made you civil. Had you singing like a nightingale, he did, on a day when you had me in worse misery even than this."

Of course I demanded to hear the story, especially when she plopped her hand over her mouth and cursed herself for mentioning a name my father the king misliked hearing. "Well, His Majesty never forbid the gifts to be here," she said. "I've even seen him stare at 'em himself as if maybe the answer to the mystery was in 'em. So he couldn't mind too much me saying who it was gave 'em to you."

Such words did nothing to cool my new fever. I was very persistent.

So she told me of my anointing day, and from a high shelf she pulled down a bell, a flute, a drum, and a painted music box. "He sent you these in the years before he disappeared." I was fascinated and made her tell me more while I watched the tiny mechanical soldiers march around in a circle as the music box played its tune. So I learned of Aidan MacAllister, beloved of the gods, a musician who could transform the hearts of men, my father's cousin who had vanished from the earth when he was but one and twenty.

To hear one has a relative on such terms with gods is a profound experience for a five-year-old, and I would not rest until I learned everything that any servant, groom, chamberlain, or tutor could tell me. Everyone older than ten had a story about him. For half a year, I pestered them . . . until the day I asked my father if he knew where his cousin had gone. "You were his only family and his king. Didn't he tell you?"

I'd never seen my father so angry—and he was not a soft-tempered man. His fury wasn't so much directed at me as at the courtiers and servants who were listening. "It is no matter where he's gone. He was nothing like these foolish stories that make him out a magician or a god. I'll not have him spoken of. He's gone and forgotten, and that's the end of it."

Well, that was not the end of it for me. I would admit that perhaps the legend was not wholly accurate, because my father said so. My father was the king, and I believed he was never wrong. But I was still obsessed with Aidan. On that same afternoon, as I groused and mumbled about my studies, old Jaston, my tutor who had also been my father's tutor and so had met the legendary Aidan, brought me a small, brass-bound box along with my lesson books. "Here's something as may interest you, Prince Donal. Yours by right, but perhaps best kept private, as you'll see."

In the box were some thirty letters, seals unbroken, all addressed to me. Jaston helped me sort them by the dates marked on them and helped me read the first one, as I was not a precocious reader.

> *To my boisterous young cousin,*
> *I've had a mind to write you since our harmonious meeting a few weeks ago. It was such a pleasure and delight to make your acquaintance. I hope you've not tormented your good nanny in like fashion again, but rather sung the chorus we made together. The counterpoint was quite nicely done, I think, and tells me that you are indeed as much my family as your father's.*
> *I've traveled quite a long distance since we met, and someday you may enjoy visiting this land beyond your realm where men wear trousers that look like skirts, and women wear gold rings poked right through their ears. It is called Maldova and is set high in the most gloriously beautiful mountains. . . .*

Those letters became my most precious possessions, read over and over again through the years until the paper was as soft as cloth. They were filled with adventure and wit, and an education about people and places and all manner of things a man could learn from them. I knew Aidan MacAllister far better than I knew anyone, for my father had little time for me, and no one else dared speak so freely to the crown prince of Elyria. Some of the letters had drawings or sketches on them, and almost all of them had snippets of musical notation attached. Aidan said he composed them especially for me.

Though I asked him repeatedly for one, my father refused to supply me a music master. But when I was nine I became friends with a squire who could play the lute and knew how to read the markings of music. I swore him to secrecy, and he spent a whole night playing my cousin's melodies. I had never heard anything so wonderful in my life. Even in my friend's awkward playing, I felt as if each phrase were plucked on strings right inside of me. It made me think my cousin knew me as well as I knew him, and I believed that if he walked into a crowded room, I would recognize him instantly, and he would recognize me.

I devised all manner of explanations as to where Aidan MacAllister had gone and what he was doing. Mostly they were things holy and mysterious and fine. Sometimes I thought he was playing a joke on everyone, and sometimes I wondered if he was just tired and had decided to rest for a while. Never, ever, did I believe he was dead. Too much of life was crowding out of his thirty letters.

When I was thirteen I came of age, and reading and

writing and mysteries gave way to more serious matters. I had very little time to think about Aidan MacAllister, for I rode as my father's squire, apprenticing at warcraft and statecraft until at seventeen I was given a command of my own. I was good at it, just as my father was. I knew it, and my father said it—as directly as he ever said anything complimentary. He had been king at eighteen, and his father at twenty, so I had to be ready.

Only once did I ever hear my father speak of his cousin. It was the night he came to my tent in the training grounds south of Vallior to order me and my troops to the Gondari border. My musician friend, now my adjutant, was playing one of Aidan's tunes as my father walked in.

"Where did you learn that?" my father demanded.

"I've heard it was composed by a famous musician from long ago, sire," said my diplomatic friend, keeping his head bowed and his knee bent.

"I thought as much." It surprised me, as my father claimed to have no ear for music. He was not angry at the sideways reference to Aidan. Telling my friend to continue playing, he sat down on my cot and handed me the paper that would send me to our most dangerous frontier. Though he hated for me to venture into such a risky theater, it was time. I was eighteen, and he could afford to show no lack of faith in me. I had no doubts of his confidence, so I didn't make him search for words that were so hard for him to say. Instead, I knelt and kissed his ring, sat back on the cot, and decided that if we were to talk of something difficult on this night, it might as well be something more intriguing than war.

"I've heard that Aidan MacAllister could make people

see visions with his music," I said. "Was he as good as that?"

"Better. He could make you live his visions . . . and be changed by them." He paused and smiled a little. "But he couldn't look at a boat without heaving up his dinner, and he couldn't shoot a bow worth dirt. Quit hunting altogether when he was ten. Said his fingers were made for harp strings, not bowstrings. I called him a sodding Florin plant-eater who couldn't stand the stink of blood. He laughed and raced me back to the stables. He could run like a fox and ride like a horse thrall. I could never beat him in a footrace or a horse race either one."

Aidan had told me the very same story in his tenth letter.

"What happened to him, Father? Why did he stop singing?"

My father did not look at me, but only shook his head. "Some things are not meant to be. There is an order to the world, not always pleasant, not always just, not always explainable. It is why you will be a king, and Vart, who sleeps across the doorway of your tent, will never be other than a slave. Aidan and his visions did not fit within that order. I don't know what happened to him. I don't know. . . ."

I believed him and promised myself that when I returned from Gondar, I would find out the truth. But three weeks from that night my horse was shot out from under me by a Gondari bowman in a surprise attack. The horse—a very large horse—fell on my leg, which snapped in protest. At least eighteen soldiers died bravely trying to rescue me, but I woke up a hostage in Gondar

Lair, facing the rest of my life in a filthy, squalid hut surrounded by dragons.

After three months of captivity, I could walk properly
again. At six months, my left arm was burned off by a
dragon, teaching me the absolute impossibility of escape.
At a year I had lost hope that my father could find any
honorable way to set me free. By the eighteenth month of
my captivity, I had determined that the dismal chill and
unending rain of Gondari winter were preferable to the
mind-destroying stink of summer in the lair. But I had not
yet learned to stay asleep when a dragon screamed. My
days and nights ran together in fits of waking misery and
too-shallow sleep.

Twenty-three dragons lived in Gondar Lair. I could
recognize their different bellows, and I gave them names:
Squealer, Volcano, Grinder, Devil . . . Devil was the one
who had taken my arm, and his throaty, malevolent
screech would inevitably leave me shaking and sick. I
laid wagers with myself as to which beast would roast me
when I went mad and ran again. When that day came I
would not fall back at the touch of flames as I had on the
day I lost my arm. I would embrace the fire and free my
father from the terrible position I'd put him in.

I thought a great deal about Aidan MacAllister in those
dreary months. I recited his letters from memory, trying
to imagine myself in the places where he'd been, instead
of the place I was. He had written a great deal about dragons, how he was always trying to figure out their role in
the world. They had fascinated him. It was perhaps the
only place where our interests diverged. Mostly I wished
my cousin would come sing to me, to make a holy vision
to replace the muddy desolation that was everything I

would ever see. I would have traded a month's rations for
him to ease my wretchedness for even one short hour.

In some nameless hour of a nameless day in a sultry,
stifling month of my second spring—I had lost track of
the exact days in the hazy horror of the time after losing
my arm—I was awakened by the bellow of an unfamiliar
dragon. I did not seek shelter in the more protected corner of my hut, but lay where I was and prayed that my father had at last decided to sacrifice me and destroy the
cursed Gondari. But it didn't sound like an attack. It
would take a legion of at least fifty dragons to attempt
Gondar Lair itself. The noise would be unimaginable: the
murderous thunder of so many wings, the continual bellowing and roar of flames. I would have heard the
Gondari legion take flight, leaving only three Riders to
protect me from the two monsters left behind to hold me
captive. And the Riders would have come to chain me up
in case they would be given the order to execute me. But
as I lay on the filthy straw and listened, I heard only the
single, strange bellow and the torrent of fire that accompanied it. Then the Gondari dragons answered with a
monumental trumpeting unlike any I'd ever heard.
Screamer first. Then Volcano.

I crept across the dirt floor and peered out the door.
The afternoon was hot and oppressive, thick, gray clouds
hanging low over the lair. Nothing appeared out of the ordinary until I looked to the south and saw a sheet of flame
so white it hurt my eyes. Again came the fierce cry that
raised the hair on my neck. Two dragons flew out of the
fire, circled the lair, and vanished into the clouds. The
Riders atop the nearest guard tower gestured frantically
toward the eastern quarter of the valley. Another white

firestorm, another eerie, trumpeting bellow, and again
two dragons flew. Three Riders appeared from the south,
running madly toward the two on the guard tower. From
the west burst white flame and booming thunder and the
screaming triumph of a dragon.

Something extraordinary was happening. Anything
that left the Dragon Riders in such frenzy was worth
knowing more of. I climbed up on the sod roof of my
hovel so as to see better, but that looked to be the worst
mistake I had ever made. From the east swooped one of
the largest dragons I'd ever seen, wings full spread,
flames pouring from its snout . . . and it was going to pass
right over me. I flattened myself to the weedy roof, trying not to get blown off by the hurricane of its passing. It
wouldn't kill me. Its Rider would never allow it to kill a
hostage so easily. I'd scarcely sat up again, wondering
why a Rider would deliberately make his mount harder to
control by riding it through the ring of bloodstones set up
to keep me captive, when I heard thunder from behind
me. I turned and saw the same beast coming back again.
I would have sworn its red eyes looked right into my
own.

I had thought myself become dead to fear. For almost
two years, fear had been my whole existence, and Devil's
hate-filled eyes blazed red in every moment of my sleep.
But when the dragon made a tighter circle and started its
third pass, talons the size of small trees fully extended, I
begged Jodar to give me strength not to bring shame upon
my father and my people. I had once seen a dragon allowed to rend a traitor with its claws. It had taken two
days for the wretch to die. Burning was a desirable ending in comparison.

I did not hide—no use in that—but knelt upon the earthen roof watching him come, my horror mounting to a fever as the five claws on one foot opened wider, then snapped around me, dragging me into the gray morning, enclosed in a cage of tissue and bone. I did not scream. I would give no watcher the satisfaction of it. In truth I don't know that I could have forced any sound from my throat. My knees plugged the gap where the tips of the claws came together imperfectly, and my left side was braced against one of the massive talons. Dragon claws were like razors, and with every jolt I expected to feel them slice through my flesh, but strangely enough I remained undamaged. I tucked my remaining arm tightly to my chest. The consideration that I might lose it and survive long enough to know of the loss was almost beyond bearing.

Wind blasted through the gaps between the claws, making my eyes stream with tears, and it took a considerable while before I convinced myself to move enough to shield them so I could see. But in the instant I did so, I understood why my flesh was intact. Thick pads of tough gray tissue were extended from the dragon's foot and curved along the inside and around the inner tip of each claw. I scarcely dared breathe. Perhaps it didn't know I was there. Perhaps it thought I was . . . I couldn't imagine. I couldn't think at all.

A monumental cry blared from just above me, ripping into me like the claws I expected, so dreadfully loud, so awesomely immense, I thought I must go mad from it. Yet strangely . . . incredibly . . . hidden in the rise and fall of the dragon's wail and in the timbre of its voice was a combination of tones that was eerily familiar.

How could it be so? I covered my head with my arm, slowed my breathing, and told myself that if I worked at it hard enough I would surely wake up on the floor of my hovel. But I lived on unharmed, the passing moments and the whipping gray clouds cooling my fevered terror, so I was able to listen with all of myself when the dragon cried out again.

No Rider flew on that dragon. My bones resonated with that truth. The beast was uncontrolled, free, and when I again heard the music in its cry of exultation, I began to tremble with something far beyond fear.

My stomach, which had not weathered events at all well, gave a fearsome lurch when the beast began its circling descent. Gingerly I leaned on one of the padded claws, grasping hold of it and peering out as we dropped below the clouds into gray daylight. We were approaching a sweeping, grassy hill, gently sloping on all sides, embraced on the south by a broad, glassy river. Once, twice, three times we circled, each time lower, until five dark blotches I'd thought were trees were revealed as two men and three horses. I dared not even think for the hope that welled up inside me, not even when we swooped low, the talon cage opened, and I tumbled gently onto the thick grass.

For a moment I lay crumpled in a ball, my face pressed against damp—oh, Jodar—such sweet-smelling grass. *If I am to die, then let it be while the soft earth holds me*. But the brimstone-laden wind of dragon wings drew my eyes to the sky. Though dizzy and half-sick, I stood and watched the dragon soar heavenward until it disappeared into the clouds. "Thank you," I yelled, as if it could understand words. Then I turned toward the brow of the hill where the men and horses were silhouetted against the sky. In my deepest heart—for no explainable reason—I believed I would walk up the hill to meet Aidan MacAllister, but in truth it was an exceptionally broad-shouldered Elhim and my weeping father.

AIDAN

Chapter 33

As prisons go, the bondage of Narim's poison was not terrible. Other than the initial nausea when he administered it every morning, little discomfort was involved. I was tired enough that a few days of immobility didn't seem cruel. The Elhim fed me and made sure all normal bodily needs were taken care of. The only thing they didn't know and I couldn't tell them—since I was quite incapable of speech—was how wickedly I itched all over once my hair started growing in again. Nothing much to do about that, even if I'd had control of my own muscles. I probably would have scratched myself to ribbons.

My mind was limp as well. I slept most of the days as we traveled. Only when the poison started to wear off could I apply any logical thought to this latest detour in my life's peculiar journey. What was Narim planning? Was it truly to speak to the dragons? To get reassurance he could not accept from me? I couldn't believe it. Nien'hak . . . that was the key. According to Davyn, Narim had been poking around in it, and according to the journal map, it was somewhere in the mountains of the Carag Huim. But I couldn't remember what it was. I tried picturing the journal entry, the lists of names and numbers, and I tried remembering where I'd heard the name

before. On the third night of our journey, as I lay paralyzed and staring into the dying coals, my thoughts
drifted to Cor Talaith, the Elhim's green valley left in cinders by the Ridemark. That led me to Iskendar and his
dying words . . . and there was Nien'hak again. "Ask him
what he found in Nien'hak," he'd said. "Ask him why
there is an Elhim named for every dragon."

It was so hard to think. A spark snapped and flew up
from a crumbling log, shooting across my vision like a
miniature dragon. The names in the journal lists were
Elhim names. No dragons, though. Narim didn't know
the dragons' names except for the Seven. The second list
was tools—unhelpful. The third list was place names. My
thoughts flitted away with the swirling ashes of the fire,
and for a while the focus of my being was how dearly I
would love to rub the grit from my eyes and take a hay
fork to my itching legs.

What did barrows and picks have to do with dragons?
And what were the place names in the journal list, and
what did the numbers attached to each place mean? Vallior—32, Camarthan—12, Aberthain—3 . . .

The truth struck me like a tower toppling on my head.
In the span of a heartbeat all of it was clear: why it was
so important that the dragons come to the lake, how
Narim planned to rescue Lara, why he had to kill me. I
thought I would burst with the horrifying certainty, and
indeed I must have groaned aloud, for Narim was soon
standing over me as I struggled to move and speak.

The place names were the locations of dragon lairs.
The numbers signified how many dragons were in each
lair. "An Elhim named for every dragon," and Narim
knew exactly how many dragons there were. And the

shovels and barrows were to use in Nien'hak—Nien'hak, the "pit of blood," the mine near Cor Talaith where the Elhim had dug out the bloodstones. What had Narim found in the pit of blood?

Narim called for Kells to hold me still as I writhed and croaked, "You can't—" That was all I managed to get out before they poured more poison down my throat.

"I was trying to keep the doses small enough so you could have some control of yourself," said Narim, "but I can't have you gathering any semblance of your wits. Certainly not enough to speak to Roelan."

I gagged and heaved, but the oily liquid slid down, burning in my stomach, leaving me limp and scarcely breathing, all sense sagging into a puddle of despair. Narim was planning to enslave the dragons again—only this time to the Elhim. And once an Elhim and his bloodstone had been bound to a dragon, only one human would know how to set them free. And I would be dead.

Narim must have judged his poisons well, for I continued in this semimindless state, drowned in panic and horror, yet unable to call on Roelan. I could not concentrate, could not draw my will together. Most of the time I could not even remember why my flesh quivered with the need to warn the dragons away from the lake. Once I felt Roelan reaching for me, his call a distant, lonely peal of thunder. I cried out after it, as will a drought-stricken farmer when the storm veers away from his sere cropland. My effort resulted in little more than a wordless moan, and all I got for it was an extra dose of Narim's poison. The Elhim had to replace the ropes around my wrists that morning, for they charred through and I almost fell under the hooves of my horse.

I could not say how many more days it took us to get to the lake after that. I was lost in terrifying dreams: of being trapped in unending dragon fire, of being dreadfully sick when my horse foundered in a river crossing, leaving me to drift on choppy water, of thrashing in mindless panic as I was returned to the chains and damp stone of Mazadine. . . .

". . . lie still. You'll hurt yourself worse if you keep this up." The calm, dry voice penetrated my dreams, but did not banish them. "I'm sorry. I'd rather do almost anything than this."

Cold darkness. Not the musty damp of prison, but sharp, chill air. Thin. Clean. Something scratchy and warm laid over me. The horror was dreams. Only dreams. If I could just get my head clear. But my head ached so fiercely, I thought my eyes were getting pushed outward from within. I tried to pull my arms over my head to hold my eyes in place, but cold iron clanked me in the face, dragging me further out of my dreams. Just not far enough.

Indeed chains bound my wrists, fastened somewhere above my head, bolted, no doubt, to the cold, rough granite beside which I lay in a pitiful heap. No chains on my ankles at least. Silver specks—blurry stars—swam in the darkness, blocked by the dark shape crouched in front of my straining eyes.

"Aidan, can you hear me?"

My tongue felt as if it were coated with a thick layer of wool; it would not obey my command. I jerked my head and wished I hadn't, as the dark world set to spin-

ning and my stomach rebelled again, heaving up nothing
and nothing and nothing. Surprisingly my eyes were still
in my head when I was done with that pointless exercise,
though they weren't functioning at all properly. Behind
the dark shape, the world tossed restlessly . . . moving toward me with little slurping noises. I shrank back against
the rock, shivering in the wool blanket laid around my
shoulders.

"Between the jenica and the boat trip, your stomach's
a mess, so I won't feed you until morning. I've no wish
to make this harder on you." A hand stroked my aching
head. "I am truly sorry for the chains. You were burning
off the ropes every time Roelan would come seeking you.
But I don't think it will be long now. A dragon has been
circling the mountains for two days. Here . . ."

Drops of cool water were dribbled on my lips, removing some of the fuzz from my tongue. "Don't. Please
don't," I mumbled. "They won't harm—" I had to close
my mouth before I started heaving again.

"I wish I could believe you, Aidan. But if you've
guessed my plan, then you know it is much more than
just protecting my people from the dragons' revenge.
What will the Ridemark do when they understand what
we've done? What will your own king do when he sees
that the Elhim have stolen the foundation of his power?
Can you imagine what it is like to be vulnerable to every
race's whim, to be despised, discounted, ignored? Never
have we been able to take our rightful place among the
peoples of the world because we are not men. That's what
caused this whole disaster to begin with. If I could go
back five hundred years and change what we did—what
I did—I'd do it. But I cannot. All I can do is to ensure the

world is ordered justly. That means Elhim must control
the dragons, and there must be no possible way to undo
it. If it gives you comfort, know that we will let them fly
as they will. We will never use them as beasts, nor force
them into war—only to defend ourselves. And only Lara
will ever ride. I promised her long ago and cannot go
back on it." Narim tucked the blanket around me and
stuffed another under my head. "I'll be back in the morning to feed you."

The midnight shape dissolved into the larger night.
Throughout the long hours that followed, his words sank
slowly into my fogged mind like snowflakes melting as
they landed on the quiet earth. Roelan would come looking for me. He would drink from the poisoned lake, and
Narim would be waiting with a bloodstone. Once bound,
bereft again of words, unable to give warning, Roelan
would draw the others. When Narim returned with the
dawn to pour thin gruel down my throat and renew his
paralyzing poison, he gently wiped the tears that ran
unchecked down my face. So sure of himself . . . so hu-
mane in his murdering . . . so kind as he schemed to enslave a race. He did not speak.

My immediate surroundings were little more than a
strip of rocky sand, stretching perhaps ten paces to the
lapping waters of the lake. Beyond the vastness of the
water were jagged cliffs of mottled red and gray granite,
and a strip of blue sky above them. I lay on my side, and
my cheek rested on the bundled wool blanket in a puddle
of drool. My mind wandered over past and present, drawing no conclusions, forming no plans, scarcely awake.

The afternoon glare was bright, and it would have
been a wretched misery indeed if I had been left exposed

to the direct sun, but the rock which supported my back had enough overhang to keep me in the shade. Though the air felt cool enough, waves of blistering heat swept over me all through the day, until the manacles on my wrists began to sear my skin. As the endless time passed, I grew desperately thirsty, a nasty torment with so much clear water so near, yet unreachable—poisoned water that would leave the dragons in a state akin to mine. Thirst captured every scattered thought, and even the flash of copper and green wings spread across the blue strip of sky could not divert my attention from it. Wild, thundering cries echoed from the cliffs and in my bones, echoing cries of distress . . . of loss . . . of pain. Yet they were only a fleeting sorrow, quickly forgotten in my craving for water.

As the angle of the sun grew steep, and the cooling air bred fogs from the waters of the lake, I saw a bit of rock detach itself from the distant cliffs and move toward me. Madness. I felt its insistent fingers scraping away the few bits of sense I had left. I struggled to move, to scream, to weep, but I could not. The rock kept coming. I closed my eyes and wished myself dead.

A quiet thump . . . some sloshing . . .

He's bringing more poison. No. No more of it! Make him kill you now.

Though I raged when the cup touched my lips, nothing but a soft moan displayed itself outside my hot skin. The drink was not the oily jenica, however, but water. I gulped and choked and came near drowning in my frenzy, sucking every drop of it down to cool the blaze that was my body. When there was no more, I opened my eyes. Two pairs of boots stood near my face, beads of water rolling off the leather onto the thirsty sand.

"Are you sure this will work?" A new voice. What was it about that voice that made my heart pound like the sea on the ice cliffs of Eskonia?

"Roelan has been hunting him all day. We've had to keep everyone inside. Clearly the beast is leery of the lake, but it won't be long until he finds what he's looking for. Once he finds Aidan, he'll touch the water. Once he touches the water, he'll drink. I'll be ready."

"I'm glad I got here in time to witness it."

"I always knew you were exceptional, but to escape from the Ridemark . . ." A counterpoint of suspicion. A minor key in the melody of his welcoming relief.

"They were distracted when Cor Neuill was emptied in a single hour. I don't think MacEachern believed the reports until he saw the dragons leaving one by one."

The boots moved, replaced by slender legs in leather breeches. A thin brown hand lifted my head, so that I looked into the face of the one who knelt beside me. I wanted to shout, to scream for joy, to leap into the air and thank every god who might exist. "Lara." Even in my living death the name burst from my lips.

"I hope events unfold quickly, Narim. This is pitiful. Why couldn't the weakling fool do as he was told?" The icy calm of her voice withered my swelling joy as frost shrivels an autumn garden, leaving a monstrous emptiness where her name had been. Despite my confusion I could recognize the gleam of red at her neck.

"Few men are capable of rational choices when their hearts are so involved."

"Better not to have a heart than to be this way."

"I thought you loved him, Lara."

"Why would I? He cared more for his beasts than for me. He saw Desmond drag me away out of Aberthain Lair, and he knew what MacEachern would do to me. A foot cut off . . . a hand . . . torture until I told him everything. That's what was going to happen, and this Senai fop did nothing to prevent it. What love is that? I despise him"—she spit into my face and dropped my head back on the blanket—"and I'll put the knife in him myself when the time comes. And this"—torn scraps of paper covered with crabbed writing drifted onto the sand beside my face—"blathering. Good riddance." One pair of boots walked away and stood by the boat.

Narim crouched down beside me. "Ah, lad, I am sorry. I thought that seeing Lara might give you some joy. She arrived here unharmed this morning and insisted on seeing you. I didn't know her feelings had changed." The Elhim gave me more water, splashing a little on my face, then before I realized what he was doing, forced one more vial of jenica into me. "Make your peace with whatever god is left to you, Aidan. Once your dragon is controlled . . . well, I promise you will feel no pain."

Never had I felt anything as urgent as the question that forced itself through the impossibilities of speech and movement—beyond madness, beyond dying, beyond mystery and love and everything that had been my life. I had to hear it. "She knew?"

"Of my plan to control the dragons? That you would have to die if it all came to pass?" He smiled sadly. "Of course she knew. She knew everything. As we told you, she very much wants to fly."

With that simple revelation did all my struggles end.

All hope was dead, all love, all strength. I could do nothing for the dragons. Nothing for Lara. Nothing for myself. Nothing. I closed my eyes as Narim's poison did its work, and I let the madness come.

LARA

Chapter 34

"Aidan. Aidan, can you hear me?" The night was far too long on its way, and the Senai . . . one would think he was already dead save for the heat that pulsed from him like fever. I shook his shoulder and slapped his cheeks; I scooped lake water in the cup Narim had tossed onto the sand and dumped it on his face. His eyes fluttered open briefly, but there was no sense in them. He didn't move. "You've got to wake up. We've no time to waste. Listen to me, Aidan MacAllister." I got more water and poured it over his head until it made a puddle around his face. He would have drowned if I hadn't hauled him upright and propped him up against the rock. "Are you a weakling fool or are you going to wake up and save these damnable beasts?"

A bird swooped across the stars, its screech echoing across the silent water. The breeze-driven lake spread across the tiny strip of sand, reaching for Aidan, while I dug in my tunic for the key I'd stolen from Narim's pocket. "Damned stupid . . ." The manacles were clogged with damp sand, almost impossible to unlock. Aidan lay slumped against the rock like a dead man. "I'll get you out of these, but you've got to wake up. I can't get you away by myself. You've got to help."

Aidan's wrists were ringed with seeping blisters crusted with sand, and I cursed Narim yet again for his single-minded cruelty. I could not reconcile it with the gentle Elhim hands that had nursed me back to life when I was thirteen. Yet who was I to condemn anyone? My own sins were beyond redeeming.

"Come on, Senai. Narim is so nervous he won't sleep. He'll come back here to see to you, to watch, to stand on the shore with his bloodstone and be ready for your dragon. You can't be here when Roelan comes, or you'll never leave this place." I slapped him again, then grabbed his lean face between my hands. "I know the paths you wander, Aidan, but I can't sing you out of them as you did for me. You've got to find the way back on your own."

His eyes dragged open again, dark holes sunk in his pale face, his scant hair and brows scarcely visible in the starlight. A death's-head. He shrank back against the rock, shivering, whether from cold or mindless fear or poison-wrought vision, I didn't know. I was afraid Narim had given him too much of the jenica. The fool Elhim had never gotten it right. I could not forget Tarwyl's description of the dead younglings. Well, Narim wasn't going to give Aidan any more poison or stick a knife in him or anything else. If Aidan MacAllister was going to die, then he would die in the arms of those who cared for him and not on a barren chip of rock in the middle of this cursed lake.

I hitched my arms around his middle and dragged his limp body across the sand to my little boat, dumping him over the bow, leaving his head dangling in the gunwales. Though he was slender, his long limbs made him blasted awkward. I lifted his sand-coated legs and flopped them over the side, then rolled him into the middle so the boat wouldn't list so badly and dump us both into the water. He ended up on his back, and I felt wickedly guilty, as I knew how painful it was for him, but it was a measure of his state that he didn't even moan. *Daughters of fire, Aidan.*

I set the oars and got to rowing. The wind had come up. The water was choppy. The boat ducked and dipped awkwardly from wave crest to wave crest. I'd never been comfortable on water. The Ridemark had no use for such skills. It had been Narim who taught me to swim and to row, as he had taught me so many things. *Damn, damn, damn you, Narim!*

The slop of the water against the bow, the creak and splash of the oars . . . it was all too loud. Sounds carried too well across the water. And it didn't help my jitters when there came a single, mournful bellow from the cliffs. Powerful. Haunting. Dragon. I picked up the pace. If I let the dragon find Aidan, its wings would touch the water, and then it would drink the poisoned stuff, and Narim would win. I hauled on the oars until my shoulders burned, but my luck ran out far too early.

"Lara!" Narim's call came faintly from behind me, somewhere across the dark water between the shore and the island. I could stop rowing and pray Narim wouldn't find me in the dark, but it wouldn't get us any farther away. Better to keep moving and hope the Elhim would check on his bait before giving chase.

Narim wasn't fooled. He knew exactly what was happening. "Lara! Don't do this!"

I glanced over my shoulder and saw the dark outline of

his boat, much closer than I'd imagined. I gritted my teeth and rowed faster.

"I trusted you. You swore an oath," he called.

A child's oath.

"You'll be our death."

I closed my ears. I'd heard it far too often, and for too long I'd let it rule my conscience. That was done with. There was no honor in torture and murder.

"Kells, Jarish! She's headed for the western shore!" Torches flared on the eastern side of the lake, where the old tunnel from the destroyed home cavern of Cor Talaith emerged from the cliff wall.

I was aiming for a spot exactly opposite the cavern, a strip of shoreline on the southwestern side of the lake near the gap in the cliffs. The lake of fire was not formed from meltwater or a captive mountain river, but from springs deep in the rocky bottom of the valley. At some time long before Narim was young, a massive rockfall had blocked a gap in the cliffs, and over the centuries the springs had filled the basin, forming the deep, cold lake. In the lonely time after I had healed from my burns and Narim had gone back to work in the city, I'd spent a lot of time exploring the trails and peaks around Cor Talaith. I had often climbed up to the rocky dam, sat, and gazed out at the breathtaking drop to the lower valleys. On one of those occasions I had discovered an unexplored maze of tunnels close by.

I hoped to reach those caverns undiscovered, for I had never told even Narim of my find. If I could just get Aidan inside, we could hide until help could reach us. I strained at the oars. I had no idea how I was going to manage once we landed, but even if I had to drag him the whole distance, Aidan would be away from the lake. Then perhaps his cursed dragon wouldn't get trapped again.

From somewhere nearby came a faint moan, and for a moment I wondered how Narim could have closed on us so fast. But the sound of choking followed, and I hauled in my oars and grabbed Aidan's shirt, rolling him onto his side. He vomited up acrid nastiness. Aidan had once told me he'd do almost anything to avoid boats.

"Well, this is fine. You come to life only enough to foul my boat." I dribbled water over his pale, hot face, making sure none of the poisoned stuff got in his mouth. He still didn't wake up. "Daughters of fire, you make this difficult."

It was a long half hour until the bow of the boat scraped against the rocks, and I jumped out to drag it onto the shore—a half hour in which torches were moving quickly around the lake toward my landing spot. "This would be a most excellent time for you to regain your senses," I said, wrestling Aidan halfway over the thwarts, then wrapping my arms around his chest again and dragging him across the splintered wood onto the land.

The west side of the lake had very little shore, only a few flat, sandy patches between steep rockfalls that stretched from the water's edge up to the clifftops. A few larger boulders jutted out from the cliffs like the bulging roots of a giant tree. I had planned to scuttle the boat and avoid the sandy patches to hide our footsteps, but there was no time and no point with pursuit so close. Speed was far more important. What I needed to do was to get a mostly dead body across two hundred paces of rough terrain up a steep path and far enough into the maze of passages that no one could find us.

I crouched behind Aidan and wrapped my arms around his chest to haul him up again, when I heard a weak cough and soft slurred words, almost indecipherable. "Am I dead?"

"No," I said, blinking back unbidden tears, pleased it was dark so he couldn't see. "You tried, but you weren't very good at it."

"Lara . . ."

Changing my approach, I folded him forward, and he promptly vomited again. When he was done with it, I moved around beside him, draping one limp arm over my shoulders.

". . . we've got . . ."

"Be quiet. Your dragon isn't captive yet, but we've got to get you away from the lake or he will be. Then your life won't be worth dirt."

"Lara, we've . . . got . . . to talk."

"You've scarcely got wit enough to know your feet from your head, Aidan MacAllister, so keep your foolishness to yourself. I'd appreciate a little help here." There was no time for this. He came near drifting off to sleep between words, and I could already hear the creak of Narim's oarlocks over the chop of the water. I heaved him upward, and we came near pitching head-forward into the boat. But by some improbable feat of will, Aidan managed to pull his feet under him, and we stood on the shore, swaying like a soggy willow tree.

"Now, step," I said. "And I don't care what blasted rhythm you use, Just move your feet in the same direction I do."

"Rather . . . dance . . ."

"You're a fool."

Slowly, far too slowly, we lurched up and over the rockfalls in the direction of the huge boulder that marked the hidden mouth of my caves. Aidan's head drooped on his chest, and at every other step he stumbled on the uneven surface. The only way I could keep us upright was to plant my feet wide apart whenever he moved. Maddeningly slow. The torches were getting closer, and Narim's boat was bumping the rocks. Like a dark, angular moon rising, a massive shape glided up from the clifftops, blocking out half the dome of the sky. No bird this time.

We staggered up a last shallow ridge of fist-sized rocks. In front of us, just across a flat strip of sand, loomed the giant boulder with rounded sides and a flat top. Behind the boulder and the water's edge was a narrow path that would take us up to the caves. "Just a little farther. Help is on the—"

Golden fire arced across the heavens, its reflection a lighted path leading down into the dark water. Then came the cry—piercing the night like a sword through flesh.

"Roelan," Aidan whispered, and stumbled. I braced him again, but soon had no choice but to let him go. Sparks snapped everywhere I touched him, his flesh searing my hands beyond bearing. He sagged to his knees on the sand and clamped his hands to his head. "Roelan, hear me . . . please . . . *Teng zha . . . wyvyr . . .*" The dragon circled the lake screaming . . . hunting . . . closer with every pass. We were still twenty paces from the boulder, maybe forty more around it to the mouth of the cave.

"Warn him away!" I said. I could see flashes of red in

the torchlight that had already advanced a quarter of the way around the lake. "Tell him to fly far from the lake."

"Can't. Can't think. Help me." Aidan's hands were shaking with his urgency, but his words were slurred, and he swayed like a drunkard.

I knelt in front of him and pulled his hands from his face. His bloodshot eyes were clouded with jenica, his eyelids heavy with drugged sleep. So with one hand I drew my knife and with the other I caught his chin, ignoring the blistering heat on my fingers. I held the knife between our faces. The sparks from his skin made the steel flicker as if the weapon contained his dragon's fire as well. "Do you see this, Aidan MacAllister? If you don't warn Roelan away, I'm going to cut your throat with it. It's the only way to save him. If you're dead, he can't find you here, and if I throw your body in the lake and foul the water with your blood, the dragons will stay away forever. Is that what you want? Live or die. Choose."

I waited. His eyes were drawn to the blade, grasping it, holding it with his gaze, as if he could use its unyielding edge to anchor his confusion. But it was taking far too much time.

"Choose, damn you. Live or die?"

I was going to have to do what I said. His eyes slid past the knife to my face. "Live," he said softly. Then his eyes sagged shut again, and, in despair, I positioned the dagger. But his skin began to glow pale in the night, and from his lips came soft words I did not know. Soon his face was shining silver like the moon. I let go of him and backed away from the blazing heat that poured from his body.

"No!" The shout came from behind Aidan, and I jumped up to face Narim, who stood at the top of the last rockfall. Even in the dark I could read his plan. In one hand he carried a dagger and in the other the coil of a dragon whip. Around his neck was the leather strap holding a bloodstone, its red glow scarring his ageless face with years and horror. "Stop him!"

I drew my sword and stepped between the Senai and the Elhim. "You'll not touch him. Not now. Not ever."

"Lara, it is our survival." Narim's voice shook as he stepped gingerly down the rockfall and walked across the strip of sand, every kindness he had done me in eighteen years of love and friendship hanging in the air between us.

"That's what you thought five hundred years ago. The world has paid the price for your mistake and will continue paying it for years to come. But sin will not heal sin. I won't let you do it."

"I thought you understood."

"You thought whatever you wanted. Never considered that you could be wrong."

"You swore to me."

"An oath means nothing without belief. I never believed in your tales or your plans or your sin or your redemption. I did what you told me because I had nothing better to do. That's where you've gone wrong, Narim. You have no faith in anyone but yourself. And so you've plotted and schemed and done terrible things, all to end up making the same mistake again. But I've learned. Don't you see? You've given me this as you've given me everything. Accept your own gift. Leave him be."

Narim's eyes kept flicking from my sword to my face

and behind me to the Senai. "Even if he warns Roelan away, I can't allow MacAllister to live. Eventually the dragons will come back here. The pull will be too strong. We'll wait—another five hundred years if we must, in hiding if we must—but we will keep the bloodstones; we will keep the lake tainted with jenica; and we will control the dragons. I can allow no one to live who is capable of undoing it." As he spoke, his glance flicked again, but this time to his left. The torches from the distant shoreline had vanished. I dared not take my eyes from Narim, but I took a step backward to get a wider view. Not ten paces to my right were two hard-eyed Elhim sneaking over the end of the rockfall nearest the water, each of them wearing a bloodstone around his neck.

"I'm sorry, Lara," said Narim, motioning his allies forward. The two took positions on either side of him, trapping Aidan and me between themselves and the boulder and the cliff, our only retreat the too-long path to my caves. "I'm too old for faith. Lay down your weapons."

I couldn't afford to look behind me to see if Aidan was capable of running. The screaming dragon swooped low across the lake, and the brimstone-tainted wind of his passing made the ground shudder. I settled my grip on the sword and drew my dagger. "I won't."

One of the newcomers, wearing a light-colored tunic, moved first. I beat back his attack, leaving him slightly off balance, and spun around just in time to catch his fellow's curved blade that was on a line for my legs. One and then the other and then the first one again, I split my attention between the two Elhim, straining to see in the weak moonlight. My arms were longer, but the Elhim were light and quick, and I had to dance and spin and dodge, all the while keeping an eye on Narim, who stood on the strip of rocks watching us. When was he going to join in? How in Jodar's name was I going to handle a third?

A rapier point glanced off my vest, and it took all my attention to discourage its owner, while preventing his friend from ripping my back open. Only when I had pushed them both back toward the lake, the rapier fellow with a bleeding thigh wound, could I spare a glance to my left. Narim no longer stood on the rocky berm. I whirled about, frantic. Almost invisible in the shadow of the cliffs, he had crept around behind me, dagger ready, heading for Aidan, who knelt glowing with more than moonlight and oblivious to the danger.

"You will not!" I screamed, and sprang toward Narim. But the other two leaped on me from behind, dragging me to the sand. "Aidan! Watch out!" Neither Elhim nor Senai paid me any mind.

But in that same moment, yellow light flared from beside the boulder at the water's edge, and a voice boomed, "Hold, Elhim! Not one more step. Not one move, or my lieutenant's arrow is in your throat. In the name of King Devlin, I command you stand down."

Men rushed out of the darkness and disarmed Narim, while others yanked the weight off my back. I pressed my head to the sand for a moment, both ragged and relieved, the burden of life, death, and the world's future lifted from my shoulders along with my attackers.

As a soldier bound his hands behind his back, Narim squinted, puzzled, into the torchlight. "Who's there? Who are you?"

"My lord." I scrambled off the sand and, without the

least resentment, nodded to the dark-haired young Senai
who stepped into the light, the same man who with his
single strong arm had rescued me from the bowels of Cor
Neuill in the very hour of my punishment. "Narim, meet
His Royal Highness Donal, the crown prince of Elyria,"
I said. Twenty more well-equipped soldiers, frayed and
bloody, followed the prince into the sandy clearing. "I
thought you'd never get here."

King Devlin's offer of protection for the Twelve Families in exchange for my release had rankled the high
commander, but Prince Donal had been very persuasive.
After all, the future of the clan was at stake, and
MacEachern was directly pledged in fealty to the king of
Elyria. The high commander, still reeling from the reports
of escaping dragons, grudgingly agreed that King Devlin
was the strongest of the clan's possible allies. But when
the prince escorted me out of the lair and into the Ridemark camp, the agreement fell apart. My brother claimed
that King Devlin had forfeited the clan's loyalty by free-
ing the dragons, and he roused the warriors to rebel
against the high commander and reclaim their ruined
honor, along with a certain traitorous daughter of the
Ridemark. And so Prince Donal and his fighters had held
off two hundred Ridemark swordsmen long enough for
Davyn and me to get away, the prince risking his life and
freedom because a man he had never met had asked him
to do whatever was needed to save my life.

"Are you well, Mistress Lara?" asked the prince, examining me carefully. Once I showed him that the blood
on me was not my own, he smiled and tipped his head to
something over my shoulder. "And he . . . we're not too
late, then?" His eyes shone with wonder . . . and I under-

stood when I turned to look on the one who knelt on the sand behind me.

Despite his filthy clothes and dirt-streaked skin, in that moment Aidan MacAllister had no kinship with any human creature. Tiny white flames danced about his body. His eyes were closed, his arms and hands spread wide apart as if to embrace the night. Only now that the blood rush of battle had faded in my ears did I hear that he had begun to sing—softly, as if soothing a child plagued with restless dreams. As we watched and listened, his powerful voice swelled into a torrent of passionate music.

Gathering what sense remained to me, I turned away.

Narim had no eye for Aidan or for the prince or even for the soldier who was binding his arms securely behind his back, but only for the Elhim who had followed Prince Donal into the torchlight. "Davyn!" said Narim, only to clamp his mouth shut again when he saw his dearest friend's face grow stone hard at the sight of him.

"I must be the greatest fool who ever walked the earth," said Davyn, striding briskly toward Narim, "and it would not be half so hard did I not love you still." With a powerful yank, Davyn snapped the leather strap that held the bloodstone to Narim's neck.

Narim did not drop his eyes.

Davyn turned on his heel, tossing the red gem on the ground by the prince's feet. "We'll find the rest of them, my lord." The prince nodded, still mesmerized by the wonder behind me. Davyn led fifteen of the Elyrian soldiers off toward the Elhim caverns. I retreated into the shadows of the great boulder, where it hung over the lake.

Almost an hour passed until the last clear note of Aidan's song fell silent. His fire died away with the music,

and the silver-white glow of his skin faded into more ordinary coloring. He pressed his hands to his eyes and
spoke softly in words that sounded very much like the ancient tongue we of the Ridemark used, but I did not know
their meanings. He tried again with the same result. After
a visible struggle, his third attempt produced, "It's all
right. It's all right." Sighing tiredly, he sat back on his
heels, lowered his hands, and blinked in astonishment at
the awestruck crowd surrounding him. He looked from
one face to the next, taking in the captive Narim, who refused to meet his eye, the other two Elhim, hands bound,
the remaining Elyrian soldiers . . . until his eye stopped
on my rescuer. Though Prince Donal wore no badge of
rank, no garb different from any of his soldiers save for
the empty left sleeve tucked into his tunic, Aidan pushed
himself to his feet and bowed deeply, wearing a smile so
brilliant it rivaled the moon. "My Lord Prince . . ."

The prince returned his grin. "You know me!"

"Were we in the grand marketplace of Vallior on the
day of first harvest, I would know you, Donal."

"And I you. Though finding you immersed in such
mystery gives me the easier part."

"Is Davyn . . . ?"

"He's well. Gone on an errand at the moment. And
you? And your . . . friend?"

"Free. Both of us." Aidan flicked his eyes upward. "He
treated you well?"

A trace of remembered despair wiped away the young
prince's smile. "My debt is everlasting."

Aidan opened his arms and the two embraced, the
bond between them more clearly visible than the torchlight.

"Don't let me singe you too badly," Aidan said, laughing and pulling away as sparks flew. "I've not learned how to manage this little problem yet."

The smiling prince shook his head, raw emotion adding a rasp to his voice. "I was afraid we'd get here too late, but Davyn swore that Lara would save you if anyone could. A number of Ridemark warriors were most displeased when we released Lara, and she insisted on coming here alone while we convinced them we were right. She even left Davyn behind, so he could guide us through the mountains."

Aidan looked around the shoreline. "Is she all right? There was fighting . . . gods, where is she?"

"She's well, I think. But I don't know where she's gotten off to."

I shrank deeper into the shadows and sank to the damp stone, wishing they would all go somewhere else. I had no place with these people.

Before the two of them could discover my hiding place, Davyn returned carrying a large leather bag. He and Aidan greeted each other as brothers.

"Davyn, have you seen Lara?" said Aidan.

The Elhim looked about sharply, then shook his head. "No. Not since I left for the cavern. She seemed unharmed."

The prince joined them, and Davyn dumped out the bag—bloodstones. "I think this is all of them, unless he's squirreled more away. I'll bring in other Elhim to search more thoroughly. Your men have rounded up a few more conspirators in the cavern; most of the villains haven't arrived as yet."

The prince jerked his head toward Narim, who stood

watching all this bleakly. "What am I to do with him? Hanging seems appropriate for one who attempts the life of King Devlin's cousin."

Sorrow shadowed Aidan when he looked on Narim. "Let him go. Let them all go. There's nothing you can do that will compare to what's going to happen. Soon, I think." He glanced up at the quiet night, and the hair on my arms and neck prickled. For even as he said it, a growing darkness obscured the stars in every direction. Wind rose beyond the heights and lightning licked the clifftops. "I would suggest you all take shelter," said Aidan. "No harm is intended, but accidents could happen."

Though looking puzzled, the prince ordered his men to take the Elhim prisoners back to the caves. When the soldiers grabbed Narim's arm, the Elhim resisted, growling furiously. At a nod of Prince Donal's head, the soldiers left Narim by the edge of the water, his hands bound and his feet tied loosely so he could not run. He said nothing more and paid no attention to anyone. I remained in my hiding place at the bottom of the great boulder. Aidan would not follow his own advice and climbed up on the boulder above my head. Neither Prince Donal nor Davyn would leave him. They stood uncertainly only a few steps away from me. And so we waited, though I didn't know for what.

Black clouds drove in from all sides. The wind whipped the lake into froth. Thunder rolled continuously, booming and crashing from the cliffs. Before very long, Narim rose slowly and awkwardly to his feet, craning his neck, scanning the sky. "MacAllister," he said, his voice choked with horror, "what have you done?"

Dragons! Fifty or a hundred of them gathered over us, blotting out the stars, and as if at a herald's trumpet blast, they released a firestorm upon the lake. The water churned and boiled, filling the air with smoke and steam. In a deafening explosion of wind and water, stone and fire, the rocky dam that held the water in the valley was blasted into dust. First a hissing stream and then a flood poured through the gaps in the rock wall and swept the remaining barrier away. As each screaming dragon released its cache of flame, it circled the valley and disappeared westward.

By the time dawn light colored the drifting fog, the air was still. The only sound was the distant rush of falling water, as the last of the lake drained into the lowlands. One dragon remained, a blot of gleaming copper, perched on the clifftops far across the gaping emptiness.

Davyn and the prince emerged from behind the boulder pile, where flying shards of broken rock and scalding spray had forced them to take shelter, and gaped at the empty lakebed. Narim stood at the edge, stunned, appalled, disbelieving. "They'll never be able to speak with us again," he said. "They'll grow wilder, farther from us."

Aidan spoke softly from atop his boulder perch. "They'll never again be slaves to anyone, humans or Elhim. Without the lake water to tempt them, they won't return here. The water was the difference, you know, the reason you were able to bind them in the first place. It wasn't just the jenica you put in it to keep them still. Whatever element of the water enabled them to understand our speech also enabled the binding of the bloodstones. That's why the Riders could never bind a dragon to a new stone."

Narim's grief was bitter. "Only the one in five hundred years, those like you, will ever hear their voices."

"You needn't fear. I'll pay the price for this as well."

I wasn't sure exactly what he was talking about; we would all pay for this night's work. The world would pay.

"What about the springs?" said Davyn. "Isn't there still a risk?"

"Keep watching," said Aidan.

After a while, the lone dragon spread its wings and glided from the clifftop, spiraling down into the fog-filled valley. A blast of white-hot fire blossomed from the deeps. When the fire receded, the dragon soared upward, returning to its distant perch. The bottom of the valley had been melted into a smooth shelf of rock, the springs irredeemably buried.

Narim sank to his knees and buried his head in his hands. How does one face the ruin of dreams carried for half a thousand years? Despite all, my heart wept for him.

Chapter 35

The prince convened a hasty trial for Narim. He took evidence from Davyn and from the Elhim who were a part of Narim's plot. I could not remain silent, which meant, unfortunately, that I could no longer stay out of sight. So I stepped out of my niche, brushed past MacAllister without acknowledging him, and told the prince I wished to speak.

Prince Donal listened carefully to my tale of Narim's tender care for me. I told him how all the Elhim, including the conspirators, had risked the safety of their sanctuary to take me in. I gave no other evidence. Whatever I knew of Narim's crimes—and my own—I left to others to tell.

The prince already knew MacAllister's mind, and only asked if he wished to add anything. MacAllister declined. Weak and foolish, as always. Even if he took no satisfaction in vengeance, how could he not see the rightness of punishment? We must pay for our deeds. Surely the prince would understand that.

I wandered over to the edge of the abyss and peered down on the scorched rocks and dried mud that were all that remained of the lake of fire, waiting to hear the verdict—to hear if my name would be listed among the condemned. After a sober deliberation, the prince announced that Narim would not hang, but that he and his Elhim conspirators would be exiled from Elyria for as long as they might live. Gods, Aidan and his cousin were two of a kind. Naive. Stupid. Who would ever be able to tell if an Elhim wandering the roads of Elyria was Narim or some other?

But the prince called forward one of his aides, his scribe who was charged with marking the wrists of those sworn to the prince's service. While three soldiers held Narim still, the man used his needles and ink to mark, not a wrist, but Narim's forehead with an X, and beside it the prince's own mark. "Wear this mark of infamy forever, Elhim, and be grateful to my cousin and Mistress Lara that you yet breathe. Never was sin healed by betrayal, and never was good built upon the abused honor of a warrior. Begone from my father's kingdom, and never tread its paths again." The other conspirators were marked in the same fashion.

Narim and the exiles left that afternoon. Ten Elyrian soldiers accompanied the Elhim, both to protect them from assault along their way to the Elyrian border and to make sure they crossed it. My oldest friend did not speak to me before he left and did not acknowledge the hand I offered. My name had not been mentioned in the prince's judgment.

Though anxious to take his place at his father's side, Prince Donal planned to remain at Cir Nakai overnight to see to his men. Many were wounded; all of them needed sleep after five days of hard riding and the ferocious action at Cor Neuill. Many had lost their gear in the fight.

The prince gratefully accepted Davyn's offer to retrieve the food, blankets, and other supplies worth salvaging that he had found in the ruined Elhim home caverns.

I needed gear, too. The desire to escape consumed me. Aidan knew everything now: I had known Narim planned to reenslave the dragons, and I had known Aidan would have to die. I could no longer pretend that my crimes were only those of a bitter child. Well and good. The temptation to keep up the deception would have been so great as to drive me mad. But I could not tolerate his looking at me, now he understood that I was as ugly inside as out.

As Davyn and a few of the soldiers set out on the shore path, I heard Aidan. "Did you see where Lara's gone?"

"The woman keeps disappearing," said the prince. "I want to speak with her, too. Recruit her, if she's willing. With what I've seen and heard . . . we could use her skills for what's to come."

As they talked, I slipped around behind the two Senai and joined Davyn on the shoreline path. I asked if he could spare a few days' rations and a blanket or two. "I need to be away from here. Today if possible."

"Whatever we have is yours," he said. "You've no need to ask."

As we hurried down the shore, a voice called after me. "We need to talk, Lara."

I called back over my shoulder. "We have nothing to say." Then I fixed my eyes on Davyn's back and put one foot in front of the other.

Davyn and I returned from the burned-out caverns just after dusk. The retrieval work had taken much longer

than we'd thought, and all my plans for leaving this
damnable valley before nightfall were confounded. We
rejoined the prince and his men, who were roasting rab-
bits and birds over small cookfires, the soldiers casting
nervous glances westward. No dragons were in sight. As
he devoured his share of the meal, the laughing prince reported that, after an afternoon of listening to him babble
like a five-year-old, Aidan had fallen asleep atop the
boulder. The Elyrians retired to the caves early, anticipat-
ing an early start the next morning.

After my week in Garn MacEachern's dungeon in Cor
Neuill, I couldn't bear to be anywhere but under the stars.
So I settled beside a rock at the edge of the abyss, well
out of the circle of firelight, wishing I dared walk away
in the dark. My pack was beside me, loaded with food
and water, ready to leave at first light. I would just have
to stay out of sight until then.

Sometime near midnight, Aidan climbed down from
his perch. He yawned and rubbed the dark stubble on his
head as if to rid himself of a year's cobwebs. Davyn offered him tea and the food that had been set aside for him.
As had happened earlier, the Senai's answer was indecipherable. Pressing the heels of his hands into his eyes, he
tried again. "Thank you," he said on his the third attempt.
"I'm as hollow as Cir Nakai."

"Will I see you in the morning?" asked Davyn. "The
prince leaves at dawn."

"I'll be awake. If not, throw a rock at me."

"Will you accept his protection and come with us? The
world will be a dangerous place for the one who has undone the power of the Ridemark."

Aidan drank his tea and shook his head. "Not for a while. I've things to do first."

"We own a part of each other's lives, Aidan MacAllister," said the Elhim. "And I've had enough grieving."

"We'll see what comes about. What of you? Are you going to watch over my young cousin the way you've watched over me?"

"He told you he'd asked me to stay with him?"

"It could be a very good thing for the Elhim—and for Donal—and for you. There's so much healing to be done, and plenty more wounds to be suffered before we can begin, I'm afraid."

"I'll consider it." The Elhim glanced my way. "We must all consider what will heal our hearts. But for now I'm off to examine the underside of my blankets. Good night, Aidan."

"Good night, my friend." The Senai was left alone, idly poking at the fire and drinking the tea Davyn had given him. He didn't seem to have noticed me in the dark. Good.

I forced myself to look at the sealed basin of the springs, the stars, the sand and shingle, anything lest he feel my eyes on him.

My strategy didn't work. "We need to talk." He had moved as quickly and quietly as a fox and now stood over me, his face unreadable in the dark.

"You keep saying that, but mostly when you're drugged or mad or half-asleep. I don't think there's much to say." Gods, why would he not leave me alone?

He sat down cross-legged in front of me, unsmiling, his brow creased. "Roelan wants me to go with them."

"With the dragons? Go where?" I could not pretend indifference.

"Wherever they go. Deeper into the Carag Huim. Beyond the mountains to the lands where they once lived."

"You'll fly. . . ." The words crept out unbidden.

"No. I suppose I'll just slog after them on foot. I'll never fly."

"But you sent him to rescue the prince." My words sounded childish, leaving me wanting to bite my tongue. I hated the way he made me feel—this unsettling confusion, as if I would fall off the edge of the world, if I took one more step.

"Donal didn't ride. Roelan carried him in his hand. But even if Roelan was willing, I couldn't do it, any more than I could put a harness on Davyn." Holy gods, he was apologizing to me! What was wrong with him?

I struggled to keep to mundane matters. "How will you live? What will you do?"

"I don't know. They won't let me starve. But Roelan is the only one who can communicate with me right now. The others are wild, lost. They need me to help them remember what they were. To help them shape words again until they can do it on their own."

"There's no lake to make it easier."

He nodded. "The consequence of their safety. I didn't have much time to choose." He was quiet for a long time after that, but I could feel the words gathering behind his silence, needing only a nudge to spill out.

"And you're going to do it?"

"It is my gift." Such simple words to carry the fullness of a man's soul. He allowed me to see all of what he felt, the things I would expect—joy, wonder, acceptance—

and, on the edges, other things—resignation, sadness, and . . .

"What are you afraid of?"

"I don't know how long I can do it and remain myself. When I speak with Roelan, even for a short time as I did today . . . Just now it took me three tries to say 'I'm hungry.' "

"I noticed."

"And this." He touched my hand and a fountain of sparks flew upward into the night. "I don't know what I am, and I don't know what I'll become. I'm terrified, because I've found a wonder that is far beyond gods and music and dragons . . . and I don't want to lose you." His dark eyes reached out to gather me in. "You are the wholeness of life, Lara, marvelous, holy, human life, filled with love and pain, joy and sorrow, courage and honor, beauty and scars. If I could be with you . . . touch all this that you are . . . then I won't forget. I don't know where I'm going or for how long, only that I want you to come with me."

Blind, stupid Senai fool! Who did he think I was? My "honor" had sent him to Mazadine . . . mutilated him. My "courage" had gotten his friends killed. I jumped to my feet—trapped on this shore by the failing moonlight, unable to untangle the jumbled mess that was threatening to burst my head and rip me apart, unable to speak anything of sense. I had no gift of music or words. "No," I blurted out. "You're a crippled madman who plans to live with monsters. I have better things to do."

He didn't argue, didn't ask why, didn't display what hurt he might have felt from my ugly jibe. Only smiled sadly as he moved around and took my place, leaning against my rock. "Ah, Lara, what are *you* afraid of?"

For a while I paced up and down the strip of sand and the rocky berm, cursing the night and my muddled head, the touch of fire that lingered on my hand, and my inability to understand the panic that filled me every time I thought of Aidan. At last I went back to retrieve my pack, so I could wait somewhere else and bolt at the first glimmer of morning.

The Senai watched me. "This is not the end," he said softly as I left him. "You heard Davyn; we own a part of each other's life. I'll not give up my share of yours that easily, even if I have to come back and ask you again in the language of dragons."

While the silver stars wheeled overhead, I forced myself to go to sleep at the mouth of the caves beyond the great boulder.

I woke to the sound of Aidan singing. He sat atop his rock, his eyes closed, white flames dancing about his head and his hands, and as I stood behind Davyn and Donal and the gaping Elyrians, watching and listening, his voice rose in a song of such haunting beauty that my skin crept over my bones. His face was a portrait of bliss as he sang the music of his heart, while on the clifftops across the gaping emptiness of Cir Nakai, a dark shape, glinting copper in the sunrise, sat and listened.

The abyss yawned beside me. I shouldered my pack and walked away.

Chapter 36

The movement of the upper airs whispers coming
   storm.
Though the days grow longer, we yearn for winter
   sleep so long denied us.
My sister Methys flew this day in the morning lands,
   soaring dawnward, joyful.
Aidan's song hath already loosed her melody.
Soon, Methys will shape her own song.

Yet my own, my beloved, doth grieve.
When his words fall silent, I hear it still.
I tell him, "Do not sorrow.
The dayfires burn and fade.
Comes the day soon when all my brothers and sisters
   will sing with thee.
My sisters weep for younglings lost, and so have
   wandered deep.
But, even so, thy giving brings them wholeness. Soon.
   Soon.
And Jodar and my brothers have tasted too much
   human blood.

But the passing season will sate their unholy hunger,
*   and, truly, their being doth move already with*
*   your teaching.*
Thy songs are true, Aidan, beloved.
With every turning of the light, thy power grows."

He says his sorrowing is for his own kind, so lost, so
*   weary, in the changing of the world.*
But when enough seasons pass, they, too, will hear
*   his songs and understand.*
Never in all its turnings hath the world seen what my
*   beloved will become.*

Yet still there is more. . . .
Ah, beloved, dost thou think I cannot see thy heart?
One alone art thou. So alone. Bound to earth. Bound
*   to me by thy ever-giving.*
Thy being incomplete . . .
I will not see thee in such pain.
Fly, old Roelan. Set right this unbalancing. . . .

LARA

Chapter 37

Three days out from Cir Nakai—or what was left of it—and I was sitting beside a small fire melting snow to drink. My little blaze was scarcely a smudge in the vastness of the night—a clear and viciously cold night, considering it was almost summer. I needed to get down lower.

I poked at the sluggish fire. Not much to burn up here so high. The brush was soggy with the warmer days melting off the snow cover. It was good to be alone. To have time to clear my head of this confusion and uncertainty that had dogged me all spring. Sons and daughters of the Ridemark were not supposed to be confused.

Soon I'd have no time to wallow in maudlin regrets. War was coming, a different kind of war than those living in the world had ever known. Swords and spears and arrows only. Human against human. I knew a man in Camarthan who could remove the Ridemark from my wrist. Best get it done before people started looking.

After the first flurry of vengeance between our own people, the true onslaught would come. As summer cleared the passes in the mountains ringing Elyria and the civilized kingdoms, the news would travel to the wild men in the vast reaches of the world beyond the mountains: the dragons were gone back into the west. The men would come down the rivers in their flat-prowed boats, wearing fur robes and horned masks and tattooed faces. They would come over land on their horses, wearing curved swords and ivory earrings and shrilling throaty cries.

An experienced scout would be useful. One who knew her way around a sword and could predict the ways of dispossessed Dragon Riders even more so. I would find the prince and let him know I was available if he wanted. Donal was a prince worth serving. Davyn had seen it. I had seen it, too, but my pigheaded nature would not allow me to admit it in front of so many. Not in front of Aidan. Not with confusion and pride and guilt standing in my way. Now Aidan was gone off with his dragons, following the demands of duty, of his gift, of his heart. . . .

Stop it! Think of something else. On every step these past three days, my thoughts kept flitting to Aidan, threatening to throw me back into confusion. Those things he'd said . . . all nonsense. I couldn't bear to be near the man. *That's* what I'd not been able to tell him. The sight of his horrid hands made me shrivel inside and live in the imagination of his torment. Did he think a lifetime of guilt and deception could be wiped out instantly? How could I tell him that I had seen his face as he sang to Roelan and knew I had no place in such mystery? Seeing him like that, bathed in the fire of the gods . . . *Stop it.*

Only one thing I'd not been able to resolve in these few days. Aidan's question kept pricking at me. What was I afraid of?

The dull flames began to jump and flare hotter; my hair whipped loose and into my eyes. A wind rising . . . a warm wind . . . The smell . . . Uneasy, I glanced over my shoulder. *Daughters of fire!* I jumped up, gawking at the dark shape that blotted out half the sky.

He swept over me so low the snow melted beneath my feet. As he circled and headed back my way, panic constricted my breast and sent my heart into my throat. Yet . . . there was something . . . the sensation came over me like the caress of sleep . . . and, despite every warning of mind and instinct, I kept breathing.

He settled on the muddy wasteland, his head not twenty paces from me, warmth enveloping me like the precursor of summer. Turning his snout upward, he bellowed—an earsplitting, rising trumpet that spewed blue and gold fire, showering me with blue sparks that teased my skin before winking out. Then he knelt and lowered his head to rest it on the thawing ground. Soft transparent lids blinked over the scarlet eyes that looked straight at me. Waiting.

"Did Aidan send you?" I wasn't so much speaking to the dragon, as to myself. To remind myself that I was not afraid. Because the rumble of the dragon's bated fire in the empty night was too huge to leave unanswered. Because if this was to be my last breath, I would hold Aidan's name on my tongue and his image in my heart as I burned.

My beloved grieves for thee.
Thou art the completion of his heart.
His yearning bade me come.

How did I know what the beast spoke? Not from the unintelligible river of noise and smoke from his mouth. Not from words. But his meaning was as clear as if I'd spoken the words myself. "I've things to do," I said. "The war . . ." But I could not lie to those scarlet eyes. "I betrayed him."

The seasons pass.
The world—this upheaving chaos—will wait for thee.
Come and learn what beauty thy deeds have wrought.
Be alone and broken no more.

The beast extended one massive leg and foot alongside its snout in a position I had never seen. With care, one could walk up the leg to the haunch, where a curled wingtip waited . . . to lift me up? *Oh, holy gods . . .*

And then, as the sharp winds of winter banish the smokes of autumn, leaving the sunlit world bright and hard-edged and new, so did the beast's offer untangle my last confusion. Clarity. Understanding. I had been changed—altered by these past weeks as surely as Aidan MacAllister had been transformed by dragon fire. And I was afraid to believe what I had learned . . . afraid to be forgiven . . . for it meant leaving behind all my certainties about who and what I was. I, too, was becoming something new. Something unknown.

"Tell him"—I closed my eyes and began to draw the broken fragments together—"tell him not yet. I've things to do. People who need my help. And I need some time. But when winter comes . . . the solstice . . . when the night is longest and the rivers freeze . . . the war will have to pause. And then for a little while . . . a few days . . . till spring perhaps . . . I'll come. But on that day, oh, child of fire and wind, I'll walk"—I gestured toward the mountains, the way he'd come, and to the place where I stood—"if you'll come back here and show me the way."

Roelan bellowed again, snuffing out my fire while starting three more in its place, scattering rocks and branches and light as he swept his green and copper wings. He circled above me, blue sparks raining from the sky. And I watched and wept and laughed until he disappeared beyond the mountains.

About the Author

Though **Carol Berg** calls Colorado her home, her roots are in Texas, in a family of teachers, musicians, and railroad men. She has a degree in mathematics from Rice University and one in computer science from the University of Colorado, but managed to squeeze in minors in English and art history along the way. She has combined a career as a software engineer with her writing, while also raising three sons. She lives with her husband at the foot of the Colorado mountains.

(0451)

See what's coming in June...

MESSIAH NODE by Lyda Morehouse
A potent mix of technology and salvation is the trademark of Lyda Morehouse's brilliant novels. Now, Messiah Node takes her uniquely-imagined world one step closer to its fate—as AIs and archangels, prophets and criminal masterminds face the final day of reckoning...
45929-6

THE GLASSWRIGHTS' TEST by Mindy L. Klasky
Glass artisan Rani's divided loyalty are tested when she is forced to choose between King and Guild...
45931-8

MECHWARRIOR: DARK AGE #4: *A SILENCE IN THE HEAVENS (A BATTLETECH NOVEL)* by Martin Delrio
From WizKids LLC, creators of the hit game Mage Knight...Duchess Tara Campbell and MechWarrior Paladin Ezekiel Crow struggle to save the planet of Northwind from the invading faction of Steel Wolves...
45932-6

To order call: 1-800-788-6262

(0-451-)

CAROL BERG

From *Revelation*
to *Transformation*...

From slave
to savior...

TRANSFORMATION   45795-1
Enter an exotic world of demons, of a remarkable
boy prince, of haunted memories, of the terrors of
slavery, and of the triumphs of salvation.

REVELATION   45842-7
Seyonne, the slave-turned-hero, returns to discover
the nature of evil—in a "spellbinding" (*Romantic
Times*) epic saga.

RESTORATION   45890-7
A sorcerer who fears he will destroy the world. A
prince who fears he has destroyed his people. Amid
the chaos of a disintegrating empire, two men
confront prophecy and destiny in the last battle of
the demon war...

To order call: 1-800-788-6262

R422

Penguin Group (USA) Inc.
Online

Your Internet gateway to a virtual environment with
hundreds of entertaining and enlightening books
from Penguin Group (USA) Inc.

*While you're there, get the latest buzz on
the best authors and books around—*

Tom Clancy, Patricia Cornwell, W.E.B. Griffin,
Nora Roberts, William Gibson, Robin Cook,
Brian Jacques, Catherine Coulter, Stephen King,
Ken Follett, Terry McMillan, and many more!

**Penguin Group (USA) Inc. Online is located at
http://www.penguinputnam.com**

PENGUIN GROUP (USA) Inc.
NEWS

Every month you'll get an inside look at our upcom-
ing books and new features on our site. This is an
ongoing effort to provide you with the most
up-to-date information about
our books and authors.

**Subscribe to Penguin Group (USA) Inc. News at
http://www.penguinputnam.com/newsletters**